Raoul De Bourbel

Routes in Jammu and Kashmir

Arranged Topographically with distances by Stages and Information as to Supplies

and Transport

Raoul De Bourbel

Routes in Jammu and Kashmir
Arranged Topographically with distances by Stages and Information as to Supplies and Transport

ISBN/EAN: 9783337142766

Printed in Europe, USA, Canada, Australia, Japan

Cover: Foto ©Andreas Hilbeck / pixelio.de

More available books at **www.hansebooks.com**

ROUTES

IN

JAMMU AND KASHMIR

ARRANGED TOPOGRAPHICALLY WITH DESCRIPTIONS OF
ROUTES; DISTANCES BY STAGES; AND
INFORMATION AS TO SUPPLIES
AND TRANSPORT.

COMPILED FROM THE MOST RECENT SOURCES BY

MAJOR-GENERAL LE MARQUIS DE BOURBEL,

R.E., RETIRED,

LATE CHIEF ENGINEER OF THE JAMMU AND KASHMIR STATE.

Calcutta:

THACKER, SPINK AND CO.

1897.

CALCUTTA

PRINTED BY THACKER, SPINK AND CO.

DEDICATED

TO

MAJOR-GENERAL HIS HIGHNESS THE MAHARAJA

SIR PRATAP SINGH, G.C.S.I.,

INDAR MAHINDAR BAHADUR, SIPAR-I-SULTANAT,

MAHARAJA OF JAMMU AND KASHMIR.

PREFACE.

THE Routes in this book are mainly compiled from the books of various authors and travellers, who have published a description and map of their journeys in or through Jammu and Kashmir. Some are taken from Lieutenant-Colonel Montgomerie's, R.E., Route book and map, and from his survey map of this country ; others are the result of my own notes when making a reconnaissance of the country for a railway to connect the Punjab with Kashmir, while the rest are collected from the information given to me at various times by traders and hunters of the country.

The notes taken during my own journeys in Jammu and Kashmir have enabled me to revise the length of the marches on some of the routes previously published, and to describe the general character of the route, whether at present fit for man on foot or horseback, or fit for laden animals, &c. The knowledge of the country acquired during a residence of 10 years has enabled me to give fairly accurate data regarding the prospect of shelter, supplies, grass, fuel, water and means of transport at each stage on many routes.

My object has been to present in a tabular and condensed form such information as may give to the traveller some idea of what lies before him, may afford him some help in his movements and may enable him to make timely arrangements to prevent detention on the march.

In the margin and foot-notes, the chief points of interest likely to attract the traveller are briefly alluded to, leaving him to form his own opinion of what he may choose to see.

All the routes in this book have been arranged into five groups, each radiating from a centre or capital of a province. Jammu, Poonch, Srinagar, Gilgit and Leh are the capitals of some chief provinces in the dominions of His Highness the Maharaja of Jammu and Kashmir, and have been selected as the most convenient centres, from which each set of routes radiate in a complete circle, extending generally to the North-Western Railway on the south, to Hazara, Kaghan and Chitral on the west, to Central Asia on the north, and to Chinese Thibet and Simla on the east. The Capitals of other provinces such as Baltistan, Zanskar, Badrawar, Ramnagar have not been taken as centres, as they are served by the other radiating routes.

This arrangement involves the recasting of the old published routes with different termini and some repetition of the parts of various routes, in order that each new route may be separate and complete. Though this adds to the bulk of the work, it will save to the traveller the trouble of making frequent reference to other parts of the same book and thus save his time, when on a journey.

Some portions of the old routes have become altered in time, through the action of glaciers, the shifting and erosion of rivers, landslips or other natural causes. Some routes have been newly constructed under the orders of H. H. the Maharaja of Jammu and Kashmir, and many local variations have taken place through gradual improvements. The names of some places have also changed. My endeavour has been to collect the most recent information available on these points for the revision of the old routes.

This book must be looked upon in the main as a selection and compilation from the works and maps of which a list is given ; from these this book takes its source, and my best acknowledgments are due to their several authors. In attempting a revision with the aid of later knowledge, many oversights or errors may have crept in, but on the whole, it is hoped, that this work may prove to be of some practical use to the public. A list of the Routes will be found at the beginning and an Index at the end of this book to facilitate reference.

The best maps for a traveller in Jammu and Kashmir are the one-inch two miles Map of Jammu and Kashmir published by the Surveyor-General of India and the Route Map of the Western Himalayas as published by the same office.

The existing rules in force as regards visitors to Kashmir should be procured from the office of the Resident in Kashmir at Srinagar or Sialkot.

The visitor to Jammu and Kashmir will find the six months, 15th May to 15th November inclusive, the best for travelling, while the last three months, 15th August to 15th November, are usually dry weather. There are shops in Srinagar, where he can purchase or hire a sufficient outfit of tents, stores, servants, &c., for a short journey, though, if not pressed for time, he had better collect at his leisure and bring such articles with him for a long journey.

As a rule the intending traveller will find it convenient to hire at his starting point at least one-half of the requisite transport for his through journey. Ponies and mules, with one man for every two animals, are procurable at every large market town. About 10 to 20 coolies are usually to be had at every intermediate stage, though there may be difficulty in getting these at times of religious and other festivals, of sowing and reaping crops. When travelling in Thibet and Central Asia, through transport for the entire baggage is essential.

DE BOURBEL.

Gupcur, Srinagar,
Kashmir, 1897.

Abu Fazl-i-Allami. Ain-i-Akbari. Translated by Colonel J. S. Jarratt, *see* Vol. II, Fasciculi IV and V of Asiatic Society of Bengal, 1891.

1820   *W. Moorcroft*—Travels in the Himalayas published in 1841.

1831   *Victor Jacquemont*—Travels in India.

1837-38   *Dr. H. Falconer*—Memoirs on Kashmir and Little Thibet.

1840   *C. F. Von Hügel*—Travels in Kashmir and Punjab.

1842   *G. T. Vigne*—Travels in Kashmir, Ladak, Iskardo.

1857   The brothers *Schlagintweit*—R. G. S. Vol. I.

1863-66   *Captain H. H. Godwin Austen* — R. G. S. Vols. 1863, 1864, 1866.

1868   *Shaw*—Yarkand and Kashgar, also R. G. S. Vol. 16, 1872.

,,   *W. H. Johnson*—Leh to Khotan, R. G. S. Vol. 11.

1869   *G. S. W. Hayward*—R. G. S. Vol. 13, also Vols. 14 of 1870 and 15 of 1871.

1870   *Dr. G. Henderson*—Lahore to Yarkand.

1872   *Havildar*—Journey through Chitral, R. G. S. Vol. XLII.

1873   *Dr. F. Stoliczka*—Geological Note on Route to Yarkand and Kashgar.

,,   *Colonel T. Gordon*—Roof of the World.

1875   *Dr. H. W. Bellew, C.S.I.*—Kashmir and Kashgar.

,,   *F. Drew*—Jammu and Kashmir territories with Maps.

1876-83   *R. Lydekker*—Geology of Kashmir and Chamba.

1878   *Captain H. Trotter, R.E.*—R. G. S. Vol. XLVIII and Routes of Yarkand Mission.

1880   *Colonel J. Biddulph*—Tribes of the Hindu Kush.

,,   *Wilson*—Itinerary in Abode of Snow.

,,   *Lieutenant H. H. Cole, R.E.*—Illustration of ancient buildings in Kashmir.

1883   *Lieutenant-Colonel T. G. Montgomerie, R. E.* — Routes in Western Himalayas with additions by Major C. E. Bates.

1884   *J. Collett*—Guide to Kashmir.

,,   *J. Northam*—Guide to Masuri, &c.

1887   *A. D. Carey*—Routes in Central Asia, R. G. S. Vol. IX.

,,   *C. F. Gilbert*—Hints to Travellers in Kashmir.

1888   *Dr. J. Ince, M.D.*—Handbook to Kashmir, with Maps, as revised by Dr. Joshua Duke.

,,   *T. D. La Touche*—Reports on Jammu Coal-fields and Sapphire Mines.

,,   *Dr. Arthur Neve*—Tourist Guide to Kashmir.

,,   *Major E. Ward, R.E.*—Sportsman's Guide to Kashmir and Ladak.

,,   *Mrs. Murray Aynsley*—Our visit to Kashmir and Ladak.

1888 Cowley Lambert—Travels to Kashmir and Ladak.
1891 H. A. Rose, C. S.—Guide to Dalhousie and Neighbouring Hills.
„   Captain H. Ramsay—Notes of Measurement of some Ladak
      Routes.
1892 Captain T. E. Younghusband, C.I.E.—R.G.S. Vols. XIV,
      also X of 1888 and V of 1895.
      Mr. H. Dauvergne—R. G. S. Vol. XIV.
1893 E. F. Knight—Where Three Empires Meet, with Maps.
„   Sir W. M. Conway—Route from Gilgit to Baltistan, R. G. S.
      Vol. I, No. II, and Climbing in the Himalayas.
„   The Earl of Dunmore—The Pamirs.
„   Doctor Edith Huntley—Notes of Journey Kangra, to Ladak.
„   H. Lansdell, D.D.—Chinese Central Asia, with Maps, by
      Messrs. Constable & Co.
„   Lieutenant-Colonel H. A. Tyacke—Sportsman's Manual to
      Kulu, Lahoul and Ladak.
„   Major E. Gordon Forbes—Route from Simla to Shipki.
1895 Major C. S. Cumberland—Sport on the Pamirs.
1896 Sir G. S. Robertson, K.C.S.I.—The Kafirs of Hindu Kush,
      and Map.
„   S. J. Stone—In and Beyond the Himalayas.

MAPS.

Sheets of the Atlas of India.
Survey Maps of Jammu and Kashmir by Lieutenant-Colonel T. G. Montgomerie, R.E.
Route Map of Punjab and Kashmir by Lieutenant-Colonel T. G. Montgomerie, R.E.
Turkistan and Central Asia by Lieutenant-General J. T. Walker, R.E., C.B.
Astor and Gilgit by Lieutenant-General J. A. Walker, R.E., C.B.
Thibet, R. G. S. Vol. IV of 1894 by Lieutenant-General J. T. Walker, R.E., C.B.

LIST OF ROUTES IN JAMMU AND KASHMIR.

LIST OF ROUTES IN JAMMU AND KASHMIR—(*Continued.*)

LIST OF ROUTES IN JAMMU AND KASHMIR—(*Continued.*)

LIST OF ROUTES IN JAMMU AND KASHMIR—(Continued.)

LIST OF ROUTES IN JAMMU AND KASHMIR--(Continued.)

LIST OF ROUTES IN JAMMU AND KASHMIR—(*Continued.*)

ABBREVIATIONS.

D. B.—Dâk Bungalow with servants and board.

B.—Road Bungalow, rest-house or *baradari* without servant or board.

F. B.—Forest Bungalow.

C.—Caravan Serai for Native traveller.

E.—Encamping ground.

P. O.—Post Office.

T. O.—Telegraph Office.

S.—Supplies or *russud* for an ordinary party of travellers.

G.—Grass or grazing for transport animals.

F.—Firewood or other fuel.

W.—Water for drinking, &c.

M. P.—Mountain Pass.

L.—Lake.

T.—Transport coolies, ponies, mules or yâks, &c., for an ordinary party of travellers.

H.—Hot spring.

ERRATA.

Page.	for		read
87 116	Poonch State		Poonch territory (*ilaka*).
329 361	Gialpoor		Gyalpo or.
371	*after* in length		343 miles.
379	Hosiharpur		Hoshiarpur.
,,	roads		road.
,,	distance		distances.
380	Kirshetwar	...	Kishtwar.
,,	Kangua	..	Kangra.
,,	*omit* from	...	
,,	Hunsa	...	Hunza.
,,	Sarikal	...	Sarikol.
,,	for Kela	...	Forbela to.

ROUTES

IN

JAMMU AND KASHMIR.

I JAMMU to AMRITSAR by PAKOI OORF, DEHRA BABA NANUK:—

NUMBER OF MARCHES.	NAMES OF STAGES.	DISTANCE IN MILES AND FURLONGS. INTER-MEDIATE m. f.	TOTAL m. f.	NATURE OF ROUTE.	MAIN VALLEYS AND MOUNTAIN PASSES.	RIVER CROSSINGS AND LAKES.	ALTITUDE ABOVE SEA LEVEL IN FEET.	SUPPLIES AND TRANSPORT AT STAGES.	REMARKS.
	Jammu *P. O., T. O., D. B., C.*	...	0 ... 4 1 ... 6 ...	Country undulating, rough cart-road.	Across Tawi drainage.	Tawi bridge. Balal ford.	1200	S. G. F. and W. abundant, T. ample.	Large town and capital of the Jammu State. Tawi Station on Branch Railway. Village.
1	**Bishenath**	11	11 ... 15 ...	Country flat, rough cart-road.	......	Aik ford.	......	S. G. F. and W. procurable, T. nil.	Village.
2	**Saidgurh**	11	22 ... 26 ...	Track across flat country.	Across Ravi drainage.	Degh ford.	......	Ditto ...	Ditto.
3	**Zufurwal** *P. O.—*	8 ... 4	30 4	Country low and subject to inundation during rains, nullahs then difficult.	......	......	......	S. G. F. procurable, W. plentiful, T. available.	Large village.
4	**Dhamtal** *D. B., E. good.—*	6 ...	36 4	......	......	......	...	Ditto ...	Ditto.
5	**Dodi**	14 ... 4	51 ... 55 ...	Road very heavy near river.	......	Ravi ferry.	......	S. after notice, T. ni	......

No.	Name of Stage	Distance	Total	Road	Drainage	Bridges		Supplies	Remarks
6	**Pakoi or Dehra Nanuk** *P. O., E. nil.—*	6 ...	57 ...	Road sandy	......	......	......	S. G. F. and W. abundant, T. available.	Large town.
7	**Fategarh** *P. O., E. nil.—*	12 ...	64 ...	Road good	......	Kiran bridged	......	S. G. F. and W. plentiful, T. available.	Town.
8	**Amritsar** *P.O., T.O., Hotel, E.—*	15 ...	69 ... 84	......	......	......	......	S. G. F. and W. abundant, T. ample.	City and junction station on N.-W. Railway.

Ia   PAKOI OORF, DEHRA BABA NANUK to JALANDHAR by BATALA.—

No.	Name of Stage	Distance	Total	Road	Drainage	Bridges		Supplies	Remarks
6	**Pakoi or Dehra Nanuk** *P. O., E. nil.—*	...	57 ...	Country level but low and subject to inundation during rains, road rather heavy.	Across Ravi drainage.	......	......	S. G. F. and W. abundant, T. available.	Large town.
7	**Batala** *P. O., T. O., D. B., E. good.—*	20 ...	71 ...	......	......	Baree Doab canal bridged. Ravi canal bridged.	......	Ditto ...	Large town and Station on Branch Railway.
			72 ...	......	......	Kussoor branch canal bridged.	......		
8	**Mehtah**	10 6	77 ...	......	Across Beas drainage.	......	......	S. after notice, T. nil.	Village.
			83 ...	......	......	Sobraon branch canal bridged.	......	......	East bank Beas Station on N.-W. Railway.
			87 6	......	......	Beas bridge of boats and ferry in rains.	......		
	Wazirghat	...	92 ...	......	......	......	......		
9	**Girana** *E. good.—*	15 4	97 ... 103 2	Grand Trunk Road	......	......	......	S. after notice, T. procurable.	Village.

Number of Marches.	Names of Stages.	Distance in miles and furlongs. Inter-mediate. m. f.	Total. m. f.	Nature of Route.	Main Valleys and Mountain Passes.	River crossings and Lakes.	Altitude above Sea Level in Feet.	Supplies and Transport at Stages.	Remarks.
1a	ROUTE—contd. ...	15 4	103 2	......	Across Beas drainage.	Veyn bridged			
	Hamira ...	...	105 ...	......	......				
		...	108 ...						
10	Kartarpur *P. O., T. O., E. good.*	8 4	111 6	......	......	......	......	S. G. F. and W. plentiful, T. available	Railway Station on N.-W. main line.
11	Jalandhar *P. O., T. O., D. B., C., E. good.—*	13 ...	124 6	......	......	......	......	S. G. F. and W. abundant, T. ample.	Cantonment, Civil Station and City, also two Railway Stations on N.-W. main line.

From Hamira, 108 miles on G. T. Road, there is a cart-road 8 miles in length to Kapurthala.
From Kartarpur, 111 m. 6 f. on G. T. Road, there is a metalled road, 9 miles long to Kapurthala, the capital of the Kapurthala State—crossing the N.-W. Railway at the end of the first mile.

II   JAMMU to AMRITSAR by SIALKOT—

	Jammu *P. O., T. O., D. B. C.*	...	0 ...	Metalled road	Across Chenab drainage.	......	1200	S. G. F. and W. abundant, T. ample	Large town and capital of Jammu State, Tawi Station on branch railway.
		1 4	...			Tawi bridge.			
		6 ...			......	Baial ford.			

No.	Station		Dist.	Country and Road	Drainage	Rivers, Canals	Elev.	Supplies (S., W., T.)	Remarks
1	**Runbir Singhpur** *P. O., T. O.—*	14	14	......	......	......	898	S. and W. scarce, T. nil.	Railway Station on branch line.
2	**Sinlkot** *P. o., T. o., D. B., C., E. good.* —	13	27 29	Country level, open and cultivated, rough cart-road, nullahs difficult during rains.	......	Aik bridged.	829	S. G. F. and W. plentiful, T. ample.	Ditto, Large Cantonment, Civil Station and City.
3	**Bhuddeeana** *E. good.—*	11	38	......	......	......	......	S. after notice, W. plentiful, T. nil.	Village.
4	**Pasrur** *E. good.—*	8 4	46 4	......	Across Ravi drainage.	Degh ford.	......	Ditto	Village, pass Nawadi 1¼ miles, Murdana 6½ miles.
5	**Dodha or Thaloh** *E. good.—*	13	55	Country flooded during rains, road fair.	......	......	......	Ditto	Village.
6	**Reyah** *B., E. good.—*	8	59	......	......	Ravi ferry.	......	Ditto	Village, pass Amkra 4½ miles, Thurpal 7 miles.
7	**Ajnala** *E. good.—*	9 ...	67 72 77 75	Country open, level, cultivated, nullahs bridged road fair, through low ground.	......	Barye Doab and Husli canals both bridged.	......	S. after notice, W. from wells, T. nil.	Ditto.
8	**Raja Sansee** *E. good.—*	8	85	......	......	......	......	S. must be collected, W. plentiful, T. nil.	Ditto.
9	**Amritsur** *P.O.,T.O., Hotel, C., E*	7	93	......	......	......	......	S. G. F. and W. abundant, T. ample.	Small Cantonment, Civil Station and City, also Junction Station on N.-W.Railway.

Branch Railway hence *viâ* Batala 24 miles, to Gurdaspur 44 miles, to Pathankot 67 miles.

III JAMMU to LAHORE and MIAN MIR by EMINABAD—

Number of Marches.	Names of Stages.	Distance in miles and furlongs. Inter-mediate. m. f.	Distance in miles and furlongs. Total. m. f.	Nature of Route.	Main Valleys and Mountain Passes.	River Crossings and Lakes.	Altitude above Sea Level in Feet.	Supplies and Transport at Stages.	Remarks.
	Jammu *P. O., T. O., D. B., C.*	... ...	0 ...	Metalled road	Across Chenab drainage.	......	1200	S. G. F. and W. abundant, T. ample.	Large town and capital of Jammu State, Railway Station on left bank Tawi river.
			1 4	......	......	Tawi bridge.			
			6 ...	......	......	Balal ford.			
1	Runbir Singhpur *P. O., T. O.—*	14 ...	14 :	......	......	......	898	S. and W. scarce, T. nil.	Railway Station on branch line.
	Sialkot *P. O., T. O., D. B., C., E. good.—*	13 ...	27 ...	Country level, open and well cultivated, cart-road fairly good but very swampy in rains, nullahs bridged.	......	......	829	S. G. F. and W. plentiful, T. ample.	Cantonment, Civil Station and Railway Station on branch line.
			31 4			Aik bridge.			
3	Bhalowala *E. good.—*	12 4	39 4	......	......	......	......	S. after notice, W. plentiful, T. nil.	Village.
4	Dharmkot *E. good.—*	13 5	53 1	......	......	......	......	S. after notice, W. plentiful, T. nil.	Village, cross road to Gujranwala 11 miles.
5	Eminabad *P. O., D. B., E. good.—*	13 2	66 3	......	Across Ravi drainage.	......	......	S. after notice, W. from wells, T. available.	Small town.

No.	Station			Road	Across Chenab drainage	Bridges, &c.	Elevation	Water and supplies	Remarks
6	Kamoke *P.O., T.O., E. good.—*	5	71 3	Grand Trunk Road	......	...	......	Ditto, T. nil.	Village and Station on N.-W. Railway.
7	Muridki *P.O., T.O., E. good.—*	12 3	83 6	......	......	...	......	Ditto	Ditto.
8	Shahdera *P.O., T.O., E. good.—*	13	96 97	6 6	......	Ravi railway bridge and ferry.	......	Ditto	Ditto.
9	Lahore *P. O., T. O., Hotels, C.*	2 5	99 102	3 3	......	Canal bridge	......	S. G. F. and W abundant, T. ample.	Capital of Panjab, Civil Station, large city, and ditto.
10	Mian Mir *P. O., T. O., D. B., C., E. good.—*	6	105 3	......	......	......	......	Ditto	Large Military Cantonment and ditto.

IV   JAMMU to GUJRANWALA by SIALKOT—

No.	Station			Road	Across Chenab drainage	Bridges, &c.	Elevation	Water and supplies	Remarks
	Jammu *P. O., T. O., D. B., C.*	::	0 ...		Across Chenab drainage	......	1200	S G. F. and W. abundant, T. ample.	Large town and capital of Jammu State, Railway Station on left bank Tawi river.
1	Runbir Singhpur *P. O., T. O.—*	14	1 6	Metalled road	......	Tawi bridge. Balal ford.	898	S. and W. scarce, T. nil.	Railway Station on branch line.
2	Sialkot *P. O., T. O., D. B., C., E. good.—*	13	27	Country level, open, well cultivated, road raised and fairly good.	......	......	829	S. G. F. and W. abundant, T. ample.	Cantonment, Civil Station, City and ditto.
3	Ghuenki *E. good.—*	9 4	31 36	4 4	......	......	Aik bridge.	......	S. after notice, W. from wells, T. nil.	Small village.

Number of Marches	Names of Stages	Distance in miles and furlongs — Intermediate m. f.	Distance in miles and furlongs — Total m. f.	Nature of Route	Main Valleys and Mountain Passes	River Crossings and Lakes	Altitude above Sea Level in Feet	Supplies and Transport at Stages	Remarks
IV	ROUTE—contd.			......	Across Chenab drainage.	......	......		
4	Duska, E. tolerable.—	9 4	36 4	Road heavy after much rain.	......	......	......	S. G. F. and W. plentiful, T. available.	Village.
		9 4	46 ..						
5	Gujranwala P. O., T O, D. B., E. good.—	16 2	62 2	......	......	......	......	S. G. F. and W. abundant, T. ample.	Small Civil Station and town on the G. T. Road, also Station N.-W. Ry.
V	**JAMMU to WUZIRABAD by SIALKOT—**								
1	Jammu P. O., T. O., D. B., C.	0 ..		Metalled road	Down Chenab drainage.	......	1200	S. G. F. and W. abundant, T. ample.	Large town and capital of Jammu State, Railway Station left bank Tawi river.
		1 4		......	......	Tawi bridge.			
		6 ..		......	......	Balal ford.			
1	Runbir Singhpur P. O., T. O.—	14 ..		......	......	......	898	S. and W. scarce, T. nil.	Railway Station on branch line.
2	Sialkot P. O., T O, D B, C., E. good.—	13 ..	27 ..	......	......	......	829	S. G. F. and W. abundant, T. ample.	Cantonment, Civil Station and City also Station on branch line.

| 3 | Samurhial D. B., E. fair.— | 13 | 6 | 40 | Country low and flooded during rains. | ...... | ...... | ...... | S. G. F. and W. plentiful, T. available. | Village track hence to Duska 10 miles. |
| 4 | Wuzirabad D. B., C., E. good.— | 13 | 4 | 54 | 2 | ...... | ...... | ...... | S. G. F. and W. abundant, T. ample. | Town and Junction on N.-W. Railway. |

Branch Railway 51 miles in length runs parallel to this road with a station at every stage.

VI JAMMU to PIND-DADUN KHAN by GUJRAT—

	Place			Total	Road	Across Chenab drainage		Elevation	Supplies	Remarks
	Jammu P. O., T. O., D. B., C.	...	0	...	Metalled road	Across Chenab drainage	......	1200	S. G. F. and W. abundant, T. ample.	Capital of Jammu State, town on right bank Tawi river, Railway Station on left bank Tawi river.
			1 4	6	......	......	Tawi bridge Balai ford.			
1	Runbir Singhpur P. O., T. O.—	14	14		......	......	......	898	S. and W. scarce, T. nil.	Small bazar and station on Branch Railway.
2	Sialkot P. O., T. O., D. B., C., E. good.—	13	27		Country flat and cultivated, road very fair.	......	......	829	S. G. F. and W. abundant, T. ample.	Cantonment, Civil Station, City and Railway Station on branch line.
3	Kulowal E. fair.—	10	2	37 40	Road difficult over heavy sand on both banks of river.	......	Chenab bridge of boats and ferry.	......	S. G. F. and W. plentiful, T. available.	Village.
4	Muhutah	4	41		......	......	......	......	S. G. F. and W. procurable, T. nil.	
5	Gujrat P. O., T. O., D. B., C., E. on G.T. road.	12	53		Road very fair	......	......	......	S. G. F. and W. plentiful, T. ample.	Small Civil Station, City and Railway Station on N.-W. main line.

Number of Marches.	Names of Stages.	Distance in miles and furlongs.		Nature of Route.	Main Valleys and Mountain Passes.	River Crossings and Lakes.	Altitude above Sea Level in Feet.	Supplies and Transport at Stages.	Remarks.
		Intermediate. m. f.	Total. m. f.						
VI	ROUTE—contd.	...	53 3	......	Across Chenab drainage.	......	......	S. after notice, T. nil	Village.
6	Dulanwala	12 ...	63 3	......		......	......	S. G. F. and W. plentiful, T. ample.	Small town and bazar, also Station on Uranchi line.
7	Dinguh *P. O., T. O., D. B.—*	12 5	76 ...	......	Across Jhelum drainage.	......	......		
8	Moong	13 ...	89 ...	Rough cart road ...	......	......	......	S. G. F. after notice, W. procurable, T. nil	Village.
9	Majee	9 ...	98 ...	......	......	......	......	Ditto ...	Ditto.
10	Malukwal *P. O., T. O.—*	10 ...	108 ...	......	......	......	693	Ditto ...	Ditto, and Station on branch line.
11	Miani *B.—*	9 ...	115 ...						
		...	117 ...						
12	Pind-Dadun Khan *P. O., T. O., D. B., C., E.*	... / 7 5	121 ... / 124 5	......	......	Jhelum bridge of boats and ferry.	731	S. G. F. and W. plentiful, T. available	Town near Salt Mines with large trade, Station on branch line.

From Jammu, branch rail to Wuzirabad 51 miles, N.-W. main line to Lala Musa 20 miles, branch rail to Pind-Dadun Khan 57 miles. Total by railway 128 miles—crossing Jhelum river by Nizam-chuk bridge.

From Muhutah 8 miles to Jalalpur and 9 miles to Gujrat. Total 17 miles good road. Muhutah and Nowshera on right bank of Chenab have been washed away by recent high floods.

The Rock Salt Mines at Khewra are 9 miles distant by road from Pind-Dadun Khan. There is also a branch line from Malukwal over the Jhelum railway bridge at Chuk Nizam to Pind-Dadun Khan 6 miles, and thence to Pind-Dadun Khan 6 miles, also another branch from Harampur to Khewra, 9 miles.

VI a   GUJRAT to PIND-DADUN KHAN by PHALIAN—

No.	Stage	Int. m.	Int. f.	Total m.	Total f.	Road	Drainage	River / ferry	Pop.	Supplies	Remarks
5	**Gujrat** P. O., T. O., D. B., C., E. on G. T. road.— Koonjah	...	...	53	3	Fair road	Down Chenab drainage.	......	......	S. G. F. and W. abundant, T. ample.	Small Civil Station, City and Railway station on N.-W main line.
6	**Mughowal** E.—	12	5	61	...	Rough cart road...	......	......	......	S. after notice, W. plentiful, T. nil.	Village.
7	**Pariwala** E.—	9	...	66	...	......	......	......	......	Ditto.	Ditto.
8	**Phalian** P. O., B., E.—	13	4	75	...	Good cart road ...	......	......	......	S. G. F and W. plentiful, T available.	Large village.
9	**Kothiala Shekhan** E.—	11	4	88	4	......	Across Jhelum drainage.	......	......	S. after notice, W. plentiful, T. nil.	Village.
10	**Miani** B.—	20	...	100	...	......	......	......	......	S. G. F. W. T. plentiful.	Ditto.
11	**Pind-Dadun Khan** P. O., T. O., D. B., C., E.—	7	5	120 / 124 / 127	5	......	......	Jhelum boat bridge and ferry.	731	S. G. F. and W. plentiful, T available.	Town near Salt Mines with large trade, Station on Branch Railway.

VII   JAMMU to JHELUM by DAULAT NAGAR—

No.	Stage	Int. m.	Int. f.	Total m.	Total f.	Road	Drainage	River / ferry	Pop.	Supplies	Remarks
	Jammu P. O., T. O., D. B., C.	...	...	0	...	Country open and cultivated, rough track over low ground, on right bank Chenab river.	Across Chenab drainage.	......	1200	S. G. F. and W. abundant, T. ample.	Large town and capital of Jammu State.
1	**Gujansu**	11	...	11	...	......	......	......	......	S. must be collected, G. and W. plentiful, T. nil.	Village on left bank Chenab river.

Number of Marches.	Names of Stages.	Distance in miles and furlongs.		Nature of Route.	Main Valleys and Mountain Passes.	River Crossings and Lakes.	Altitude above Sea Level, in Feet.	Supplies and Transport at Stages.	Remarks.
		Inter- mediate. m. f.	Total. m. f.						
VII	ROUTE—contd.	......	......	......					
2	Amirpur	11 ...	11 ...	......	Across Chenab drainage.	Chenab ferry and 5 offshoots.	......	S. scarce, G. and W. plentiful, T. nil.	Village on right bank Chenab offshoot.
3	Minawur P. O., B., E.—	12 ...	23 ...	Rough cart-road	......	Tawi ford.	......	S. procurable, G. and W. plentiful, T. available.	Small town.
	Mutianwala	7 ...	30 ...	......	......				
4	Kureeanwala P. O., E. good.—	10 ...	40 ...	Fair road from mile 32	......	Bhundur ford.	...	S G F. and W. plentiful, T. available.	Large village.
5	Daulatnagar P. O., D. B.—	12 4	52 4	Good road, but very sandy in crossing river beds.	......	......	1029	S. G. F. and W. procurable, T. nil.	Ditto.
6	Kharian Serai P. O., T. O., D. B., C., E. good.—	14 4	67 ...	Join the Grand Trunk Road.	Kharian Pass over Pabbi range. Across Jhelum drainage.	......	......	S. G. F. and W. plentiful, T. available.	Large village and Station on N.-W. Railway.
7	Alumgir Serai P. O., T. O., E. good.	9 4	76 4	......	......	Jhelum railway bridge	......	Ditto	Naurangabad village and Karyala Station on N.W. Ry.

No.	Name			Remarks on road	Drainage	Ford	Elevation	Supplies	Remarks
8	Jhelum P. O., T. O., D. B., C. B. good.—	4	4	81	......		Ditto	......	827	S. G. F. and W. abundant, T. ample.	Cantonment, Civil Station and City, also Railway Station on N.-W. main line.

VIII JAMMU to JHELUM by BHIMBER.—

No.	Name			Remarks on road	Drainage	Ford	Elevation	Supplies	Remarks
1	Jammu P. O., T. O., D. B. C.	...	0	...	Country open and well cultivated.	Across Chenab drainage.	......	1200	S. G. F. and W. abundant, T. ample.	Large town and capital of the Jammu State.
	Akmoor P. O., F. B.—	16	16	Rough cart-track, very sandy at river crossings.	......	Chenab ferry.	1142	S. G. F. and W. plentiful, T. available.	Small town, bazar and fort on right bank Chenab.
2	Amirpur E.—	16	32	......	......	......		S. scarce, G. and W. plentiful, T. nil.	Village.
		37			Tawi ford.			
3	Minawur P. O., E.—	7	39	......	......	......		S. procurable, G. and W. plentiful, T. available.	Small town and tehsil.
4	Barnali E.—	18	52	......	Across Bhimber drainage.	......		S. scarce, G. and W. plentiful, T. nil.	Village.
		60				Bhundar ford		
5	Bringh E.—	12	64	......	......	......		S. scarce, G. and W. plentiful, T. nil.	Ditto.
		68				Bhimber ford		

Number of Marches.	Names of Stages.	Distance in miles and furlongs. Intermediate. m. f.	Total. m. f.	Nature of Route.	Main Valleys and Mountain Passes.	River Crossings and Lakes.	Altitude above Sea Level, in Feet.	Supplies and Transport at Stages.	Remarks.
VIII	*ROUTE—contd.*	...	...						
6	**Bhimber** *P. O., B., E.—*	...	68 ...	Country track ...	Across Bhimber drainage	......	1100	S. G. F. and W. plentiful, T. available	Small Town, head-quarters of district.
	Chance Gotreala	5	69 ...	......	Across Jhelum drainage.	......	......	S. scarce, G. and W. plentiful, T. nil.	Village.
		...	76 ...						
7	**Besuh Khoord**	16	85 ...	......	......	Jhelum railway bridge.	......		
	Nawangabad	...	94 ...	Join Grand Trunk Road.	......	......			
		...	96 ...						
8	**Jhelum** *P. O., T. O., D. E., C., E. good.—*	13	98 ...	......	......	......	827	S. G. F. and W. abundant, T. ample.	Cantonment, Civil Station and City, also Railway Station on N.-W. main line.

VIIIₐ BHIMBER to RAWUL PINDI by MIRPUR—

Number of Marches.	Names of Stages.	Distance in miles and furlongs. Intermediate. m. f.	Total. m. f.	Nature of Route.	Main Valleys and Mountain Passes.	River Crossings and Lakes.	Altitude above Sea Level, in Feet.	Supplies and Transport at Stages.	Remarks.
6	**Bhimber** *P. O., B., E.—*	...	69 ...	Country undulating and much cut up by ravines. Track across drainage.	Across Bhimber drainage.	......	1100	S. G. F. and W. plentiful, T. available.	Small Town and head-quarters of district.
	Sukasin	...	78 ... / 80 ...		Ditto	Branch of Sukatar.	......		

No.	Place		Total	Road	Crossing	Ferry / Branch	Elevation	Supplies	Remarks
7	Selar	14 ...	83 ... / 86 -	......	Across Poonch drainage.	Branch of Sukatar.	......	S. scarce and G. F. W. plentiful, T. nil.	Village.
8	Mirpur *P. O., B., E.—*	15 ...	98 -	Fair hill road	......	......	1236	S. G. F. and W. plentiful, T. available	Town of some size, and large bazar.
9	Chaomukh *P. O., E.—*	10 ...	109 ...	Hill Track	Sensar Pass	Poonch Toi or Palasta ferry.	1902	S G F and W. plentiful, T. available.	
10	Hil	10 ...	118 ...	......	Across Jhelum drainage.	Jhelum ferry	......	S. nil, W. from river, T. nil.	
11	Bewal *E.—*	13 ...	131 ...	Fair road over broken ground.	......	......	......	S. after notice, G. and W procurable, T. nil.	Village.
12	Kalar *E.—*	8 ...	139 ...	......	......	......	1790	S. G. F. and W plentiful, T. available.	Large place.
	Manikiala	...	149 ...	......	Across Sohan drainage.	...	1916	......	Ancient tope.
13	Rewat *P. O., T. O., B., E.—*	14 4	153 4	Grand Trunk Road	......	......	1871	S. scarce, W. scarce. T. nil	Village and Station on N.-W. Railway
14	Rawul Pindi *P. O., T. O., D. B., Hotels, C., E.—*	13 4	167 ...	.....	......	......	1700	S G F and W. abundant, T. ample.	Large Cantonment Civil Station and City; also Railway Station on N.-W. main line.

From Bhimber 69 miles, another track to Kalaris 87 miles and to Mirpur 100 miles.

From Sukasin 78 miles there is a track by Alibeg to Sukchainpur on left bank Jhelum river 88 miles, whence Jhelum City is distant 10 miles or 98 miles and Mirpur 15 miles or 103 miles from Jammu.

Between Chaomukh and Kalar there is an alternative route by the Danguli or Palalan ferry over the Jhelum river, Chaomukh, 108 miles; Sanor, 118 miles; Palalau, 128 miles; Kalar, 141 miles.

IX JAMMU to RAWUL PINDI by KOTLI—

Number of Marches	Names of Stages	Distance in miles and furlongs		Nature of Route	Main Valleys and Mountain Passes	River Crossings and Lakes	Altitude above Sea Level in feet	Supplies and Transport at Stages	Remarks
		Intermediate m. f.	Total m. f.						
	Jammu P. O., T. O., D. B.—	...	0 ...	Country open and cultivated, rough cart road	Across Chenab valley.	......	1200	S. G. F. W. and T. ample.	Large town and capital of Jammu state
1	Aknoor P. O., F. B.—	16	16	......	......	Chenab ferry	1142	S. G. F. W. plentiful, T. available.	Small town and bazar on right bank Chenab.
2	Choki Chowra E.—	13 4	29 4	Fair hill road used by troops in marching to Srinagar by Pir Punjal.	Ambi Pass.	Kurna Khad	2150	S. G. F. after notice, W. procurable, T. nil.	Halting place.
3	Thanda Pani B., E.—	12 4	42	......	Kalidhar range.	Rud bridge and ford.	1460	S. scarce, W. plentiful, T. nil.	Village 1 mile distant.
4	Siot	10	52	Track across broken ground.	Up Tawi valley.	Tawi ford ...	......	S. scarce, T. nil.	Village.
5	Naoshera P. O., B., C.—	12 4	64 4	Fair hill road fit for mules on a fine plain, well cultivated.	Makri range	......	3000	S. G. F. W. plentiful, T. available.	Town and bazar 300ft. above right bank Tawi.

No.	Name			Road / Track	Direction	Ferry	Elevation	Water supply	Remarks
6	**Laroka**	15	79	......	Down Ban valley	......	......	S. scarce, T. nil. S. G. F. precarious, W. from wells, T. available.	Village.
7	**Koireta**	10	89	......	......	......	2500	......	Ditto.
	Dhunna		97	......	......	Ban ford.	......	......	Town of 300 houses and bazar.
8	**Kotli** P. O., B., E.—	16	100 105	Rough stony track, difficult for mules.	Across Poonch valley	Poonch Toi or Palasta ferry.	2000	S. G. F. plentiful, W. from springs, T. available.	
9	**Sensar** E.—	13	106 114 118	Steep ascent	Across Brunian gully		3158 2320	S. G. F. W. T. procurable.	Bachlon Pass. Village and thanna.
10	**Salgraon**	12	123 130	......	Khaira gully. Across Jhelum valley	Jhelum ferry	......	S. G. F. scarce, W. plentiful, T. nil. S.G.F.W. procurable. T. available.	Village.
11	**Thoa** E.—*Chinton*	12	142 147	Fair track across broken ground.	Down Sohan valley	......	2208		Village.
12	**Rewat** P. O., T. O., B., E.—	15	4 157	Grand Trunk Road.	......	......	1871	S. G. F. W. scarce, T. nil.	Village and Station on N. W. Ry.
13	**Rawul Pindi** P.O., T.O., D.B. C., E.	13	4 166 171	......	......	Sohan bridge.	1700	S. G. F. T. abundant. W. precarious.	Large Cantonment, Civil Station, City and Railway Station on N.W. main line. Water supply being added.

Between Naoshera and Koirta, there is an alternative track by Dooral Pass and down the Ban valley by Seri—*riz*, Naoshera 64 miles, Dooral 74, Seri 83, Koireta 88 miles, Kotli 104 miles.

2 From Sensar there is an alternative track by Owen ferry and Kahoota to Rawul Pindi—*riz*, Sensar 118 miles, Owen ferry over Jhelum River 13g miles, Kahoota 147 miles, Siala 160 miles, Rawul Pindi 171 miles.

From Sensar there is a track 10 miles long to Samor falling into the route from Bhimber by Palalan ferry to Rawul Pindi.

IXa KOTLI to ABBOTTABAD by MURREE—

Number of Marches	Names of Stages	Distance of miles and furlongs		Nature of Route.	Main Valleys and Mountain Passes	River crossing and Lakes.	Altitude above Sea Level in feet.	Supplies and Transport at Stages.	Remarks.
		Intermediate m. f.	Total m. f.						
8	Kotli *P.O., B., E. good —*	...	105	Rough stony hill track, difficult for mules.	Across Poonch valley.	......	2000	S. G. F. plentiful, W. from springs, T. available.	Town and tehsil, large bazar.
			106	...		Poonch Toi or Palasta ferry.			
9	Sarsawa *E.—*	6 ...	111	...	...	...	......	S. G. F. after notice, W. procurable, T. nil.	Village.
10	Palandri *P. O., E.—*	16 ...	127	...	......	......	4250	Ditto, T. available.	Fort and tehsil.
11	Mangh *E.—*	11 ...	128 / 133 / 138	...	Palandri ridge Up Jhelum valley.	Goon ford.	......	Ditto, T. nil	Village and fort.
12	Tain *E.—*	10 ...	148	...	...	......	......	Ditto „	Ditto.
	Dhara	...	152	...	...	Jhelum ferry.			

13	Dhanda E.—			159	...	Fair hill track, passable for mules.	......	......	Ditto ,	Ditto.
14	Murree P. O., T. O., Hotels C.	13		172	...	Across hilly country; road fair for riding and mules.	Murree range	......	7108	S. G. F. W. plentiful, T. ample.	Summer Cantonment, Sanitarium and large bazar.
				184	4	......	Across Hurroo valley	Branch Hurroo ford.		
15	Nagri B.—	13	2	185	2	......			S. G. F. after notice, W. plentiful, T. nil.	Village.
	Mari B.—			188	6	......	Mari ridge.	......		
				190	2	......				
16	Sajkot	10		185	2	Netlahs easy	Across Dohr valley.	......	S. G. F. after notice, W. plentiful, T. nil.	Village.
				103	2	......		Dohr ford.		
17	Abbottabad P. O., T. O., D. B., C. E.—	16	4	211	6	......	......		4166	S. G. F. and W. plentiful, T. available.	Cantonment, Civil Station, town and bazar.

This is the lower road from Murree to Abbottabad. It leaves the main road from Murree towards Rawal Pindi at 4 miles 4 furlongs, descends by a steep zig-zag, crosses two branches of the Hurroo river with Gurini between and from Nagri Dhoondhan ascends easily in 3 miles 4 furlongs to Mari ridge, then descends and crosses the Hurroo river at 1 mile 4 furlongs beyond. From Sajkot it ascends a low ridge and descends down the Godawala nullah to the Dohr river, which it crosses between Itajoia and Haveliyan.

From the Mari bungalow there is a direct road along the top of mountain spur to Chunglagully, distant about 7 miles, and passable for mules.

From Sajkot a road ascends the ridge to Kalabagh on the upper road, distant about 10 miles.

From Sajkot, a road runs past Nara Police Station, 3 miles, southwards to Hurripur, distant about 25 miles.

For the upper road from Murree to Abbottabad by the gullies, see Route XXVII.

X JAMMU to GILGIT by KOTLI and KISHENGUNGA VALLEY.—

Number of Marches	Names of Stages	Distance in Miles and Furlongs		Nature of Route	Main Valleys and Mountain Passes	River crossings and Lakes.	Altitude above Sea Level in Feet.	Supplies and Transport at Stages.	Remarks.
		Intermediate m. f.	Total m. f.						
	Jammu *P. O., T.O., D. B.—*	... ...	0 ...	Country open and cultivated, rough cart-road.	Across Chenab valley.	.....	1200	S. G. F. and W. abundant, T. ample.	Large Town and Capital of Jammu State.
1	Aknoor *P. O., F. B.—*	16 ...	16 ...	Fair hill road used by troops in marching to Srinagar *viâ* Pir Punjal Pass.	.....	Chenab ferry	1142	S. G. F. and W. plentiful, T. available.	Small town and bazar on right bank of Chenab river.
			26 ...		Ambi range.				
2	Choki Chowra *E.—*	13 4	29 4	......	......	Kurna Khad	2150	S. G. F. after notice, W. procurable, T. nil.	
			34 ...		Kalidhar range.				
4	Thandapani *B., E.—*	12 4	42 4	......	......	Rud bridge and ford.	1400	S. scarce, W. plentiful, T. nil.	Village 1 mile off.
	Siot	10 ...	52 ...	Track across broken ground.	Up Tawi valley.	.....	......	S. scarce, T. nil.	Village.
5	Naoshera *P. O., B., C.—*	12 ...	64 ...	Fair hill road fit for mules on a fine plain, well cultivated.	Makri range	Tawi ford	3000	S. G. F. and W. plentiful, T. available.	Town and bazar.
			77 ...			.....			

No.	Stage		Distance (miles)	Total (miles)	Road	Direction	Ford / Bridge	Altitude	Water & Supplies	Remarks
7	Laroka	...	15	79	...	Down Ban valley.	...	......	S. scarce, T. nil.	Village.
	Koireta	...	10	89	...	......	......	2500	S. precarious, W. from wells, T. available, W. scarce.	Village.
	Dhanna	...	...	97	...	......	Ban ford.	......	......	......
8	Koti *P. O., B., E.—*	...	16	100, 105, 106	Rough stony hill track, difficult for mules.	Across Poonch valley.	......	2000	S. plentiful, W. from springs, T. available.	Village and town of 300 houses, bazar and tehsil.
9	Sarsawa *E.—*	...	6	111	......	......	Poonch Toi or Palasta ferry.	......	S. after notice, W. procurable, T. nil.	Village.
10	Palandri *P. O., E.—*	...	16	127, 128, 133	......	Palandri range	Goon ford.	1250	Ditto, T. available.	Fort and tehsil.
11	Mangh *E.—*	...	11	138	......	Up Jhelum valley.	......	......	Ditto, T. nil.	Village and fort.
12	Tain *E.—*	...	10	148	......	......	......	......	Ditto ...	Ditto.
13	Khodar	...	9	150, 157	......	......	Mal or Bagh bridge. Jhelum ferry.	......	S. from Jhanjhana, W. from river, T. nil.	Jhanjhana village.
14	Kohala *P. O., D. B.—*	...	12	169	... ...	......	......	1915	S. G. F. and W. plentiful, T. after notice.	Small bazar, border of Kashmir.

Number of Marches	Names of Stages	Distance in miles and furlongs — Intermediate m. f.	Distance in miles and furlongs — Total m. f.	Nature of Route	Main Valleys and Mountain Passes	River Crossings and Lakes	Altitude above Sea Level, in Feet	Supplies and Transport at Stages	Remarks
X	*ROUTE—contd.*	...	...						
	Bareda B.—	...	169 2	Kashmir metalled and bridged road.	Up Jhelum valley				
		...	170	......	......	Agar bridge	2029	S. scarce, F. and W. plentiful, T. nil.	Village.
15	**Dulai** *D.B.—*	12	177 3	......	......	......	2103		
		9 2	181	......	......	Jhelum bridge	2225	S. G. F. and W. procurable, T. after notice.	Village and bazar at junction of Kishenganga. Town on left bank Kishenganga bazar, head-quarters of district.
16	**Dumel** *P. O., T. O., D. B., E.— Muzafferabad*	...	190 2	......	Up Kishenganga valley left bank.	......	2470	......	
17	**Nuraseri**	12 6	193	Hill track passable for laden mules, though difficult in parts, especially for 6 miles at Titwal, 7 miles near Doarian, 13 miles between Shardi and Khel and 21 miles over the Shontar Pass.		......	2750	S. W. F. G. plentiful, T. nil.	
18	**Punjgram**	4	203			......	2900	S. W. F. G. plentiful, T. available.	Village.
19	**Nowsnda**	9	210 4			...	3425	Ditto, T. nil.	
20	**Titwal** *E.—*	6 4	219 4			Karna.	3250	S. W. F. G. plentiful, T. available.	Village and tehsil.

No.	Name						Elevation	Supplies	Remarks
21	Phalak	6	232	...	...	......	3550	S. W. G. F. plentiful, T. available.	Village.
22	Rampura	6	238	...	......	......	4050	Ditto, T. nil.	Ditto.
	Salkota	...	242 4	......	Cross to right bank.	Kishenganga Jhula bridge.		...	
23	Shahkot	6	244	......	......	......	4300	Ditto	Ditto.
24	Karen	8	252	......	......	Wooden bridge over Kishenganga.	4650	Ditto, T. available.	Ditto.
25	Doarian	7	259	......	......	......	5050	Ditto	Ditto.
26	Dudnial	7	266	......	......	......	5050	Ditto, T. nil.	
27	Kharigam or Shardi. *F.—*	9	275	......	......	......	5850	S. procurable, W. G. F. plentiful, T. available.	Village and fort.
28	Seri	7	282	......	......	......	6000	No supplies, W. G. F. plentiful, T. nil.	
29	Khel *E.—*	8	290	......	Up Khel valley.	......	6250	S. scanty, ditto.	Village.
30	Dumel *E.—*	8	298	......	......	......	7300	S. nil,	
31	Bala *E.—*	8	306	Easy hill track passable for mules.	Shentar Pass Down Mir Malik valley	......	10000	Ditto	Southern foot of Pass.
	Ghazinbilli	...	312 316				13000 11700	Ditto	Northern foot of Pass.
32	Shingardodar	12	318	......	......	Dabin ford	10500		

Number of Marches	Names of Stages	Distance in miles and furlongs		Nature of Route.	Main Valleys and Mountain Passes.	River Crossings and Lakes.	Altitude above Sea Level in Feet.	Supplies and Transport at Stages.	Remarks.
		Intermediate. m. f.	Total. m. f.						
X	ROUTE—contd.	......	......	......	......	......			
33	Mir Malik *E.—*	12	318	......	......	......	9400	S. procurable, W. G. F. plentiful, T. nil.	Small village.
	Ratta	8	326	......	......	......	8500	......	Village.
34	Chugaon *E. confined.—*	......	333	......	Down Astor valley left bank.	......	8750	S. and G. scanty. W. and E. procurable, T. nil.	Ditto.
35	Gurikot *E. confined.—*	10 4	336 4	......	......	Astor bridge	7800	Ditto	Ditto.
36	Astor (Idgah) *P.O., T.O., B., E. Polo ground.—*	10 4	347	Join new 10ft. road from Srinagar by Gurais and Astor to Gilgit, fully bridged and of easy gradients.	......	......	7800	S. and G. procurable, W. and F. plentiful, T. moderate.	Village, fort and lazar, bungalow will be built.
	Harcho	7	354	......	......	......	......		
37	Dashkin *E. confined.—*	......	363	......	......	......	......	Ditto, T. available.	Village.
38	Doian *R. B., E.—*	15	369	......	......	......	......	Ditto, T. nil.	Ditto.
39	Ramghat	11	380	......	......	Astor bridge	......	S. G. F. nil, W. plentiful, T. nil.	Guard House.
		10 4	380 4						

No.	Station			Total miles	Road	Direction	Bridge	Elevation	Water and supplies	Remarks
40	**Bawanji** P. O., T. O., B., E.—	7	4	398	...	Up Indus valley left bank.		4635	S. and G. procurable, W. plentiful, F. scarce, T. available.	Village and bazar with fort.
41	**Pertabpul** C., E.—	7	...	405	...	...	Indus bridge wire rope suspension.	...	S. G. F. oil, W. plentiful, T. nil.	
42	**Safedpari**	10	...	415	...	Up Gilgit valley right bank.	...	...	Ditto.	
43	**Minawar**	10	...	425	...	...	...	...	Ditto.	
44	**Gilgit** P. O., T. O., E.—	9	...	431	...	...	...	4890	S. G. F. W. moderate, T. available.	Military Cantonment, fort and bazar.

East of Shontar Pass there is another gully which has been partially explored and is said to be 13,500 feet high. There is snow along this route between Shardi and Astor 80 miles during the winter, and the Shontar gully is then impassable. This road is usually closed for half the year. There is plenty of grass and wood fuel from Jamun to Astor, abundant water throughout, and supplies are procurable. Through transport is necessary from Jamun to Gilgit, with occasional aid from Naoshera, Kotli, Mozufferabad, and Astor.

From Doarian 260 miles, there is a road up the valley of same name which branches by 2 passes, Doarian and Rattigulli into the Klagan valley.

Xa PARALLEL ROUTE MOZUFFERABAD to KAREN by RIGHT BANK KISHENGUNGA RIVER—

No.	Station			Total miles	Road	Direction	Bridge	Elevation	Water and supplies	Remarks
16	**Mozufferabad** P. O., E.—	...	...	192	Country undulating, well cultivated, fair road to Pala, hence difficult for laden mules.	...	...	2470	S. W. G. F. plentiful. T. moderate.	Town and bazar, head-quarters of district.
17	**Kowri** E.—	8	...	200	...	Up Kishengunga valley right bank.	...	...	Ditto ...	Large village.
18	**Pala** E.—	7	...	207	...	...	...	...	Ditto ...	Ditto.

Number of Marches	Names of Stages	Distances in miles and Furlongs. Intermediate. m. f.	Distances in miles and Furlongs. Total. m. f.	Nature of Route.	Main Valleys and Mountain Passes.	River crossings and Lakes.	Altitude above Sea-Level in Feet.	Supplies and Transport at Stages.	Remarks.
Xa	ROUTE—contd.								
19	**Jaggian**	... 12 ...	207 219 225 ...	......	Saraugo Pass	......	......	S. scarce, W. G. F. plentiful, T. nil.	
20	**Patian** E.—	... 12 ...	231 ...	......	......	Jagran	...	Ditto, T. available.	Village.
21	**Shahkot** E.—	... 7 ...	238 ...	......	......	......	4300	S. W. G. F. plentiful, T. nil.	Ditto.
22	**Karen** E.—	... 8 ...	246 ...	......	......	Kishenganga wooden bridge	4650	Ditto, T. available.	Ditto.

From Kowri 200 miles, there is a fair road for pack animals over the Galontia gully, 208 miles, to Balakot, 218 miles, in the Khagan valley
From Patian 231 miles, there is a road up the Jagran valley eastwards which leads by 3 passes, Bidela, Shikara and Torgulli into the Khagan valley.

Xb SHARDI to GURAIS ACROSS HILLS—

Number of Marches	Names of Stages	Distances in miles and Furlongs. Intermediate. m. f.	Distances in miles and Furlongs. Total. m. f.	Nature of Route.	Main Valleys and Mountain Passes.	River crossings and Lakes.	Altitude above Sea-Level in Feet.	Supplies and Transport at Stages.	Remarks.
27	**Shardi** E.—	... ...	275 ... 280 ...	Rough mountain path not passable for miles across four mountain spurs and intervening valleys.	...... Spur ridge	Kishenganga bridge.	5850 11000	S. procurable, W. G. F. plentiful, T. available.	Fort on left bank Kishenganga.

No.	Name	Miles	Total	Remarks on road	Direction	River crossings	Elevation	Water, grass, fuel	General remarks
28	Moktah Malik-ka-kothi. E.—	11	286	......	......	......	......	W. G. F. plentiful. T. nil.	In open forest about 1800 feet above Thien.
29	Camp	10	296	......	Spur ridge	......	......	Ditto	Village at junction of Kretsinar and Zemindhar Khan nullahs.
30	Thien. E.—	6	302	......	......	......	......	S from Kroras, W. G. F. plentiful, few coolies.	Village.
31	Matsil. E.—	13	315	......	Spur ridge	......	......	S. scanty, W. G. F. plentiful, T. nil.	
	Dudi	...	324	......	......	Tsandan Khul torrent.	...	......	
32	Geshart. E.—	16	331	......	Naosara ridge	Hanti nullah.	......	S. nil, W. G. F. plentiful, T. nil.	
	Bakthaor	...	335	......	......	......	......	......	
33	Kanzilwan. E.—	7	342	Join new road Srinagar to Gurais.	Up Kishengunga valley.	Kishengunga bridge.	7300	Ditto.	
34	Gurais. P. O., B., C., E.—	12	354	......	......	......	7800	S. W. G. F. plentiful, T. moderate.	Large village, fort and tehsil.

Xc KHEL to GURAIS UP KISHENGUNGA VALLEY.—

No.	Name	Miles	Total	Remarks on road	Direction	River crossings	Elevation	Water, grass, fuel	General remarks
29	Khel. E.—	...	29C	Rough hill path difficult for new and impassable for laden animals	Up Kishengunga valley.	......	6200	S. scanty, W. G. F. plentiful, T. nil.	

Number of Marches	Names of Stages	Distance in miles and furlongs		Nature of Route	Main Valleys and Mountain Passes	River crossings and Lakes	Altitude above Sea Level in feet	Supplies and Transport at Stages	Remarks
		Inter- mediate m. f.	Total m. f.						
Xc	ROUTE—contd.	...	290 ...				......		
30	Phulmai	13 ...	303 ...	...	......	Phulmai ford.	......	W. G. F. plentiful, T. nil.	
	Sirdari	...	308 ...	Rough path pass- able for miles.	......	......	......	......	Village.
31	Thaobut E.—	10 ...	313 ...	......	......	......	......	S. scanty, W. G. F. plentiful, few coolies.	Ditto.
32	Kanzilwan E.—	10 ...	323 ...	New road from Srinagar to Gurais.	......	......	7400	S. nil, W. G. F. plentiful, T. nil.	Ditto.
33	Gurais P. O., B., C. E.—	12 ...	335 ...	......	......	......	7800	S. W. G. F. plentiful, T. moderate.	Fort and tehsil.

A path ascends the Phulmai nulla over the Dohban Pir Pass 14,000 feet and descends down to Shingar Dodar about 22 miles in length.

XI JAMMU to POONCH by KOTLI—

| Jammu P. O., T. O., D. B.— | ... | ... | 0 ... | Country open and cultivated, rough cart-road. | Across Chenab valley. | ...... | 1200 | S. G. F. and W. abundant, T. ample. | Large town and capital of Jammu State. |

No.	Name			Road description	Pass / Direction	Crossing	Elevation	Supplies	Remarks
1	**Aknoor** *P. O., F., B.—*	16	16	Fair hill road used by troops in marching from Jammu to Srinagar by Pir Punjal Pass.	......	Chenab ferry	1142	S. G. F. and W. plentiful, T. available.	Small town and bazar on right bank of Chenab.
2	**Choki Chowra** *E.—*	13	26 ... 4 / 29 / 34	......	Ambi Pass. Kalidhar range.	Kurna Khud	2150	S. F. G. after notice, W. procurable, T. nil.	Halting place.
3	**Thandapani** *B., E.—*	12	42 ... 4	......	Up Tawi valley.	Rtud bridge and ford.	1460	S. scarce, W. plentiful, T. nil.	Village 1 mile off.
4	**Siot**	10	52	Track across broken ground.	......	......	......	S. scarce, T. nil.	Village.
5	**Naoshera** *P. O., B., E.—*	13	64			Tawi ford	......	S. G. F. and W. plentiful, T. available.	Town, bazar and tehsil.
6	**Dooral** *Seri*	11	75 / 84	Fair hill road fit for mules on a fine plain, well cultivated.	Dooral Pass Down Ban valley.	......	......	S. scarce, T. nil.	
7	**Koireta**	14	89		......	......	2500	S. precarious, W. from wells, T. available.	Village with ziarat and well.
8	**Kotli** *P. O., B., E.—*	16	100 / 105 / 107	Rough stony hill track, passable for mules, but difficult in places.	Up Poonch valley.	Ban ford. ...... Nela nuldee.	2000	S. G. F plentiful, W. from springs, T. available.	Town of 300 houses, bazar and tehsil.
	Tui		114	......	......	......	2170	130° Fahr.	Hot springs from limestone rocks on right bank Poonch river, cross by boat.
9	**Saira** *B.—*	14	119 / 122	......	......	Mehndur ford.	3000	S. G. F. plentiful, W. from river distant, T. available.	Large village.

Number of Marches.	Names of Stages.	Distance in miles and furlongs. Inter-mediate m. f.	Total. m. f.	Nature of Route.	Main Valleys and Mountain Passes.	River Crossings and Lakes.	Altitude above Sea Level in Feet.	Supplies and Transport at Stages.	Remarks.
XI	*ROUTE—contd.*	... ...	122 ...						
10	**Poonch** P. O., D. B., C., E.	16 ...	135 ...	......		Suran ferry	3300	S. G. F. and W. abundant, T. ample.	Capital of Poonch State, town, fort, large bazar.

From Kotli a track ascends the Dharan Range to the Nilliadheri gully 4,200 feet and descends down to Mankot Fort across the Mendola or Mehadur river, about 16 miles in length. After going 3 miles down the latter to Sagra, it ascends the Haveli Range to Sonra gully 4,500 feet, and descends into the Suran valley, and after crossing the latter river by a boat ferry reaches Poonch about 12 miles. Total distance 31 miles.

From Aknoor there is a road by Berk to the Sangarmarg iron mines which avoids the high ground thus: Jammu to Aknoor 16, Gerahti 26, Serai 37, Berk 44, and Sangarmarg 50 miles passable for laden mules.

From Thanhapani a road leads by Prat Tehsil to the Mehugala coalfield thus: Thandapani 42, Prat 52, Mehugala 64, Kalakot 70 miles from Jammu.

This Route XI was one of the three imperial roads of the Mogul period from the Punjab to Kashmir, and was the one selected for the passage of elephants. From Poonch it continued up the Bitarh valley over the Haji Pir Pass to Uri and thence up the Jhelum valley to Baramulla and Srinagar, for details of which see Route XXX. Though circuitous and of great length, it could be made suitable for a railway and the cultivated Doon country between Aknoor and Kotli would yield traffic.

XII JAMMU to SRINAGAR, by PIR PUNJAL PASS: OLD IMPERIAL ROUTE :—

Number of Marches.	Names of Stages.	Distance in miles and furlongs. Inter-mediate m. f.	Total. m. f.	Nature of Route.	Main Valleys and Mountain Passes.	River Crossings and Lakes.	Altitude above Sea Level in Feet.	Supplies and Transport at Stages.	Remarks.
	Jammu P. O., T. O., D. B.—	... ...	0 ...	Country open and cultivated, rough cart road.	Across Chenab valley.	......	1200	S. G. F. and W. abundant, T. ample.	Large town and capital of the Jammu State.
1	**Aknoor** P. O., F. B.—	16 ...	16 ... 26 ...	Fair hill road used by troops and passable for laden mules.	Ambi Pass.	Chennb ferry.	1142	S. G. F. and W. plentiful, T. available.	Fort, timber depôt, small town and bazar on right bank Chenab river.

No.	Name			Total	Remarks	Pass or range crossed	River, bridge, &c.	Elevation	Supplies	Description
2	Choki Chowra E.—	13	4	20 34	......	......	Kurwa Khud	2150	S. G. F. after notice, W. procurable, T. nil.	Halting place.
3	Thandapani B., E.—	12	4	42	......	Kalidhar range. Up Tawi valley.	Rud bridge and ford.	1460	S. scarce, W. plentiful, T. nil.	Village 1 mile off.
4	Dhurmsal E.—	10	4	52	......	Cross low spur.	......	......	S. procurable, W. plentiful, T. nil.	Village.
5	Sialsui E.—	10	...	62	......	Cross steep range.	......	......	S. scarce, W. plentiful, T. nil.	Ditto.
6	Rajaori (Rampur) P. O., B., C.—	14	...	76	......	......	Tawi ford bridge unfinished.	3094	S. G. F. and W. plentiful, T. ample.	Town and bazar well built on right bank Tawi. Bon left bank opposite.
7	Thana Mandi B., C., E. small.—	14	...	90	......	......	......	8200	S. G. F. and W. plentiful, T available.	Village, Bon right bank Tawi.
				95	......	Ratan Pir	......		......	Shelter huts on Pass.
8	Baramgalla B., C.—	10	4	100	The length between Barangalla and Shupiyon over the Pir Punjal Pass has got out of order and become difficult in places; the scenery is very beautiful.	Up Suran valley.	Puraai bridge waterfall. Cross Suran river by numerous bridges.	5800	S. scarce, G. F. W. plentiful, T. nil.	Small village and fort in deep gorge near confluence of Puraai nullah and Suran river.
9	Poshiana B., C., E. on house tops.—	8	4	109		......	......	8150	S. and W. scarce, G. and F. plentiful, T. nil.	Village deserted in winter months.
				115		Pir Punjal	......	11400	......	Shelter huts on pass.
10	Alinabad Serai B., C.—	11	...	120		Down Hem-biara valley.	......	10000	S. nil, G. F. W. plentiful, T. nil.	Halting place.
	Dubchi B.—	...	...	128						
				129		......	Rupri bridge.			

Number of Marches	Names of Stages	Distance in miles and furlongs		Nature of Route.	Main Valleys and Mountain Passes.	River crossings and Lakes.	Altitude above Sea Level in Feet.	Supplies and Transport at Stages.	Remarks.
		Intermediate m. f.	Total m. f.						
XII	*ROUTE—contd.*	...	129 ...						
11	**Hirpura** E., C.—	12 ...	132 ...		...	...	7700	S. procurable, G. F. W. plentiful, T. nil.	Small village on right bank Rembiara.
12	**Shupiyon** P. O., B., C., E.—	8 ...	140 ...	Good road in the Kashmir valley with bridges over small nullahs.	Down Jhelum valley.	......	6714	S. G. F. W. abundant. T. ample	Town, bazar, tehsil, and head-quarters of district.
			141 4		......	Rembiara ford			
			144 4		......	Maukund ford			
			150		......	Ranchu ford.			
	Rama B., E. confined.—	...	151 ...	......	......		...	S. and W. procurable, T. available.	Large village on Ranchn river.
13	**Khanpur** C.— *Wahtor*	16 ...	156 ...	......	......	......	...	S. nil, G. F. and W. procurable, T. nil.	Village.
		...	162 ...	......	......		...		
14	**Srinagar** P. O., T. O., C. E.—	13 ...	169 ...	......	......	Jhelum bridge	5235	S. G. F. W. abundant. T. ample.	Large village. Capital of Kashmir State, large city, Hari Parbat Fort, Maharajah's Palaces, Residency, several bazars on both banks of Jhelum river.

There is no dak bungalow for travellers at Srinagar, but there are a few quarters for residence of visitors, for occupation of which early application in the season to the Assistant Resident in Kashmir at Srinagar should be made.

The Pir Punjal Pass is usually closed by snow from the 15th November to 15th April.

XIIa. RAJAORI to POONCH by BHIMBER GULLI—

No.	Place	Miles	Cumulative	Road	Valley	Ford/Ferry	Elevation	Water supply	Remarks
6	Rajaori (Rampur) P. O., B., C., E.—	...		76	Fair hill road, passable for mules.	Tawi valley	.....	3094	S. G. F. and W. plentiful, T. ample.	Town and bazar well built.
7	Derian E.—	14		90	.....	Bhimber gulli Down Mehndur valley.	.....	.....	S. scarce, G. F. W. plentiful, T. nil.	Village.
	Dhurmsal			92	.....			5170		
				100	.....		Mehndur ford	3000	.....	Tehsil.
8	Mankot E.—	16		106	......	.....	.....		S. and W. plentiful, T. available.	Fort and village.
	Sagra			109	.....					
9	Ban E.—	11		117	.....	Poonch valley	.....	.....	S. scarce, W. plentiful, T. nil.	
10	Poonch P. O., D. B., B., C., E.—	11		128	.....	.....	Suran ferry.	3300	S. G. F. and W. abundant, T. ample.	Capital of Poonch State, fort, town, large bazar.

From Sagra 109 miles a road ascends either to the Soona gulli or to the Chilnai gulli and descends down to the Suran valley, and across this river by boat ferry to Poonch 121 miles.

XIIb. ALTERNATIVE ROUTE RAJAORI to SHUPIYON by DARHAL PASS—

No.	Place	Miles	Cumulative	Road	Valley	Ford/Ferry	Elevation	Water supply	Remarks
6	Rajaori (Rampur) P. O., B., C., E.—	...	...	76	Fair hill road passable for laden mules.	Tawi valley	.....	3094	S. G. F. and W. plentiful, T. ample.	Town and bazar well built.

3

Number of Marches	Names of Stages	Distance in miles and furlongs		Nature of Route.	Main Valleys and Mountain Passes.	River Crossings and Lakes.	Altitude above Sea Level in Feet.	Supplies and Transport at Stages.	Remarks.
		Inter-mediate. m. f.	Total. m. f.						
XIIb	*ROUTE—contd.*								
7	**Darhal** E.—	...	76 ...	......	......	......	......	S. G. F. and W. plentiful, T. available.	Large village.
		12 ...	88 ...		Ratan Pir range.				
		...	94 ...	Pass not open before June.					
8	**Beloh** E.—	7 ...	95 ...	......	Darhal Pass	Nil Sar, L. Nundun Sar, L.	13080	S. nil, F. procurable, G. and W. plentiful, T. nil.	Shepherds' huts.
		...	99 ...						
9	**Aliabad Serai** B., C.—	12 ...	107 ...	......			10000	S. nil, G. F. W. plentiful, T. nil.	Halting place.
		...	116 ...	......	Jhelum valley.	Rupri bridge.			
10	**Hirpura** E., C.—	12 ...	119 ...	......			7700	S. procurable, G. F. W. plentiful, T. nil.	Small village.
11	**Shupiyon** P. O., B., C., E.—	8 ...	127 ...	......	......	......	6715	S. G. F. and W. abundant, T. ample.	Town, bazar, tehsil and head-quarters of district.

Loop route from Beloh 95 miles crosses another Darhal Pass 13,460 feet, more to the South-East, and descends by the Bhag Sar or Lake to Roopro 103 and Aliabad Serai 112 miles.

These two Darhal Passes are seldom open before June, and close in November on the first fall of snow.

XIIc BARAMGALLA to SRINAGAR by CHHOTI GULLI PASS—

No.	Stage			Total	Direction	Nature of road	Crossing	Elevation	Water and supplies	Remarks
8	Baramgalla C.—	...	...	100	4 — Across Suran valley.	Fair hill road passable for laden mules, though not open before July.	Suran ford	5800	S. scarce, G. F. W. plentiful, T. moderate.	Small village.
9	Hilloh	10	4	111	......	......	......	......	S. nil, G. F. W. plentiful, T. nil.	Good grazing ground. Two roads from Pass.
10	Kachgal River	12	...	115	Chhoti gulli	Easy ascent and descent	......	14090	Ditto.	
11	Pakapura	11	...	123	Down Kachgal valley.	......	......	......	S. procurable, G. F. W. plentiful, T. available.	Village.
	Chrar	...	...	134	......	......	......	6400		Town and bazar.
12	Khanpur C.—	10	...	139	Down Jhelum valley.	Good road along well cultivated plain.	......	......	S. nil, F. and W. procurable, T. nil.	
13	Srinagar P. O., T. O., C., E.—	13	...	157	......	......	Jhelum bridge	5235	S. G. F. and W. abundant, T. ample.	Capital of Kashmir State, town, fort, and bazar.

From Chhoti gulli 115 miles another road leads down the Sangsofed valley to Fras Nag 125 miles, Dragaon 141 miles, and to Srinagar 166 miles, also passable for laden animals. The Chhoti gulli Pass is not open before July.

XIId POSHIANA to SRINAGAR by CHITTAPANI PASS—

No.	Stage			Total	Direction	Nature of road	Crossing	Elevation	Water and supplies	Remarks
9	Poshiana B., C., E. on house tops.—	...	...	109	... — Up Chitta valley.	Rough hill track not open before July.	Suran ford	8150	S. and W. scarce, G. and F. plentiful, T. nil.	Village deserted in winter.

Number of Marches	Names of Stages	Distance in miles and furlongs — Intermediate m. f.	Total m. f.	Nature of Route	Main Valleys and Mountain Passes	River Crossings and Lakes	Altitude above Sea Level in Feet	Supplies and Transport at Stages	Remarks
XIId	*ROUTE—contd.*								
10	Chittapani	...	109	......	......	......	......	S. nil, G. F. W. plentiful, T. nil.	Halting place.
11	Sangurwini	6	115	......	Chittapani	......	14540	S. scarce, G. F. W. plentiful, T. nil.	Village.
12	Pakapura	12	127	......	Down Kachgal valley.	......	......	S. procurable, G. F. W. plentiful, T. available.	Ditto.
	Chor	12	139	Good road over well cultivated plain.	Down Jhelum valley.	......	6400	......	Town and bazar.
13	Khanpur *C.—*	10	149	......	......	......	......	S. nil, F. and W. procurable, T. nil.	......
14	Srinagar *P. O., C., E.—*	13	162	......	......	Jhelum bridge	5235	S. G. F. and W. abundant, T. ample.	Capital of Kashmir State, large town, fort and bazar.

The Chittapani Pass is not open before July, and closes on the first fall of snow in November.

XIII JAMMU to SRINAGAR by BUDIL PASS.

Number of Marches	Names of Stages	Distance in miles and furlongs — Intermediate m. f.	Total m. f.	Nature of Route	Main Valleys and Mountain Passes	River Crossings and Lakes	Altitude above Sea Level in Feet	Supplies and Transport at Stages	Remarks
1	Jammu *P. O., T. O., D. B.—*	...	0	Rough cart-road	Chenab valley.	......	1200	S. G. F. and W. abundant, T. ample.	Capital of Jammu State, large town and bazar.

No.	Stage	Inter.	Total	Road	Pass / Feature	River	Elev.	Supplies	Remarks
2	Akhnoor *P. O., F. B.—*	16	16	Road passable for laden mules throughout.	.....	Chenab ferry	1142	S. G. F. W. plentiful, T. available.	Small town, fort and bazar.
3	Jandrai Kapaion Ki Baoli	7	23	.....	.....	.....	2000	S. nil, W. scarce, F. plentiful, T. nil.	Jungle.
			24	.....	Jendar gala.	Katundra ford			
			27	Stair descent					
4	Poni *E.—*	8	28	Steep and stony ascent.	Dal gala.	.....	2000	S. and W. plentiful, T. available.	Large village.
			32	.....	Chili gala.	.....	4000		
5	Jandi Upper *Jargin*	8	38	Fair road	Nar valley	Nar ford		S. G. F. and W. procurable, T. nil.	Village.
			40						
			44						
6	Nar	12	52	.....	.....	.....		S. precarious, F. W. procurable, T. nil.	Scattered village.
			55		Choroo Sira	.....	7807		
7	Bhagoli	8	60	Road stony and bad	Ans valley	.....		S. nil, F. and W. plentiful, T. nil.	One or two huts.
			62	.....	.....	Ans bridge.			
8	Budil *E.—*	5	65	.....	.....	.....		S. G. F. and W. plentiful, T. available.	Large village and fort.
9	Abid *E.—*	4	69	.....	.....	.....		S. nil, G. F. W. plentiful, T. nil.	
			70	Ascent and descent very steep.	Beberi spur.				

Number of Marches.	Names of Stages.	Distance in Miles and Furlongs.		Nature of Route.	Main Valleys and Mountain Passes.	River Crossings and Lakes.	Altitude above Sea Level in Feet.	Supplies and Transport at Stages.	Remarks.
		Inter-mediate. m. f.	Total. m. f.						
XIII	ROUTE—contd.	... ...	70 ...			......	......	S nil, G. F. W. plentiful, T. nil.	
10	Delhi or Yamrush E.—	7 ...	76 ...		Budil or Sedau				
			81 ...	Ascent steep and awkward, and easy descent.		......	14120		
11	Harshin Tower or Nazamdhi Garhi. *Rock Shelter.*	14 ...	90 ...	Fair road	Veshau valley.	......	......	Ditto	Halting place, guard house.
	Sedau	... ...	96 ...			......	......	......	Large village and customs post.
12	Shupiyon P. O., B., C., E.—	11 ...	101 ...	Good road		......	6715	S. G. F. and W. abundant, T. ample.	Town, bazar, tehsil, and head-quarters of district.
			102 4		Jhelum valley.	Rembiara ford.			
	Rawa B., E. confined.—	... ...	112 ...	Over well cultivated plain.		......	......	S. and W. procurable, T. available.	Large village on Ramchu river.
13	Khanpur C.—	16 ...	117 ...			......	......	S. nil, F. and W. procurable, T. nil.	
14	Srinagar P. O., T. O., C., E.—	13 ...	130 ...			Jhelum bridge	5235	S. G. F. W. abundant, T. ample,	Capital of Kashmir State, large town, fort and bazars.

The Budil Pass is generally closed by snow from December to May inclusive.

From Poni north-west to Berk 6 miles by good road. From Poni eastwards to Riassi 10 miles, crossing the Chenab river at Talwara ferry, also by a good road.

From Poni 32 miles after crossing the Chilli Pass 4,000 feet, there is a route down the Nar valley by Thakera Kot 44 miles to Chenka on the right bank of the Ans river, opposite Aarnas 50 miles, thence up the Ans valley along this same bank over a difficult and rugged path by Kurla and Tiloo to Chaona 71 miles from Jammu.

From Jaryin 44 miles west by Puidur to Sangarmarg iron mines 9 miles, crossing the range at Ichni or Inkan 5,200 feet, where there is a thick coal outcrop.

From Dhurmsal a road ascends up the Golabgurh valley passing by Mehugala coal mines and Teliri, and after crossing over the Chooroo Sira range 7,800 feet, descends either to Nar or to Bhagoli in the Ans valley, distance about 26 miles.

From Bhagoli 60 miles, and Budil 65 miles, are parallel routes on either bank of the Ans river westwards, which join in at Obhi 70 miles on right bank, hence there are 3 routes, one westwards to Rajaori 87 miles, one north-west by Putli Fort to Durhal 85 miles, and the third up the Panchgabbar valley northwards by Boorjari 80 miles, over the Rupri Pass 13,620 feet and 85 miles, descends to Roopro 90 miles, and to Aliabad Serai 99 miles on the Pir Punjal road from Jammu.

XIIIa. LOOP ROUTE from NAR to SHUPIYON by KONSA NAG AND VESHAU VALLEY—

No.	Stage		Miles		Total	Remarks			Elevation	Supplies	Notes
6	Nar E.—	...	...	...	52	......	Chooroo Sira range.	......	7800	S. precarious, G. F. W. procurable, T. nil.	Small village.
7	Chaona E.—	...	14	...	66	Rough hill track passable for miles, and open from June.	Ans and Chuniperal valleys.	Ans bridge	......	W. S. procurable, G.F. plenty, T. available.	Village.
8	Sartoto or Nund-Kot E.—	...	10	...	76	......	......	......	......	S. precarious, G. F. W. plentiful, T. nil.	Ditto.
		...	...	...	83	......	Konsa Nag Pass.	......	13250		
9	Konsa Nag E.—	...	9	...	85	......	Veshau valley	Konsa Nag Lake.	......	S. nil, F. scarce, G.W. plentiful, T. nil.	Celebrated place of pilgrimage.
10	Kungwatta E.—	...	10	...	95	......	......	......	......	S. nil, G. F. W. plentiful, T. nil.	Halting place.

Number of Marches	Names of Stages.	Distance in miles and furlongs. Intermediate. m. f.	Total. m. f.	Nature of Route.	Main Valleys and Mountain Passes.	River Crossings and Lakes.	Altitude above Sea Level in Feet.	Supplies and Transports at Stages.	Remarks.
XIIIa	*ROUTE—contd.*								
11	Sedau E.—	10 ...	95 .	......	......		......	S. procurable, G. F. W. plentiful, T. nil.	Large village and customs post.
		6 ...	101 ..			Veshau ford			
12	Shupiyon P. O., B., C., E.—	5 ...	106 ...	......	......	......	6715	S. G. F. and W. abundant, T. ample.	Town, bazar, tehsil, and head-quarters of district.

XIIIb SHUPIYON to BARAMULLA—

Number of Marches	Names of Stages.	Distance in miles and furlongs. Intermediate. m. f.	Total. m. f.	Nature of Route.	Main Valleys and Mountain Passes.	River Crossings and Lakes.	Altitude above Sea Level in Feet.	Supplies and Transports at Stages.	Remarks.
12	Shupiyon P. O., B., C., E.—	...	101 ..	Hill track passable for laden animals, across undulating ground along the eastern foot of Pir Punjal range.	Across Jhelum drainage.	......	6715	S. G. F. W. abundant, T. ample.	Town, bazar and tehsil, head-quarters of district.
			102			Rembiara ford			
			106			Mankund „			
			111			Kachgal „			
13	Chrar E.—	14 ...	115	......	......	Dudhganga ford.	6400	Ditto, W. distant	Small Town, Musjid with tomb of Shah Nur-uddin.
			120			Yechara ford.			
14	Khan Baba Sahib's Ziarat—	10 .	123 ...	......	Across Suknag drainage.	......	......	S. scanty, G. F. W. procurable, T. scarce.	
			125 ...						

15	**Kag** E.—	10	133	......	Ditto	......	......	S. G. F. W. procurable, T. available.	Large village, ancient spring Gunjnag.
	Firozepur	...	135	......	Poshkar gulli	Suknag bridge.	......		
		...	140	......	......	......	......		
16	**Baba Marishi** B., C.—	13	145	......	......	Bahun ford.	......	S. scanty, G. F. W. plentiful, T. nil.	Ziarat of Baba Pam Din, place of pilgrimage.
		...	148	......	......	......	7000		
	Kontra	...	154	......	......	Ningal ford.	......		
17	**Baramulla** P. O., T. O., D. B., E., C.—	16	164	......	Jhelum valley.	Jhelum bridge.	5175	S. G. F. W. abundant, T. after notice.	Small town, bazar and tehsil on right bank Jhelum.

This is the most direct route with beautiful scenery and occasional fine views of the Panjal Range; there is another route from Shupiyon to Kag by Sangarwini, Eosa, Dudhi Patri, Ringa Zabal, and Urzal or Ryar more inside the hills through lovely scenery.

From Firozepur there is a good road to Gulmarg about 6 miles in length up the mountain side, while about 3 miles above Firozepur along the right bank Bahun valley, there are the ruins of two ancient temples on the Durrung Plain, which appear to have been partly destroyed by earthquakes.

From Baba Marishi there is also a short road 2 miles long to Gulmarg Bazar, this was made in 1891.

Baramulla was severely injured by the great earthquake of 1885. About 5 miles off, the earth suddenly opened and swallowed up part of a village with its inhabitants, jets of hot water and sand gushing out.

XIV JAMMU to SRINAGAR by GULABGURH or KURI PASS—

Jammu P. O., T. O., D. B.—	...	0	...	...	1200	S. G. F. and W. abundant, T. ample.	Capital of Jammu State.
Negrota	...	6	...	Diroomi valley	Rough road over-beds of stony ravines to Riassi and passable for laden animals.	1150	H. H. Maharaja's Rest-house and garden.

Number of Marches.	Names of Stages.	Distance in miles and furlongs. Inter-mediate. m. f.	Distance in miles and furlongs. Total. m. f.	Nature of Route.	Main Valleys and Mountain Passes.	River crossings and Lakes.	Altitude above Sea Level in Feet.	Supplies and Transport at Stages.	Remarks.
XIV	ROUTE—contd.								
1	Dunga ...	...	6 ...	......		......	......	S. nil, G. F. procurable,	Small village.
	Tandapani	11	11	......	Gundla ridge	......	1650	W. scarce, T. nil.	Temple and spring.
2	Kanjili	12	16 18	...		......	1400	S. precarious, G. F. W. procurable, T. nil.	Small village.
	Dera		23	... ...	Chenab valley	Doda ford	1330 1330	......	Sikh temple.
3	Riassi P.O., T.O., B., C., E.—	12	26 33 4	Fair road over the Salar range down to Chenab and along right bank to Aarnas.	......		1800	S. G. F. W. plentiful, T. ample.	Town, bazar, tehsil and castle.
	Bidar		35			......	2450		On Salal hill spur. Huts.
4	Banasu	10	39 42 45	......	Tor gulli		3300 1540		
5	Aarnas E.—	6	51	......	......	Chenab rope bridge or ferry.	......	S. nil, G. F. procurable, W. plentiful, T. nil. S. G. F. W. procurable, T. available.	Large village on right bank Chenab, facing Salar Fort on left bank Chenab.
6	Toroo E.—	10	61	Rough road with many ups and downs over spurs and ravines.	Ans and Gulabgurh valleys left bank.	......	......	S. procurable, G. F. W. plentiful, T. nil.	Cluster of villages.
7	Angril E.—	14	75 ...			...	......	Ditto ...	Small village.

No.	Place	Miles	Total	Road description	Valley / Range	River / Ford	Elevation	Water supply	Remarks
	Dowal	... ...	76, 79	.....	.....	Golabgurh ford.	.....	.....	Ditto.
8	**Kinderali or Gulabgurh Fort** *E.—*	9	84	Steep ascent and easy descent over pass.	Gulabgurh or Kuri, Chitti valley.	.....	.....	S. nil, G. F. W. plentiful, T. nil.	Ditto.
9	**Gogulmarg** *E.—*	11	90, 95	.....	...	...	12530	Ditto ...	Marg and huts.
	Koond Koolloo	... ...	100, 102	Good road over fine plain, well culti-vated.	Pahargurh range.	.....	.....	S. procurable, W. scarce, G. F. plentiful, T. available.	Ditto.
10	**Kuri** *E.—*	11	106		Veshau valley.	.....	.....	S. G. F. plentiful, T. available.	Large village.
11	**Shupiyon** *P. O., E., C., E.—*	12	112, 118	.....	.....	Veshau ford.	6715	S. G. F. and W. abundant, T. ample.	Town, tehsil and head-quarters of district.
	Ramu *E. confined.—*	4	119, 129	.....	Jhelum valley.	Rembiara ford.	.....	.....	Large village.
12	**Khanpur** *C. E.—*	16	134	.....	...	.....	.....	S. nil, G. F. W, procurable, T. nil.	...
13	**Srinagar** *P. O., T. O., C., E.—*	13	147	.....	.....	Jhelum bridge	5235	S. G. F. W. abundant, T. ample.	Capital of Kashmir State, large town, cantonment, fort and bazars.

This was said to be the best horse road into Kashmir, but is not so much used at present. From Jammu to Riasi there is an alternative route, also up stony beds of ravines by Negrota 6 miles, to Dumun 14 miles, thence along the Sarna ridge to Katera 26 miles, 1,760 feet and across numerous ravines to Riasi 37 miles. The celebrated temple and place of pilgrimage, Trikoota Devi, is situated on the mountain of three peaks, about 3 miles north of Katera, up the Balan Khud, where copious springs of pure water issue from the limestone rock at an elevation of 3,000 feet ; at Katera is a fine State garden.

XIVa. BRANCH TRACK from GULABGURH to SHUPIYON by DEDAM PASS—

Number of Marches.	Names of Stages.	Distance in miles and furlongs. Intermediate. m. f.	Distance in miles and furlongs. Total. m. f.	Nature of Route.	Main Valleys and Mountain Passes.	River Crossings and Lakes.	Altitude above Sea Level, in Feet.	Supplies and Transport and Stages.	Remarks.
8	Gulabgurh E.—	...	84 ...	Difficult path for men only.	......	......	.....	S. nil, G. F. W. plentiful, T. nil.	Fort.
		...	94 ...	......	Dedam Pass.	......	.....		
9	Dedam E.—	12 ...	96 ...	......	Kolnarawa valley.	......	.....	Ditto	Large marg.
10	Bo E.—	8 ...	104 ...	Good road for laden animals.	......	......	.....	S. procurable, G. F. S. plentiful, T. nil.	Fair village.
11	Hanjipur E.—	6 ...	110 ...	......	Veshau valley	Veshau ford	.....	S. G. F. and W. plentiful, T. available.	Large village.
12	Shupiyon P. O., B., C., E.—	10 ...	120 ...	......	......	......	6715	S. G. F. and W. abundant, T. ample.	Town, bazar, tehsil and head-quarters of district.

This is a rugged mountain path known only to Gujars. The pass is above 12,500 feet high with fairly easy ascent and descent. From Gogulmarg 95 miles after crossing the Pahargurh Range, there is a shorter route by Hanjipur 105 miles, to Shupiyon 115 miles. From Koond Koolloo there is a road 6 miles in length to Kungwattu on the Konsa Nag Pass road. These Routes XIII and XIV up the Ans valley are the most direct from Jammu to Srinagar, and traverse a less width of the friable Murree rock formation than any other route. The passes from 12,500 to 14,120 feet are very high, and these roads are, therefore, blocked by snow during one-half of the year. If the money could be found for a 10-mile tunnel through these mountains this direction would probably be suitable for a railway.

XV JAMMU to SRINAGAR by BANIHAL PASS—

There are three branches to this route, by the Chenab valley, by the Singipal Pass, and by the pass over the Larulari Range, all converging to the iron suspension bridge over the Chenab river at Ramband, hence a single route up the Bichlari valley over the Banihal Pass to Islamabad and Srinagar.

Firstly, BY THE CHENAB VALLEY—

	Name			Road			Elevation	Supplies	Remarks
	Jammu P. O., T. O., D. B.—	...	0	Rough cart road over fertile country.	Up Chenab valley.	......	1200	S. G. F. and W. abundant, T. ample.	Capital of Jammu State, large town and bazar.
1	**Merh**	9	9	......	......	......	925	S. G. F. W. plentiful, T. available.	Village and H. H. Maharajah's garden.
	Akuoor	...	18	......	......	......	1142		
2	**Gaura**	11	20	Hill track over broken ground and stony beds of ravines.	......	......	1200	S. and W. plentiful, T. available.	
3	**Dera**	12	32	...	......	......	1330	S. G. F. nil, W. plentiful, T. nil.	Sikh temple.
			39 4		......	Doda ford	1330		
4	**Riassi** P. O., T. O., B., C., E.	9	41	Fair road over Salar range and along Chenab valley, left bank, passable for mules.	...	......	1800	S. G. F. and W. plentiful, T. ample.	Fort town, bazar and tehsil.
	Muri		43 4		......	......	2000		
			45 4		Serli Pass	......	4300		
	Ser		48		Kirkhari gully	......	2950		
			49			......	2875		
5	**Kansur** E.—	10	51	......	......	...	1600	S. moderate, G. F. W. plentiful, T. available.	Village.

Number of Marches	Names of Stages	Distance in miles and furlongs — Intermediate. m. f.	Distance in miles and furlongs — Total. m. f.	Nature of Route.	Main Valleys and Mountain Passes.	River crossings and Lakes.	Altitude above Sea Level in feet.	Supplies and Transport at Stages.	Remarks.
XV	ROUTE—contd.	...	...						
6	**Kotroo**	...	51 ...		......	......	2075	S. moderate G. F. W. plentiful, T. nil.	Village.
	Harej	6	57 ..4		......	......	1800		
7	**Parand**	7	60 ...		......	......	2450	Ditto, T. available.	Ditto. Ancient ruins.
	E.—								
	Kartal	...	64 ...		......	Pinkia river ford.	1900		
		...	67 ...	Road diverges round Kaonsal mountain over limestone formation to avoid cliffs on Chenab.	Simni gully	......	6100	......	Spur of Mandi peak.
8	**Madial**	11	72 ...		......	......	3900	Ditto, T. nil.	Ditto.
		...	75 ...		Bilkot gully	......	4408		
	Tangar	...	77 ...	Fair hill road passable for mules.	......	......	2650		
		...	79 ...		......	......			
9	**Dharamkoond**	8	83 ...		......	......	2200	Ditto, T. available.	Ditto. Rope sling bridge over Chenab.
	E.— *Gunga*	...	85 ...	...	......	......	3800		
	Maitra *B.—*	...	92 ...		......	......	......	S. nil, G. F. procurable, W. plentiful.	Old baradari.

| 10 | Ramband P. O., T. O., B., C., E. | 11 | ... | 94 | ... | | ... | ... | Chenab bridge | 2324 | S. G. F. and W. plentiful, T. available. | Tehsil and bazar. |

Between Riassi and Kansur, the Chenab river makes a remarkable bend, changing from a westerly to a southerly course through a deep gorge of limestone cliffs. The Salar Fort is situated in the angle of this bend and the road from Riassi avoids the latter, crosses the limestone range by the Serli Pass in a N. E. direction and descends to Kansur in the Chenab valley. It passes by Sir, near which are situated the mines of lead and antimony which have been worked for a long period.

Between Karlat and Tangar, the Chenab cuts through a spur of the limestone range forming a deep gorge walled in by high cliffs, with a great fall. From Karlat the road diverges S. E. to Madial over the Simni Pass, and comes round the base of a limestone peak N. E. to Tangar, back on the Chenab. In the vicinity of Dharamkoond up the Chenab valley, there are large deposits of Gypsum called nakol.

This route up the Chemab and Bichlari valleys has been reconnoitred for a railway. It passes through 40 miles of the Murree rock formation, and would meet difficulty at the Tangar and Salar limestone gorges.

Secondly, BY THE SINGIPAL PASS—

No.	Stage				Road	Range	Khud / ford	Elev.	Supplies	Remarks
	Jammu P. O., T. O., D. B.—	...	...	0	Good road but stony.	Up Tawi valley.	......	1200	S. G. F. and W. abundant, T. ample.	Capital of Jammu State, large town and bazar.
	Negrota	...	...	6	......	......	......	1150		
				16	......	Nadaini gully	......	2275		
1	Dunsal	17	6	17	......	......	ChupperKhud	1800	S. G. F. procurable, W. scanty, T. scarce.	Village.
				20	......	Shegala range	Doodur Khud	2800		
				24	......	......	......			
	Periam	...	...	25	Old road now seldom used.	......	......			
				32	......	......	......			
2	Krimchi	14	2	35	......	Siraoli range.	Biru ford.	2500	Ditto, W. baoli and nullah.	Ditto Old fort in ruins.
				39	......					

Number of Marches	Names of Stages	Distance in miles and furlongs Intermediate m. f.	Total m. f.	Nature of Route.	Main Valleys and Mountain Passes.	River crossings and Lakes.	Altitude above Sea Level in Feet.	Supplies and Transport and Stages.	Remarks.
XV	ROUTE—contd.	...	...						
3	Mir	...	39	......	Across head Pinkia valley.	Pinkia ford.	4800	S. nil, G. F. W. procurable, T. nil.	Halting place.
	Bakul	10	42	......					
4	Landra	9	47	......	Singpal		4700	S. scarce, G. F. W. and T. available.	Fort.
			51	Steep descent	Across Chenab valley.		8200		
	Bilkuta		56	......					
	Maitra		59						
5	Ramband P. O., T. O., B., C. E.	12	63	......		Chenab bridge.	2234	S. G. F. W. plentiful, T. available.	Tehsil and bazar.
			65						

Thirdly, MAIN ROUTE BY THE SARTARGURH PASS OVER THE LARULARI RANGE—

Number of Marches	Names of Stages	Distance in miles and furlongs Intermediate m. f.	Total m. f.	Nature of Route.	Main Valleys and Mountain Passes.	River crossings and Lakes.	Altitude above Sea Level in Feet.	Supplies and Transport and Stages.	Remarks.
1	Jammu P. O., T. O., D. B.—	...	0	Made road through-out and partially bridged.	Up Tawi valley.	...	1200	S. G. F. and W. abundant, T. ample.	Capital of Jammu State.
	Negrota B.—	...	6	......		...	1150	......	H. H. Maharaja's Baradari and garden.
			16	......	Nadaini gully.	...	2275		
2	Dunsal B.—	17 6	17 6	Between Jammu and Udampur very stony over boulder forma-tion.	Shegala range	ChupparKhud	1800	S. G. F. procurable, W. scanty, T. scarce.	Village.
			20 6			Doodur Khud.	2800		
	Periam		24						
			25 6						

	Place					Road	Crossing	Bridge	Elev.	Supplies	Description
3	Udampur P. O., T. O., Palace, C., E.—	12	6	30	4	Good section	......	......	2500	S. G. E. plentiful, W. scarce in dry summer, T. ample.	Town and bazar, head-quarters of district.
4	Dramthal B.—	13	6	44	2	......	......	......	3300	S. G. F. procurable, W. moderate, T. scarce.	Village.
	Chineni	...	...	49	...	Steep and stony ascent & descent.	......	......	3900	S. and W. abundant, T. ample.	Small town and bazar.
	Putai Talao	...	...	53	...	......	Larulari	......	6600	......	Near Sartargurh.
5	Batoti B. E.—	11	6	56	...	Steep descent which might be improved.	Across Chenab valley.	......	5050	S. G. F. plentiful, W. moderate, T. scarce.	Village.
6	Ramband P. O., T. O., B., C., E.	13	2	69	2	Rough road through shale, subject to snow, avalanches from Loonkot mountain and liable to land-slips.	......	Chenab bridge	2324	S. G. F. W. plentiful, T. available.	Tehsil and bazar.
	Digdihol	...	...	77	...	......	Up Bichlari valley.	......	3300		
	Klalna	...	...	80	...	......	......	Bichlari bridge.	3200		
7	Ramsu Hut.—	12	6	82	...	......	......	Ditto	3700	S. G. F. procurable, W. plentiful, T. nil.	Small village.
	Nachlana	...	...	84	...	......	......	Ditto.	4400	......	Customs post.
8	Deogul or Banihal B.—	11	...	86	...	Good section	......	Mohu bridge	5450	......	
		...	...	89	...	......	......	Bichlari bridge.	6300	S. G. F. W. moderate, T. scarce.	Village.
	Takia C.—	...	...	93	4	Steep ascent and descent, road fair.	......	......	9200	......	Village, foot of pass.
		...	...	98	4	......	Banihal				
				100							

4

Number of Marches.	Names of Stages.	Distance in miles and furlongs.		Nature of Route.	Main Valleys and Mountain Passes.	River Crossings and Lakes.	Altitude above Sea Level in feet.	Supplies and Transport at Stages.	Remarks.
		Intermediate. m. f.	Total. m. f.						
XV	*ROUTE—contd.*	... ...	100 4						
9	**Verinag** P.O., T.O., B. E.—	11 2	104 2	Good road	Down Jhelum valley	Sandri bridge, Bringh bridge.	6000	S. G. F. and W. plentiful, T. available.	Large village and tehsil.
10	**Islamabad or Anant Nag.** P.O., T.O., B.,C., E.—	16 2	120 4	......	Right bank	Sulphurous springs.	5450	Ditto, T. ample.	Town, bazar and head quarters of district.
	Kanabal B.—	... ...	122 ...	Hence travellers mostly go by boat down the Jhelum.			5400	Ditto "	On right bank Jhelum
	Bijbehara B. C.—	... ...	126 ...	Fair road	......	......	......	......	Town and bazar, numerous temples and mosques.
11	**Awantipur** E.—	17 ...	137 4	......	......	......	5300	S. nil, T. nil.	Ruins of ancient city and temple.
	Pandrethan	... ...	149 ...	......	......	......	......		Ancient city and temple in ruins.
12	**Srinagar** P. O., T. O., C., E.—	18 ...	155 4	......	......	......	5235	S. G. F. and W. abundant, T. ample.	Capital of Kashmir State, large town and bazar, Military Cantonment.

This route is reserved by H. H. Maharajah of Jammu and Kashmir, and no visitor can travel this way without his express permission. When the latter is given, the traveller should arrange for the through transport of his camp and baggage from Jammu to Islamabad, otherwise much trouble and difficulty may be felt, the local coolies frequently putting down their loads on the roadside and running away. The Banihal Pass is usually closed by snow during two months of the year, 15th December to 15th February inclusive.

Through Dansal a cross route starting from Riassi runs along the Dansal plain generally in a south-east direction by Jindrar, and after crossing the Tawi river at Negrota comes to Munwal, where the two roads from Jammu to Rannagar and Bisaoli diverge. Near this place are the ruins of some fine Pandoo temples which are little known. The distances from Riassi are to Katera 11 miles, Dunsal 25 miles, Jindrar 33 miles, Negrota 38 miles, and Munwal 40 miles.

From Ramband 69 miles 2 furlongs, an old road ascends the Loonkot Range 8,000 feet, and crossing over above Bilhoot 74 miles, descends into the Peristan valley by Barargadh 80 miles, to Ramsu 85 miles.

From Ramband 69 miles 2 furlongs, a loop track ascends N. E. over the same range under Saroo Peak by Gunhot 75 miles, and after crossing the Pass descends down the Peristan valley by Peristan 86 miles, to Ramsu 98 miles.

XV.—UDAMPUR to RIASSI.—

No.	Stage	Dist.		Total	Country / road	Drainage / spur	Stream	Elevation	Supplies	Remarks
3	Udampur P. O., T. O., Palace, C., E.—	...		30	4	Open country, well cultivated, but broken by numerous deep ravines, road fair.	Across drainage of Thwi.	.....	2500	S. and G. F. plentiful, W. scarce in dry summer, T. ample.	Town and bazar, head-quarters of district.
4	Cymbal Sui E.—	10	4	41	...	Sandran spur	Sukhul Kud	.....	S. precarious, W. scarce, T. nil.	Village.
5	Katera C., E.—	8	...	49	...	Trikoota spur / Across Chenab drainage.	Balan Kud	1760	S. and W. plentiful, T. available.	Large village.
6	Riassi P. O., T. O., B., C., E.—	11	...	58	60	...	Dooda stream.	.....	1800	S. and W. plentiful, T. ample.	Fort, town, bazar and tehsil.

From Udampur 30 miles 4 furlongs there is another route by Siraoli 43 miles, and over two spurs of the Siraoli Peak to Gurg 52 miles, thence down the Doodavalley to Riassi 65 miles.

XVb CROSS ROUTE from PARAND to SAD MAHADEO by LANDRA and CHINENI.—

Number of Marches	Names of Stages	Distance in miles and furlongs — Intermediate m. f.	Total m. f.	Nature of Route.	Main Valleys and Mountain Passes.	River crossings and Lakes.	Altitude above Sea Level in feet.	Supplies and Transport at Stages.	Remarks.
	Parand E.—	...	0 ...	Hill track not passable for laden animals.	Up Pinkia valley.	......	2450	S. moderate, G. F. W. plentiful, T. available.	Village and ruins of temple.
			5 ...	......	......	Pinkia ford.			
1	Landra	15 ...	15 ...	......	......	......	4700	S. scarce, G. F. W. T. procurable.	Fort.
			21 ...	......	Larulari range				
2	Chineni P. O., C., E.—	12 ...	27 ...	Good road	Across Tawi drainage.	...	3900	S. G. F. W. plentiful, T. ample.	Small town and bazar. Residence of Raja of Chineni.
3	Sad Mahadeo C., E.—	8 ...	35 ...	......	......	......	......	Ditto.	Place of pilgrimage, with temples and bazar.

XVc NACHILANA to SHUPIYON by MOHU PASS.—

Number of Marches	Names of Stages	Distance in miles and furlongs — Intermediate m. f.	Total m. f.	Nature of Route.	Main Valleys and Mountain Passes.	River crossings and Lakes.	Altitude above Sea Level in feet.	Supplies and Transport at Stages.	Remarks.
8	Nachilana	... ...	86 ...	Rough hill track passable for mules.	Up Mohu valley.	Mohu bridge	4400	......	Customs post.

9	Mohu E.—	11 ...	97 ...	......	......	......	S. nil, G. F. W. plentiful, T. nil.	Marg.
10	Dunnouf E.—	14 ...	101 ... 111 ...	Mohu Pass. Down Koinerawa valley.	... ...	......	S. procurable, G. F. W. plentiful, T. scarce.	Village.
11	Hanjipur E.—	6 ...	117 ...	......	Veshau ford	......	S. and W. plentiful, T. available.	Large village.
12	Shupiyon P. O., B., C. E.—	10 ...	127 ...	......	......	6715	S. G. F. and W. abundant, T. ample.	Town, bazar, tehsil and head-quarters of district.

Over the mountain range S. E. from Banihal, which separates the Bichlari valley from the Shahabad valley, are 3 passes :

Nandmarg ascended from Ramsu 82 miles, up the Pogal stream by Maligam 92 miles, to Choan, Custom House, 105 miles at the upper end of the Shahabad valley.

Ramsoor ascended from Ramsu 82 miles, up the Marwan stream by Prihanta 92 miles, to Ingrawarru in the Shahabad valley 102 miles.

Halan ascended from Deogul 93 miles, by Halan 104 miles, to Nowraon 107 miles, and Verinag 110 miles, in the Shahabad or Upper Jhelum valley.

On the west side of Banihal Pass is the Traj Pass, which may be ascended from Deogul 93 miles, by Dunnahar 102 miles, to Rozlu valley 112 miles, and Islamabad 127 miles.

From Verinag westwards there is a pleasant road with fine scenery along the northern foot of the Punjal Range by the Rozlu valley and Dunnouf to Shupiyon, viz., Verinag to Hillar 6 miles, Rozloo valley 15 miles, Dardgound 23 miles, Dunnouf 33 miles, Hanjipur 39 miles, Koond Koolloo 48 miles, Kingwattu 54 miles, Sedau 60 miles, Shupiyon 65 miles. Supplies and coolies are procurable throughout except at Koond Koolloo and Kingwattu.

XVd EXTENSION ROUTE VERINAG to INSHIN in WURDWAN VALLEY by MARGAN PASS.—

9	Verinag P. O., T. O., B.—	... ...	... ... 104 ... 105 ... 108 ... 111 ...	2	Good road passable for laden animals.	Shahabad valley. Shail Nag range. Bringh valley	Sandrin ford Bringh ford.	6000	S. G. F. & W. plentiful, T. available	Large village and tehsil.

Number of Marches	Names of Stages	Distance in Miles and Furlongs		Nature of Route	Main Valleys and Mountain Passes	River Crossings and Lakes	Altitude above Sea Level in Feet	Supplies and Transport at Stages	Remarks
		Intermediate m. f.	Total m. f.						
XVd	ROUTE—contd.	...	...						
10	Soph	.. ..	111 ...	......	......	......	......	S. G. W. plentiful, F. scarce, T. available.	Two large villages employed in working iron mines.
	E.—Kharpura	9 6	114 ...						
			117 ...						Large village.
11	Nowbug E.—	9 ...	120 ...	......	Nar Snogar. Up Nowbug valley.	......	......	S. G. F. W plentiful, T. available.	
			123 ...						
12	Guran E.—	9 ...	132 ...	Road over pass steep and stony.	Margan Pass or Ikpattan. Up Wardwan valley.	......	11000	Ditto ...	Small village
			138 ...						
13	Inshin	16 ...	148 ...	......	......	Meru Wardwan bridge.	8143	S. precarious, G. F. W. plentiful, a few coolies procurable.	Village.

From Verinag 2 roads lead to Soph over the Shail Nag range between the Shahabad and Bringh valleys, both equally good.

XVe	EXTENSION ROUTE ISLAMABAD to AMARANATH by LIDAR VALLEY—								
10	Islamabad or Anant Nag P.O., T.O.,B.,C., E.—	......	120 4	Good road passable for laden animals	Up Lidar valley left bank.	......	5450	S. G. F. W. abundant, T. ample.	Town and bazar, head-quarters of district, sulphurous hot springs.
11	Bawan E.—	4 4	125 ...	......	......	......	......	Ditto	Beautiful spring, temple and caves.

No.	Name			Road	Ranges	Rivers, &c.	Elevation	S. G. F. W., plentiful, T. available.	Remarks
12	Bishmakarm E.—	10	135	......	......	......	......	S. G. F. W., plentiful, T. available.	Mahomedan shrine, old copper mines at Harpat Nag.
	Buthot	...	141	......	......	......	......	......	Village.
	Ganeshbal	...	146	......	......	......	......	......	Chief stage of pilgrimage.
13	Pailgam E.—	14	149	Fair road practicable for ponies and janpans.	......	......	8500	Ditto	Cluster of villages.
	Preslang	...	166	......	......	......	......	......	Small village, last up valley.
14	Tanin or Chandanwara. E.—	10	169	......	......	......	10500	S. nil, G. F. W. plentiful, T. nil.	Halting place.
15	Shisha Nag E.—	10	169	......	Sach Kach range.	Shisha Nag	12500	Ditto	Ditto.
16	Panjitarni E.—	11	180	......	......	......	......	Ditto, Juniper bushes.	Ditto.
17	Amaranath Cave	5	185	......	......	Cave in the Gypsum rock.	13000	Nil.	Celebrated place of pilgrimage, sacred to Siva.

Between Tanin and Panjitarni, there is another route by Astan Marg about 16 miles, rougher but shorter. From Panjitarni there is a path down the Sangam Kol river to Baltal on the Srinagar and Larlak road at the southern foot of the Zoji La. The distance is about 8 miles and is traversable only while this river is covered by snow bridges during winter and generally until the end of June.

XVI JAMMU to SKARDU by KISHTWAR and SURU—

Number of Marches.	Names of Stages.	Distance in miles and furlongs. Inter-mediate m. f.	Total m. f.	Nature of Route.	Main Valleys and Mountain Passes.	River Crossings and Lakes.	Altitude above Sea Level, in feet.	Supplies and Transport at Stages.	Remarks.
	Jammu *P. O., T. O., D. B.—	... ...	0 ...	Fair road passable for laden animals, very stony over boulder formation.	......	......	1200	S. G. F. & W. abundant, T. ample.	Capital of Jammu State, Military Cantonment, large town and bazar.
	Negrota B.—	... 6	6 ...	......	Up Tawi valley.	......	1150	......	H. H. Maharajah's Baradari & Garden.
1	**Dunsal** B.—	11 6	17 6	......	......	......	1800	S. G. F. procurable, W. scanty, T. scarce.	Village.
2	**Udampur** P.O., T.O., *Palace*—	12 6	30 4	Good road	......	......	2500	S. G. F. plentiful, W. scarce, in dry summer T. ample.	Town and bazar, head-quarters of district.
3	**Dramthal** B.—	13 6	44 2	......	......	......	3500	S. G. F. plentiful, W. moderate, T. scarce.	Village.
	Chineni P. O.—	...	49 ...	Steep ascent	......	......	3900	W. and S. abundant, T. ample.	Small town and bazar.
	Putri Talao	...	53 ...	......	Larulari range.	......	6600	......	Near Sartarghur.

No.	Station			Total dist.	Road	Route	Bridge	Elevation (feet)	Supplies	Remarks
4	Batoti B.—	...	11	6 · 56	...	...	......	5050	S. G. F. plentiful, W. moderate, T. scarce	Village.
5	Asar E.—	...	14	... 70	Hill road fairly passable for mules.	Up Chenab valley.	......	3150	S. G. F. W. procurable, T. moderate.	Ditto.
6	Kullen B., E.—	...	12	... 82	...	...	......	3800	Ditto	Ditto.
	Doda	...	...	... 85 · 86	...	...	Neru bridge or raft.	......	......	On right bank of Chenab river.
7	Bhela E.—	...	12	... 94	Rough hill road passable for laden animals.	Up Chenab valley or Chandra Bhaga left bank.	......	3670	S. G. F. W. procurable, T. scarce.	Village.
8	Zanglwar E.—	...	13	... 107 · 108	...	...	Karney bridge.	3670 · 2950	Ditto	Ditto.
9	Joshni E.—	...	6	... 113	Cross numerous ravines.	...	......	3200	S. G. F. W. scarce, T. nil.	Ditto.
10	Kishtwar P. O., B., C., E.—	...	15	· 128	...	...	......	5400	S. G. F. W. plentiful, T. ample.	Fort, small town, bazar, and head-quarters of district on high plateau.
11	Phalma	...	6	... 134	This part of road not practicable for mules owing to very difficult places.	Up Maru Wurdwan valley.	Chandra Bhaga rope bridge.	3664	S. precarious, G. F. W. procurable, few coolies.	Small village.
	Bandarkoot									

Number of Marches.	Names of Stages.	Distance in Miles and Furlongs.		Nature of Route.	Main Valleys and Mountain Passes.	River crossings and Lakes.	Altitude above Sea Level in feet.	Supplies and Transport at Stages.	Remarks.
		Intermediate. m. f.	Total. m. f.						
XVI	*ROUTE—contd.*	...	134	......			......		
12	Ekali	14	148	......	Up Maru Wurdwan valley.	......	......	S. nil, G. F. W. procurable, T. nil.	Huts.
13	Sanger *Zawl*	16	164	......	......	Maru Wurdwan bridge.	......	Ditto	Ditto.
14	Hanja	15	179	......	......	Maru Wurdwan bridge.	......	Ditto	Ditto.
15	Petgam or Maru	13	192	......	......	Farriabad bridge.	......	S. G. F. W. procurable, few coolies.	Village.

Hence there are two routes to Sarru, one up the Maru Wurdwan valley by the Bhutkhol Pass and the other up the Farriabad valley by the Chiloong Pass, the latter much longer. See Route XVIa.

Number of Marches.	Names of Stages.	Distance in Miles and Furlongs.		Nature of Route.	Main Valleys and Mountain Passes.	River crossings and Lakes.	Altitude above Sea Level in feet.	Supplies and Transport at Stages.	Remarks.
		Intermediate. m. f.	Total. m. f.						
16	Hajka *E,—*	11	203	Road bad along precipices.	Up Maru Wurdwan valley.	......	......	S nil, G. F. W. procurable, T. nil.	Halting place.

No.	Place	Miles	Total	Road	Route	River	Elevation	Supplies	Remarks
17	Inshin P. O., E.	9	212	......	......	......	8143	S. precarious, G. F. W. procurable, few coolies.	Village.
	Afth	...	216	......	......	......	......	......	
	Basmaa	...	219	Road passable for ponies not laden.	......	Maru Wurtwan bridge.	......	......	Old fort.
18	Suhnis E.—	15	222	......	......	Ditto.	......	Ditto	Last village up this valley.
19	Dumhoi E.—	9	227	......	......	Ditto.	......	S. nil, G. F. W. procurable, T. nil.	Halting place.
20	Morse Khol E.—	12	248	Snow track over glacier.	Bhatkhol or Lauwi La.	......	......	S. G. nil, W. procurable, F. scarce, T. nil.	Ditto at foot of glacier.
			260	......	......	......	14370	......	Kwaj Kur track.
21	Dunore E.—	20	268	......	Down Suru valley left bank.	......	......	S. G. F. nil, W. procurable, T. nil.	Halting place.
22	Suru E.—	10	278	Road passable for men and led ponies only.	......	......	10624	S. G. F. W. procurable, few coolies and ponies.	Village and fort.
23	Sankho E.—	18	296	......	......	......	......	S. G. F. W. obtainable, T. available.	Large village.
24	Chaliskot E.—	12	308	......	......	......	......	S. G. F. W. procurable, T. nil.	Village.

Number of Marches.	Names of Stages.	Distance in Miles and Furlongs. Intermediate. m. f.	Distance in Miles and Furlongs. Total. m. f.	Nature of Route.	Main Valleys and Mountain Passes.	River Crossings and Lakes.	Altitude above Sea Level, in Feet.	Supplies and Transport at Stages.	Remarks.
XVI	ROUTE—contd. ...	...	...						
25	Kargil E.—	12 ...	308 ...	......	......	......	8787	S. G. W. plentiful, F. moderate, T. available	Large village and fort, and headquarters of district.
26	Kirkitchu E.—	14 ...	322 ...	Difficult road not passable for ponies or mules.	......	Dras bridge	......	S. G. F. W. procurable, T. nil.	Village Chamagand on right bank.
27	Gangany E.—	10 ...	332 ...	......	......	......	......	Ditto ...	Small village.
28	Olting Thang E.—	10 ...	342 ...	......	Down Iuins valley left bank.	......	......	S. G. F. W. procurable, few coolies	Village.
29	Tarkuty E.—	12 ...	354 ...	Bad parts over rugged spurs with scaffolding.	......	......	7800	Ditto ...	Ditto.
30	Kartaksho E. confined—	14 ...	368 ...	......	......	......	8500	Ditto ...	Ditto.
31	Tolti E.—	17 ...	385 ...	......	......	......	......	Ditto ...	Ditto.
32	Parkuta E.—	12 ...	397 ...	Fair hill road ...	......	......	......	S. G. F. W. plentiful, T. available.	Large village.

33	Gol E.—	13	424	......	......	......	......	Ditto	... Ditto.
	Kepchang	...	441	......	......	......	......	Ditto	... Ditto.
34	Skardu P. O., T. O., E.—	21	445	......	......	......	7,440	S. G. W abundant, F. scarce, T. ample.	Capital of Baltistan, fort and bazar.

There are two routes over the Bhut khol Pass between Suknis and Suru. The Kwaj Kur Route, as above given, generally open from June to November, and the Saga Route by the Rang marg, 73 miles long, which, though it has easier gradients, is not safe after the snow melts. As changes occur in the glaciers, the tracks are altered, and this may account for the different routes given by travellers.

It is remarkable that in this road from Jammu to Skardo, 445 miles in length through the mountains, there are only two passes—the Larulari, 6,600 ft. and the Bhut khol, 14,370 ft. With a large camp, through transport is necessary for the bulk of the baggage.

XVIa ALTERNATIVE ROUTE from PETGAM to SURU by CHILOONG PASS—

15	Petgam E.—	...	192	...	Hill track used by men only, difficult path.	Up Farriabad valley.	......	S. procurable, G. F. W. moderate, few coolies.	Village.
	Zabbas	...	...	...	......	...	......	......	Hot Spring.
16	Metwan E.—	14	206	...	......	......	......	S. nil. G. F. W. procurable, T. nil.	Hamlet.
17	Maharran E.—	10	216	...	......	......	......	Ditto	Halting place.
18	Kailgan Rocks E.—	12	228	...	......	......	......	Ditto	Ditto.
19	Camp E.—	12	240	...	......	......	......	S. F. G nil, W. plentiful, T. nil.	Ditto.

Number of Marchings.	Names of Stages.	Distance in miles and furlongs. Intermediate. m. f.	Total. m. f.	Nature of Route.	Main Valleys and Mountain Passes.	River crossings and Lakes.	Altitude above Sea Level in Feet.	Supplies and Transport at Stages.	Remarks.
XVI	ROUTE—contd.	12 ...	240 ...	......			......		
20	Ramdun Sankpo E.—	20 ...	260 ...	......	Chiloong Pass down Ramdun Sankpo valley.	......	......	S. F. G. nil, W. plentiful, T. nil.	Foot of Penge La.
21	Gonpa LamaSeroi or Ringdom E.—	13 ...	273 ...	Track improves as the valley widens.	......	......	......	S. precarious, F. G. procurable, W. plentiful, T. nil.	Lama Monastery
22	Gulmatongo E.—	17 ...	290 ...	Heavy road	......	......	......	Ditto	Huts.
23	Purkatse E.—	12 ...	302 ...	Steep ascent	...... Purkatse spur.	......	......	Ditto	Small village.
24	Suru E.—	6 ...	308 ...	......	......	......	10624	S. G. F. moderate, W. plentiful, few coolies.	Fort and village.

From Purkatse another road winds round the spur along right bank of river to Suru 12 miles long.

XVII JAMMU to LEH by BADRAWAR and ZANSKAR—

No.	Station	Dist. between	Total	Road	Direction	Ford / Pass	Elevation	Supplies	Remarks
1	Jammu P.O., T.O., D.B., C.—	...	0	Fair hill road passable for laden animals but stony.	Up Tawi valley.	Tawi ford	1200	S.G.F.W. abundant, F. dear, T. ample.	Capital of Jammu State, Military Cantonment, large town and bazar.
	Pergulta E.—	10	10			......	......	S.G.F.W. procurable, few coolies.	Village.
2	Suruin Sar E.—	9	19			Suruin Sar L.	1825	S.G.F.W procurable, few coolies.	Ditto.
	Munsnd		28				......		Ruins of Pandoo temples in vicinity.
3	Chian E.—	11	30				......	Ditto	Village.
			32		Belsi or Sunádhar range, Pulasu spur				
			38			Silokad.			
4	Ramnagar P.O., T.O., E.—	13	43	Good road	Up Ramnagar valley.		2700	S.G. F. W. plentiful, T. ample.	Capital of Ramnagar Jagir. Town, fort and bazar.
5	Korta E.— Kroide Garoo	9	52		From Korta to Kroide Garoo road ascends spur and runs along high ridge Kalatil.		......	S.G.F.W. procurable, few coolies.	Village.
			62				......		
6	Dooder E.—	13	65				......	Ditto	Ditto.

Number of Marches	Names of Stages	Distance in miles and furlongs — Intermediate m. f.	Distance in miles and furlongs — Total m. f.	Nature of Route.	Main Valleys and Mountain Passes.	River crossings and Lakes.	Altitude about Sea Level is feet.	Supplies and Transport at Stages.	Remarks.
XVII	ROUTE.—contd.	...	...						
7	Asmas E.—	13 ...	65 ...	......	Up Room-mutta valley.	......	......	S. nil, G. F. W. procurable, T. nil.	Halting place.
		10 ...	75 ...	Short deep descent and easy road.	Siwulidar or Seyagi.	......	10148		
8	Badrawar P. O., E.—Chinta	12 ...	78 ...	Summer road follows high ridge to 2 miles beyond Jaora.	Down Neru valley.	Neru bridge	5427	S. G. F. W. abundant, T. ample.	Capital of Badrawar Jagir. Town, fort and bazars.
		...	87 ...	In winter lower road by Jagud is taken.					
9	Jaora E.—	17 ...	90 ...		......	......		S. G. F. W. plentiful, T. available.	Village.
		...	104 ...	......	Chira gully.				
10	Zanglwar E.—	8 ...	106 112 ...	Fair road	Up Chandra Bhaga valley.	Karney Gad bridge.	3670	S. G. F. W. procurable, T. available.	Ditto.
11	Joshni E.—	6 ...	118 ...	Road crosses numerous ravines and is bad in places.	......	......		S. nil, G. F. W. procurable, T. nil.	Ditto.
12	Kishtwar P. O., E.—	15 ...	133 ...	......	......	......	{5400 {5000	S. G. F. W. plentiful, T. ample.	Town, fort, bazar, head-quarters of district.

No.	Name of place	Stage		Total		Route remarks	Valley direction	Bridges	Elevation	Supplies	Character of place
13	Bagni	13	...	146	...	Difficult path high above river, crossing numerous side gorges with considerable ascents and descents, practicable for unladen ponies.	Up Chandra Bhaga valley left bank.	......	......	S. scanty, G. F. W. plentiful, T. available	Small village.
14	Piyas	11	...	157	...	......	......	......	6320	S. nil, G. F. W. procurable, T. nil.	Hamlet.
15	Siri	9	4	166	4	......	......	......	8700	Ditto	Ditto.
16	Atholi or Gulabgarh E.—	14	...	180	4	Up Bhutna valley, open and well cultivated.	......	Chandra Bhaga rope bridge and Bhutna wooden bridge	6360	S.G. F. W. procurable, T. available.	Village and fort, chief place of Padar.
17	Kundhel Umshil	11	...	191 / 194	4 / ...	Easy path to Soomjam for laden animals.	......	Bhutna bridge	7680	Ditto	Village.
18	Machail E.— Soomjam	11 / ..	...	202 / 207	4 / ...	......	......	......	9700 / 11000	Ditto	Ditto. Sapphire mines in vicinity.
19	Bujwas	8	4	211	...	......	......	......	11570	S. nil, G. F. W. procurable, T. nil.	

Hence there are three tracks to the Zanskar valley. Firstly, up the Kaosh nullah over the Hagshu La 16,660 feet down the Hagshu Tokpho, across the Zanskar valley over the Rulakun La 17,500 feet by Rulagourg, Linshot 12,580 feet to Yelchung 12,735 feet. Secondly, the route over the Umasi La 17,370 feet to Yelchung which follows, and thirdly, over the Muni La a deserted track leading direct to Padam and Yelchung. The Umasi La is usually open for 3 months, June to August, inclusive.

No.	Name of place	Stage		Total		Route remarks	Valley direction	Bridges	Elevation	Supplies	Character of place
20	Bugian Hiwan E.—	7	...	218 / 223	...	Steep ascent over snow to glacier, level plateau and steep descent.	Umasi La or Bardhar.	......	15500 / 17370	G. and W. procurable, F. S. T. nil.	Halting place.
21	Gowra E.—	13	...	231	...	......	......	......	......	Ditto	Ditto.

5

Number of Marches.	Names of Stages.	Distance in Miles and Furlongs.		Nature of Route.	Main Valleys and Mountain Passes.	River crossings and Lakes.	Altitude above Sea Level in Feet.	Supplies and Transport at Stages.	Remarks.
		Intermediate. m. f.	Total. m. f.						
XVII 22	ROUTE.—contd. Ating E.— Tungring	13 ... 10	231 ... 241 ... 247 ...	......	......	......	12020	S. G F. W. procurable, few coolies	Village.

Hence there are two routes down the Zanskar valley on either bank to Yelchung. A Jhula bridge at Tungring to left bank Doda river.

Number of Marches.	Names of Stages.	Distance in Miles and Furlongs.		Nature of Route.	Main Valleys and Mountain Passes.	River crossings and Lakes.	Altitude above Sea Level in Feet.	Supplies and Transport at Stages.	Remarks.
		Intermediate.	Total.						
23	Semi Gonpa E.—	9 ...	250 ...	Fair hill track, passable for laden animals.	Down Doda or Zanskar valley right bank.	......	11560	Ditto	Ditto and temple.
24	Padam E.—	9 ...	259 ...	......	......	Tsarap Lingti Chu or Sindit Jhula or rope bridge.	11373	S. G. F. W. procurable, few coolies, T. available.	Former capital of Zanskar, village and fort.
25	Thonde E.—	9 ...	268 ...	......	......	......	11460	Ditto, T. nil.	Small village.
26	Zozar E.—	7 ...	275 ...	......	......	......	11583	Ditto	Hamlet and bridge over Zanskar river.
27	Zangla E.—	6 ...	280 ... 281 ...	......	......	Sumdo.	11050	S. G W plentiful, F. scarce, T. available.	Village.
			289 ...	......	Chelong Labho.	......	14530		
28	Khurma foo E.—	13 ...	294 ...	Rough hill road passable for ponies.	......	......	13050	S. nil, G. F. W. procurable, T. nil.	Halting place.
29	Pangot E.—	10 ...	304 ... 308 ...	......	Nira La.	......	16000	Ditto	Ditto.

No.	Place	Miles		Road	Passes	Zanskar bridge	Elevation	Supplies	Hamlet
30	Nira or Naorung *E.—*	10	314 . 4 / 315 .	......	...... Chochu Bori La.	...... Zanskar bridge.	10819	Ditto	Small village.
31	Yelchung *E.*	6	318 ... / 320 ...	......	......	......	12730	S. precarious, G.F.W. scanty, T. nil.	

Here the route leaves the Zanskar valley, although the most direct line would be down this river to its junction with the Indus river at Nimu. The Zanskar river from Yelchung down to Chiling is bordered by rugged and lofty cliffs, which are said to be inaccessible.

No.	Place	Miles		Road	Passes	Zanskar bridge	Elevation	Supplies	Hamlet
	Meling		325 ...	......	Singri La.	......	16600	......	
32	**Photaksur** *E.—*	16 ...	328 ... / 336 ...	Fair hill road passable for ponies.	......	......	13900	S.G.F.W. procurable, few coolies.	Village.
33	**Honupatta** *E.—*	13 ...	340 ... / 349 ...	......	Sirsir La. Down Marling valley.	......	16372 / 12400	S. G. F scarce, W. plentiful, T. nil.	Ditto.
	Phanjila / *Turchik*		356 . 3 / 359 ...	......					
34	**Wanla** *E.—*	12 ...	361 ...	......	......	......	10900	S. G. F. procurable, W. plentiful, T. available.	Ditto.
35	**Lamayuru** *E.—* / *Khalsi*	6 ...	367 ... / 375 ... / 379 . 2	Good road passable for laden animals.	Prinkiti La	......	12500 / 11520	S. G. F. W. plentiful, T. available.	Village and monastery.
36	**Nurla** *B., E.—*	18 . 2	383 . 2	......	Up Indus valley right bank	Indus bridge.	10000	S. G. F. W. procurable, few coolies.	Village.
37	**Saspul** *B., E.—*	14 . 6	400 ...	......	......	......	......	Ditto, T. nil.	Small village.
38	**Nimu** *B., E.—*	11 . 4	411 . 4	......	......	......	......	Ditto, few coolies.	Village.
39	**Leh** *P. O., B. C. E.—*	18 . 2	429 . 6	......	......	......	11400	S. G. F. W. plentiful, T. ample.	Capital of Ladak, town, fort & bazar.

From Zozar there is another difficult path to Leh north-eastwards over the Charcha La, Riberang La and Kunda la, open only when the rivers are low. From Phanjila 356 miles 3 furlongs, a track branches off up the Ripchar nullah to Hinju 365 miles, over the Choke La 13,513 feet down the Semda foot to Drogulika 375 miles, Ezas 384 miles, whence there are two ways to Leh; either up the Zanskar river and crossing the latter near Chiling to Skio 400 feet, 11,120 feet, over the Kunda La, 16,211 feet to Zinchan 420 miles, Chushot 436 miles, crossing by bridge over the Indus river 10,500 feet, and onwards to Leh 446 miles; or down the Zanskar and Indus rivers left bank by Umlung Goongma 402 miles, to Saspul 414 miles, crossing the Indus river by bridge at this place and onwards by Nimu 426 miles, to Leh 444 miles.

XVIIa ATING to YELCHUNG by LEFT BANK DODA or ZANSKAR RIVER

Number of Marches.	Names of Stages.	Distance in miles and furlongs. Intermediate. m. f.	Distance in miles and furlongs. Total. m. f.	Nature of Route.	Main Valleys and Mountain Passes.	River Crossings and Lakes.	Altitude above Sea Level in Feet.	Supplies and Transport at Stages.	Remarks.
22	Ating E.—	...	241	Easy path to Pidmu	Down Doda or Zanskar valley left bank.	......	12020	S. G. F. W. procurable, few coolies.	Village.
23	Tungring	6	247	......	......	......	.....	Ditto, T. nil.	Ditto.
24	Kursha	8	255	......	......	Doda bridge	.....	S. G. F. W. moderate, few coolies.	Large village, Lama Monastery.
25	Zozar left bank	12	267	......	......	......	11583	S. G. F. W. procurable, T. nil.	Halting place.
26	Pidmu	11	278	Difficult path crosses deep gorges and high ridges in the massive limestone and slate formation.	......	......	.....	Ditto	Village.
27	Hansmil	6	284	......	......	......	.....	S. precarious, G.F.W. procurable, T. nil.	Hamlet.
			292	......	Purfi La.	......			
			293	......	......	Omachu.			
			295	......	Khlangpu spur.	......			
28	Sneatse	13	297	......	Hulooua La	......	15453	S. nil, G. F. W. scanty, T. nil.	Halting place.
			303	......	......	Lazungchu.			
		4	304	......	Chupkun La.	......			
			306	......	......	......			
29	Linshot	11	308	......	......	......	12850	S. G. F. W. scanty, T. nil.	Small village.
			311	......	Mitookse La.	......			
			313	......	......	Sholo Kurpochu.		Ditto	Ditto.
			315	......	Kuba La.	......			
30	Yelchung E.—	10	318	......	......	......	12730	Ditto	Ditto.

XVIII JAMMU to HANLE by CHAMBA—

No.	Station		Total	Road	River / Ford	Elevation	Supplies	Remarks
	Jammu *P. O., T. O., D. B.*—	...	...	Fair hill road passable for laden animals, rises up the range to the two mountain lakes and descends to Ramkot.	......	1200	S.G. F. W. abundant, T. ample.	Capital of Jammu State, Military Cantonment, large town and bazars.
1	Pergulta *E.*—	10	10	......	......	......	S. nil, G. F. W. procurable, T. nil.	Small village.
2	Suruin Sar *E.*—	9	19	Along Suruin hill range.	Saruin Sar L.	1825	S. G. F. procurable W. plentiful, T. nil.	Or by Munwal 9m., Tial 9m., Ramkot 9m.
3	Man Sar *E.*—	10	29	......	Man Sar L.	......	S. G. F. procurable, W. plentiful, T. nil.	Lake and temple.
4	Ramkot *E.*—	16	45	Ramkot plain.	......	......	S. G. F. W. plentiful, T. available.	Fort.
5	Sambarta *E.*—	8	53 ... 56	Across Wooj valley.	Wooj ford.	2320	S. after notice, C. T. W. procurable, T. nil.	Village.
6	Padua *E.*—	7	60 ... 62	......	Pine ford.	......	S. G. F. W. plentiful, T. available.	Large village.
7	Mandpur *E.*—	8	68	Up Ravi valley right bank.	......	......	S. after notice, G. F. W. procurable, few coolies.	Village.
8	Bisaoli *P. O., C. E.*—	11	79	Good road for laden animals.	Ravi ford and ferry.	2170	S. G. F. W. abundant, T. ample.	Town, fort and bazar on right bank Ravi.
9	Mail *E.*—	6	85	......	......	......	S. G. F. W. plentiful, T. available.	Village.
10	Rampur *E.*—	12	97	......	......	......	Ditto	Ditto.

Number of Marches	Names of Stages	Distance in miles and furlongs		Nature of Route.	Main Valleys and Mountain Passes.	River crossings and Lakes.	Altitude above Sea Level in feet.	Supplies and Transport at Stages.	Remarks.
		Intermediate. m. f.	Total. m. f.						
XVIII	ROUTE.—contd. ...	12 ...	97 ...	......	......				
11	Chamba ... P. O., D. B., C. E.—	14 ...	111 ...	......	......	Ravi bridge	3033	S. G. F. W. abundant, T. ample.	Capital of Chamba State. Large town and bazars.
12	Rakh ... D. B., E.—	12 ...	123 ...	......	......	......	......	S. G. F. W. plentiful, T. available.	Village.
13	Chitrali ... E.—	10 ...	133 ...	......	......	......	5883	Ditto	Ditto.

From Chitrali there are two routes to Thandi at the junction of the Chandra and Bhaga rivers, one by the Kukti pass, the other by the Bara Bhagal pass as under : though on the latter, a difficult glacier has to be crossed 8 miles long. Both passes are impracticable for ponies.

BY KUKTI PASS :—

Number of Marches	Names of Stages	Distance in miles and furlongs		Nature of Route.	Main Valleys and Mountain Passes.	River crossings and Lakes.	Altitude above Sea Level in feet.	Supplies and Transport at Stages.	Remarks.
14	Oolasa ...	11 ..	144 ...	Fair hill track	Up Barmaor branch of Ravi valley.	Ravi bridge	......	S. G. F. W. procurable. T. available.	Village.
15	Barmaor ... P. O.—	10 ...	154 ...	......	......	......	7076	S. G. F. W. plentiful, T. available.	Large village.
16	Harsa ...	10 ...	164 ...	......	......	......	6650	S. F. G. W. procurable, T. available.	Village.

No.	Name					Road	Valley/Ridge	River	Elevation	Supplies	Remarks
17	Kukti *F. B.—*	12	...	176 187	...	Difficult path	Kukti pass Chandra Bhaga valley.	......	17400	Ditto	Ditto.
18	Rupeh	25	...	201	...	......	......	......	......	Ditto	Ditto.
	Lota	...	...	203	...	......	......	Chandra Bhaga bridge			
19	Tandi	12	...	213	...	......	......	......	......	Ditto	Ditto.

OR BY BARA BHAGAL PASS :—

No.	Name					Road	Valley/Ridge	River	Elevation	Supplies	Remarks
14	Chanota	12	...	140 145	...	Fair hill track	Hulasa ridge. Up Ravi valley.	......	......	S. G. F. W. plentiful, T. available.	Village.
15	Sutket	9	...	154	...	......	......	......	......	Ditto	Ditto.
16	Channir *Kunaur*	12	...	166 176	...	......	......	Ravi bridge	......	S. G. F. procurable, T. available.	Ditto.
17	Bara Bhagal	16	...	182	...	Very difficult path	......	......	8535	Ditto	Ditto.
18	Camp	12	...	194 200	...	......	Bara Bhagal pass.	......	......	S. F. T. nil, G. W. plentiful.	Halting place.
19	Tandi	18	...	212	...	......	Chandra Bhaga.	......	......	S. G. F. W. procurable, T. available.	Village.
20	Kailing(Kardang) *P. O., B., E.—*	5	...	218	...	Good road passable for laden animals to the Tsarap valley.	Up Bhaga valley right bank.	......	......	S. G. F. W. plentiful, T. available.	Chief place Lahoul, Moravian Mission. D.B. at Kardang on left bank of Bhaga river.

Number of Marches.	Names of Stages.	Distance in miles and furlongs.		Nature of Route.	Main Valleys and Mountain Passes.	River crossings and Lakes.	Altitude above Sea Level in Feet.	Supplies and Transport at Stages.	Remarks.
		Inter-mediate. m. f.	Total. m. f.						
XVIII	*ROUTE.—contd.*	...	...						
21	**Kulang** E.—	5 ...	218 ...	......	......	......	......	S. G. F. W. procurable, T. procurable.	Village.
		12 ...	230 ...	......	......				
22	**Sumdeo Darcha** C, E.—	10 ...	238 ...	......	......	Kada Tokpo bridge.	10844	Ditto	Ditto, last on road.
23	**Patsio** C, E.—	9 ...	240 ...	......	......	Bhaga bridge	12464	S. T. nil, G. F. W. plentiful.	Encamping ground for traders.
	Tapachand	...	249 ...	......	......	:	......		
24	**Zing Zingbar** *Hal.—*	8 ...	255 ...	......	......	Bhaga bridge	......	S. G. F. T. nil, W. plentiful.	Halting place on road to Bara Lacha pass. Pasture across river.
		...	257 ...						Ditto.
25	**Suruj Dul**	6 ...	263 ...	Gradual ascent and descent.	Under Bara-lacha pass not crossed.	Chukum L. Yunan Tso L.	 15417	S. T. nil, W. plentiful. G. F. available.	
		...	270 ...	......					
26	**Kenlung**	12 ...	275 ...	......	Down Yunan valley.	Yunan bridge.	... ...	Ditto	Ditto.
	Phatangidanda	...	283 ...						

No.	Stage	Dist.	Total	Remarks on track	Landmark	Reference	Height	Supplies	Remarks
27	Sarchu (Lingti) ... E.— *Zamdang Zampa*	13	288 293	....	......	Sarchu bridge	......	S. T. nil, W. plentiful, G. F. available.	Boundary of Lahoul and Ladak, at junction of Lingti and Yunan rivers.
28	Lama Guru	13	301	Track becomes more difficult and is used by men, sheep and goats.	Up Tsarap or Maling valley.	......	......	Ditto	Halting place.
29	ThungChungKiri	13	314 325	......	Pangpo La Down Lankpol valley.	Maling bridge.	......	Ditto	Ditto.
30	Tso Kum	17	331	......		......	17500	Ditto	Ditto.
31	Khiang Shisa	12	343	......	Down Phirse foo valley.	Phirse foo.	......	S. T. nil, G. F. W. procurable.	Hamlet.
32	Latok *Khulmoche*	14	350 357 363	Gentle descent from Pangpo La to Tso Morari Lake.	......	......	......	S. G. F. T. nil, W. procurable.	Halting place.
33	Kiangdom	16	373 377 383	Easy track	Narbu La. Across head of Parechu valley.	Tso Morari Lake. Phirse foo.	14900	G. W. scanty, F. S. T. nil.	Plain at south end of Lake.
34	Lam Tso	20	393	......	......	......	......	S. G. F. T. nil, W. procurable.	
35	Larsa-le	13	406 409	Easy ascent and descent, stony path.	Lenak La down Kongrachu.	......	18100	S. G. T. nil, F. W. procurable.	Two tracks over this pass.

Number of Marches	Names of Stages	Distance in miles and furlongs.		Nature of Route.	Main Valleys and Mountain Passes.	River crossings and Lakes.	Altitude above Sea Level in Feet.	Supplies and Transport at Stages.	Remarks.
		Intermediate. m. f.	Total. m. f.						
XVIII	*ROUTE.—contd.*	...	409				......		
36	Gongra-le	11	417		......	......	......	S. G. T. nil, F. W. procurable.	
	Togra-le	...	422						
37	Sango Plain	15	432	Swampy track in places.	......	......	......	S. F. and T. nil, G. W. procurable.	
38	Hanle *E.—*	14	446	......	Up Hanle valley left bank.	......	14276	S.G. F. W. procurable, T. available.	Village, large monastery, head-quarters of district.

From Gongra-le there is a path direct to Hanle over the high table land, Thungangeri plain, about 20 miles in length.

XVIIIa ALTERNATIVE ROUTE from TANDI to HANLE by SPITI:—

Number of Marches	Names of Stages	Distance in miles and furlongs.		Nature of Route.	Main Valleys and Mountain Passes.	River crossings and Lakes.	Altitude above Sea Level in Feet.	Supplies and Transport at Stages.	Remarks.
		Intermediate. m. f.	Total. m. f.						
19	Tandi *E.—*	...	219	Fair hill road passable for mules, which must swim across Chandra river at Koksor.	Up Chandra valley right bank.	Bhaga bridge	......	S. G. F. W. plentiful, T. available.	Village.
20	Gundla *E.—*	8	227	......	......	......	10514	S.G. F. W. procurable, few coolies.	Ditto.
21	Sisu *E.—*	9	230	......	......	......	9938	Ditto	Small ditto.
22	Koksor *E.—*	10	240	......	Ditto left bank.	Chandra rope bridge.	10201	Ditto	Ditto.

No.	Name of place	Miles	Total	Remarks on road	Direction	River	Elevation	Supplies	Halting place
23	Chahtru opposite Old Kokser. E.—	13	253	Road difficult in places and stony.	......	......	......	S, nil. G. F. W. procurable, T. nil.	Halting place.
24	Puti Runi E.—	12	265 268	......	Bara Shigri torrent and glacier. Chota Shigri moraine.	......	......	Ditto	Ditto.
25	Karcha E.—	11	276 280	Easy ascent and descent.	Kunzam pass Down Lichu ravine.	......	14931	Ditto	Ditto.
26	Loisar E.—	16	292	Fair road	Down Spiti valley.	Spiti ford	12395	Ditto	Village.
27	Kioto E.—	12	304 308	......	Up Lagurdasi valley.	......	......	S G. F. precarious, W. procurable, few coolies.	Small ditto.
28	Lagudarsi E.—	11	315	Road difficult, not passable for laden mules.	......	......	......	Ditto	Halting place.
			320	......	Takling La or Sanna La.	......	......	W. procurable, T. nil	
29	Dakar Kuru E.—	19	334	......	Down Parechu valley.	......	......	Ditto	Ditto.
30	Tradang E.—	15	349	......	......	......	......	Ditto	Ditto.
31	Narbu Sumdo E.—	9	358	Bad path	Right bank	......	15300	Ditto	Ditto.
32	Chumar E.—	18	376	......	Down Parechu valley.	Parechu	......	S. G. F. precarious, W. procurable, T. nil.	Lama monastery

Number of Marches.	Names of Stages.	Distance in miles and furlongs.		Nature of Route.	Main Valleys and Mountain Passes.	River crossings and Lakes.	Altitude above Sea Level in Feet.	Supplies and Transport at Stages.	Remarks.
		Intermediate. m. f.	Total. m. f.						
	XVIIIa ROUTE.—contd.								
33	Chepzi	18 ...	376 ...	......	Up Kyumsan Lang.	......	......	S. G. F. precarious, W. procurable, T. nil.	Chinese frontier.
34	Nakkero-le	10 ...	386 ...	......		......	......	W. procurable, T. nil	Spring do.
		9 ...	395 ...						
			402 ...	......	Kyung Zing La.				
35	Kar-Le	17 ...	410 ...	......		Hanle ford.	......	Ditto	Halting place.
			412 ...	......	......	......		Ditto	Ditto.
36	Trakarpo E.—	12 ...	419 ...	......	Nara pass.		......		
			424 ...	......	......	......			
37	Hanle E.—	10 ...	429 ...	......	......	Hanle ford.			
			434 ...	......	......	......	14276	S. G. F. W. procurable, T. available.	Village and Buddhist Monastery on left bank Hanle river.

Between Kioto and Narbu Somdo there is an alternative track by the Parang La as under, open from July to September inclusive, the scenery wild and magnificent.

27	Kioto	... ...	304 ...	Track fit for men and yaks only.	......	......	......	S. G. F. precarious, W. procurable, few coolies.	Small village.
		... ...	305 ...	......	......	Lagularsi			

28	Kiwar	...	15	...	319	...	......	......	......	13400	S. G. F. W. and T. available.	Large village.
29	Jugtha	...	12	...	331	...	Steep and rough ascent and four miles of glacier on descent.	Parang La	......	16000	G. F. W. procurable, T. nil.	Halting place.
30	Dutung	...	10	...	341	...			......	18300	W. procurable.	Ditto.
										16000		
31	Umdung	...	17	...	358	...	......	......	......	......	Ditto	Ditto.
32	Narbu Sumdo	...	20	...	378	...	......	......	......	15300	G. F. W. procurable, S. T. nil.	Ditto.

From Kiwar 319 miles down Spiti valley right bank, in a S. E. direction Ki Monastery 324 miles, Kaja 331 miles, Lara 339 miles, and Dankar 12,774 feet 317 miles, chief place of Spiti are reached.—S. G. F. W. and T. available throughout.

XIX JAMMU to HURDWAR by SIMLA—

Jammu P. O., T. O., D. B.,—	...	...	0	...	......	......	......	1200	S. G. F. W. abundant, T. ample.	Large town, cantonment and capital of Jammu State.
			1	4		Across Tawi drainage.	Tawi bridge.			
1	Ismaailpur	...	12	...	9	12	Track across undulating country at foot of hills, broken by ravines and well cultivated.	...... Across Degh drainage.	Balal ford.	......	S. G. F. W. scarce, T. nil.	Hamlet.
					23	...			Basantha ford.			
2	Samba	...	13	...	25	...	......	......	......	......	S. G. F. W. moderate, T. available.	Small town and tehsil.
	E.—											
3	Aleh	!	12	...	37	...	......	Across Ravi drainage.	......	......	S. G. F. W. scarce, T. nil.	Hamlet.
4	Jasrota	...	12	...	49	...	......	......	Chalybeate spring, Woojh ford.	......	S. G. F. W. procurable, T. available.	Small town and bazar, head quarters of district.

Number of Marches	Names of Stages	Distance in miles and furlongs. Inter- mediate m. f.	Total m. f.	Nature of Route.	Main Valleys and Mountain Passes.	River Crossings and Lakes.	Altitude above Sea Level in feet.	Supplies and Transport at Stages.	Remarks.
XIX	ROUTE.—contd.								
5	Kuttoah P. O.—	12 ...	49 ...	......	......	......	......	S. G. F. W. plentiful, T. ample.	Small town and tehsil on right bank of Ravi river.
		12 ...	61 ...	......	......	Ravi ferry.			
6	Madhopur P. O., D. B., E.—	6 ...	64 ... 67 ...	Road fit for wheeled traffic during year.	......	......	1137	Ditto	Bazar and canal workshop.
7	Puthankot P. O., T. O., hotel, C., E.—	8 ...	73 ...	......	......	......	... ...	Ditto	Bazar and terminus of branch railway from Amritsar.
			81 ...	......	......	Chukee bridge			
8	Nurpur P. O., D. B., E.—	16 ...	91 ...	Fair weather, cart-road through low hill country, well cultivated.	Across Reas drainage.	......	2050	S. G. F. plentiful, W. scarce and bad, T. ample.	Town and bazar, old fort.
9	Kotla or Triloknath. P. O., B., E. small.—	14 ...	105 ...	......	......	Daira bridge	3184	S. G. F procurable, water plentiful, T. available.	Ancient town.
			107 4	......	......	Burhal bridge.			
10	Shahpur P. O., B., E. fair.—	11 ...	116 ...	......	......	Khouli bridge.	3148	Ditto	Village.
			120 ... 124 ...	......	......	Guj nullah Manji nullah.			

No.	Name of stage	Intermediate distance (m.)	(f.)	Total distance (m.)	(f.)	Nature of road	Direction	Rivers and streams crossed	Height above sea	Supplies	Remarks
11	Kangra *P. O., D. B., E. fair—*	13	...	129	...	......	......	......	2419	S. G. F. W. plentiful, T. ample.	Fort on top of rock 150 feet above Bangunga.
12	Ranital *B., C.—*	9	...	136	4	......	......	Bangunga nullah.	......	S. G. F. W. procurable, T. nil.	Small village.
13	Jualamukhi *B., C., E.—*	11	4	138	...	......	......	Naphtha springs under Changa mountains.	1883 } 3284 }	S. G. F. W. plentiful, T. available.	Small town, celebrated place of pilgrimage.
14	Nadaon *P. O., E.—*	6	4	149	4	Good road through low hill country, well cultivated, pretty scenery.	Across Beas drainage	Beas ferry	...	S. G. F. W. plentiful, T. ample.	Small town on left bank Beas.
15	Hamirpur *P. O., B.—*	14	2	156	...	......	Across Sutlej drainage.	Koman nulla.	......	S. G. F. after notice, W. plentiful, T. nil.	Village.
	Mairki Hati	...	...	161	2	......	......	......	......	Ditto	Small village.
16	Dangoh	16	...	170	...	......	......	......	......	Ditto	Small village.
17	Kunar Hati	8	...	180	2	Fair hill road	......	Sher Khud	......	S. G. F. after notice, W. plentiful, T. nil.	Ditto.
18	Belaspur *E. extensive.—*	9	...	186	2	Good broad road	......	Sutlej ferry	......	S. G. F. W. plentiful, T. available.	Town on left bank Sutlej, bazars.
	Bujaum	...	...	194	2	......	......	......	......	S. G. F. scarce, W. procurable, T. nil.	Hamlet.
19	Sahiki Hati	21	6	203	5	Road fair with steep ascent.	Ascending spur.	......	......	S. G. F. after notice, W. plentiful, T. nil.	Village.
	Kunur	...	...	213	...	......	......	......	......	Ditto	Small village.
20	Sairi *B., E. small.—*	20	...	225	...	Road fair for laden animals.	Along ridge of spur.	Ghumbur bridge.	......	S. G. F. W. procurable, T. nil.	Small bazar.

Number of Marches	Names of Stages	Distance in miles and furlongs — Intermediate m. f.	Distance — Total m. f.	Nature of Route	Main Valleys and Mountain Passes	River crossings and Lakes	Altitude above Sea Level in Feet	Supplies and Transport at Stages	Remarks
XIX	ROUTE—contd.		...						
21	Simla P. O., T. O., hotels, C.— Sanjoli	20	245	......	......	......	7084	S. G. F. abundant, W. scarce, T. ample.	Summer Capital of India. Large town and bazars.
		10	255						
			257 2	Road good, through Tunnel, thick forest, with fine scenery.					
22	Phagu B.—	12	267				8178	S. G. F. procurable, W. scarce in dry season, few coolies.	Small bazar.
			273 4		Across Giri drainage.				
23	Sainj	8	275	......		Giri ford.	8300	S. G. F. W. procurable, few coolies.	Village, Bunniahs' shop half mile off.
24	Dhar or Godhna	7	282	Along top of spur through oak forest.		......	......	Ditto	Small village.
25	Patar nala	6	288		Across Tonse drainage.	Giri ford.	9368	S. nil, G. F. W. procurable, T. nil.	Hamlet.
26	Chipal	10	298			......	7695	S. scarce, G. F. W. procurable, few coolies.	Village.
27	Piantra or Kedi	11	300 311			Shallu ford.	......	Ditto	Small village.

No.	Stage			Road	Rivers	Bridges	Elevation	Supplies	Remarks
28	Tikri or Pehri	8	317	Fair hill road through forests and beautiful scenery through precipitons country.	Across Tonse drainage.	......	......	S. scarce, G. F. W. procurable, T. nil.	Village.
29	Mandholi B.— Zeeni	5	322	......	......	......	......	Ditto	Ditto.
	Maindrot F. B., E. good.—		327	......	......	Tonse bridge wire suspension.	......	S. nil, G. F. W. procurable, T. nil.	
30		9	331	......	......	......	......	Ditto, W. far off.	
31	Kutiyan F. B.—	9	340	......	Jakna Leni	......	......	Ditto, W. near.	
	Lokur F. B.—		346	...	Across Jumna drainage.	......	......	Ditto.	
32	Kinanipani E. extensive—	12	352	Road good, easy gradient top of ridge between Tonse and Jumna.	......	......	...	Ditto.	
	Deobun F. B.—		363	......	......	......	9000		
33	Chakrata P. O., B.—	15	367	......	......	......	7364	S. G. F. W. plentiful, T. ample.	Military Cantonment.
34	Pokri B.—	9 4	376 4	Good hill road fit for riding and laden animals.	......	......	......	S. nil, G. F. W. procurable, T. nil	
	Shevalia D. B.—		379	......	......	......	......	Ditto	Usual halting place.
35	Nagtat	8	384 4	......	......	......	......	Ditto.	
36	Lekwar B.—	7	391 4	......	......	Jumna bridge iron suspension.	......	S. G. F. W. procurable, few coolies.	Village.
			395	......	......				
37	Masuri or Landour P. O., T. O., hotels, C.	17 4	409	Good hill road	......	Jumna bridge iron suspension.	6580 } 7433 }	S. G. F. W. abundant, T. ample.	Hill sanatarium, convalescent depot, town and bazar.

6

Number of Marches	Names of Stages	Distance of Miles and Furlongs — Intermediate m. f.	Total m. f.	Nature of Route	Main Valleys and Mountain Passes	River Crossings and Lakes	Altitude above Sea-level in feet	Supplies and Transport at Stages	Remarks
XIX	*ROUTE—contd.*	17 4	409 ...		......	......	......		
38	Rajpur *P. O., hotels, C.—*	7 4	416 4	Metalled cart-road	......	......	......	S. G. F. W. abundant, T. ample.	Small town.
39	Dehra *P.O., T.O., hotels, C.*	7	423 4	......	......	......	2347	Ditto	Military Cantonment, Civil Station, town and bazar.
40	Lachiwala	10 6	434 2	Fair weather, rough cart-road.	Down Ganges drainage.		1680	S. G. F. W scarce, T. nil.	
41	Kunsrao	8	442 2	......	......	Sugwa ford.	1360	Ditto.	
42	Hurdwar *P.O., T.O., D.B., C., E.*	12	454 2	......	......	......	1050	S.G. F W abundant, T. ample.	Small town and bazar, celebrated bathing ghat on Ganges river.

XIXa ALTERNATIVE ROUTE from JAMMU to PUTHANKOT—

Number of Marches	Names of Stages	Distance of Miles and Furlongs — Intermediate m. f.	Total m. f.	Nature of Route	Main Valleys and Mountain Passes	River Crossings and Lakes	Altitude above Sea-level in feet	Supplies and Transport at Stages	Remarks
	Jammu *P. O., T. O., D. B.—*	0	0 ...		Across Chenab drainage.	Tawi bridge.	1200	S. G. F. W. abundant, T. ample.	Capital of Jammu State, cantonment, town and bazars.
			1 4	Rough cart-road		Balal ford.			
			7 ...						
1	Bishenath	11	11 ...				......	S. G. F. W. procurable, T. nil.	Village.
	Keri		15 ...			Aik ford.			

No.	Place			Road remarks	Drainage	Ford	Elevation	Water & Supplies	Description
2	Bagnlade Chuk...	11	22	Track across flat, open and cultivated country.	......	......	......	Ditto	Small village.
3	Rajpur	13	26 / 35	......	......	Degh ford.	......	Ditto	Village.
4	Rampur	12	37 / 47	......	Across Ravi drainage.	Beyn ford.	......	Ditto	Small village.
5	Kuttoah *P. O.—*	13	50 / 60	......	......	Oojh ford.	......	S. G. F. W. plentiful, T. ample.	Small town and tehsil.
6	Madhopur *P. O., D. B., E.—*	6	63 / 66	Road fit for wheeled traffic during year.	......	Ravi ferry.	1137	Ditto	Bazar and canal workshop.
7	Puthankot *P. O., T. O., hotel, C. E.—*	8	74	......	......	......	......	Ditto	Bazar and terminus of branch railway from Amritsar.

XX JAMMU to LUDIANA by GURDASPUR and HOSHIARPUR :—

No.	Place			Road remarks	Drainage	Ford	Elevation	Water & Supplies	Description
	Jammu *P. O., T. O., D. B.—*	...	0 / 1 / 4	Rough cart-road over cultivated country.	Across Tawi drainage.	Tawi bridge.	1200	S. G. F. W. abundant. T. ample.	Capital Jammu State, cantonment, town and bazar.
1	Bishenath	11	6 / 11 / 15	......	Across Aik drainage.	Balal ford. Aik ford.	......	S. G. F. W. procurable. T. available.	Village.

Number of Marches.	Names of Stages.	Distance in Miles and Furlongs.		Nature of Route.	Main Valleys and Mountain Passes.	River Crossings and Lakes.	Altitude above Sea Level in Feet.	Supplies and Transport at Stages.	Remarks.
		Inter-mediate. m. f.	Total. m. f.						
XX	ROUTE—contd.	...	15	Track across open country.	Across Degh drainage.	......	......	S. F. nil, G. W. procurable, T. nil.	Hamlet.
2	Saidgurh	12	23	......	......	Degh ford.	......		
		...	27	......	......	......	......		
3	Zafarwal E. nil.—	10	33	Cart-road well raised, nullas overflow during the rains and are difficult to cross.	Across Ravi drainage.	......	......	S. G. F. procurable, W. plentiful, T. available.	Large village.
		9 4	42 4	......	......	......	......		
4	Ghurib Shah E. good.—	...	45	......	......	Kerf river.	......	S. G. F. after notice, W. plentiful, T. nil.	Small village.
		...	49	......	......	Choa river.	......		
5	Nurkikot E. good.—	9 2	51 6	......	......	......	......	Ditto	Village.
		...	55	......	......	Beyn ford.	......		
6	Nynakot E. good.—	8 3	60 1	......	......	......	......	Ditto	Ditto.
		...	64	......	......	Ravi ferry.	......		
7	Trimu Ghat E. one mile from river.—	5	65 1	Road metalled and bridged, flat, open country, fairly cultivated.	......	......	......	Ditto	On left bank Ravi.

No.	Name of place			Miles		Character of road	Drainage	Rivers, canals, ferries	Elevation	Water supply	Remarks
8	Gurdaspur P. O., T. O., D. B., E. good.—	9	6	74 / 76 / 79	7 / 4 / ..	......	......	Ravi canal. / Baree Doab Canal. / Beas ferry.	......	S. G. F. W. abundant, T. ample.	Small civil station and railway station on branch line from Amritsar.
9	Nowshera Ghat.. E. good near river.—	10	2	85	1	Road unmetalled and nullahs unbridged, good in fair weather; flat, open and well cultivated country, along foot of Sohan range.	Across Beas drainage.	......	......	S. G. F. procurable in vicinity, W. plentiful, T. nil.	On right bank Beas.
10	Mokerian P. O., E. good.—	5	2	90	3	......	......	......	......	S. G. F. procurable, W. plentiful, T. available.	Small town.
11	Dassohah P. O., E. good.—	9	..	99	3	......	Across large number of ravines, roads and nullahs from the Sohan hill range.	......	......	Ditto	Village. Hence road to Jullunder 37¾ miles south.
12	Ghurdeewala E. good.—	7	7	107	2	......	......	......	......	Ditto, T. nil.	Small village.
13	Hurriana P. O., E. good.—	9	1	116	3	......	......	......	......	Ditto	Village.
14	Hoshiarpur P. O., D. B., C. E. confined.—	8	4	124	7	Unmetalled road fit for wheeled traffic.	Flowing southwards.	Chow.	1066	S. G. F. W. plentiful, T. ample.	Small civil station.
15	Muhtianah E. good.—	12	..	136 / 142	7 / ...	......	......	Beyn ford.	......	S. G. F. W. procurable, T. available.	Village.

Number of Marches	Names of Stages	Distance in miles and furlongs — Intermediate m. f.	Total m. f.	Nature of Route	Main Valleys and Mountain Passes.	River crossings and Lakes.	Altitude above Sea Level in Feet.	Supplies and Transport at Stages.	Remarks.
XX	ROUTE—contd. ...	...	142 ...						
16	Phagwara ...	11 2	148 1	......	Across Sutlej drainage.	......	......	S. G. F. W. plentiful, T. available.	Large village and station on N. W. main line.
17	Phillour P. O., T. O.—	11 6	159 7	Grand Trunk road and N. W. Railway.	...	......	......	S. G. F. W. plentiful, T. ample.	Fort, town, and station on N. W. main line.
		...	163 ...	......	......	Sutlej bridge of boats and ferry.			
18	Ludiana P. O., T. O., D. B., C. E. confined.—	9 4	169 3	......	......	......	......	S. G. F. W. plentiful, T. ample.	Large city, civil station and railway station on N. W. main line.

From Zafarwal there is an alternative track to Nynakot thus: Zafarwal 33 miles, Sheikopur Chak 43 miles, Shukargarh 53 miles and Nynakot 61 miles 5 ft.

From Gurdaspur there is an alternative route to Hoshiarpur thus: Gurdaspur 74 miles 7 furlongs, Satiali 87 miles, Beyt ferry over Beas river 99 miles, Tandah 107 miles, Bulawal 119 miles, Hoshiarpur 129 miles. From Tandah, however, to Hoshiarpur, the road is bad across broken country.

From Tandah 107 miles a branch road by Kalabukra 120 miles, to Jullundur 134 miles.

From Dussohah there is a good branch road to Jullundur thus: Dussolah 99 miles 3 furlongs, Tandah 110 miles 1 furlong, cross Beyn river twice, Kalabukra 123 miles 1 furlong, Jullundur 137 miles 1 furlong.

From Hoshiarpur there is a metalled and bridged road to Jullundur thus: Hoshiarpur 124 mile. 7 furlongs, Adumpoor 138 miles 1 furlong, Jullundur 149 miles 1 furlong, crossing the Beyn bridge at 139 miles.

XXI POONCH to JAMMU by RAJAORI—

No.	Stage	Intermediate	Distance	Road	Direction / Drainage	Rivers, Fords, Bridges	Elevation	Supplies	Remarks
1	**Poonch** P. O., D. B., B., E.—	......	0	Fair hill road passable for laden animals throughout, parts in this section cut up by recent high floods.	Up Suran valley.	...... Dungli bed. Maudi ford.	3300	S. G. F. W. abundant, T. ample.	Town, fort, bazar and capital of Poonch State.
	Suran B., E.—	14	2			Suran bridge.	4300	S. G. F. procurable, W. plentiful, T. scanty.	Small village.
			6						
			14						
	Bifflici	......	16	......	......	Ditto	7000		
			22	Last mile of ascent steep, descent easy.	Milidheri gulli.	Ditto			
			26						
2	**Thanna Mandi** B.—	16	28	......	......	......	......		
	Saj	......	30	Old made road in fair order, kept up and in use by traders.	Down Tohi valley left bank.	Tohi ford.	4580	S. G. W. F. T. plentiful.	Road to Baramgalla. Bazar and trade depôt. Imperial serai on top of hill.
			31						
	Futtehpur	......	38			......			Imperial serai.
			41	......	......	Durhal ford.	......		
			42						
3	**Rajaori (Rampur)** P. O., B., E.—	14	44	......	......	Kandal ford.	3094	S. G. F. W. T. plentiful	Small town, tehsil, bazar, stone built.
			46			Jamoola ,,			
			47			Dilcoori ,,			
			50						
4	**Sialsui** B., C., E.—	14	58	......	Sialsui spur Across Golabgarh drainage.	......	......	S scarce, G. F. W. procurable, T. scanty.	Small village.
			59			Golabgarh bridge.			
			66						
5	**Dharmsal** B., C., E.—	10	68	......	Dharmsal spur Across Rud drainage.	......	......	S.G. F. procurable, W available, T. scanty.	Ditto.

Number of Marches.	Names of Stages.	Intermediate m. f.	Total m. f.	Nature of Route.	Main Valleys and Mountain Passes.	River Crossings and Lakes.	Altitude above Sea Level in Feet.	Supplies and Transport at Stages.	Remarks.
	ROUTE—contd.								
XXI 6	Thandapani *B., C., E.—*	10 ...	68 ...	Rough and stony road in crossing both ranges to Aknoor, narrow and steep at the passes.	......	Rad bridge.	1460	S. scarce, W. plentiful, T. nil.	Village one mile distance from Baradari.
		10 ...	78 ...		Kalidhar range.				
			86 ...						Halting place.
7	Choki Chowra *E.—*	12 4	90 4		Ambi pass.	Koonar Knd.	2150	S. G. F. after notice, W. procurable, T. nil.	Halting place.
			94 ...						
8	Aknoor *P. O., F. B., C., E.—*	13 4	104 4	Rough cart-road after crossing the Chenab river.	Chenab valley	Chenab ferry.	1123	S. G. F. W. plentiful, T. available.	Small town, fort and bazar on right bank Chenab.
9	Jammu *P. O., T. O., D. B., C., E.*	16 ...	120 ...	......	Tawi valley.	......	1200	S. G. F. W. and T. ample.	Large town, bazar and capital of Jammu State.

This old Imperial road is at present in use for the march of troops.

From Rajaori 44 miles a track branches off eastwards up the Kandal nullah to Piri 56 miles across the Jaoli spur to Obhi on the Ans river 65 miles, and crossing the latter the road goes to Bodil 76 miles.

About three miles east of Sialsui is a Tatapani or hot spring, which is much frequented locally for cure of rheumatism, &c. There is a coal outcrop close by and others at Kalakot, Seri, Mehugala, &c. in the vicinity. This appears to have been the locality visited by Mr. Vigne and mentioned by him in his book; the place is worth seeing.

XXI. POONCH to RAJAORI by BHIMBER GULLI:—

Number of Marches.	Names of Stages.	Intermediate m. f.	Total m. f.	Nature of Route.	Main Valleys and Mountain Passes.	River Crossings and Lakes.	Altitude above Sea Level in Feet.	Supplies and Transport at Stages.	Remarks.
	Poonch *P. O., D. B., E.—*	0 ...		Fair road to Chilas, stony hill track on ascent to gulli, easy descent.	......	Suran ferry.	3300	S. G. F. W. and T. ample.	Town, fort, bazar and capital of the Poonch State.
		5 ...			Chilasi gulli	......	4500		

					Road		Water	Elevation	S. G. F. W. and T.	Remarks
Gani	...	...	...	9 ...	Good road along the valley passable for laden animals.	Up Mehndur valley right bank.	......	2800	S. G. F. W. and T. procurable.	Village.
1 Sagra	...	12 ...	12 ...							
Mankot	...	...	15 ...							
Sukhi Sarwar	...	...	20 ...	......	......	Tatti baoli	......	......	Ancient temple in ruins.
2 Dharmsal *E.—*	...	9 ...	21 ...	Gentle ascent to pass along the Tar ridge and easy descent down Charkot valley, crossing numerous ravines.	......	Mehndur ford	3100	Ditto	Large village and tehsil.
			27 ...			Narayan baoli	4650	......	Spring pure water
			29 ...		Bhimber gulli Down Charkot valley	......	5170		
3 Petrara	...	12 ...	33 ...	Cross Charkot river several times.	......	......	S. and T. precarious, G. F. W. procurable.	Small village.
4 Rajaori	...	12 ...	45 ...	......	......	......	3094	S. G. F. W. and T. plentiful.	Small town, bazar, tehsil, stone built.

This route is usually taken in winter when the Milildheri pass 7,000 feet, above Bitllaj, is closed by snow.

The water in this Mehndur valley is not of good quality, though drinkable.

In the first march, the camp can be pitched at Gani about one mile beyond the pass, if preferred. Supplies not procurable, but all else can be furnished.

Good water available at Tatti baoli built by Raja Buldeo Singh and at Narayan baoli built by order of Maharaja Golab Singh.

The ordinary route from Poonch, after crossing the Suran River, follows down the left bank of this river to its junction with the Mehndur river and ascends the right bank of the latter to Sagra, distance 18 miles passable for laden animals.

The hill range between the Suran and Mehndur rivers may be crossed at other gullies, which though higher, give a more direct line between Poonch and Dharmsal.

An alternative route is up the Suran right bank to Suran, where cross river by bridge, ascend the Gerawali pass, and go across three intervening spurs by Parat to the Sangiot gulli, thence descend down the Sangiot nala, which falls into the Charkot river, one march above Rajaori.

Cross roads go from Dharmsal northwards to Suran, by Uri and the Gosai pass 5,150 feet, 12 miles long, and by Herin and the Gerawali pass 5,230 feet, 12 miles long; the latter is said to be the best for ponies.

XXII   POONCH to GUJRAT by RAJAORI—

Number of Marches	Names of Stages	Distance in miles and furlongs. Inter-mediate. m. f.	Total. m. f.	Nature of Route.	Main Valleys and Mountain Passes.	River crossings and Lakes.	Altitude above Sea Level, in Feet.	Supplies and Transport at Stages.	Remarks.
	Poonch P. O., D. B., E. —	...	0 ... 4	Fair hill road, passable for laden animals throughout. Parts in this section cut up by recent high floods.	Up Suran valley.	...... Dangli bed. Mandi ford.	3300	S. G. F. W. abundant, T. ample.	Town, fort, bazar and capital of Poonch State.
			2		......				
			6						
1	**Suran** B. —	14	14		......	Suran bridge. Ditto	4300	S. G. F. procurable, W. plentiful, T. scanty.	Small village.
			16						
	Bigltaj		22	Last mile of ascent steep, descent easy.	Miiidheri gully.	Ditto	7000		
			26						
2	**Thanna Mandi** B., C.—	16	30	Old made road in fair order, kept up to Naoshera and much used by traders.	Down Tohi valley left bank.	...... Tohi ford.	4580	S. G. F W. T. plentiful.	Imperial serai, bazar and trade depot.
	Saj		31						Imperial serai on top of hill.
	Futtehpur		38		......	Durhal ford.			Imperial serai.
			41						
			42						
3	**Rajaori (Rampur)** P. O., B., E.—	14	44	......	Ditto right bank.	Tohi ford.	3004	S. G. F. W. T. plentiful.	Small town, tehsil, bazar, stone built.
			45						
	Moradpur		48	......	......	Panda ford.			Old serai in ruins.
	Talmakot		54	......					
4	**Chingas Serai** B., C.—	15	59	......	......	Lituli baoli. Chopi ford.	2340	S. G. F. W. plentiful, coolies available.	Serai and village.
			64 ... 4	......			2000		
			67	......					
	Nadpur Serai		70	......	Chaini spur	......	2400	......	Spring pure water.

No.	Stages and places	m.	f.	Total m.	f.	Remarks on road	Drainage	Range	River crossings	Height	Supplies	Remarks
5	**Naoshera** P. O., B., C., E.—	13	4	72	4	Hence the road, though made, has in many parts fallen into bad order, very rocky and stony in crossing both ranges.	Koman Gosha	......	Janbir „	1800	Ditto	Small town, bazar, serai, fort, tehsil 200 feet above Tohi.
				78	...					2870		
6	**Saidabad** B., C., E.—	12	4	85	...		Down Bhimber valley.		Crossed river bed 4 times. Samani ford.	2000	S. G. F. W. plentiful, T. available.	Samani village 2 miles off westwards.
				86	4			Aditak range	Bhimber river forded 6 times.	2800		
	Mitret			92	...							
		...	...	95	...							
7	**Bhimber** P. O., B., C., E.—	14	...	99	...	Cart - road hence, cut up in places to Kotla, fair dry weather road, unbridged and unmetalled to Gujrat, over which ekkas and tongas can travel.	Down Bhimber valley.		Bhimber ford	1060	Ditto	Small town, bazar, head-quarters of district or zillah.
				100	...							Small village.
8	**Kotla** D. B.—	8	4	107	4				...	......	S. G. F. procurable, W. from wells, few coolies.	Larger village.
9	**Daulatnagar** P. O., D. B.—	8	...	115	4				Bhandur ford	980	Ditto.	Large city and civil station.
	Gujrat City P. O., T. O., C., E. on G. T. Road.	...	...	121	...	Gujrat, over which ekkas and tongas can travel.					S. G. F. W. plentiful, T. ample.	
				127	...							
10	**Gujrat Railway Station** P. O., T. O., D. B.—	13	4	129	...	......			......	......	......	On N. W. Railway.

From Bhimber 99 miles there is a tract by Barnata 117 miles, Minawur 129 miles, where the Tohi river is crossed by ford or boat, Amirpur 137 miles, Phulkian 143 miles, where the Chenab river is crossed by ferry boat, and a rough cart-road thence to Sialkot 160 miles on the branch railway Wazirabad to Jammu. There are Dâk Bungalows at Phulkian and Sialkot. This route is not recommended, owing to the difficulty of crossing baggage over the quicksands of the Tohi river, over the low inundated country between Minawur and Amirpur, and over the five branches of the Chenab met between Amirpur and Phulkian, two of which are deep, after which the Chenab river has to be crossed.

From Daulatnagar 115 miles 4 furlongs there is a cross-country road eastwards by Julalpur 126 miles, over the Chenab ferry at Muhatah 136 miles to Sialkot, 150 miles from Poonch.

Imperial serais of the Mogul period are met with at Thanna Mandi, Saj, Futtehpur, Rajaori in ruins with garden and Baradari on the opposite bank of the river, Moradpur in ruins, Chingas, Narya in ruins, Nadpur, Naoshera with Baolibagh, Koman Gosha Choki, Saidabad with garden and remains of stone bund or dam across river and at Bhimber. At Naoshera, there are inscriptions on stone tablets on north side of the Baoli well and over the entrance gateway to Serai fort.

The bungalow of four rooms at Suran, Thanna, Rajaori (Baradari), Chingas Serai, and Naoshera are in fair order, that at Saidabad is at present in bad order, that at Bhimber requires much repair, the Dâk Bungalows at Kotla, Daulatnagar and Gujrat are excellent.

At one mile west of Saidabad on the road to Samani, an ancient Hindu temple in ruins called Dera may be seen with a platform and stone wall enclosure.

XXIII   POONCH to LALA MUSA by KOTLI—

Number of Marches	Names of Stages	Distance in miles and furlongs — Intermediate m. f.	Distance in miles and furlongs — Total m. f.	Nature of Route.	Main Valleys and Mountain Passes.	River Crossings and Lakes.	Altitude above Sea Level in Feet.	Supplies and Transport at Stages.	Remarks.
	Poonch P. O., D. B., E.—	...	0 ...	Rough hill road, very stony, passable for mules, steep ascent to	Down Poonch valley left bank.	Suran ferry.	3300	S. G. F. W. abundant, T. ample.	Village and thanna.
			13 ...	Saira; thence over	...	Mendola ford.			
1	**Saira** B.—	16 ...	16 ...	rugged broken ground difficult in places to Kotli.	...	......	2950	S. G. F. procurable, W. from river, T. available.	Large village, bazar and tehsil.
			28 ...			Neli ford.			
2	**Kotli** P. O., B., E.—	14 ...	30 ...	Good road over fine plain, well cultivated, passable for laden animals.	Up Ban valley.	......	1980	S. G. F. plentiful, W. from spring, T. ditto	Town, fort, bazar and capital of the Poonch State.
			36 ...		...	Ban ford.			
	Dunna	...	38 ...		...	......	......	W. scarce.	Hamlet.
3	**Koireta**	16 ...	46 ...	......	...	......	2450	S. G. F. procurable, W. from wells, T. scanty.	Large village, encamp at Guri Ziarat.
	Bundal	...	52 ...	......	...	......	......		Hamlet.
4	**Dhurmsala**	12 ...	58 ...	Fair hill road over easy slopes.	...	Waterfall	2700	S. G. F. scanty, W. from nullah, few coolies.	Ditto.
	Makri	...	61 ...	......	Panch Pir gulli.	......	2925		

No.	Station	Dist.	Total	Road	Direction	Ford	Elev.	Water & Supplies	Remarks
5	**Saidabad** B., C., E.—	21	75	Fine cultivated plain, steep ascent and descent over Aditak range, rocky and stony; hence, first section to Kotla cut up by rains, thence a fair weather road to the railway without bridges.	Down Samani valley.	......	2000	S. G. F. W. plentiful, T. available.	Samani, large village and thanna, distant 2 miles.
			80 4		Aditak pass.	Samani ford.	2800	......	Custom house.
	Mitiret		85		......				
			88		......	Bhimber forded 6 times.			
6	**Bhimber** P. O., B. C., E.—	14	93		Down Bhimber valley.	......	1060	Ditto	Small town, bazar and head-quarters of zillah.
			94	......	......	Bhimber ford.			
7	**Kotla** D. B.—	8 4	101 4	......	......	......	......	S. G. F. procurable, W. from wells, few coolies.	Small village.
8	**Daulatnagar** D. B.—	8	109 4	......	......	......	980	Ditto	Large village.
			116 4	......	......	Bhimber ford.			
9	**Lala Musa** P. O., T. B., E.—	9 4	119	......	......	......	......	S.G. F. W. T. available	Junction Station of Salt range branch, on N. W. Railway.

From Makri 61 miles there is a cross hill track to Mirpur about 24 miles distant, which passes the Castle of Kambir at the 2nd mile. For mile 70, there is a shorter road down the rocky bed of the Samani river to Samani, and over the plain to Saidabad, which shortens this march by 3 miles. This way is, however, quite impassable for laden animals. Half way between Samani and Saidabad are the remains of an ancient Hindu temple called Dera.

From Bhimber 93 miles, there is a track by Pindi and along the eastern foot of the Pabbi range, about 20 miles in length, to the Kharian Station on the N. W. Railway or 113 miles from Poonch. This avoids any crossing of the Bhimber river, and is used in the rainy season. At Kharian there is a road Bungalow, a serai, good encamping ground, and supplies are plentiful.

XXIV POONCH to JHELUM by KOTLI and MIRPUR—

Number of Marches.	Names of Stages.	Distance in miles and furlongs.		Nature of Route.	Main Valleys and Mountain Passes.	River crossings and Lakes.	Altitude above Sea Level in Feet.	Supplies and Transport at Stages.	Remarks.
		Intermediate. m. f.	Total. m. f.						
	Poonch	...	0 ...	Rough hill road very stony, steep ascent in steps to Saira; thence over rugged broken ground to Kotli, passable for mules, but difficult in places.	Down Poonch Toi or Palasta left bank.	Suran ferry.	3300	S. G. F. W. abundant, T. ample	Town, fort, bazar and capital of Poonch State.
1	Saira	16 ...	13 ... 16 ...			Mendola ford	2950	S. G. F. procurable, W. from river, T. available.	Village and thanna.
2	Kotli	14 ...	30 ...	Very rough hill road not passable for baggage animals.	......	......	1980	S. G. F plentiful, W. from springs, T. available.	Large village, bazar and tehsil.
	Berarli	...	36 ...		......	Ban ford.			
3	Goalpur	12 ...	42 ...	Riding pony can be led by taking detours. Most of these 3 marches must be done on foot.	......	......	......	S. G. F. scarce, W. from spring, T. nil.	Hamlet.
	Trochi fort	...	43 ...						
	Nark	...	44 ...			Mamuli ford.			
		...	48 ...						
4	Radan E.—	15 ...	57 ...	......	......	......	......	S. G. F. scarce, W. plentiful, few coolies.	Village.

				Road	Direction	Ferry / Water	Elevation	Supplies	Remarks
5	Chaomukh	... 9 ...	66 ...	Fair hill road passable for laden animals over stony ground.	Leave valley and cross Mirpur plateau.	Poonch ferry	1118	Ditto	Large village.
6	Mirpur	... 10 ...	76 ...		Bialar pass	.....	1236	S. G. F. W. plentiful, T. available.	Small town, bazar and tehsil.
			80 ...	......		.....	1672		
7	Katiali	... 13 ...	89 ...	Rough cart-road	Jhelum valley	Jhelum ferry	......	S. G. F. scarce, W. plentiful, T. nil.	
8	Jhelum	... 10 ...	99 ...		.....	.....	765	S. G. F. W. abundant, T. ample.	Cantonment, civil station, city and head-quarters of district.

This is the line that would probably be taken by a cart-road or railway, if one be ever made between Poonch and Jhelum.

From Poonch, after crossing the Suran river, there is a direct track to Kotli crossing two hill ranges by the Chilasi gulli and Nilidheri-ki gulli and the Mehndur river between at Mankot. The Chilasi gulli is 4,500 feet, the Mehndur river crossing 2,700 feet, and the Nilidheri-ki gulli 4,195 feet above the sea. The distances from Poonch are Chilasi gulli 5 miles, Mankot 15 miles, Nilidheri-ki gulli 18 miles, and Kotli 30 miles.

From the 43rd mile a road ascends up the Mamuli valley by Bai to Dharmsala about 20 miles in length.

From Mirpur 76 miles, there is another track to Mangla ferry under the old fort on the Jhelum river, 87 miles, and a road thence to the Dina Station on the N.-W. Railway 97 miles from Poonch.

XXV POONCH to JHELUM by SENSAR and TANGROT —

				Road	Direction	Ferry / Water	Elevation	Supplies	Remarks
1	Poonch	... ...	0 ...	Rough hill track, very stony throughout to Tangrot, and difficult in places for laden mules, which, however, can get through; the ascent and descent over the Chumba pass is most trying.	Down Poonch valley right bank.	.....	3300	S. G. F. W. abundant.	Town, fort, bazar and capital of Poonch State.
	Note	... ...	7 ...			Baoli.			Hamlet
	Ser	... 10 ...	9 ...			.....	2830	S. G. F. W. procurable.	
	E. on Kai bed	... ...	10 ...			Kai ford	2830		
	Mendol	... 15 ...	15 ...			Baoli	2460		
2	Tai	... 10 ...	20 ...			.....	2170	Ditto 150° Fahr.	Old ruined temple called Dera.
	E. on Poonch bed	... ...	27 ...		Chumba gully	Hot springs			Large village, hot springs in limestone rocks on edge of Poonch river.
		... ...	36 ...			Sarsawa ford	3900 2000		

Number of Marches	Names of Stages	Distance in miles and furlongs. Intermediate m. f.	Total m. f.	Nature of Route.	Main Valleys and Mountain Passes.	River crossings and Lakes.	Altitude above Sea Level is Feet.	Supplies and Transport at Stages.	Remarks.
XXV	ROUTE—contd.	...	...						
3	Sarsawa	...	36 ...	......	......	Baoli	2500	Ditto	Large village and bazar.
	E.—Nori	17 ..	37 ...	......		Karnoti ford	2100		
	Branion	...	40 ...	.. ...	Baroi pass	Baoli	3158		
		...	43 ...						
4	Sensar	10 ...	47 ...	......		Ditto	2300	Ditto, W. scarce in Jammu.	Village and shop.
	E.—Choch	...	51 ...	......	Khaira gully	......	2936		
		...	54 ...	......	......	Baoli	2650		
	Biari	12 ...	59 ...	......		Ditto	1492	S. G. F. T. scarce, W. indifferent.	Hamlet.
	E.—Dadial	...	66 ...	......	......	......	1200	... ..	Small bazar.
	Tangrot	15 ...	72 ...	......	Chana spur.	......	1000	S. G. F. W. T. procurable.	Junction of Poonch and Jhelum rivers.
	D. B.—	...	74 ...	Rocky ascent and stony descent. Fair road to Shikarpar, whence rough cart-road to Jhelum over cultivated plain.	......	Jhelum ferry			
7	Shikarpur	12 ...	86 ...	......	......	......	......	Ditto	Hamlet.
	B.—								
8	Jhelum	13 ...	99 ...	......	......	......	765	S. G. F. W. T. abundant.	Cantonment, civil station, town, head-quarters of district and station on N.-W. Railway.
	P.O., T.O., D.B., C.E.								

This route follows the right bank of the Poonch, Toi or Palasta river down to its junction with the Jhelum at Tangrot and crosses the Jhelum by a boat ferry. Good fishing at Tangrot and in many places up the Poonch river to Poonch. From Tangrot, small and large boats can be floated down the rapids of the Jhelum river to Jhelum City.

At Tai hot springs there is a boat ferry, by which people can cross to left bank and join the road to Kotli, distant 9 miles.

From Sarsawa and Sensar are also roads to Kotli, distant 6 and 12 miles respectively.

From Sensar 41 miles there is a track north-west by Tara Kila to the Owen ferry on the Jhelum in length 16 miles, another west to the Salgraon ferry over the Jhelum 59 miles, thence to Kolar 77 miles, and to Mandra Railway Station 88 miles, and a third to the Dangali ferry over Jhelum, thence by Bewal to Gujar Khan Railway Station.

From Shikarpor 86 miles, there is a cart-road 6 miles long to Dina Station on N.-W. Railway.

XXVI POONCH to RAWUL PINDI by LUCHMUN BATEA—

No.	Names	Stage dist. (m. f.)	Total dist. (m. f.)	Description of road	Direction	Fords	Elevation (feet)	Supplies	Remarks
1	Poonch — P. O., D. B., E.—	... ...	0 ...	Rough hill tract, very stony, passable for laden animals.	Down Bitarh valley.	Bitarh ford.	3300	S. G. F. W. and T. ample.	Town, fort, bazar and capital of Poonch State.
	Note	... ...	7 ...			Baoli.	2830		
	Ser	... ...	9 ...2		Up Kai valley.	......	2900		
	Deorand	... ...	12 ...3			Baoli.	3200		
	Hinzira	15 ...3	15 ...3		Up Palungi valley.	Kai ford.		S. G. F. moderate, W. plentiful, few coolies.	Post and hamlet fort on ridge.
	E.— Palasgi	... ...	21 ...6	Track has fallen out of order, and has become very difficult for laden animals.	Cross spur	......	5330		
		... ...	25 ...		...	Tilni ford.	4510		
2	Nar	11 ...3	26 ...6		......	......	5130	Ditto	Village.
	E.— Nehrian	... ...	28 ...		Tangri gully		5700		
	Betora	... ...	29 ...		Across head Sarsawa valley.	Nehrian ford	5030		
		... ...	35 ...		......	Runga ford.	3800	Ditto	Ditto and thanna.
3	Palandri	14 ...	40 ...6	Track covered with loose boulders; old made road on British side, right bank Jhelum, quite out of repair and difficult for laden animals.	Cross ridge	......	4250	......	Village.
	E.— Bhotea	... ...	49 ...		......	......	... ...	Ditto	
4	Luchmun Patun	10 ...2	51 ...		Across Jhelum valley.	Jhelum ferry	1480	Ditto	Ferry post.
	E. very small— Soha	... ...	59 ...		......	......	2600	Ditto	Village.

Number of Marches	Names of Stages	Distance in miles and furlongs		Nature of Route	Main Valleys and Mountain Passes	River crossings and Lakes	Altitude above Sea Level in Feet.	Supplies and Transport at Stages.	Remarks.
		Intermediate. m. f.	Total. m. f.						
XXVI	ROUTE—contd.	...	...						
5	Panjar E.—	...	59	Steep zigzag ascent to Soha, whence fair track to Kahuta.	Panjar watershed.	...	2650	S. G. W. scarce, F. plentiful, T. nil.	Hamlet.
	Duberai	12	63	......	Down Ling and Sohan valleys.	...	2096		
		...	67						
6	Kahuta P. O., E.,—	8	71	Rough cart-road	......	Ling ford.	2050	S. G. F. W. plentiful.	Large village and bazar.
		...	72	......					
7	Sinla E.—	11	82	......	......	Ling ford	......	S.G.F.W. procurable, T. nil.	Village and station on N.-W. Railway.
		...	84	......	......	Sohan bridge.			
		...	90	Joins G. T road	......				
8	Rawul Pindi P. O., T. O., D. B., Hoida, C., E.—	12	94	......	...	......	1700	S. G. F. W. abundant.	Large cantonment, fort, civil station, city, head-quarters of district and station on N.-W. Railway.

There are other routes from Poonch to Latchmun Bates, the foregoing is said to be the most direct and crosses two hill spurs at Nehrian and Palandri. There is another way in better order and passable in summer from Hazira 15 miles 3 furlongs by Sudnuti tehsil, Haila 24 miles, village where S. G. F. W. and T. procurable, Danna 6,500 feet, to Palandri 37 miles, which is used by camels, &c.

An alternative route might be from Haila 24 miles ascend the Tilni nullah to its source at Girhali 28 miles, cross the pass just above this place, descend into the Goon valley by Garar fort to Lajana 34 miles, and follow this river down to its junction with the Jhelum river, one mile above Luchmun Katea, 45 miles from Poonch. This line, as far as the Goon valley, would also be on the most direct route from Poonch to Murree crossing the Jhelum river at the Rampatun ferry beneath Kotli on the British side.

Near Panjar 63 miles, this road passes south of an I under the Nerth plateau, a fine site for a military sanitarium.

From Kahuta 71 miles a cart-road runs south direct to Mandra Station on the N.-W. Railway, 1,695 feet and 91 miles from Poonch. It passes by Chinani 78 miles, 2,208 feet, Pindorian 81 miles 4 furlongs, 2,031 feet and Bhata 86 miles 4 furlongs, 1,779 feet above the sea.

XXVII POONCH to ABBOTTABAD by MURREE—

There are several tracks between Poonch and Murree and two routes hence to Abbottabad.

The easiest route at present crosses the Kai gulli to Parl, descends down the Kein nullah to Raoli in the Mal or Bagh valley and follows down this river to its junction with the Jhelum near Dhara ferry, where the road crosses the Jhelum and rises up to Murree.

	Place					Description of road	Valley / route	Crossing	Elev.	Supplies	Remarks
1	**Poonch** P. O., D. B., E.—	...	...	0	...	Rough hill track, very stony and difficult in places for laden animals.	Down Bitarh valley.	......	3300	S. G. F. W. T. ample.	Town, fort, bazar and capital of Poonch State.
	Ser	...	...	9	...	Very steep and stony ascent to pass.	Up Swan or Kai valley.	......	2830		
	Hazira E.—	15	3	15	3	......	Kai gulli.	......	3200	S. G. F. moderate, W. plentiful, few coolies.	Post and hamlet.
2	**Parl** E.—	12	5	24	...	Fine plateau with good road to Parl, then rocky steep descent and after crossing Kein river, easy gradient to Raoli and Maugh.	Down Kein valley.	......	5530	S. G. F. W. T. available	Cluster of villages on extensive plateau, well cultivated.
				28	...		......	Kein ford.	5225		
	Raoli			36	...		......	Mal bridge.	2920		Wide valley, well cultivated.
3				40	...		Down Mal or Bagh valley.	Mal ferry.			
	Mangh E.—	16	...	44	...	......	......		2880	Ditto	Ditto
				58	...						

Number of Marches.	Names of Stages.	Distance in miles and furlongs. Intermediate. m. f.	Distance in miles and furlongs. Total. m. f.	Nature of Route.	Main Valleys and Mountain Passes.	River Crossings and Lakes.	Altitude above Sea Level in Feet.	Supplies and Transport at Stages.	Remarks.
	XXVII ROUTE—contd.								
4	**Dhulkot** *E. very small—*	16 ...	62 ...	Steep, rough, stony approaches to ferry on both sides of Jhelum river.	Cross Jhelum valley.	......	......	S. G. F. W. scanty, T. nil.	Fort.
	Dhara	......	60 ...		......	Jhelum ferry	1677.		
5	**Dhanda**	10 ...	70 ...	Fair road made to Murree.	Along the Kotli spur to Murree.	......	......	S. G. F. W. scanty, T. nil.	Small village.
6	**Murree** *P.O., T.O., Hotels, C., E.*	13 ...	83 ...	Good hill road along the top of range and down the spur, passable for laden animals throughout.	Along the range of gullies and down the spur to Bagnota.	......	7000	S. G. F. W. plentiful, T. ample.	Military and Civil Sanitarium, town and bazar.
7	**Chungla gulli** *D. B.—*	10 ...	93 ...			......	8200	S. G. scarce, W. and F. moderate, T. nil.	Military post.
8	**Dunga gulli** *D. B.—* *Kalabagh*	9 ...	102 ...	......	......	......	7600	Ditto	Ditto.
9	**Bagnota** *D. B.—*	12 ...	107 ... 114 ...	......	Across head of Dor drainage.	......	7190. 4800	Ditto	Small village.
10	**Abbottabad** *P.O., T.O., D.B., C., E.*	10 ...	115 ... 124 ...	......	......	Kala Nuddee	3663. 4166	S. G. F. W. and T. abundant.	Cantonment, Civil Station, town, bazar and head-quarters of district.

Another route goes from Poonch to Kohala 74 miles (see Route XXVIII), and after crossing the Jhelum bridge, either joins the cart-road 27½ miles long to Murree (Sunny bank), or rises straight up the spur by Nuttia gulli to Dunga gulli 15 miles or 89 miles from Poonch. This last march is practicable only for lightly laden coolies.

A third route to Murree, by Parl and Mangh, crosses the Jhelum by the Kwadra ferry, and rises up the Birgraon nullah to Murree. This is not passable for laden mules.

A fourth route to Murree, also by Parl 28 miles and Mangh gala 40 miles, crosses the Jhelum river by the Rampatan ferry 52 miles, and rises up the hill range to Parana 64 miles and Murree 76 miles from Poonch. This is passable for laden mules.

A fifth route might be made from Poonch up the Swan and Palungi valleys, over the Girhali pass to Lejana 34 miles, then follow down the Goon river to its junction with the Jhelum, ascending the latter to Rampatan 48 miles, where cross this river by the ferry boat and rise up the Kotli spur by Kotli to Murree 72 miles from Poonch.

For lower road between Murree and Abbottabad.—See Route IXa.

A new water-supply has recently been added at Murree.

XXVIII POONCH to MOZUFFERABAD by KOHALA—

	Station			Miles	Description of road	Route	Ford	Elevation	Supplies	Remarks
	Poonch P. O., D. B., E.—	...	...	0 ...	Rough hill track, very stony and difficult in places for laden animals.	Down Bitarh valley.	Bitarh ford.	3300	S. G. F. W. T. ample	Town, fort, bazar and capital of Poonch State.
	Ser	...	...	9 ...	......	Up Swan or Kai valley.	......	2830	......	......
1	Hazira E.—	...	15	15 ...	......	......	......	3200	S. G. F. moderate, W. plentiful, few coolies.	Post and hamlet.
	Dethan	3		20 ...	Steep ascent to pass.	......	......	5530		
				24 ...				5225		
2	Parl E.—	12		28 ...	Fine plateau and good road to Prat then rocky steep descent and after crossing Kein river, easy gradient to Raoli and Arja.	Kai gulli Down Kein valley.	......	3250	S. G. F. W. T available	Cluster of villages on extensive plateau, well cultivated.
	Raoli	5		36 ...		......	Kein ford.	2920		
3	Arja E.—	20		40 ...		Across Mal valley.	Mal bridge.	2840	S. G. F. W. moderate, T. available.	Village.
				48 ...		Tirkot neck	......	5150		
				59 ...	......		......			

Number of Marches	Names of Stages	Distance in Miles and Furlongs — Intermediate m. f.	Distance in Miles and Furlongs — Total m. f.	Nature of Route	Main Valleys and Mountain Passes	River Crossings and Lakes	Altitude above Sea Level in Feet	Supplies and Transport at Stages	Remarks
XXVIII	ROUTE—contd. ...	...	59						
4	Chumiatti	15	63	Fair hill road across head of valley to Chumiatti, then keeps along topof range with steep zigzag stony descent to Kohala.	Along the top of Chaman-kot range with sharp descent to Jhelum.	......	4870	S. G. F. W. moderate, T. available.	Village.
5	Kohala P. O., T. O., D. B.—	11	74			......	1916	S. G. F. W. procurable, T. after notice.	Small bazar and customs post.
			82	Join Jhelum cart-road to Dumel.	Up Jhelum valley left bank.	Agar bridge	2020		
6	Dulai D. B.—	12	86			......	2105	Ditto	Hamlet.
	Dumel P. O., T. O., D. B., E.	9 2	95 2		Up Kishen-gunga valley.	Jhelum bridge.	2225	S. G. F. W. plentiful, T. available.	Bazar.
7	Mozufferabad C.—	1 6	97		......		2344	Ditto	Small town and head-quarters of district.

From Dethan 20 miles, a detour can be made northwards over the Neja gulli, crossing the Ramkot stream, one of the principal effluents of the Mal river, at Koderi, and coming down the Mal valley by Bagh, a large village and tehsil, to Raoli, in length about 24 miles. From Arja there is another hill track northwards over the Rangla pass, which descends down the Agar valley by Danna and joins the Jhelum cart-road at the Agar bridge, in length about 27 miles, thus shortening the distance to Mozufferabad.

XXIX POONCH to HATIAN or CHAKOTI by BAGH—

No.	Station	Intermediate distance	Total distance	Road	Valley / pass	Ford	Elevation	Supplies	Remarks
	Poonch	...	0	Rough hill track, very stony and passable for mules.	Up Tat valley	Bitarh ford.	3300	S. G. F. W. T ample.	Town, fort, bazar and capital of Poonch State.
1	Tat	10	10	Steep ascent and descent over pass.	Taoli pass.	...	...	S. nil, G. F. moderate, W. plentiful, T. nil.	Fort.
			18	...	...	Ramkot ford.			
			22	...	...				
2	Ramikot	14	24	Fair hill road	Down Mal valley right bank.	...	...	S. G. F. moderate, W plentiful, few coolies.	Small village.
3	Bagh	12	36	...	...	...	...	S. G. F. W. plentiful, T. available.	Large village and tehsil.

Hence, there are two routes, firstly, over the Tok pass to Hatian; secondly, over the Kalan pass to Chakoti or Uri.

FIRSTLY—

No.	Station	Intermediate distance	Total distance	Road	Valley / pass	Ford	Elevation	Supplies	Remarks
3	Bagh	...	36	Rough hill track with difficult places and passable for mules.	Up Malwan valley.	...	...	.....	Pir Panjal range.
			46	...	Tok pass				
4	Timberkot	13	49	...	...	...	...	S. and T. nil, G. F. W. moderate.	Small village.
5	Hatian	9	58	Join Jhelum cart-road.	Down Hatian nullah.	...	3000	S. nil, G. F. moderate, W. plentiful, few coolies.	Ditto.

SECONDLY—

Number of Marches	Names of Stages	Distance of Miles and Furlongs — Intermediate m. f.	Total m. f.	Nature of Route	Main Valleys and Mountain Passes	River crossings and Lakes	Altitude above Sea Level, in Feet.	Supplies and Transport at Stages.	Remarks.
3	Bagh	...	36 ...	Rough hill track with difficult places and passable for mules.	Up Malwan valley. Kalan jass.	......	......	......	Pir Panjal range.
			46 ...						
4	Kilana	13 ...	49 ...	......	Down Opi nullah.	......	......	S. G. F. W. plentiful, coolies available.	Residence of Raja of Kilana.
	Opi	...	55 ...	Join the Jhelum cart-road.					
5	Chakoti *or*	10 ...	59 ...	......	Jhelum valley	......	3700	S. G. F. W moderate, T. available.	Small village.
5	Uri	15 ...	65 ...	......	......	......	4390	Ditto W. scarce, T. difficult.	Fort, tehsil and village, large plateau, well cultivated.

Both the Tok and Kalan passes are on the Pir Panjal range, while further east between the Pir Kantha and Bisari peaks, there are two more passes at the head of the Mal valley above Barikot and Rahkot, which lead down the Islamabad nulla by Sing to Uri. These two paths are used only by shepherds and woodmen in the summer and autumn. The ascent on Poonch side is steep, the descent on the Kashmir side is gradual, and the road from Sing to Uri could be improved. The total distance from Poonch to Uri would be about 45 miles and 40 miles respectively.

XXX   POONCH to SRINAGAR by HAJI PIR PASS—

No.	Stage	Dist. between	Total	Road	Direction / Valley	Ford / Bridge	Elevation	Supplies	Remarks
	Poonch P. O., D. B., B., E.—	...	0	Road very rough and stony in bed of river excepting 3 miles over Daigwar plateau and last 2 miles into Kahuta.	Up Bitarh valley.	......	3300	S. G. F. W. T. ample	Town, fort, bazar and capital of Poonch State.
			6		......	Bitarh ford.			
1	**Kahuta** B., E.—	10	10	Fair road hence to Aliabad.	Up Gungi valley.	......	4560	S. G. F. W. moderate, T. available.	Village.
2	**Aliabad Serai** E.—	7	13	Steep ascent to pass very stony and descent very rocky.	......	Gungi ford.	6700	S. G. F. after notice, W. plentiful, T. nil.	Hamlet.
			17		Haji Pir pass	......	8500	......	Pir Panjal range.
3	**Haidrabad** E. very small—	7	20	Road into Uri most execrable, most troublesome to laden animals.	......	......			
			23		Down Namila valley.	Namila ford.	6000	Ditto	Hamlet.
			24						
4	**Uri** E. confused—	10	34	Join the Jhelum cart-road, bridged and metalled to Baramulla.	Up Jhelum valley.	Namila bridge.	4390	S. G. F. procurable, W. scarce, T. difficult.	Village on fine plateau, well cultivated, fort and tehsil.
			36						
5	**Rampur** E.—	13	47	......	......	......	4900	S. G. F. W. moderate, a few coolies.	All supplied by Nawab of Bhunniar.
	Bhunniar		49	......	......	Harpet-kai bridge.	5000.	......	Old Panchiah temple.
			50	......					
6	**Baramulla** E.—	15	63	Cart-road under construction to Srinagar.	......	......	5175	S. G. F. W. plentiful, T. after notice.	Town, bazar and tehsil.

Number of Marches.	Names of Stages.	Distance in miles and furlongs. Intermediate. m. f.	Total. m. f.	Nature of Route.	Main Valleys and Mountain Passes.	River Crossings and Lakes.	Altitude above Sea Level, in Feet.	Supplies and Transport at Stages.	Remarks.
7	**Patan** *E. with chunar trees—*	16	79 ...	......	......	......	5200	S. F. G. T. available, W. from springs.	Village, 2 fine Mahadeo temples in ruins.
8	**Srinagar** *P. O., T. O., C., E.—*	19	98 ...	......	......	Amiri Kadal over Jhelum.	5235	S. G. F. W. and T. abundant.	Large city, cantonment, bazars, palaces of H. H. Maharaja and capital of Kashmir State.

This was one of the Imperial roads in the Mogul period.

From Poonch there is an alternative track up the Sudroon valley by Nanganari, over the Haribamba pass, which is about the same height as the Haji Pir pass, and down the western branch of the Namila nullah, by Haidrabad to Uri. The distance is about the same as the foregoing route, the length between Nanganari and Haidrabad is at present quite unfit for laden animals.

Both these passes are closed by snow in winter, December to March inclusive, and are liable to avalanches, when the snow melts.

From Baramulla, travellers usually take boat up the Jhelum river, starting about mid-day to Sopoor 14 miles, where there is a Rest-house, and supplies are plentiful, and extra boatmen can be obtained for crossing the Woolar Lake, or to Ningul 16 miles at the entrance of the Woolar lake. The boats leave at 3 A.M. in the morning to cross the Woolar Lake and avoid the high wind which generally sets in sudden squalls any time after 11 A.M. The high waves are then dangerous to these flat-bottomed boats. An ordinary boat will generally reach Shadipur in the evening and stay the night. Leaving early next morning the boat will arrive at Srinagar about mid-day. Total distance by river and lake from Baramulla about 60 miles, by river and canal about 48 miles.

When the river is high, the Nora Canal between Shadipur and Ningul is navigable, and the boats can travel through by this short cut reaching Srinagar in about 24 hours.

XXXI POONCH to BARAMULLA by PAJJA PASS—

Stage	Place	Miles (stage)	Miles (total)	Road	Pass / spur / valley	Ford / bridge	Elevation	Supplies	Remarks
	Poonch P.O., D. B., E.—	...	0	Road for half the march very stony up bed of river, is passable for mules throughout.	Up Bitarh valley.	......	3300	S. G. F. W. T. ample,	Fort, town, bazar and capital of Poonch State.
			6		......				Village.
1	**Kahuta** B, E. small—	10	10	Very rough and stony but of easy gradient.	......	Bitarh ford.	4560	S. G. F. W. moderate, T. available.	
			11		......		4300		
2	**Kalamulla** E. very small—	10	20	......	......	Gungi ford.	6050	S. G. F. moderate, W. plentiful, few coolies.	Cluster of villages.
			26	The ascent and descent of this pass are both very steep and slippery. There is a second ascent and descent over the Tilpatoo spur down to Gaggerhil, whence easy path to Bhunniar, where Jhelum road is joined.	Pajja pass	Keeran ford.	10000	......	Pir Panjal range.
			30		Tilpatoo spur	......	9300		
3	**Gaggerhil** E. very small—	15	35		Down Harpet-kai valley.	Harpet-kai bridge.	6100	S. after notice, G. F. W plentiful, T. nil.	Hamlet.
	Maidan		37		......	......	......		
	Trekan		40		......	......	......	......	Residence of Nawab of Bhunniar.
4	**Bhunniar** Hospital—	8	43	......	Up Jhelum valley.	Harpet-kai bridge.	5000	Ditto	Old Buddhist Temple.
5	**Baramulla** P.O., T.O., D. B., E.—	14	57	......	......	......	5175	S. G. F. W. plentiful, T. after notice.	Town, bazar and tehsil.

This route is usually closed after the first fall of snow in November until the end of April, and avalanches are frequent on the snow melting. There is another pass westwards about 4 miles called Dunk, under the Budaori peak, which is used by shepherds only. The approach on the Poonch side is most precipitous, while that on the Kashmir side winds round the flank of the Budaori peak on to the Tilpatoo spur, descending the latter to Gaggerhil. The Dunk pass is slightly higher than the Pajja pass. The nulla which drains from Dunk into the Harpet-kai river was covered by a snowbridge 4 miles long in August, showing that immense avalanches must fall into it from the Budaori peak across the path to Tilpatoo.

XXXIa POONCH to BARAMULLA by GAJAN PASS—

Number of Marches	Names of Stages.	Distance in miles and furlongs.		Nature of Route.	Main Valleys and Mountain Passes.	River Crossings and Lakes.	Altitude above Sea Level in Feet.	Supplies and Transport and Stages.	Remarks.
		Intermediate. m. f.	Total. m. f.						
	Poonch *P. O., D. B., E.—*	...	0 ... 6	Very stony road in the bed of the Bitarh for half this march.	Up Bitarh valley.	Bitarh ford.	3300	S. G. F. W. T. ample	Town, fort, bazar and capital of Poonch State.
1	Kahuta *B., E.—*	10	10 ... 11 ... 18 ... 20 ...	The track though stony improves, and is passable for laden animals.	... ...	Gungi ford Kalamulla ford. Pent ford.	4560 4300 5160	S. G. F. W. moderate, T. available.	Village, 200 feet above Bitarh river. At Koongulla.
2	Palan *E. small—*	11	21 ... 25 ...	Hence men only can travel on foot, owing to difficulty of fording the Bitarh bed.	Up Sakrala valley.	Cross Bitarh numerous fords.	5640	S. and T. nil, G. F. W. plentiful.	Hamlet.
3	Hillun *E. in fields—*	6	27 ... 35 4	Easy gradient, all the way up to the pass and down the other side, practicable for laden animals.	Gajan gulli	....	6300 9135	S. moderate, G. F. W. plentiful, T. available.	Village.
4	Gajan *E. small—*	10	37 ...		Down Harpet-kai valley.	.....	.....	G. F. W. plentiful, S. and T. nil.	Glade in forest.

No.	Name											
5	**Gaggerhil** *E. small—*	8	...	45	...	Good road down this valley.	......	Harpet-kai bridge.	......	6100	Ditto S. after notice	Hamlet.
	Maidan	:	...	47	:	......	......	Ditto	......	......	......	Residence of Nawab of Bhunniar.
	Trekan	...	...	50	:	......	......	......	......	......	......	......
6	**Bhunniar** *Hospital, E. small—*	8	...	53	:	Joins Jhelum road	Up Jhelum valley.	Ditto	......	5000	S. & T. after notice, G. F. W. plentiful.	Old Buddhist Temple.
7	**Baramulla** *P.O., T.O., D.B., E*	14	...	67	:	......	......	......	......	5175	S. G. F. W. plentiful, T. after notice.	Town, bazar and tehsil.

Above Hillun, there is a splendid plateau called Mairn 6,600 feet situated at the fork of the Nilkanta and Sakrala rivers, which united form the Bitarh river.

The Gajan pass is about 3 miles east of the Pajja pass, 10,000 feet, and is the lowest point in this part of the Pir Punjal range. Half-way between them is the Durbut gulli, very steep on the Poonch side at the head of the Pent nullah, which falls into the Bitarh river near Palan. The approaches to the Gajan pass on both sides are through lovely and wild scenery.

The encamping ground at Gajan is at the foot of both passes Gajan and Pajja, and there are two roads from it to Gaggerhil. One over the Jabar plain and Tilpatoo spur is fit for beasts of burden, the other descending down the Gajan nullah and Harpet-kai river is fit for men only. A sharp descent brings it to Toong 6,800 feet on the Harpet-kai river, which it follows by Somali 6,630 feet with bridge to Chotali 6,430 feet, a small basin above a rocky gorge. To avoid the latter the path surmounts a spur 7,300 feet and descends to Gaggerhil 6,100 feet.

From Toong 41 miles, a track crosses the Harpet-kai river by a ford and rises straight up the steep spur opposite to a ledge 10,000 feet at the foot of the Sellar peak. It then flanks the western face of this mountain crossing the Marpatra pass 10,580 feet at the northern end 48 miles, and goes eastwards to Lilian Marg 9,400 feet and 53 miles, whence a number of tracks diverge.

I. The approach from Toong just mentioned.
II. To Trekan in the Harpet-kai valley, where the Nawab of Bhunniar resides, 9 miles long.
III. To Bhunniar at the mouth of this valley 12 miles long.
IV. To Naoshera on the Jhelum road 10 miles long.
V. To Sher on the Jhelum road down the Kechana valley by Nambal, 12 miles long.
VI. To Baramulla on the Jhelum road by Murun and Gohan 17 miles long or 70 miles from Poonch.
VII. To Gulmarg 10 miles or 63 miles from Poonch.
VIII. To Hillun back over the Jharni gulli at the head of the Harpet-kai valley and down the Jharni nullah, which falls into the Sakrala about
    Hillun at the 29½ mile from Poonch.

XXXII POONCH to GULMARG by NILKANTA PASS—

Number of Marches.	Names of Stages.	Distance in miles and furlongs. Inter-mediate. m. f.	Total. m. f.	Nature of Route.	Main Valleys and Mountain Passes.	River Crossings and Lakes.	Altitude above Sea Level in Feet.	Supplies and Transport and Stages.	Remarks.
	Poonch P. O., D. B., E.—	...	0 6	Very stony road in bed of Bitarh for half this march.	Up Bitarh valley.	Bitarh ford.	3300	S. G. F. W. and T. ample.	Town, fort, bazar and capital of the Poonch State.
1	Kahuta B., E.—	10	10 11	The track though stony improves, and is passable for laden animals.	...	Gungi ford	4560 4300	S. G. F.W. moderate, T. available.	Village 300 feet above river.
2	Palan E. small—	11	21	Hence men only can travel on foot owing to diffi-culty of crossing Bitarh bed.	...	Cross Bitarh river several times.	5640	S. and T. nil, G. F. W. plentiful.	Hamlet.
3	Hillun E. in fields—	6	27	Rough and rugged track, rocky and steep to top of pass.	Up Chunwara valley.	...	6300	S. moderate, G. F. W. plentiful, T. available.	Village.
4	Dangar Allan E. small plain—	5	32 39	The descent on the Kashmir side is easy with a fair path to Gulmarg, over the Aphar-wat shoulder of the Pharpat peak.	Nilkanta pass	Cross Chun-wara bed often.	7260 11930	S. and T. nil, G. F. W. plentiful.	Small grassy terrace. Pir Panjal range.
5	Pharpat Marg ... E.— Killan Marg—	12	44 47 51		Apharwat spur.	... ...	...... 12000. 11000.	W. and G. available.	

| 6 | Gulmarg P. O., T. O., Hotel, E. | 10 | ... | 54 | ... | ...... | ...... | ...... | 8500 | S. and T. moderate, in season, W. distant G. F. ample. | Sanitarium and bazar in season. |

Above Hillan in the fork of the Nilkanta (Chumwara) river and Sakrala, there is a fine plateau called Maira, a splendid encamping ground. There are two gullies on the Nilkanta ridge, the north one is said to be bad and precipitous, the south one should be taken. Neither are fit for ponies. This route is open during four months of the year, July to October inclusive, as soon as the rivers subside after the melting of the snow. On the Poonch approach, the rivers have to be forded in numerous places. It is seldom used, and travellers now prefer the route by the Firozepur pass which is shorter and easier.

XXXIII   POONCH to SRINAGAR by FIROZEPUR PASS—

No.	Stage	Dist.	Total	Road	Route	Intermediate	Elev.	Supplies	Remarks
	Poonch F. O., D. B., E.—	...	0	Good road passable throughout for laden animals.	Up Suran valley.	......	3300	S. G. F. W. T. ample.	Town, fort, bazar and capital of Poonch State.
			2 4			Dangli bed.			
			6		U p Mandi valley.	Mandi bridge.			
			12						
1	Mandi or Koondah E. small— Gogri lower	13	13		...	Loran "	5000	S. G. F W plentiful, T. available.	Large village and tehsil. Summer residence of Raja of Poonch.
			21						
2	Gagri upper E.—	10	23	Steep ascent to pass on Poonch side and easy descent on Kashmir side.	Firozepur pass	......		S. nil, G. F. W. moderate, T. scanty.	Cluster of village.
			31		Down Palate valley.		12000		
3	Banabali Nag	12	35	......		Banabali Nag or Kontar Nag.		S. and T. nil, G. F. W. plentiful.	Lake.
	Drung	...	44	......				......	Two ancient temples in ruins.
4	Firozepur E.—	11	46	Road enters a n highly cultivated plain.	Down Bahun valley.	Bahun ford.		S. and T. scarce, G. F. W. plentiful.	Large village.

Number of Marches.	Names of Stages.	Distance in Miles and Furlongs.		Nature of Route.	Main Valleys and Mountain Passes.	River Crossings and Lakes.	Altitude above Sea Level in Feet.	Supplies and Transport at Stages.	Remarks.
		Inter-mediate. m. f.	Total. m. f.						
XXXIII ROUTE—contd.									
5	Magam	11 ...	46 ...	Joins the Srinagar and Gulmarg road, and crosses low swampy ground.	.....	...	.....	S. and T. moderate, G. F. W. available.	Small village.
	B., E. very small—	12 ...	58 ...						
	Narbal	...	64 ...		.....	Suknag bridge.			
6	Srinagar	16 ...	74 ...		.....	Amiri Kadal over Jhelum.	5235	S. G. F. W. abundant, T. ample.	Large city, Hari Parbat fort, cantonment, summer palaces of H. H. Maharaja and Court, Residency; capital of Kashmir State.
	P. O., T. O., C., E.								

This route is open during four months of the year July to October inclusive.

At Mandi there is no encamping ground. It is usual to camp either at Koondah, when ascending higher up the Mandi valley or at Rajpur near, when ascending the Loran valley.

A detour can be made through another gulli south of the Firozepur pass by the Kontar Nag, which lengthens the route to Banabali Nag by 2½ miles. From this latter lake a track branches northwards by Barzatah 38 miles, joins the Nilkanta pass route at 40 miles and passing over the Apharwat shoulder 12,000 feet of the Pharpat peak 14,500 feet of the pass direct to Barzatah, 15 miles from Gagri upper, avoiding the lake if they intend taking this upper route, or go to Banabali Nag, whence they can follow the Palata river down to its junction with the Bahun river along the foregoing road and 2 miles beyond on the left bank, whence strike up the face of the hill to Gulmarg 50 miles from Poonch.

Travellers for Gulmarg can go from the pass direct to Barzatah, 15 miles from Gagri upper, avoiding the lake if they intend taking this upper route, or go to Banabali Nag, whence they can follow the Palata river down to its junction with the Bahun river along the foregoing road and 2 miles beyond on the left bank, whence strike up the face of the hill to Gulmarg 50 miles from Poonch.

From Firozepur 46 miles a track branches northwards by Baba Marishi 7,000 feet 50 miles and Kontra 55½ miles, to Baramulla 67 miles, passable for laden animals.

From Kontra another road of easy descent leads down the Ningul valley by Minagam, Wogan and Natpur to Sopoor 5,185 feet and 70 miles from Poonch. Sopoor is the head-quarters of Zillah Kamraj.

XXXIII. GAGRI to SRINAGAR by ZAMIR PASS—

No.	Name			Remarks	Direction	Bridges and fords	Elevation	Supplies	Description
2	Gagri lower	...	... 21 ..	The ascent of this pass on the Poonch side is steep and rugged, fit for men only.	Up Zamir valley. Zamir pass	Maoli bridge	......	S. nil, G. F. W. moderate, T. scanty.	Cluster of villages.
			30 ..				13470		
3	Shinamani E.—	11	32 ..	On the Kashmir side the descent is easy, and from Dunwas the track is fair, though it crosses low and swampy ground about Syboog liable to inundation in the high floods of the Jhelum river.	Across Bahun drainage.	Bahun ford.	......	S. and T. nil, G. F. W. available.	Marg.
			38 ..						
4	Dunwas E.— Badshot	9	41		Down Suknag valley.	......	......	Ditto	Tower.
			47						
5	Aripatan E.—	14	55		......	Suknag bridge.	......	S. F. T. scanty, G. and W. available.	Village.
			56						
6	Syboog	10	65		Across Hokarsar swamp.	......	......	Ditto	Ditto.
7	Srinagar P. O., T. O., C., E.—	8	73	......	......	Amiran Kadal over Jhelum.	5235	S. G. F. W. abundant, T. ample.	Large city, fort, bazar, and capital of Kashmir State.

At the 26th mile from Poonch a track branches off in a south-east direction over the Tosha Maidan pass 29 miles and descends by the Damam Sar to the Tosha Maidan 40 miles, an extensive Marg, the resort of numerous herds of cattle, ponies, sheep, &c, in the summer and autumn—See next Route XXXIV. Hence a track goes northward down the Bahun valley, through Vehinar to the Dunwas tower 50 miles.

XXXIV. POONCH to SRINAGAR by TOSHA MAIDAN PASS—

Name				Remarks	Direction	Elevation	Supplies	Description
Poonch P. O., D. B., E.—	...	...	0 ...	Good road passable throughout for laden animals.	Up Suran valley.	3300	S. G. F. W. T. ample.	Town, fort, bazar and capital of Poonch State.

Number of Marches	Names of Stages	Distance in miles and furlongs		Nature of Route.	Main Valleys and Mountain Passes.	River crossings and Lakes.	Altitude above Sea Level in Feet.	Supplies and Transport at Stages.	Remarks.
		Inter-mediate. m. f.	Total. m. f.						
	XXXIV ROUTE—contd.								
			0						
			2						
			4			Dungli bed.			
			6		Up Mandi valley.				
1	**Mandi or Rajpur** P. O., E.—	13	13	......	Up Loran valley right bank.	Mandi bridge	5000	S. G. F. W. plentiful, T. available.	Large village and tehsil. Summer residence of Raja of Poonch. Fork of Loran and Dali Nar rivers.
	Biarah		20	......			......	......	
2	**Sultan Patri** E.—	12	25	The ascent over the Phulwaran spur to the top of pass is rather steep, while the descent is gentle over an extensive plateau covered with good pasture, the scenery is beautiful.			......	S. and T. nil, G. F. W. moderate.	Dak deserted in winter.
			31		Mineagol		12500		
			32		China marg.		12000		
			33			Damam Sar.			
			37			Geditur Nag ford.			
3	**Tosha Maidan** E.—	16	41	......	......	......	10000	S. and T. nil, G. F. W. available.	Grazing ground.

	Stage		Interm.	Total	River / Bridge	Elev.	Road	Supplies	Remarks
	Zanigam	...	::	48		......	The road crosses low and swampy ground liable to inundation.		
4	Watrehel E.—	...	13	54	Across Suknag and Jhelum drainage.	......		S. G. W. available, F. and T. moderate.	Large village.
5	Srinagar P. O., T. O., C., E.—	...	14	68	Amiran Kadal over Jhelum.	5235		S. G. F. W. abundant, T. ample.	Large city, fort, bazar and capital of Kashmir State.

This appears to be the most direct route from Poonch to Srinagar. The pass is fairly easy without obstructions, and is usually open from June to the first fall of snow in November. At the 37th mile, instead of crossing the stream, which flows from the Gaditur Nag, the traveller may branch off due east across the Koot Nag stream, south of the Laishah Alum peak, cross the Suknag river by a bridge 43 miles and follow down this valley on the left bank by Ringazabal 48 miles and Urzal to Watrehel 70 miles. The scenery down the Suknag valley surpasses that on the other route. Tosha Maidan is an extensive marg on undulating ground at the summit of the Pir Punjal, is frequented in summer and autumn by herds of all kinds of cattle, ponies, mules, sheep and goats for grazing. The scenery on all the approaches is beautiful, and the views from the edges of the marg or from the peaks on it are fine.

XXXIVa MANDI to SRINAGAR by NURPUR and SANGSOFED PASSES—

	Stage		Interm.	Total	Road	Direction / Valley	Elev.	Supplies	Remarks
1	Mandi or Rajpur E.—	...	::	13	Good road to Nurpur passable for laden animals.	Up Loran valley.	5000	S. G. F. W. plentiful, T. available.	Large village and tehsil.
	Biarah	...	::	20		Up Dali Nar valley.	......		
2	Batulkot E.—	...	10	23	......	......	......	S. and T. nil, G. F. W. plentiful.	Small village of iron miners.
3	Nurpur	...	8	31	Ascent to pass steep and difficult in places, descent is also sharp and difficult. Traversed by laden animals.	Nurpur pass	......	Ditto	Iron working.
		...		36					
		...		37		Kala Sar.	13610		
4	Doodhi Patri E.—	...	16	47		Down Yechara valley.	......	Ditto	Hamlet.

Number of Branches	Names of Stages	Distance in miles and furlongs — Intermediate m. f.	Total m. f.	Nature of Route	Main Valleys and Mountain Passes	River crossings and Lakes	Altitude above Sea Level in Feet	Supplies and Transport and Stages	Remarks
	XXXIVa *ROUTE—contd.*								
5	**Dragam** ...	16 ...	47 ...	Good road hence along the well cultivated plain.	Across Jhelum drainage.	......	......	S. and T. moderate, G. F. W. available.	Village.
	Yechgam	14 ...	61 ...	......	......	......	......	S. G. F. W. and T. available.	Large village.
		......	65 ..			Dudh Gunga bridge.			
		......	74 ...						
6	**Srinagar** *P.O., T.O., C., E.—*	14 ...	75 ...	......	......	Amiran Kadal over Jhelum.	5225	S. G. F. W. abundant, T. ample.	Large city, fort, bazars and capital of Kashmir State.

At the 29th mile, a path strikes up over the Chorgulli pass, a most difficult and rugged ascent, and descends by the Bagh Sar to the Suknag valley above Ringzabal.

At the 33rd mile, a track branches off southwards over the Sangsofed pass 36 miles and descends across two spurs into the Sangsofed valley to Frasnag 48 miles, and continues to Nilnag near Gogipatri 58 miles; thence by Surus and Dragaon to Yechgam 73 miles, and to Srinagar 83 miles from Poonch.

After accomplishing the rather steep ascent to this pass, there is a fair road downwards to Gogipatri, and a good road hence to Srinagar. These three passes are open only during four months of the year, July to October inclusive. The Nurpur pass is said to be the easiest of the three for beasts of burden.

XXXV POONCH to ISLAMABAD or ANANT NAG by PIR PUNJAL PASS—

Names of Stages	Intermediate m. f.	Total m. f.	Nature of Route	Main Valleys and Mountain Passes	River crossings and Lakes	Altitude above Sea Level in Feet	Supplies and Transport and Stages	Remarks
Poonch *P. O., D. B., E.—*	0 ...		Good road, practicable for laden animals throughout.	Up Suran valley right bank.	...... Dungli bed. Maudi bridge.	3300	S. G. F. W. T. ample.	Town, fort, bazar and capital of Poonch State.
	2 4							
	6 ...							

No.	Stage	Dist.	Total	Road remarks	Direction / valley	River / bridge	Elevation	Supplies	Description
1	Suran B.—	14	14	......	Ditto left bank.	Suran "	4300	S. G. F. & T. moderate; W. plentiful.	Village.
2	Baramgalla B.—	12	26	Road along stony bed of Chittapani for half this march with numerous crossings of the stream, steep ascent to Poshiana.	......	Suran "	5800	Ditto	Small village.
	Chandimar	...	27		......	Suran bridge.		Ditto	
		...	28		Up Chittapani valley.	Alatopa "			
3	Poshiana E. on roofs of houses	10	36		Up Nilana valley.	......	8140	S. and T. nil, G. F. W. moderate.	Ditto deserted in winter.
4	Aliabad Serai B., C., E.—	11	41	Severe climb to top of pass over fair road. Easy descent by good road.	Pir Punjal pass.	......	11400		
			47		Down Rembiara valley.	......	10100	Ditto	Old serai built by the Mogul Emperors. Tower.
	Dubchi	...	48		......	......	9700	...	Sheds in forest.
			55		......	......	......	......	
5	Hirpura B., E.—	12	56			Rembiara bridge.			
			59	Valley widens and opens out into the plains of Kashmir.	......	......	7760	Ditto	Scattered village.
6	Shupiyon P. O., E.—	8	67	Good road across a highly cultivated plain.	Across Veshau and Jhelum drainage.	......	6714	S. G. F. W. and T. plentiful.	Town and tehsil.
7	Kulgam E.—	15	82			......	...	S. G. W. and T. plentiful, F. scanty.	Large village.
	Khaimoo	...	91			Veshau bridge			
	Kanabal	...	94			Jhelum "			

NUMBER OF MARCHES	NAMES OF STAGES	DISTANCE IN MILES AND FURLONGS.		NATURE OF ROUTE.	MAIN VALLEYS AND MOUNTAIN PASSES.	RIVER CROSSINGS AND LAKES.	ALTITUDE ABOVE SEA LEVEL IN FEET.	SUPPLIES AND TRANSPORT AT STAGES.	REMARKS.
		INTERMEDIATE. m. f.	TOTAL. m. f.						
XXXV	*ROUTE—contd.*		94 4						
8	Islamabad **or** Anant Nag *P. O., T. O., C., E.—*	14 ...	96 ...	......	Across Veshau and Jhelum drainage.	......	5460	S. G. F. W. and T. plentiful.	Town, bazar, tehsil and head-quarters of zillah.

This route is usually open from the 1st May to the middle of November. Storms and keen winds are frequent on this high pass. Travellers should avoid crossing in bad weather, and should start about dawn to get over the pass before the wind rises.

At Chaandimar 28 miles, two tracks branch out, one north-east over the Chhoti gulli pass 14,090 feet (see Route XXXVa), and the other south-east over the Mastan pass 13,780 feet.

The latter track rises up the Puran spur to the Mastan pass and descends to the foot of the Pir Punjal pass, being about 3 miles longer than the ordinary road.

From Poshiana 36 miles, a track branches up the Chittapani valley to its head over the Chittapani pass 14,540 feet and 44 miles, and descends down the Kachgul valley by Upper Sangarwini 56 miles, and Pakapura 68 miles, to Chrar 73 miles. This pass is said to be difficult and bad for laden animals.

From Dubchi 55 miles, there is a path by Phudar 61 miles, to Pakapura 72 miles, and Chrar 77 miles from Poonch.

XXXVa BARAMGALLA to SRINAGAR by CHHOTI GULLI PASS—

	NAMES OF STAGES	INTERMEDIATE	TOTAL	NATURE OF ROUTE.	MAIN VALLEYS	RIVER CROSSINGS	ALTITUDE	SUPPLIES AND TRANSPORT	REMARKS.
24	Baramgalla *B., E.—*	...	26 ...	Road good and passable throughout for laden animals.	Up Suran valley.	...... Suran bridge.	5800	S. scarce, F. G. and T. moderate, W. plentiful.	Village on elevated plateau.
		...	27 ...						

No.	Name of stage	Intermediate distance	Total distance (miles)	Description of road	Route notes	River crossed	Height (feet)	Supplies	Remarks
	Chundinar	...	28	.....	Ascend Alatopa spur of Pir Punjal range and continue along the top of this ridge.	.....	.....	.....	Iron works and village.
	Alahuri	...	30	.....		.....	.....	.....	Halting place.
	Baramuri	...	34	.....		.....	.....	.....	Ditto on spur.
3	**Hilloh** E.—	10 4	36	Good road of easy gradient up to pass. Gradual descent from pass.	Chhoti gulli	.....	.....	S. and T. nil, G. F. W. plentiful.	Halting place at head of valley.
			41	.....		.....	14090		
4	**Loodur Marg** E.—	13 4	50	.....	Down Sang-sofed or Dudh Gunga valley on right bank.	.....	.....	Ditto	Pasture ground.
5	**Surus** E.—	13	63	.....		.....	.....	S. precarious, T. nil, G. F. W. available.	Small village.
			65	Road emerges from the hills on to the well-cultivated plain of Kashmir.		Dudh Gunga.	.....		
			74			Yechara.	.....		
6	**Kralpoora** E.—	14	77	.....		.....	.....	S. G. F. W. moderate, T. nil.	Village.
7	**Srinagar** P. O., T. O., C., E.	8	84	.....		Dudh Gunga. Amiran Kadal over Jhelum.	5235	S. G. F. W. abundant, T. ample.	Large city, fort and capital of Kashmir State.
			85						

At foot of the Chhoti gulli pass on the Kashmir side at mile 44 a track turns to the east and follows down the Kachgul valley to Pakapura 64 miles, Chrar 69 miles, Nagam 74 miles, Wahtor 78 miles, and Srinagar 87 miles from Poonch.

Or joining the track from the Chittapani pass it follows the same Kachgul valley by Upper Sangarwini 56 miles, to Pakapura 68 miles, and to Chrar 68 miles, and so on.

At mile 60, instead of going down the valley to Surus, there is a track eastwards to Gogipatri 62 miles, and is the easiest of all the roads into Kashmir, though open only from July to October inclusive. All the approaches to it on the Kashmir side have grass, wood and water in abundance, and are quite passable for laden animals. The Chhoti gulli pass is of very gradual ascent and descent, and is the single road on the Poonch side has access to grass, wood and water in the valley below the Alatopa spur. Food-supplies must be taken through from Poonch or Srinagar.

NUMBER OF MARCHES.	NAMES OF STAGES.	DISTANCE IN MILES AND FURLONGS.		NATURE OF ROUTE.	MAIN VALLEYS AND MOUNTAIN PASSES.	RIVER CROSSINGS AND LAKES.	ALTITUDE ABOVE SEA LEVEL IN FEET.	SUPPLIES AND TRANSPORTS AT STAGES.	REMARKS.
		INTERMEDIATE. m. f.	TOTAL. m. f.						

XXXVI SRINAGAR to JAMMU—*See Route* XII by Pir Punjal ..... Pass 11,400 feet 169 miles.
　　　　　　　　　　　　　　　　　XIII 　" 　Budil 　14,120 　" 　130 　"
　　　　　　　　　　　　　　　　　XIV 　" 　Golabgurh or Kuri 　" 　12,530 　" 　147 　"
　　　　　　　　　　　　　　　　　XV 　" 　Banihal 　" 　9,200 　" 　155 　" 　4 furlongs.

XXXVII SRINAGAR to SIALKOT by BUDIL PASS—

NUMBER OF MARCHES.	NAMES OF STAGES.	INTERMEDIATE. m. f.	TOTAL. m. f.	NATURE OF ROUTE.	MAIN VALLEYS AND MOUNTAIN PASSES.	RIVER CROSSINGS AND LAKES.	ALTITUDE ABOVE SEA LEVEL IN FEET.	SUPPLIES AND TRANSPORTS AT STAGES.	REMARKS.
	Srinagar *P. O., T. O., C., E.—*	...	0 ...	Good made road along the cultivated plain to Wahtor, whence fair road onwards to Shupiyon, crossing the boulder beds of rivers.	Up Dodh Ganga valley right bank.	Amiran Kadal	5235	S. G. F. W. abundant, T. ample.	Capital of Kashmir State, cantonment and fort, large town and bazar.
	Rambagh	...	2 ...			.....	.....	.....	Temple of Moharajah Golab Singh.
	Kralpura	...	6 ... 4			.....	.....	.....	Large village.
1	**Wahtor** *Khanpur C.—*	3 ...	9 ... 13 ...		Across western drainage of Upper Jhelum valley.	.....	.....	S. G. F. W. procurable, S. nil, G. F. W. procurable, T. available.	Ditto. Halting place.
2	**Ramu** *B., E. confined—*	9 ...	17 ... 18 ...			Ramchu ford.	.....	S. G. F. and W. procurable, T. available.	Village on Ramchu river, bungalow destroyed by fire, room in old dharmsala.

	Stage / Place			Road	Direction	Ford / Bridge	Elevation	Supplies	Remarks
	Shahju marg	...	...	...	...	Mankund ford. Rembiara „	...	...	Old Imperial serai.
3	Shupiyon P. O., B., E.—	11	22 25 27	...	...	...	...	...	...
			29	Fair road to Budil pass, passable for laden animals.	...	...	6715	S. G. F. W. and T. ample.	Town, bazar and tehsil.
	Sedau		...	...	...	...	...	...	Large village and customs post.
4	Nazamdi Garhi ... E. rock shelter—	11	34	...	...	...	...	S. and T. nil, G. F. W. plentiful.	Halting place, guard tower.
			40	Easy ascent to pass but descent steep and difficult, though passable for laden animals.	Up Urseni valley left bank.	...	...		
5	Delhi E.—	14	49		Budil pass.	...	14120	Ditto	Halting place, a few huts.
			54		Across head of Chuniperal valley.	...	...		
	Abid, E. limited		50	Stiff ascent and descent.	Beberi spur. Down Budil valley.	Budil ford.	...	Ditto	Few scattered huts.
			61						
6	Budil E.—	11	64	...	Across Ans valley.		...	S. G. F. W. plentiful, T. available.	Large village and small fort.
			65	Road stony and difficult, but passable for laden animals.	...	Ans bridge.	...		
			67 4						
7	Bhagoli	6	71	...	Choroosira ridge.	...	...	S. and T. nil, G. F. W. procurable.	Hamlet.
			75	Steep ascent 2 miles, along crest of hill 3 miles and descent 3 miles.					
8	Nar	8	79	Road stony and difficult, though passable.	Down Nar valley.	...	...	S. precarious, G. F. W. procurable, T. nil.	Scattered village.

Number of Marches	Names of Stages	Distance in miles and furlongs — Intermediate m. f.	Distance in miles and furlongs — Total m. f.	Nature of Route.	Main Valleys and Mountain Passes.	River crossings and Lakes.	Altitude above Sea Level in Feet.	Supplies and Transport at Stages.	Remarks.
	XXXVII *ROUTE—(contd.)*								
9	Chelo or Jandi ...	... 8	79 ...	.....	.....	Nar ford	......	S. G. F. W. procurable, T. nil.	Village.
10	Poni *E.—* ...	11 ...	90 ...	Steep and stony descent.	Chele gala	......	4000	S. G. F. W. plentiful, T. available.	Large village and State garden.
		... ...	92 ...	.....	......	Poni ford.	2000		
		8 ...	98 ...	Stair ascent	Dal gala.	Katundra ford			
		... ...	100 ...	......	......				
		... ...	101 4	......	......				
		... ...	103 ...	......	Jendar gala.				
11	Jandrai Kapaion-ki baoli ...	... ...	106 ...	......	......	...	2000	S. and T. nil, G. and F. plentiful, W. scarce.	Resting place in jungle.
12	Akrnoor ...	8 4	106 4	Stony road	......	...		S. G. F. W. plentiful, T. available.	Small town, fort and bazar.
	Kaneki Chuk ...	7 4	114 ...	Rough road passable for laden animals.	Down Chenab valley.	Chenab ferry	1142		
		... ...	120 ...						
13	Gujjanso ...	12 ...	126 ...	Rough cart-road along open cultivated plain to Sialkot.	...	......		S. G. F. T. scanty, W. plentiful.	Small village.
		... ...	133 ...		...	Tawi ferry.			
14	Chaprar ...	10 ...	136 ...	......	...	......		S. G. F. T. after notice, W. plentiful.	Village.

| 15 | Sialkot | ... | 13 ... | 149 ... | ... | ... | 829 | S. G. F. W. and T. abundant. | Military cantonment, civil station, town, fort, bazar and head-quarters of district. |

Between Shupiyon and Budil, two alternative loop routes are available.

Firstly, up the valley of the Veshau river to its source the Konsa Nag 13,000 feet, a large lake of great sanctity and frequented by pilgrims, over the pass of the same name 13,250 feet, down the Chumiperal valley and across the Beberi spur range to Budil, the marches being through Sedau 5 miles, crossing the Veshau river near the falls of Harihal 2½ miles, Kungwattan 7 miles, Konsa Nag 10 miles, Pass 3 miles, Nundkot 6½ miles, Beberi ridge 4 miles, and Budil 5 miles. Total 43 miles.

Secondly, up the Rembiara valley to Alialsad Serai, thence crossing a spur ridge and up the Rupri valley to the mountain lakes which form its source; hence are 2 tracks over the Rupri pass 13,620 feet, one down the Laktal and Putsar spur, crossing the Beberi range to Budil, the other down the Panchgabier or Upper Ans valley to Budil : the marches from Shupiyon being up the Pir Punjal road to Hirpura 8 miles, and Aliabad Serai 12 miles ; thence to Rupri 10 miles, Rupri pass 5 miles, Boorjarj 5 miles, Kundi 10 miles, and Budil 13 miles. Total 63 miles.

All these 3 passes Budil, Konsa Nag and Rupri are usually closed by snow from the first fall in November to the end of May.

From Budil a cross road westwards connects Rajaori and Kotli, the marches being Kundi 13 miles, Piri 6 miles, down Kundul valley and across Tohi river to Rajaori 12 miles, up Charkot valley to Ajeengurh pass 10 miles, down Ban valley to Koireta 16 miles, and to Kotli 16 miles. Total 73 miles.

From Poni are cross routes eastwards to Rinssi 10 miles, crossing the Chenab river at the Talwara ferry at the 8th mile, and westwards to Thandapani 14 miles, and to Naoshera 20 miles further.

From Aknoor, there is a rough cart-road eastwards, 16 miles to Jammu, half way is Nagbani, where are the stud stables of the Jammu State.

XXXVIII SRINAGAR to GUJRAT by PIR PUNJAL PASS—OLD IMPERIAL ROUTE—

Srinagar *P. O., T. O., C., E.*—							
	... ...	Good made road along the cultivated plain to Wahtor and fair road onwards to Shupiyon, fording the boulder beds of rivers and with bridges over small nullahs.	Up Dudh Gunga valley right bank.	Amiran Kadal	5235	S. G. F. W. abundant, T. ample.	Capital of Kashmir State, cantonment and fort, large town and bazars.
Rambagh	... ...	2	...	...	...	...	Temple containing ashes of Maharaja Golab Singh.
Kralpura	... ...	6 4	...	...	...	...	Large village.

XXXVIII ROUTE—(contd.)

Number of Marches	Names of Stages	Intermediate m. f.	Total m. f.	Nature of Route	Main Valleys and Mountain Passes	River Crossings and Lakes	Altitude above Sea Level in Feet	Supplies and Transport at Stages	Remarks
1	**Wahtor**	......	6 4	......		......	......	S. G. F. W. procurable	Large village, halting place.
	Khanpur C.—	9	9 .. 13 .. 17 ..	......	Across Western drainage of Upper Jhelum valley.	Ramchu ford.	......		
2	**Ramu** B., E. confined—	9	18 ..	......		......	......	S. G. F. W. procurable, T. available.	Village on Ramchu river. Bungalow destroyed by fire, room in old dhurmsala.
	Shahju mary	......	22 .. 25 4	......	....	Mankund ford. Rembiara ford.	......	......	Old Imperial serai.
3	**Shupiyon** P. O., B., E.—	11	27 4 29 ..	From Shupiyon the old made road has got out of order to Baramgalla and is difficult in places, though passable for laden animals.	Up Rembiara valley.	Rembiara ford.	6715	S. G. F. W. and T. ample.	Town, bazar and tehsil.
4	**Hirpura** B., C., E.—	8	37 ..	......	......	......	7700	S. procurable, G. F. W. plentiful, few coolies.	Small village on right bank Rembiara.
	Dubchi B.—	......	40 ..	......	......	Rembiara.	......		
	Suk Serai	......	41 .. 42 ..	The scenery is very beautiful.	......	......	......	......	Shahkot on right bank. Halting place.
5	**Aliabad Serai** B., C.—	12	49 ..	......	......	......	10000	S. and T. nil, G. F. W. plentiful.	

No.	Stage			Miles	Road	Route	River crossing	Elevation	Supplies	Description
6	**Poshiana** C., E. on house tops—	11	...	64 ...	......	Pir Punjal pass.	......	11400	...	Shelter hut on pass.
			...	60 ...	......	Down Chittapani or Suran valley.	Cross Chittapani and Suran river by numerous bridges.	8150	S. W. scarce, G. F. plentiful, T. nil.	Village deserted in winter.
	Chandimar	...	:	66 :	......			......	......	Village and iron works.
7	**Baramgalla** B., C. —	8	4	68 4	......	Ratan Pir pass.	Purnai bridge and water-falls.	5800 / 8200	S. scarce, G. F. W. plentiful, few coolies.	Small village and fort in deep gorge near confluence of Purnai nullah and Suran river.
				74						
8	**Thana Mandi** B., C., E. small—	10	4	79 :	Old made road in fair order to Naoshera and much used by traders.	Down Tohi valley left bank.	Tohi ford.	4580	S. G. F. W. plentiful, T. available.	Village on right bank Tohi, salt depot.
				80						
	Saj Serai	...	:	87 :						
	Futtehpur Serai	...	.	90 .				......	......	On top of hill.
9	**Rajaori (Rampur)** P. O., B., C.—	14	...	92 :	......	Down Tohi valley along right bank.	Darhal ford. Tohi ford bridge unfinished.	3094	S. G. F. W. plentiful, T. ample.	Town and bazar, well built on right bank Tohi. R. opposite on left bank.
				93 :						
	Moradpur Serai	...	:	94 :						
	Tulmakot	...	:	97 :			Panda ford.	......	......	
				103 :						
10	**Chingas Serai** B., C.—	15	...	108 :	...	......	...	2340	S. G. F. W. plentiful, coolies available.	Serai and village.
	Nadpur Serai	...	4	113 4	......:		Lilali baoli Chopi ford.	2000	......	Spring pure water.
			:	116 :	......	Chaini spur				
			4	119 4	Hence the road though made, has fallen into bad order in many parts and become very rocky and stony in crossing both ranges.	Koman Gosha				
11	**Naoshera** P. O., B., C., E.—	13	...	121 4			Janbir ford Forded river bed 4 times.	2400 / 1800 / 2870	Ditto	Small town, serai fort, tehsil and bazar.
			:	127 :						
12	**Saidabad** B., C., E.—	12	4	134 :		Down Bhimber valley.	Samani ford.	2000	S. G. F. W. plentiful, T. available.	Samani village 2 miles off westwards.
				135 4						
				141		Aditak range.	......	2800		

NUMBER OF MARCHES	NAMES OF STAGES	DISTANCE IN MILES AND FURLONGS.		NATURE OF ROUTE	MAIN VALLEYS AND MOUNTAIN PASSES.	RIVER CROSSINGS AND LAKES.	ALTITUDE ABOVE SEA LEVEL IN FEET.	SUPPLIES AND TRANSPORT AND STAGES.	REMARKS.
		INTERMEDIATE. m. f.	TOTAL. m. f.						
XXXVIII	*ROUTE—(contd.)*								
	Mütiret	... ...	141 ...	......	......				
13	**Bhimber** P. O., B., C., E.—	14 ...	144 ...	......	......	Bhimber river forded 6 times.	1090	S.G.F.W. plentiful, T. available.	Small town, bazar, head-quarters of zillah.
		......	148 ...	Cart-road hence cut up in places to Kotla: fair, dry weather, road un-metalled and un-bridged to Gujrat over which ekkas and tongas can travel.	Down Bhimber valley.	Bhimber ford.			
14	**Kotla** D. B.—	8 4	149 ...						
			156 4	......	......	......	980	S. G. F. procurable, W. from wells, few coolies.	Small village.
15	**Daulatnagar** P. O., D. B.—	8 ...	164 4	......	......	......	......	Ditto	**Large village.**
			170 ...			Bhimber ford.			
16	**Gujrat City** P. O., T. O., C., E. on G. T. road—	......	176 ...	......	......	......	......	S.G.F.W. plentiful, T. ample.	Large city and civil station on N.-W. Railway.
16	**Gujrat Railway Station.** P. O., T. O., D.B.—	13 4	178 ...	......	......	......	......		

From Aliabad Serai 49 miles, there are alternative Routes over the two Durhal passes as under, both passable for laden animals. Aliabad Serai 49 miles up the Indili valley to its source the Nandun Sar 58 miles, over the first Durhal pass 13,080 feet, 59 miles, down by Nilsar to Beloh, 63 miles in the Poran valley, thence crossing the Ratan Pir range at 64 miles, the road drops to Durhal pass 13,080 feet, and to Rupri 69 miles, and to Rajaori 83 miles. The other route from Aliabad Serai crosses the spur ridge between the Indili and Rupri rivers, and ascends to Rupri 59 miles, and Bhagsar 61 miles, over the second Durhal pass 13,460 feet and 62 miles, and drops to Beloh 67 miles, where it joins the first route towards Rajaori.

The Pir Punjal pass is open from May to about the middle of November, the two Durhal passes are open only from July to end of October. The route over the first Durhal pass is said to be the easiest to travel when the rivers are low and fordable.

From Baramgalla 68 miles 4 furlongs; a good road goes west down the Suran valley by Suran 80 miles, to Poonch 94 miles. There are 7 bridges over the Suran river, and the passage of traffic depends upon these being maintained in good order.

From Rajaori 93 miles, there is a cross road through the hills to Kotli, it ascends the Charkoh valley to the Ajeemgurh pass 103 miles, and descends down the Ban valley to Koireta 119 miles, and to Kotli 135 miles.

From Bhimber 148 miles, a road goes direct S.-W. under the Pubbi hills to the Kharian Railway Station 165 miles, and is used in the rainy season to avoid any crossing of the Bhimber river.

From Dualtangar 164 miles 4 furlongs, a road goes westwards crossing the Bhimber river at 174 miles to the Lala Musa Railway Station 174 miles, and another goes eastwards by Julalpur 175 miles, to Sialkot 189 miles, crossing the Chenab river by the Muhatah ferry at 185 miles.

XXXIX SRINAGAR to POONCH — See Route.—

Route	by	Pass	Height	Miles
XXX	by Haji Pir	Pass	8,500 feet,	98 miles.
XXXI	" Pajja	"	10,000 "	92 "
XXXIa	" Gajan	"	9,135 "	102 "
XXXIII	" Firozepur	"	12,000 "	74 "
XXXIIIa	" Zamir	"	13,470 "	73 "
XXXIV	" Tosha Maidan	"	12,500 "	68 "
XXXIVa	" Nurpur or	"	13,610 "	75 "
	Sangsofel			83 "
XXXVa	" Chhoti gulli	"	14,090 "	85 "

In May and June the Haji Pir or Gajan route should be selected; in July to October inclusive, the Firozepur, Tosha Maidan and Nurpur routes are shortest, while the Chhoti gulli is the easiest of all, and the Pir Punjal route is the longest. There is lovely scenery with fine views on every route, the Gajan, Tosha Maidan and Pir Punjal being perhaps superior in this respect. From November to April, all these routes are, as a rule, closed by snow, while in April, when the snow melts, they are all liable to avalanches of snow, especially on the Haji Pir, Pajja, Firozepur and Zamir passes.

XL. SRINAGAR to RAMPUR by GULMARG—

	Srinagar	0 ...		Good road to Parana Chowni,	Amiran Kadal Dudh Gunga bridge.	5235	S.G.F.W.T. abundant.	Capital of Kashmir State, large city, &c.
	P.O., T.O., C., E.—	1 ... 4		thence narrow	Suknag bridge.			
	Parana Chowni	4 ...		raised bank				
	Narbal	10 ...		through swamps,				
1	Magam	16 ...	16 ...	very muddy and slippery after rain to Magam.			S.G.F.T. procurable in season, W. plentiful.	Small village.
	B., E. small—							

Number of Marches	Names of Stages	Distance in miles and furlongs		Nature of Route	Main Valleys and Mountain Passes	River crossings and Lakes	Altitude above Sea Level in Feet.	Supplies and Transport at Stages.	Remarks.
		Intermediate. m. f.	Total. m. f.						
XL	ROUTE—(contd.) ...	16 ...	16 ...						
2	Gulmarg P. O., T. O., hotel, E.	14 ...	30 ...	Good road hence to Gulmarg, though stony in places.	......	......	8500	S. and T. moderate in season, W. distant, G. F. ample.	Sanitarium and bazar in season.
		...	35 ...		......	Ningul ford			
3	Linian marg E.—	10 ...	40 ...	Fair road through alternate pine forest and marg down to Nowshera, where it joins the Jhelum cart-road.	......	Kechama ford	9400	S. and T. nil, G. F. W. ample.	Shepherd's huts.
	Nowshera	...	49 4		......	......			
	Bhaaniar	...	52 4		......	Harpetkai bridge.	5000	......	Ancient Buddhist temple.
		...	53 ...			......			
4	Rampur P. O., T. O., D. B., E.	14 ...	54 ...			......	4900	S. G. F. W. moderate a few coolies.	All supplied by Nawab of Bhunniar.

There is another track from Srinagar to Gulmarg across the Hokarsar swamps to Syboog 8 miles, Hardu 16 miles, where the Suknag river is crossed by a ford, Khundabama 18 miles, Firozepur 26 miles, Gulmarg 30 miles. At Firozepur several streams of the Bahun river have to be crossed. There is no advantage in this route, and during the rainy season the swamps and Bahun streams are often unfordable.

XLa SRINAGAR to GULMARG viâ PATAN—

	Srinagar P. O., T. O., C., E.—	0 ...	...	Carriage road under construction to Patan.	......	Amiran Kadal Dudt. Gunga bridge.	5235	S. G. F. W. T. abundant.	Capital of Kashmir State, large city, &c.
		2 ...	...		......				

	Place			Suknag bridge.	Route	Supplies	Ht.	Remarks
1	*Harprat*	...	13	.....	......	S. G. F. T. available, W. from spring.	...	Village and ancient ruins.
	Hanjipur	...	16	Hanjipur bridge.	......		...	Mahomedan shrine.
	Patan E.—Chandesir	19	19 26 4	.....	Good mule track over Karewah land and through pine forest to Gulmarg.	S. G. F. W. procurable, T. nil.	...	
	Baba Mariahi B., C., E.—	...	34	.....	......		...	Sanitarium a n d bazar in season.
2	**Gulmarg** P.O., T.O., hotel, E.—	17	36	......	......	S. T. moderate in season, W. distant, G. F. plentiful.	8500	

This though longer is likely to become the favourite land route as soon as the carriage road between Srinagar and Patan to Baramulla is finished. Visitors will drive in their carriage or tongas to Patan in 3 hours and either rest there, when a bungalow is built for the accommodation of travellers, or ride over at once to Gulmarg, doing the whole journey in one day. Eventually a carriage road from Patan to Gulmarg is quite feasible with a ruling gradient of 1 in 20.

XLb SRINAGAR to GULMARG by POLHALLAN—

	Place				Route	Supplies	Ht.	Remarks
	Srinagar P. O., T. O., C., E.—Shadipur	...	0	.....	By boat down the Jhelum river to Shadipur, thence by Noroo canal and western branch to Polhallan. Good mule track over Karewa land and through pine forest to Gulmarg.	S. G. F. W. T. abundant.	5235	Capital of Kashmir State, large city, &c.
1	**Polhallan** E.—Chandesir	25	15 25 31	.....		S. G. F. W. T. procurable.	......	Large village.
	Baba Mariahi B., C., E.—	...	40	.....		S. G. F. W. procurable, T. nil.	.....	Mahomedan shrine.

9

NUMBER OF MARCHES	NAMES OF STAGES	DISTANCE IN MILES AND FURLONGS.		NATURE OF ROUTE	MAIN VALLEYS AND MOUNTAIN PASSES	RIVER CROSSINGS AND LAKES.	ALTITUDE ABOVE SEA LEVEL IN FEET.	SUPPLIES AND TRANSPORT AT STAGES.	REMARKS.
		INTERMEDIATE. m. f.	TOTAL. m. f.						
XLb	ROUTE—contd.	...	40 ...	......	......	......			
2	Gulmarg P.O., T.O., hotel, E.—	17 ...	42 ...	......	......	......	8500	S. T. moderate in season, W. distant, G. F. plentiful.	Sanitarium and bazar in season.

This route is often taken in May and June when there is water enough in the **Noru** canal, and its western branch through the **Rurangaru** swamp to Folhallau. In July and August the musquitoes and insects are a **terrible pest**, and mosquitoe nets are indispensable. **From Folhallau the** march to Gulmarg is done in one day, being reckoned as 1½ stages.

XLc SKINAGAR to GULMARG by SOPUR—

	NAMES OF STAGES	INTERMEDIATE. m. f.	TOTAL. m. f.	NATURE OF ROUTE	MAIN VALLEYS AND MOUNTAIN PASSES	RIVER CROSSINGS AND LAKES.	ALTITUDE ABOVE SEA LEVEL IN FEET.	SUPPLIES AND TRANSPORT AT STAGES.	REMARKS.
	Srinagar P.O., T.O., C., E.—	...	0 ...	By boat down Jhelum river and across Woolar Lake to Sopoor.	Down Jhelum river.	......	5235	S. G. F. W. T. abundant.	Capital of Kashmir State, large city, &c.
	Shadipur	...	15 ...						
1	Hajan	27 ...	27 ...	......		Across Woolar Lake.		......	Large village of boatmen at mouth of Woolar Lake.
2	Sopur P.O., T.O., B., C., E.	18 ...	45 ...	Good mule track to Gulmarg	Up Niagul valley.	......	5185	S. G. F. W. T. plentiful.	Town, bazar and head-quarters of Kamraj zillah.
	Munagam	...	57 ...						

No.	Place			Bridge	Road	Elevation	S.G.F.W.T.	Remarks
3	Kontra E.— Baba Marishi R, C, E.—	15	60 65	......	......	......	S.G.F.W.T. procurable.	Up Nambalnar valley and spur.
4	Gulmarg P.O., T.O., hotel E.—	7	67	......	......	8500	S.T. moderate in season, G.F. plentiful, W. distant.	Sanitarium and bazar in season.

There is another road to Gulmarg by Baramulla, the whole distance from Srinagar to Baramulla being by water 60 miles round by Woolar Lake, or 50 miles by the Noru canal between Shadipur and Sopur, or by carriage road via Patan 35 miles. From Baramulla there is a good road ascending a spur on to the table land and along this watershed to Kontra 11 miles, where it crosses the Ningul river and joins the Sopur road onwards by Baba Marishi to Gulmarg 7 miles. Total 18 miles.

XLI SRINAGAR to JHELUM by JHELUM VALLEY :—

No.	Place			Down Jhelum	Road	Bridge	Elevation	Supplies	Remarks
1	Srinagar P.O., T.O., C., E.— Herpot	0 3	13 19	Down Jhelum left bank to Kohala.	Carriage road bridged and metalled under construction to Baramulla.	Amiran Kadal Dudh Gunga bridge Sukuag bridge	5235	S.G.F.W. and T. abundant	Capital of Kashmir State, military cantonment and fort, large city and bazar, &c.
	Patan E.— Bulgaon	19	27	......	......	Ningul bridge	5200	S.G.F.T. available, W. from springs.	Village and ancient ruins, road turns off to Gulmarg.
2	Baramulla P.O., T.O., D.B.C.E. Sher Buoninar	16	35 39 49	......	Carriage road through to Kohala, bridged and metalled.	Kechama bridge. Harpetkai bridge.	5175 5000	S.G.F.W plentiful, T. after indice.	Town, bazar and tehsil. Ancient Bhuddist temples.

Number of Marches	Names of Stages	Distance in Miles and Furlongs — Intermediate m. f.	Total m. f.	Nature of Route.	Main Valleys and Mountain Passes.	River Crossings and Lakes.	Altitude above Sea Level in Feet.	Supplies and Transport at Stages.	Remarks.
XLI	ROUTE—contd.	...	49 4						
3	**Rampur** P.O., T.O., D.B., E.—	15 5	50 5	This hill road recently constructed passes through metamorphic rocks between Baramulla and Uri and the Murree rock formation, hence to Kohala.	...	...	4900	S. G. F. W. moderate, few coolies.	Beautiful camping ground on terrace lined with deodars.
4	**Uri** P. O., T. O., D. B., E. continued—	13 3	62 ...		...	Namila bridge	4390	S. G. F. procurable, W. scarce, few coolies.	Village on fine plateau well cultivated. Fort and tehsil.
			64 ...			...	...		
			63		...	Islamabad „			
			75 ...		...	Opi „			
5	**Chakoti** D. B., E. very small—	13 4	77 4	After heavy rain landslips are liable to occur owing to the friable nature of the shaly rocks.	Down Jhelum valley on left bank.	...	3700	S. G. F. W. moderate, T. available.	Small village on cultivated plain.
	Chenar stage	...	82 2						
	Neli	...	86 2						
6	**Hatian**	10 6	88 2		...	Hatian bridge	3000	S. G. F. T. moderate, W. plentiful.	Police post, old D. B. in ruins.
	Ser neck	...	93 6						
7	**Garhi** P. O., E., D. B.—	10 4	98 6	...	...	...	2700	S. G. F. W. and T. available.	Open, cultivated plain, large village on opposite bank.

No.	Stage / Place	m.	f.	Total m.	f.	Remarks (geology / route)		Bridges	Elevation	Water & Supplies	Remarks
8	**Dumel** (P. O., T. O., D. B., E. moderate—)	13	4	112	2	The same Murree rock formation continues down the Jhelum valley to Owen ferry where it gradually merges into the Sewalik or tertiary formation.	......	......	2225	S. G. F. W. plentiful, T. available.	Bazar, junction of Jhelum and Kishengunga rivers.
	Rara			117	6						
9	**Dulai** (D. B., E. very small—)	9	2	121	4		......	......	2105	S. G. F. W. procurable, few coolies after notice.	Hamlet.
	Chatar			125	..			Agar bridge	2029		
	Barsala			132	..				2010	......	Bungalow reserved for H. H. Maharaja.
10	**Kohala** (P. O., T. O., D. B., E. very small—)	12		133	4	From Kohala ascend cart-road 7 m. 3,108f., and descend footpath sharply to Kojadar, thence keep along old road made by Captain Hall, Dy. Commr. of Pindi, along right bank down to Soha.	Down Jhelum valley right bank.	Jhelum bridge	1916	Ditto	Small bazar, customs post. Jhelum river.
				140	4			......	1868 / 3108		
11	**Kopadar ferry**	10	4	144	..			......	1815	S. from Jhanjhana, G. F. W. plentiful, T. nil.	Used by men carrying timber to Murree.
12	**Malot or Dhara ferry**	10		154	..			......	1677	S. from Malot, G. F. W. plentiful, few coolies.	Crossing of road from Poonch to Murree.
13	**Rampatan**	10		164	..	This old road much neglected and in bad order, has become very difficult for laden animals.		......	1568	S. precarious, G. F. W. plentiful, T. nil.	Ditto.
	Makroch	+		167	..				2205		
14	**Luchmun Bhatea**	7		171	..			......	1480	S. from Baroi, G. F. W. plentiful, T. nil.	Crossing of Poonch and Rawal Pindi road.

Number of Marches	Names of Stages	Intermediate m. f.	Total m. f.	Nature of Route	Main Valleys and Mountain Passes	River Crossings and Lakes	Altitude above Sea Level in Feet	Supplies and Transport at Stages	Remarks
XLI	ROUTE—contd.								
	Soha	7	171	From Soha there is only a footpath down the valley to Tangrot. This path leaves the river in many places to surmount high cliffs which project into the river.	......	......	1409	......	Soha village 2,650ft.
15	Owen ferry	11	176		......	......	1360	S. & T. from Bewar, G. F. plentiful, W. springs.	Crossing of road from Poonch to Mandra Railway Station.
	Kanzard		182				1380	S. from shop, W. springs.	
	Sokberi		186				......		
			191					S. from shop, G. F. plentiful, few coolies.	
16	Salgraon ferry	14	195		......	......	1210		Crossing of road from Kotli to Mandra Railway Station.
17	Dangrali or Palalian ferry	13	209	Only coolies lightly laden can traverse this track, and ponies cannot be led over it.	......	......	1080	S. from Palalan, G. F. W. plentiful, few coolies.	Crossing of road from Kotli to Gujarkhan Railway Station.
	Hti ferry		216				1010		
18	Bagham ferry	10	219		......	......	970	S. G. F. W. plentiful, T. available.	Large village.
19	Tangrot ferry	10	229	From Tangrot fair road passable for laden animals to Shikarpur, whence rough cart-road over open cultivated plain to Jhelum.	Down Jhelum valley right bank	......	870	S. G. F. W. T. procurable.	Junction of Poonch and Jhelum rivers.
	Mangla ferry		237		......	......			Fort on left bank in Kashmir territory.
20	Shikarpur B.—	12	241				810	S. G. F. W. and T. procurable after notice.	Small village.

No.	Place						Remarks
	Kutidli ferry	...	344	...	......	......	Crossing of road from Mirpar to Jhelum.
	Sukchainpur	...	297	...	......	780	Forest depot on left bank in Kashmir.
21	Jhelum P.O., T.O., D.B., C., E.	13	254	...	S.G.F.W and T. abundant.	740	Cantonment, civil station, town, head-quarters of district, station on N.-W. Ry.

On this route from Kohala to Jhelum, the heights of river at each crossing are given. The section Kohala to Tangrot is not passable for laden mules or riding ponies, and is used only by occasional fishermen who find grand sport. From Tangrot small and large boats can be floated down the rapids to Jhelum City.

Where vertical cliffs project into the river, the only way is to cross over to left bank, if there is a convenient ferry or to surmount the hill spur above and descend again to right bank.

The halting places are at the ferries, and the ground for camping very small. A traveller should take through transport, unless he can afford to wait at each stage and give notice to the nearest large village for coolies.

From Uri 64 miles, a road branches off southwards over the Haji Pir pass to Poonch 98 miles, see Route XXX, and for its continuation to Kotli 128 miles, and to Jhelum 197 miles, see Route XXIV, which is much shorter and easier than following down the Jhelum valley.

For the Poonch and Murree road crossing at Dhara ferry, see Route XXVII.
For the Poonch and Rawal Pindi road crossing at Latchman Bhatea, see Route XXVI.

XLII SRINAGAR to RAWUL PINDI by MURREE:—

No.	Place							Remarks
	Srinagar P.O., T.O., C., E.—	...	0 ...	Amiran Kadal Dudh Gunga bridge.	Down Jhelum valley on left bank.	Carriage road under construction bridged and metalled to Baramula.	5335	S.G.F.W.T. abundant.	Large city, fort, summer capital of Kashmir State. Road branches to Gulmarg.
	Parrwa Chowa	...	9 ...	Sukting bridge.			......	
	Harprat	...	5 ... 13 ...	......				
1	Patan E.—	19 ...	19 ...	...		......	5200	S.G.F.T. available, W. from springs.	Small village, two ancient Hindu temples in ruins.

Number of Marches.	Names of Stages.	Distance in miles and furlongs.		Nature of Route.	Main Valleys and Mountain Passes.	River crossings and Lakes.	Altitude above Sea Level in Feet.	Supplies and Transport at Stages.	Remarks.
		Inter-mediate. m. f.	Total. m. f.						
XLIII	ROUTE—contd.								
	Pokhallan	19	19	.....	.....	.....	.....	.....	Road branches to Gulmarg.
	Bulgaon	.....	21	.....	.....	.....	.....	.....	Road branches to Sopur.
		.....	27	.....	.....	Niugul bridge	.....	.....	
2	Baramulla P. O., T. O., D. B., E.	16	35	Carriage road through to Rawul Pindi used by all wheeled traffic, bridged and metalled.	.....	.....	5175	S. G. F. W. plentiful, T. after notice.	Town, bazar, tehsil, temple ruins at Uskam.
	Sher	.....	39 4	.....	.....	Kechama bridge.	.....	.....	Wide plain, cultivated.
	Naoshera	.....	46	.....	.....	Naoshera bridge.	.....	.....	Road branches to Gulmarg.
		.....	48	.....	.....	.....	.....	.....	Ancient Buddhist temple.
	Bhunsiar	:	49 2	.....	.....	Harpetkai bridge.	5000	.....	Saw mill, workshop, residence of Road Engineer.
3	Rampur P. O., T. O., D. B., E.	15 5	50 5	From Baramulla to Uri, the road traverses metamorphic rocks, and from Uri to Tret passes through the Mur-	.....	.....	4900	S. G. F. W. T. moderate.	Beautiful camping ground on terrace lined by deodar trees.
		::	57	.....	.....	.....	.....	.....	Ancient temple in ruins.
		::	62	.....	.....	Namila bridge.	.....	.....	

No.	Name of place			Total miles		Remarks on road	Bridge	Elevation	Supplies	Description
4	**Uri** *P.O., T.O., D.B., E.—*	13	3	64	...	ree rock formation. This road is liable to landslips after heavy rain and snow owing to the friable nature of the shaly rocks.		4390	S.G.F.T. procurable, W. scarce.	Village on fine plateau, well cultivated, small fort, tehsil.
	Bujadanga			65	4		Islamabad bridge.		......	Cliffs gorge.
	Dardkot			69	2				......	Ditto.
	Baranbat			71					......	Ditto.
	Opi			74, 75			Opi bridge.			
5	**Chakuti** *D.B., E. small—*	13	4	77	4			3700	S.G.F.W. moderate, T. available.	Small village on cultivated plain.
	Chenar stage			82	2				......	Kathai, residence of Nawab Sultan Mahomed Khan, on right bank.
	Neli			86	2	The worst months are usually March and April when the snow melts, and the spring rain sets in.	Neli bridge			Plateau above road.
6	**Hatian** *Ser neck*	10	6	88	2		Hatian bridge	3000	S.G.F.T. moderate, W. plentiful.	Police post, old D.B. in ruins.
				93	6					
7	**Garhi** *P.O., D.B., E.—*	10	4	98	6			2700	S.G.F.W. and T. available.	Cultivated plain. Large village, Hatian on right bank.
8	**Dumel** *P.O., T.O., D.B., E. small—*	13	4	112	2	This road is usually closed to wheeled traffic from the middle of December to the middle of March, when it is covered by snow between Srinagar and Uri and for about 16 miles over the Murree hill.		2225	S.G.F.W. plentiful, T. available.	Bazar at junction of Jhelum and Kishengunga rivers.
	Kara			117	6					
9	**Dulai** *D.B., E. very small—*	9	2	121	4		Agar bridge	2105	S.G.F.W. procurable, T. after notice.	Hamlet.
	Chatar			124	4			2029		
	Bareala			126				2010		Bungalow reserved for H. H. Maharaja, and shop.
	R.—			132						

Number of Marches	Names of Stages	Distance in Miles and Furlongs		Nature of Route	Main Valleys and Mountain Passes	River Crossings and Lakes	Altitude above Sea Level in Feet	Supplies and Transport at Stages	Remarks
		Intermediate m. f.	Total m. f.						
XLII	ROUTE—contd.								
10	Kohala P. O., T. O., D. B., E. very small—	... 12	132 133		... Down Jhelum valley right bank.	Jhelum bridge	1916 1925	S. G. F. W. procurable, T. after notice.	Small bazar and customs post.
11	Phagwari Resot, Road bungalow	... 12 2½	135 145 147	When this Murree section is blocked by snow, travellers follow the old bridle road between Kohala and Dewal to Murree	Ascent of Murree hill.	Kunair bridge		S. G. F. W. available, T. nil.	Village with two shops.
	Jhika gully	...	157				6800		Bridle road from Murree to Dewal crosses.
	Keldauka	...	160	.....	.....			......	Road branches to the gullies and Abbottabad.
12	Sunny bank under Murree Lodging house—	... 15 2½	161	Excellent hill carriage road, hence to Rawul Pindi, well maintained.	Descent of Murree hill.		6600	S. G. F. plentiful, W. from new supply, T. ample.	Murree is a civil and military sanitarium with large bazar.
	Murree Brewery Gora Gali	...	165 166				5200		
13	Tret P. O., D. B., E.— Chottar garden	... 11 2½	172 174 179	.....	.....	Salgram bridge.	2900	S. G. F. W. procurable, T. nil.	Small bazar.

14	Barakao *D. B., E.—*	12	...	184 2 / 188 2	......	......	Barakao causeway. Pungrel causeway.	1950	Ditto	Two shops and police post.
15	Rawul Pindi *P. O., T. O., D. B., hotels, C., E.—*	13 4	197 6	...	......	......	......	1700	S. G. F. W. and T. abundant.	Large military cantonment, civil station, large city, head-quarters of district and station on N.-W. Ry.

At Domel 112 miles 2 furlongs, a road 1¼ mile long after crossing the Jhelum river by at present a temporary wire rope suspension bridge branches to Mozufferabad, a town and head-quarters of zillah at the entrance of the Kishengunga valley.

Another road forks out to Abbottabad, see Route XLIII.

Murree Church is distant 3 miles, from Sunny bank 161 miles, and, as a rule, most travellers prefer halting in Murree, where there are good hotels and a club.

From Murree there are 2 roads westwards to Abbottabad, for the upper, see Route XXVII, and for the lower, see Route IXa.

From Kohala there is an old bridle road up the hill spur to Dewal 11 miles, Jhika gully 18 miles, and Murree 20 miles.

XLIIIa HATIAN to KOHALA by OLD ROAD—

6	Hatian	...	...	88 2	Fair track ascending to Chikar.	......	Hatian bridge. Hatian ford	3000	S. G. F. T. moderate, W. plentiful.	Police post.
7	Chikar	10	...	98 2 / 99 ... / 102 ...	......	Basoli gully Across Agar valley.	...	......	S. G. F. T. W. procurable.	Village. Pir Punjal range.
8	Maira	8	...	106 2 / 109 4	......	Agar ford	......		Ditto	Village.
9	Danna	7	...	113 2	Steep descent to Jhelum river.	......	......	......	S. G. F. W. plentiful.	Large village.

Number of Marches	Names of Stages	Distance in miles and furlongs — Intermediate m. f.	Total m. f.	Nature of Route.	Main Valleys and Mountain Passes.	River Crossings and Lakes.	Altitude above Sea Level, in Feet.	Supplies and Transport at Stages.	Remarks.
XLII	*ROUTE—contd.*	7 ...	113 2						
10	Kohala	7 ..	120 2	......	.....	Jhelum bridge	1916	S.G. F. W. procurable, T. after notice.	Small bazar and customs post.

From Garhi 98 miles 6 furlongs another short cut may be made by climbing up the hill at the back of the Dak Bungalow to the Kot village, 3,000 feet, thence descending gradually down the Agar valley to Chatar on the Jhelum road 114 miles, thus saving 12 miles. The path is fair but stony, and fit only for men on foot.

XLIII SRINAGAR to KALAKE SERAI or HASSAN ABDAL by ABBOTTABAD—

Number of Marches	Names of Stages	Distance in miles and furlongs — Intermediate m. f.	Total m. f.	Nature of Route.	Main Valleys and Mountain Passes.	River Crossings and Lakes.	Altitude above Sea Level, in Feet.	Supplies and Transport at Stages.	Remarks.
1	**Srinagar** *P. O., T. O., C., E.—*	...	0 ...	Carriage road under construction to Baramulla, or go by boat down Jhelum river and through Woolar Lake 60 miles. If Noru canal between Shadipur and Sopur be open, then 50 miles.	Down Jhelum valley on left bank.	Amiran Kadal	5235	S.G. F. W. and T. abundant.	Large city, fort, bazar and summer capital of Kashmir state.
	Purana Chowni	...	2 ...			Dudh Gunga bridge.			
	Harprat	...	5 ..						
		...	13 ..			Soknag bridge.			
	Patan *E.—*	19 ...	19 ...			......	5200	S.G. F. T. available, W. from springs.	Small village, two ancient Hindu temples in ruins.
	Pothallan	...	21			......	...	......	Road branches to Gulmarg 17 miles.
	Bulgaon	...	27 ..	.....	......	Ningrul bridge	...	......	Road branches to Sopur 4 miles.

No.	Name of stage and place	Dist.		Total		Road	Cross Jhelum river to right bank.	Ford or bridge.	Elevation in feet.	Supplies, water, fuel.	Remarks.
2	**Baramulla** P.O., T.O., D.B., E.—	16	...	35	...	......	Cross Jhelum river to right bank.	Jhelum bridge.	5175	S. G. F. W. plentiful, T. after notice.	Town, bazar, tehsil.
	Bhimbiar	...	...	45	...	......	......	Limber ford.	......	......	Gypsum alabaster quarries 3 miles up side valley.
				47			......				
	Tatamulla	...	...	49	...	Fair hill road passable for laden animals but difficult in places.	......	......	4846	......	Jagir of Dewan Lachmun Doss.
3	**Gingl** E.—	18	...	53	...	......	......	Bijhama bridge.	4618	S. G. F. W. procurable, few coolies.	Bijhama 2 miles up side valley, summer residence of Nawab Sultan Mahomed Khan.
				55			......	Dodiali bridge.			
	Dawaren Old Imperial serai in ruins	...	...	56	...	......	......	......	......	......	Ancient ruins of city and temple.
	Dína	...	...	59	...	......	......	......	4283	......	
4	**Shadera** B.—	12	2	63	2	Rough hill road stony with many ascents and descents and much cut up after heavy rain.	......	......	4798	Ditto	Ditto.
				65			Kumar must	......	4294		
				69				......	4682		
5	**Kathai** E.—	10	6	76	...	......	......	Kathai ford.	3665	S. G. F. W. and T. available.	Winter residence of Nawab Sultan Mahomed Khan.
	Peliasa	...	...	79	2	......	Cowlanda	......	4045	......	
				80			......	Peliasa ford.			
6	**Khunda**	8	6	84	6	......	......	......	3540	S. scarce, G. F. W. procurable, T. nil.	Small village.
	Dopatta	...	...	92	...	......	......	Dopatta ford.	......	......	Old fort.
7	**Hattian** *Medsi*	10	...	94	6	Good hill road onwards.	......	......	2665	S. G. F. W. and T. available.	Large village.
				97			......	Dwarsida ford.			

No. of Marches	Names of Stages	Distance Inter. m. f.	Distance Total m. f.	Nature of Route	Main Valleys and Mountain Passes	River Crossings and Lakes	Altitude above Sea Level in Feet	Supplies and Transport at Stages	Remarks
XLIII	ROUTE—contd.	...	97						
8	Muzafferabad P. O., T. O., D. B. at Dumel, C., E.—	13 2	108	Rough track very stony and much cut up, steep approaches to pass on both sides.		Kishenganga bridge.	2252	S. G. F.W. plentiful, T. after notice.	Town, fort, bazar, head-quarters of zillah. Old Imperial serai.
			109				4556		
			115 4	Fair hill road passable for ekkas.	Doob gully	......	2848		
9	Garhi Habibulla P. O., D. B., C., E. small	10 4	118 4			Nausook or Kunhar bridge	4004	S. G. F W and T. available.	Large village and bazar.
			125 6			Ichur bridge	3360		
10	Mansera P. O., D. B., E.—	18	133 4	Fair cart-road earthen.	Batrasi gully	Batti „	3540	S. G. F. W. and T. plentiful.	Large village and tehsil.
			136 4						
11	Abbottabad P. O., T. O., D. B., E.—	16	152 4	Good road bridged and metalled.	Sulhud pass		4005	S. G. F. W. and T. ample.	Military cantonment, civil station, town, head-quarters of district Hazara.
			153	Tonga dak runs to Hassan Abdal.	......	Dor ford	2700		
			161						
	Chamba E. C., E.—		163	......			2010	S. G. F. W. after notice, T. nil.	Halting place.
	Haripur P. O., T. O., D. B., C., E.—	23 2	175 6	......			1730	S. G. F. W. and T. plentiful.	Town, bazar, tehsil.
	Hattar		189	......		Haro ford	......	S. G. F. after notice, W. from well, T. nil.	Halting place.
	Batar tope		191	......			1600		

13	Kala-ke Serai P.O., T.O., D.B.— or	21	2	197	...		1690	S.G.F.T. after notice, W. from well.	Railway station on N.-W. Railway.
	Hassan Abdal P.O., T.O., D.B.; 1¼ mile from railway station.	19	...	194	6		1400	S.G.F.W. and T. available.	Ditto.

From Pellasa 80 miles there is a track up the side valley northwards over the Hattian gulli of the Kajnag range which descends into the Karna valley to Titwal on the Kishengunga river 20 miles.

From Malsi 97 miles there is a track up the Dwarsida valley across the Kajnag range and descends down the ravine which leads to Noseri Nausada on the Kishengunga river about 16 miles in length.

From the old Imperial serai at Mozufferabad 109 miles there is an alternative route by the Lohar gulli 3,459 feet 112 miles, to Garhi Habibulla 118½ miles. This track is passable for laden animals.

From Garhi Habibulla northwards, there is a good road up the Kunhar valley on both banks to Balakot 12½ miles, a populous town and trading mart of the Kaghan valley.

XLIIIa BARAMULLA to MOZUFFERABAD by TUTMARI GULLI—

2	Baramulla P.O., T.O., D.B., E.—	...	...	35	...	Fair hill road, 6 ft for riding and passable for laden animals, through to the Kishenganga valley.	5175	S.G.F.W. plentiful, T. after notice.	Town, bazar, tehsil.
	Arkaaas	:	...	40	4		5400	Vij ford. Hamal "	...	Large village.
	Yarbagh	...	...	41	...				
				42	4				
3	Ashpura E.—	14	...	49	...	Up Marwar valley left bank.	...	S.G.F.W. available, few coolies.	Ditto.
	Ashterhama	:	...	50	4	Tirna ford. Marwar "	5700	...	Ditto.
	Lach	:	...	52	...				
				54	...				
4	Lansar Naugaon E.—	9	...	58	...	...	...	S. scarce, G.F.W. moderate, few coolies after notice.	Hamlet.

Number of Marches	Names of Stages	Distance in Miles and Furlongs — Intermediate m. f.		Total m. f.		Nature of Route.	Main Valleys and Mountain Passes.	River Crossings and Lakes.	Altitude above Sea Level, in Feet.	Supplies and Transport at Stages.	Remarks.
	XLIIIa ROUTE—contd.										
5	Gruzen E.—	9	...	58	...	......	Up Jetti ravine. Tutmari gulli.	Hudnar ford	......	S. and T. nil, G. F.W. procurable.	Dak.
6	Nakot or Chanian E.—	12	..	70	..	......			......	S. scarce, G. F. W. available, few coolies.	Small village.
7	Budipura E.—	9	...	79	...	......	Down Karna valley.		......	Ditto	Ditto.
8	Titwal P. o., E.—	9	...	88	...	Hence rough and stony road, difficult for laden animals, with many steep ascents and descents, some rocky and precipitous.	Down Kishenganga valley left bank.	Karna bridge	3250	S. G. F. W. plentiful, T. available.	Village and tehsil, small fort.
9	Noseri Nausada E.—	7	...	95	...			......	3425	Ditto, T. nil.	Village.
10	Panjgram E.—	6	4	101	4			......	2900	S. G. F. W. plentiful, T. available.	Ditto.
11	Nuraseri E.—	9	...	110	4	A riding pony may be led and taken round bad places by long detours.		......	2750	Ditto, T. nil.	Ditto.

12	Mozufferabad or Dumel P. O., T. O., D. B., C., &c.—	11	...	129	..	Good road	......	2470 }	S. G. F. W. plentiful, T. after notice.	Town, bazar, head-quarters of zillah.
		1	4	130	4	Join Jhelum road	Jhelum bridge	2225 }		

The traveller might go by boat from Srinagar to Sopar or *vid* Patan by land 32 miles. Hence march up the Pohru and Marwar valleys to Langyat 46 miles, Jagir of Raja Sir Anar Singh, K.C.S.I., and join the foregoing route at Lach 54 miles. From Lach 54 miles instead of going up the Marwar valley to Tutmari gulli, the traveller might strike northwards through the beautiful undulating country of the Lolab by Nichihama to Shalura.

From Lach 54 miles this route, which is passable for laden animals, skirts the eastern flank of the Danhu or Trebella mountain, descends to Daren, and after crossing the Punjlar river comes to Rajpore 60 miles, the Jagir of Raja Akbar Ali Khan. Hence proceeding up the left bank of the Punjlar through the fine Chokchi gorge, the route forks into two branches, one westwards and one northwards.

The western track leads to Nichihama village 64 miles, where the burnt and sunken acre, Syun Nar, mentioned by Abu Fazl-i-Allani in the Ain-i-Akbari and described by Dr. Falconer and Mr. Vigne may be seen. The ground was at times so hot that, after scraping the surface, the natives used to cook their rice by placing the pans upon the cleared space.

On examination there are clear indications of the burning of an underground seam of coal from 3 to 5 feet in thickness; the outcrop of the latter is yet visible in the ravines at both extremities of the burnt acre, which has subsided, and in a section of the soil thus exposed above it, where the seam is reduced to a white ash and the adjoining clay shales to a red brick.

Similar burnt soil is found at Rampuru, in Budishung 65½ miles with coal shale outcrops in the two ravines on the borders, and again at Suktoji 67 miles in the bed of a ravine, where the coal is said to have been set on fire by the blazing pine trees and long grass of the forest, which occasionally takes fire and burns fiercely. After crossing the Tahnt river at Suktoji and ascending the hill spur northwards, the road passes through a pine forest, where the remains of artificial tanks on the ridge may be seen, to Lutchmapura 69 miles, Wyss 71 miles, Lihun 72 miles, and emerges into the open country, where it crosses a sheet of rice cultivation and the Kamil river, on the left bank of which stands Shalura 75 miles.

The northern route from Chokchi gorge goes up a glen along the western flank of the Kronbkar mountain to Sarmarg 6,400 feet, a village and pond on a lovely site 65 miles, and descends down another winding glen northwards to Kokrum 68 miles, and thence through the rice plain to Shalura 75 miles. The coal seen in the outcrops at Nichihama, Budishung and Suktoji, is of inferior quality between brown coal or lignite and peat. Other outcrops are reported at Nagi, &c., in the vicinity. The material burns well, however, and the burning ground above has been considered a phenomenon during a long period.

XLIIIb MANSERA to OGHI—

10	Mansera P. O., D. B., C., E.—	...	...	136	4	Good hill road passable for laden camels.	Across Pukli and Sirun valleys.	......	3540	S. G. F. W. and T. plentiful.	Large village and tehsil.
		...	...	143	...		Sirun ford.				

Number of Marches	Names of Stages	Distance in miles and furlongs — Intermediate m. f.	Total m. f.	Nature of Route	Main Valleys and Mountain Passes	River Crossings and Lakes	Altitude above Sea Level in Feet	Supplies and Transport at Stages	Remarks
	XLIIIb ROUTE—*contd.*	.. ..	143 ..				......		
11	Khanki E.—	8 ..	144 4		Susal pass.	......	......	S. G. F. W. procurable, T. nil.	Village.
		.. ..	147 ..	Easy pass through hills thickly wooded.					
12	Oghi P. O., E.—	10 ..	154 4	......	Agror valley at base of Black Mountain.	Oonar nala	......	S. G. F. W. and T. procurable.	Village, police and military outpost.

From Oghi there is a road through Shergurh and Nila Pani to Derband.

XLIIIc ABBOTTABAD to THANDIANI—

Number of Marches	Names of Stages	Distance in miles and furlongs — Intermediate m. f.	Total m. f.	Nature of Route	Main Valleys and Mountain Passes	River Crossings and Lakes	Altitude above Sea Level in Feet	Supplies and Transport at Stages	Remarks
11	Abbottabad P. O., T. O., D. B., E.—	.. ..	152 4	Fair hill road for riding ponies and passable for laden mules level to Nawashahr and rises beyond.	......	Jub nala	4005	S. G. F. W. and T. ample.	Head-quarters of district Hazara.
		.. ..	155 ..		......	Darhan „	......		
	Nawashahr	.. ..	157 ..		Across head of Dor river.	......	......	......	Large village.
		1 ..	165 ..		......	Dor nala.			
12	Thandiani	.. ..	169 ..	......	......	......	8600	S. and T. moderate in season, G. F. W. plentiful.	Small sanitarium.

XLIIId HARIPUR to DERBUND—

No.	Place			Miles		Road	Valley	Ford	Elev.	Supplies	Remarks
12	Haripur P.O., T.O., D.B., C., E.	...	...	175	6	Rough cart-road passable for ekkas.	Down Dohr valley.	......	1730	S. G. F. W. and T. plentiful.	Town, bazar, tehsil.
13	Barukot or Torbela P.O., E.—	8	2	184	:	......	......	Dohr forded twice. Sirun ford.	......	S. and T. after notice, G. F. W. procurable.	Village.
14	Nawangiran	10	...	194	...	No water, road between Barukot and Nawangiran, rocky and difficult.	Up Indus valley left bank.	......	......	S. and T. precarious, G. F. W. available.	Small village.
15	Derbund P.O., E.—	10	...	204	...	......	......	......	......	S. and T. after notice, G. F. W. procurable.	Village in Tanawal opposite Uab, where Nawab resides.

The route by Torbela on the left bank of the Indus is longer by 10 miles but preferable for water.
There is another route across the hills and down Sirun valley from Abbottabad by Sherwan, Bhir, Tapla to Torbela.

XLIV SRINAGAR to MOZUFFERABAD by NESCHAU or NATTISHANAR GULLI—

No.	Place			Miles		Road	Valley	Ford	Elev.	Supplies	Remarks
	Srinagar P.O., T.O., C., E.—	...	.	0	...	Carriage road under construction to Buḷgaon, might be continued across plain to Sopur where there is a good bridge across Jhelum river.	Down Jhelum valley.	Amiran Kadal	5235	S. G. F. W. and T. abundant	Capital of Kashmir State.
	Harpat	...	:	13	...			Suk nag ″			Large town, bazar and Hari Parbat fort.
1	Patan E.—	19	...	19	...			......	5200	S. G. F. T. available, W. from springs.	Small village and ancient ruins.

Number of Marches	Names of Stages	Distance in miles and furlongs. Intermediate m. f.	Total m. f.	Nature of Route.	Main Valleys and Mountain Passes.	River Crossings and Lakes.	Altitude above Sea Level in Feet.	Supplies and Transport at Stages.	Remarks.
XLIV	ROUTE—contd.	...	...						
	Balgaon	...	19	...	...	Ningrl Kadal			
2	Sopur P.O., T.O., B., C., E.—	13	27	...	Up Pohru valley left bank.	Jhelum bridge	5185	S. G. F. W. and T. plentiful.	Town, bazar and head-quarters of Zillah Kamraj. Road branches to Lalpura 12 miles.
	Arenu	...	32	From Sopur the road is good and passable for laden animals through to Titwal on Kishengunga.	...	...	...		Village.
3	Chogul E.—	15	43		...	...	...	S. G. F. W. and T. available.	
	Wadpoora Warpoora	...	47		...	...	...		
	Shalura E.—	...	51 57	...	Right bank	Pohru river.			
4		16	63		Up Kamil valley left bank.	Kamil ford or bridge.	5300	Ditto after notice	Do. old fort, shop.
	Panagram	...	66 71	Easy and gradual ascent to pass and short steep descent.	...	Kamil bridge		S. G. F. W. and T. available.	Large village.
5	Drungiari E.—	12	75	...	Up Pulhai ravine. Neschau gulli Down Karma valley to Titwal.	...	...	S. and T. nil, G. F. W. procurable.	Hamlet.
	Hajinar	...	80 85	...		...	10400.		

No.	Name of stage	Dist.	Total	Remarks on road	Direction	Bridge	Elevation (feet)	Supplies	Remarks
6	Tungta or Karna E.—	14	89	......	......	......	......	S. G. F. W. moderate, few coolies	Small fort.
	Tikeal P.O. E.—	...	95	......	......	Karna bridge	3250	Ditto	Tehsil and small fort.
7	Panjhot E.—	12	101	The road rises up from Kishengunga river to higher region, is more difficult but cooler than lower road.	Down Kishengunga valley left bank.	......	......	S. and T. scanty, G. F. W. available.	Small village.
8	Partan E.—	12	113	......	......	......	......	Ditto	Ditto.
9	Dunna E.—	10	123	Long descent from Dunna to the Kishenganga river.	......	......	......	Ditto	Ditto.
10	Nura Seri E.—	10	133	Road along left bank of river bal.	......	......	2750	S. G. F. W. plentiful, T. nil.	Ditto.
11	Mozufferabad or Dumel P.O., T.O., B., C., E.—	11	144	......	......	......	2470	S. G. F. W. plentiful, T. after notice.	Town, bazar and head-quarters of zillah.
		1	145	......	......	Jhelum bridge	2225	......	

This pass is closed by snow from November to February inclusive, when another adjoining pass to the north, Kukwa gulli 9,550 feet from the Karna valley into the Rungwari ravine, which flows into the Kamil river, one mile below Drungiari, is used. The approaches are steeper, but the through distance is the same.

XLIVa SHALURA to KAGHAN VALLEY by KAREN—

No.	Name of stage	Dist.	Total	Remarks on road	Direction	Bridge	Elevation (feet)	Supplies	Remarks
4	Shalura E.—	...	63	This track is easily passable for laden animals to Karen.	Up Wurassoon valley.	......	5300	S. G. F. W. and T. after notice.	Village, shop, old fort.

No. of Marches	Names of Stages	Intermediate m. f.	Total m. f.	Nature of Route	Main Valleys and Mountain Passes	River Crossings and Lakes	Altitude above Sea Level in Feet	Supplies and Transport at Stages	Remarks
XLIV.	ROUTE—contd.								
5	Wurassoon E.—	...	63 ...	......	......	......	......	S. G. F. W. and T. after notice.	Village.
6	Doodi E.— Monaiyan	6 ...	69 ...	Easy approaches to pass on both sides.	Down Doodi valley.	Putran-ke gali.	10175.	S. and T. nil, G. F. W. plentiful.	Halting place.
		...	74 ...				7400	S. G. F. W. plentiful, T. available.	Village.
7	Karen E.— Nogdara	10 ...	77 ...	Hence the road becomes more difficult and is bad in many places.	Up Babun-ka Katta.	Kishenganga wooden bridge	4650	......	Ditto.
		...	84 ...						
8	Karka E.—	10 ...	87 ...	......	Chirik gali	......	......	S. and T. nil, G. F. W. plentiful.	Halting place.
		...	90 ...						
9	Kensi E.—	10 ...	97 ...	From the Jagran valley to the Kaghan valley the track is rather better.	Across Jagran valley. Shikara gali Down Shikara valley.	......	......	S. and T. nil, G. F. W. available.	Small village.
		...	100 ...						
10	Shikara E.—	12 ...	109 ...			......	......	Ditto	Halting place.
		10 ...	119 ...						
11	Jared E.—	11 ...	130 ...	...	Kaghan valley	......	......	S. and T. scarce, G. F. W. available.	Small village.

Between Wurasoon and Doodi, there is a choice of 3 passes over this mountain range, of which Putrao-ke gali is the middle one. The other two are Treldubul and Mulla passes.

From Karen there are other routes to the Kaghan valley by going up or down the Kishenganga valley and striking up one of the side valleys leading westwards, the foregoing is said to be the one at present used by traders in ghi and salt.

From Kenzi, in the Jagran valley, there are 3 passes, Bichla, Shikara and Tor gali into the Khagan valley, and the middle one is here shown.

Jared is a stage on the Kaghan valley road, 5 miles from Bhunja, 25 miles north of Balakot, and 15 miles south of Khagan, all three trading marts.

XLV SRINAGAR to KAGHAN VALLEY by DRAWAR—

No.	Stage		Total	Road	Direction	River/crossing	Elev.	Supplies	Remarks
	Srinagar *P. O., T. O., C., E.—*	...	0	Carriage road under construction to Bulgaon, might be continued to Sopur, where there is a good bridge over the Jhelum river.	Down Jhelum valley.	Amiran Kadal	5235	S. G. F. W. and T. abundant.	Capital of Kashmir State. Large town, bazar and Hari Parbat fort.
	Harpat	...	13			Suknag "			
1	Patan *E.—*	19	19				5200	S. G. F. W. and T. available, W. from springs.	Small village and ancient ruins.
	Bulgaon	...	27			Ningul "			
2	Sopur *P.O., T. O., B., C., E.*	13	32	From Sopur the road is good and passable for laden animals through to the Kishenganga river in Drawar.	Up Pohru valley.	Jhelum bridge	5185	S. G. F. W. and T. plentiful.	Town, bazar and head-quarters of Zillah Kamraj. Road branches north to Lalpura 12 miles.
	Arwan	...	43			......		......	
3	Chogul *E.—*	15	47					S. G. F. W. and T. available.	Village.
	Wadpoora	...	51			Pohru river.			
4	Mogulpur *E.—*	11	58					S. G. F. T. after notice, W. plentiful.	Ditto.
		...	61			Kamil bridge.			
5	Lodrdona *E.—*	8	66	Easy gradual ascent and descent.	Seetalwan or Zurkaima gal.	......	9800	Ditto	Ditto.
		...	70						

Number of Marches.	Names of Stages.	Distance in miles and furlongs. Intermediate. m. f.	Total. m. f.	Nature of Route.	Main Valleys and Mountain Passes.	River crossings and Lakes.	Altitude above Sea Level in feet.	Supplies and Transport at Stages.	Remarks.
XLV	ROUTE—contd.								
6	Jimagun E.—	...	70 ..	...	Down Chor-baila valley.	......	7000	S. and T. nil, G. F. W. plentiful.	Halting place.
7	Dudnial in Dra-war. E.—	9 ...	75 ..	...	Kishengunga river.	......	5850	S. G. F. W. plentiful, T. nil.	Village.

Hence there are two routes to the Rutti gali leading into the Kaghan valley, one by Deorian and the other by Kurigam.

FIRSTLY—

Number of Marches.	Names of Stages.	Distance in miles and furlongs. Intermediate. m. f.	Total. m. f.	Nature of Route.	Main Valleys and Mountain Passes.	River crossings and Lakes.	Altitude above Sea Level in feet.	Supplies and Transport at Stages.	Remarks.
8	Deorian E.—	7 ...	91 ..	This track is used by laden mules, though difficult in many places.	Up Seri valley	Kishengunga river.	5050	S. G. F. W. plentiful, T. available.	Village.
9	Dari E.—	12 ...	103 .. 108 ..	This pass is said to have steep approaches on both sides.	...... Rutti gali. Down	......	......	S. and T. nil, G. F. W. plentiful.	Halting place.
10	Jora E.—	16 ...	119 ..	...	Dhawartala or Jora Katta	......	......	Ditto	Ditto.
11	Burawai E.—	9 ...	128 ..	...	Kaghan valley.	......	......	Ditto	Ditto.

Burawai is 17 miles 6 furlongs distant and north of Narung the highest village up the Kaghan road.

SECONDLY—

No.	Name	Int.	Total	Nature of road	Pass / valley	River crossed	Elevation	Supplies	Remarks
8	**Kurigam** E.—	9	93 / 102	......	Kurigam gali.	Kishenganga river.	5850	S. and T. procurable, G. F. W. plentiful.	Village near Shardi.
9	**Dari** E.—	12	105 / 110	Steep ascent and descent over pass.	Rutti gali.	Across head of Seri nala.	......	S. and T. nil, G. F. W. plentiful.	Halting place.
10	**Jora** E.—	16	121	......	Down Dhawar-tala nulla or Jora Katta.	......	......	Ditto	Ditto.
11	**Burawai** E.—	9	130	......	Kaghan valley.	......	9330	Ditto	Ditto.

Burawai has excellent pasture and is much frequented in summer by numerous flocks of sheep and goats and by herds of cattle.

XLVI SRINAGAR to CHILAS by KAMAK DURI PASS—

No.	Name	Int.	Total	Nature of road	Direction	River / Bridge	Elevation	Supplies	Remarks
	Srinagar P. O., T. O., C., E.—	......	0	Carriage road under construction to Bulgaon and might be continued 5 miles further to Sopur where there is a good bridge over the Jhelum river.	Down Jhelum valley.	Amiran Kadal	5235	S. G. F. W. and T. abundant.	Capital of Kashmir State. Large town, bazar, Hari Parbat fort.
	Harpat	......	13	......	......	Suknag ,,	......	S. G. F. T. available, W. from springs.	......
1	**Patan** E.—	19	19	......	......	......	5200	S. G. F. T. available, W. from springs.	Village and ancient ruins.
	Bulgaon	......	27	......	......	Ningul ,,	......	......	......
2	**Sopur** P. O., T. O., B., C., E.	13	32	......	......	Jhelum bridge	5185	S. G. F. W. and T. plentiful.	Town, bazar and head-quarters of Zillah Kamraj.

Number of Marches	Names of Stages	Distance in miles and furlongs — Inter-mediate. m. f.	Distance in miles and furlongs — Total. m. f.	Nature of Route	Main Valleys and Mountain Passes.	River crossings and Lakes.	Altitude above Sea Level in feet.	Supplies and Transport at Stages.	Remarks.
XLVI	ROUTE—contd.								
3	Arwan E.—	13 ..	32 ..		.....	.....	.....	S. and T. after notice, G. F. W. available.	Village.
4	Lalpura P. O., G., E.—	12 ..	44 ..	Hence a good road passable for laden animals through to Shardi on the Kishengunga. The Wyana pass is quite easy both ways.	Wyana pass. Down Lolab valley.	.....	5600	S. G. F. W. and T. plentiful.	Capital of Lolab, town, bazar and tehsil.
		10 ..	46 ..						
			54 ..						
5	Kroras E.—	12 ..	66 ..	Up Seh valley	Up Seh valley	.....	5700	S. G. F. W. and coolies procurable.	Village.
6	Camp E.—	8 ..	74 ..	The Kuslona pass is of gradual ascent and descent.	..... Kuslona pass. Down Mokta valley.	.. ..	10500.	S. and T. nil, G. F. W. procurable.	Halting place at foot of pass.
			77 ..						
7	Mokta malik E.—	10 ..	84 ..	The Lachidal pass is very steep in both ascent and descent.	Lachidal pass.	.....	.....	Ditto	Ditto.
			87 4						
8	Shardi P. O., E.—	10 ..	94 ..	From Sardi the road goes up a wide valley well wooded with a few hamlets.	Up Kankatori valley.	Kishengunga river.	5850	S. and T. procurable, G. F. W. plentiful.	Village and fort.
	Sargaon E.—	...	102 ..			.....	6550.		
9	Samgam E.—	13 ..	107 ..	....	.....	.....	6900	S. and T. precarious, G. F. W. plentiful.	Small village.
	Ganot E.—	...	112 ..	....	.....	.....	7600.		

No.	Name of place	Int.	Total	Country / direction	Nature of road	Supplies	River / bridge	Height	Remarks
10	Hole Nar E.—	10	117	...	The road is good to the foot of the pass where the climb up and run down are both very stiff and severe.	S. and T. nil, G. F. W. plentiful.	......	......	Halting place at foot of pass.
11	Nihat E.—	20	137	Kamakduri pass. Down Nihat valley.		Ditto	......	15008.	Ditto.
12	Basha E.—	11	148	Down Kanogha valley.	From Basha there is a good road to Chilas.	S. and T. after notice, G. F. W. procurable.	Kanogha bridge.	......	Village.
13	Chilas P. O., T. O., B., E.—	11	159	Indus valley.		S. G. F. W. and T. plentiful.	......	4000	Village and military post.

From Surgaon 102 miles there is a track N. E. up the Nuri Nar valley over the Nuri Nar or Julkhud pass 116 miles down the Julkhud-ka-katta to Seri 130 miles on the Kaghan road.

From Gamot 112 miles there is a track N. E. up the Siralgot nala which leads to a group of 5 passes over the dividing range. The northern pass Katora gali is said to lead down a ravine to Thak on the Kaghan road to Chilas, the north-eastern pass Siral gali leads to Dudibat Sar or glacier lake and descends down the Purbidin-ka-katta to Kotawai on the Khagan road.

At the 115th mile, a path goes west up the Kahjundi nala across the Kundi pass to Mora, see Route XLVII.

At the 117th mile, a path ascends N. W. up the Hole Nar nala to the Hole Nar pass 14,637 feet and Barai pass, 14,000 feet and descends down the Barai nala to Paloi and Bunar.

All these high passes are closed by snow during 8 months of the year from November to June inclusive, glaciers are numerous in this range which is a S. E. offshoot of Nanga Parbat Peak 26,620 feet.

XLVIa.—SRINAGAR TO LALPURA BY NAGMARG—

No.	Name of place	Total	Country / direction	Nature of road	Supplies	Point / bridge	Height	Remarks
1	Srinagar P. O., T. O., C., E.—	0	Down Jhelum valley left bank.	Carriage road for 6 miles and thence along 10-foot road earthen and bridged to Bandipura, quite passable for camels and laden animals.	S. G. F. W. and T. abundant.	Amiran Kadal	5235	Capital of Kasmir State.
	Shadipur	11 4	Right bank.			Noru bridge.		Large town, bazar, Hari Parbat fort.
	Sumbhul E.—	15 4	Right bank.		S. G. F. W. procurable, T. after notice.	Jhelum „	......	Village and some shops.
	Ajas	23 4	Along eastern border of Woolar Lake.					

Number of Marches	Names of Stages	Distance in miles and furlongs — Intermediate m. f.	Distance in miles and furlongs — Total m. f.	Nature of Route.	Main Valleys and Mountain Passes.	River Crossings and Lakes.	Altitude above Sea Level in Feet.	Supplies and Transport at Stages.	Remarks.
	XLVIa *ROUTE—contd.*	......	23 4						
2	**Bandipura** P. O., T. O., E.—	19	34 4	Road fair	Along northern shore of Woolar Lake.	......	5200	S. G. F. W. and T. plentiful.	Large village and bazar.
3	**Alsu** E.—	7 4	42	......	......	......	5200	S. G. F. W. and T. available.	Village.
4	**Nagmarg** E.—	6	48	Steep ascent and easier descent.	Tewa or Burchhai gully.	......	8100	S. and T. nil, G. F. W. available.	Sanitarium.
	Deosar	......	52						
5	**Lalpura** P. O., C., E.—	8	56	......	Lolab valley.	......	5600	S. G. F. W. and T. plentiful.	Capital of Lolab Town, bazar and tehsil.

The usual plan is to go by boat from Srinagar down the Jhelum river, and across the Woolar Lake to Alsu about 40 miles, there land and cross over the Nagmarg range into the Iolab. Nagmarg is situated along the ridge to the north of the pass. A few old huts in bad order. One of the summer resorts of Kashmir with lovely scenery and beautiful views on a fine day.

From Alsu is a fair road 12 miles to Sopur by land, passing the Shukr-ud-din Ziarat on the Watlab hill, one of the celebrated shrines of Kashmir at the 4th mile.

XLVII SRINAGAR to ASTOR by LOLAB and SHONTAR PASS—

Number of Marches	Names of Stages	Distance in miles and furlongs — Intermediate m. f.	Distance in miles and furlongs — Total m. f.	Nature of Route.	Main Valleys and Mountain Passes.	River Crossings and Lakes.	Altitude above Sea Level in Feet.	Supplies and Transport at Stages.	Remarks.
	Srinagar P. O., T. O., C., E.—	......	0	Carriage road under construction	Down Jhelum valley.	Amiran Kadal	5235	S. G. F. W. and T. abundant.	Capital of Kashmir State. Largetown,

No.	Name of stage	Intermediate	Total	Remarks on road	Direction	River	Elevation	Supplies and water	Remarks
	Harprot	......	13	......	......	......	......	......	bazar, Hari Parbat fort.
1	**Patan** *E.—*	19	19	to Bulgaon, which might be continued 5 miles further to Sopur bridge over the Jhelum river.	......	Suknag „	5200	S. G. F. and T. available, W. from springs.	Village and ancient ruins.
	Bulgaon	...	27	......	......	Ningal „	......	......	
2	**Sopur** *P.O., T.O., E., C., E.—*	...	32	Hence a good road passable for laden animals to Kroras.	Up Pohru valley left bank.	Jhelum bridge	5185	S. G. F. W. and T. plentiful.	Town, bazar and head-quarters of Zillah Kamraj.
3	**Arwan**	12	44 ... 46	...... Easy ascent and descent.	Wyana pass.	......	......	S. and T. after notice, G. F. W. available.	Village.
4	**Lalpura** *P. O., C., E.—*	10	54	......	Down Lolab valley.	......	5600	S. G. F. W. and T. plentiful.	Capital of Lolab town, bazar, tehsil.
5	**Kroras or Thien** *E.—*	12	66	From Thien above Kroras at the junction of the 2 rivers, an old road turns off north eastwards over the Ura gully, an easy pass on both sides, and thence northwards down the Machil valley to the Kishengunga. This old road is much cut up, but is passable for laden moles. After crossing the wooden bridge over the Kishengunga	Up Seh valley	......	5700	S. G. F. W. and coolies procurable.	Village.
	Sirkuli	...	70			......	6400.		
6	**Ura gully**	8	74		Down Machil valley.	......	9500.		
7	**Santwari** *E.—*	9	83		......	——!	7000.		
8	**Khel** *E.—*	13	96		Cross Kishengunga valley. Up Khel valley.	Kishengunga Bridge.	6134	S. scanty, W. G. F. plentiful, T. nil.	Ditto.
9	**Dumel Pain** *E.—*	8	104		......	...	7300	S. and T. nil, W. G. F. plentiful.	Junction of Barai river.
10	**Shontar** *E.—*	8	112 ... 122		Shontar pass	....	10000 15052	Ditto	Halting place south of pass.

Number of Marches	Names of Stages	Distance in miles and furlongs — Intermediate m. f.	Distance in miles and furlongs — Total m. f.	Nature of Route	Main Valleys and Mountain Passes	River crossings and Lakes	Altitude above Sea Level in Feet	Supplies and Transport at Stages	Remarks
	XLVII ROUTE—contd.	...	122	river, the track continues good to the foot of the Shontar pass, where there is a stiff climb to the top, on the north side the road is of easy gradient over marg country to Rattu where is the junction of Kamri pass route. Join 10-foot road Srinagar to Gilgit earthen and bridged.			...		
11	**Duman** E.—	18	130		Down Mir Malik valley.	Dabin ford	...	S. and T. nil, W. G. F. plentiful.	Junction of ravine which leads to Dolaban Pir.
12	**Mir Malik** E.—	8	138		......	......	9083	S. procurable, T. nil, G. F. W. plentiful.	Village.
	Rattu	...	146			......	8299		
13	**Chugam** E.—	10 4	148 4		Down Guraigah or Astor valley left bank.	Rupal bridge.	...	S. and G. scanty, W. and F. procurable, T. nil.	Ditto.
		4	152						
14	**Gurikot** E. confined.—	10 4	159		......	Astor bridge	7800	S. and G. scanty, F. W. available, T. nil.	Ditto.
15	**Astor (Idgah)** P. O., T. O., B.— E. polo ground.—	7	166	......	......	......	7838	S. and G. procurable, F. and W. plentiful, T. moderate.	Village, fort, bazar, bungalow will be built, residence of Raja of Astor or Hasora.

From Lalpura 54 miles there is another route by Kranan over the Bhatnar Pir gully down the Machil valley.

From Sirkuli 70 miles there is another track eastwards up the Kunchali river over the Machil pass into the Machil valley.

From Uta gully down the Machil valley are the remains of an old road once constructed by the State and bridged.

From Dumel Pain 104 miles a route branches northwards up the Barai nala by Moree 110 miles over the Barai pass 14,000 feet and 122 miles, and descends down the Barai or Bunar nala by Paloi 140 miles, and Diamirai 148 miles, to the Indus 156 miles, where it joins the Bawanji and Chilas road along left bank of this river. Bunar fort is about 3 miles west of this Bunar nala on a commanding plateau, about half way between Paloi and Diamirai.

The Shontar pass 15,052 feet b. p. according to the map, is said to be the highest of 3 gullies in this vicinity, but there is no path at present to the other two.

About 15 miles S. E. along this range, there is another pass Dohlban Pir gully 14,045 feet to which there is access on both sides, by the Phulmai nala on the south from the Kishenganga valley, and by the Daman nala on the north side from the Mir Malik valley. The easiest approach from Srinagar to the Dohlban Pir would be by Kanzilwan on the Gilgit road 62½ miles, see Route XLVIII ; thence down the Kishenganga valley by Bakhtaor 66 miles, Thaobut 73 miles, Sirdari 80 miles, the last village in this direction, Phulmai nala 87 miles, Dohlban Pir gully 100 miles, Daman 112 miles, and Mir Malik 120 miles. This would be shorter than the foregoing route, but the march from Sirdari along the right bank of the Kishenganga river to the Phulmai nala is said to be extremely difficult from the rocky cliffs projecting into the river.

XLVIII SRINAGAR to GILGIT by BURZIL (DORIKUN) PASS—

	Place					Description of road	Direction / bank	River crossed	Elevation	Supplies	Remarks
	Srinagar P. O., T. O., C., E.—	...	...	0	...	Carriage road for 6 miles and thence 10-foot road bridged and passable for all laden animals through to Gilgit.	Down Jhelum valley left bank.	Amiran Kadal	5235	S. G. F. W. and T. abundant.	Capital of Kashmir State. Large town, bazar, Heri Parbat fort.
	Shadipur	...	...	11	4			Noru bridge.			
1	Sumbhul E.—	15	4	15	4		Right bank	Jhelum bridge		S. G. F. W. procurable, T. after notice.	Village and shop.
	Ajas	...	...	16	4		Skirts eastern shore of Woolar Lake.	Manus Bal bridge			
	Nadihal	...	...	23	4		Road nearly level to Bundipura with a few ups and downs over spurs, skirting Manus Bal and Woolar Lakes.			......	Baoli and ruins.
		...	...	32	...						
		...	...	33	4			Erin bridge.		......	
2	Bundipura P. O., T. O., E.—	19	...	34	4				5200	S. G. F. W. and T. plentiful.	Large villa e and bazar.

Number of Marches	Names of Stages	Distance in miles and furlongs — Intermediate. m. f.	Distance in miles and furlongs — Total. m. f.	Nature of Route.	Main Valleys and Mountain Passes.	River Crossings and Lakes.	Altitude above Sea Level in Feet.	Supplies and Transport at Stages.	Remarks.
	XLVIII ROUTE—contd. ...								
	Sonerwein ...	19 ...	34 4	Ascent by sharp zigzag of 1 in 7, gradient of 1 in 7	......	Budhkul bridge.			
	Serbal ...	...	36 ...	gradient to top of hill, and 3	Tragbal spur.				
3	Tragbal B. E., C.—	11 4	43 ...	miles easy gradient up to pass.	......	......	9160	S. and T. nil, W. scanty, G. F. plentiful.	Halting place in forest of pine trees.
		...	46 ...	......	Rajdiangan pass.	......	11950		
	Safed Pattan	...	51 ...	Similar gradual descent for 2 miles and sharp	Down Zudkusu valley.				
4	Gorai B. E.—	12 4	53 4	zigzag down for 3 miles, the road	...	......	...	S. and T. nil, W. from river, G. F. plentiful.	Small maidan.
			58 4	then falls with a gradient of 1 in 10 to Kanzilwan,	Up Kishenganga valley.				
	Kanzilwan	...	62 4	and continues with a gentle		Kishenganga bridge.	7400.	S. G. F. and T. plentiful.	
	Mullakadal	...	67 4	rise to Gurais.					
5	Gurais P. O., T. O., B., E.—	15 ...	73 4		...	Kishenganga bridge.	7800	S. G. F. W. and T. plentiful.	Fort situated between 2 villages Daner and Mankoot with bazar.
	Bungla ...	...	83 4		Up Burzil valley.	Cross Burzil river twice by bridges.			
6	Peshwari B. E.—	14 4	88 ...	Hence road continues with an easy gradient up the	......	Rathak bridge.	......	S. and T. nil, G. F. W. available.	Hamlet.
			91 ...						

No.	Place	Dist.	Total	Description of road	Feature	Bridge	Elevation	Supplies	Remarks
	Minimarg T. O.—	...	93	open grass valley with a few clumps of pine trees.	......	......	9700		Maidan and forest patches.
7	**Burzil Choki** B, E.—	11	99	Easy ascent to pass by zigzag and gradual descent along open stony valley over ancient moraines.	......	Burzil bridge	10740	Ditto	Ditto
	Sirdarkoti B, E.—	...	103		Dorikun pass	......	13900		
		4	109 4		Down Burzil valley.		......		Ditto
8	**Chillum** B, E.—	17 4	116 4	......	......	Claachor bridge	11500	Ditto	
		4	118 4	......	......				
	Das Khirin	...	124	......	......	Das bridge.	10500		
9	**Godhai** B, E.—	15	131 4	......	......	Bubind bridge	9100	S. and T. precarious, G. F. W. available.	Small village.
	Gurikot	...	142	Sharp rises and falls over several spurs.	......	Astor bridge.	7800		
10	**Astor (Idgah)** P. O., T. O., B., E.—	17 4	149	The road descends gradually to the Astor river at Turpi and Harcho whence it rises gradually to Dashkin, and after passing through the edible pine forest at Mushkin, it rises up the flank of the Hatu Pir to	Down Astor valley left bank.	......	7838	S. G. F. W. and T. available.	Fort, village and bazar, residence of Raja of Hasora.
	Harcho	...	161		......	Harcho bridge	6200		
11	**Dashkin** B, E., C.—	14 4	163 4		......	......		S. G. F. W. and T. moderate.	Village.
	Mushkin	...	167						
12	**Doian** B, E.—	10	173 4		Hatu Pir spur	......	7800	Ditto	Ditto

Number of Marches	Names of Stages	Distance in miles and furlongs — Intermediate m. f.	Distance in miles and furlongs — Total m. f.	Nature of Route.	Main Valleys and Mountain Passes.	River crossings and Lakes.	Altitude above Sea Level in Feet.	Supplies and Transport at Stages.	Remarks.
	ROUTE XLVIII—contd.								
13	Ramghat or Shaitan Nara.	10 . / 10 4	173 4 / 175 ...	Doian, whence it descends by long zigzags down the shaly sides of a spur to the Astor river at Ramghat.	Up Indus valley left bank.	Astor bridge	3700	S. G. F. and T nil, W. procurable.	Military post.
14	Bawanji or Bunji P. O., T. O., B., E.— Pratabpul B., C., E.—	7 4 / 7 ...	192 4 / 199 4	Good road over stony plain. Ascent by zigzags over spur and gentle descent intoGilgit valley, after crossing the Safed Pari cliffs,	Indus valley left bank. / Right bank.	...... Indus iron suspension bridge.	4631 / 3850	S. G. W. and T. moderate, F. scarce. / S. G. F. and T nil, W. from Indus river.	Fort, village and bazar. / On left bank Indus.
15	Safed Pari B., E.—	17 ...	209 4		Up Gilgit valley right bank.	......	......	Ditto, W. from river.	Cliff.
16	Minawar B., E.—	10 ...	219 4	gentle descent to Minawar, and thence road rises gradually through open plain.	......		4000	S. and T nil, F. W. available, G. scarce.	Small village.
17	Gilgit or Gilit P. O., T. O., B., E.—	9 ...	228 4	Ascent to Jutial barracks and through plain to Gilgit.		......	4390 5025	S. G. F. T. moderate, W. plentiful.	Military Cantonment, town and bazar, residence of Political Agent, head-quarters of province.

The first two marches are usually done by boat from Srinagar down the Jhelum river and along the eastern shore of Woolar Lake to Bandipura. This road is usually closed by snow between Bandipura and Astor from the 1st November to the 31st May. Footmen can travel through in fine weather during this time. There are block houses on both the passes for shelter and protection from snow-storms. There is much risk in travelling during winter from avalanches, especially in the Zsulkusu valley, and in the narrow valley between Burzil Choki and Dorikun bordered by cliffs, where any vibration of the air may shake down the snow.

About a mile west of Sumbhul are interesting ruins at Andarkot or Indrakot.

About one mile beyond Sumbhul the road crosses the canal from the Manus Bal Lake and follows the high bank of the lake to Safeepoor where there is a hot spring and some ruins.

From Bandipura, there is a direct path for footmen only up the Budhkut nala by Atawat over the Dienoor pass, stiff and rugged on both sides to Gurais above 30 miles in length.

A cross road through the hills connects Lalpura in the Lolab with the Zsulkusu valley at Gorai. Lalpura 0, Nachhani spur 3 miles, across head of Arpan valley, Kimsaran spur 10 miles, across head of Bunar valley through forest 14 miles, Sata spur 16 miles, down Gorai valley to Gorai 20 miles. Through supplies and transport are needful.

A road has been made on both sides of the Kishenganga river from Kanzilwan to Gurais. In the dry summer the one on left bank is preferable as it passes through much forest and is shaded from the sun. There are bridges over the Kishenganga river at Kanzilwan, Mullakadul, Murkoot, and Gurais.

Gurais is a beautiful valley, one of the sights of Kashmir, a fine open plain about 10 miles in length and 2 miles in width bordered by high mountains topped by cliffs and clothed with fine forest. An azure river, the Kishenganga, stocked with fish, flows down the valley. At the eastern end is a tall pyramidal mountain of limestone, at foot of which is a copious spring said to be the source of the Kishengunga proper. This valley is famous for a hardy race of ponies, who are surefooted and excellent for mountain work.

From Minimarg 93 miles is a track up the Nagai valley eastwards over the Deosir pass and down into the Shingo valley which leads to Kargil. Between Burzil Choki and Astor, several routes branch out eastwards up the side valleys over the Deosai plains to Skardu, the principal of which are entered below.

From Ramghat there is a road along the left bank of the Indus river westwards to Chilas, see Route LXII. At 159 m. 4f. the iron wire suspension bridge over the Indus river, 327 feet span, is named in honour of His Highness the Maharaja Sir Pratap Singh, G.C.S.I.

XLVIII₂ KANZILWAN to ASTOR by GUGAI PASS—

	Kanzilwan	...	...	62	4	Rough hill track	Down Kishengunga valley.	Kishengunga bridge.	7400	S. G. T. moderate, F. and W. plentiful.	Small village.
	E.— Bakthaor	...	...	65	...					
5	Thaobut	9	4	72	...	Path fit for men only.	Up Gugai valley.	Ditto	......	s. and T. nil, G. F. and W. plentiful.	Village.
	E.—									

Number of Marches.	Names of Stages.	Distance in miles and furlongs. Intermediate. m. f.	Total. m. f.	Nature of Route.	Main Valleys and Mountain Passes.	River Crossings and Lakes.	Altitude above Sea Level in feet.	Supplies and Transport at Stages.	Remarks.
	XLVIII a ROUTE—contd.								
6	Gugai	9 4	72 ...	Stiff ascent to pass and steep and rugged descent.	...	...	...	S. and T. nil, G. F. W. plentiful.	Halting place.
7	Brazil	10 ...	82 ...	...	Gugai pass.	...	...	Ditto	Ditto.
	Riat	...	87 ...						
8	Lohin Hadol E.—	10 ...	92 ...	Fair track of easy gradient used by traders on return journey into Kashmir.	Down Gnraigah valley.	...	9600	Ditto	Ditto.
	Marmai	...	102 ...						
		14 ...	106 ...						
		...	109 ...						
9	Pulkarkot E.— Rattu	10 ...	116 ...	Mir Malik route joins.	...	Mir Malik bridge.	8284	S. and T. scanty, G. F. W. procurable.	Small village.
		...	125 ...						
10	Chugam E. confined—	12 ...	128 ...	...	...	Rupal bridge.	...	S. and G. scanty, T. and F. procurable, W. plentiful.	Village.
		...	132 ...		Down Astor valley.				
11	Gurikot of Astor E.—	10 4	138 4	Join highway from Srinagar to Astor.	...	...	7800	Ditto	Ditto.

| 12 | Astor (Idgah) ... P. O., T. O., B., C., E. | 7 | ... | 145 | 4 | ... | ... | ... | 7838 | S. and G. procurable, W. and F. plentiful, T. moderate. | Village, fort, bazar, residence of Raja of Hasora. |

There is little known about this route, though it is in a direct line from Rajdiangan pass northwards to Astor. It is used by shepherds and sportsmen only and is a path for footmen only. At 132 miles the Rupal river flows into the Guraigah river, and the joint river below is called Astor. The Rupal drains a wide valley of beautiful scenery with some villages, in one Tashing, the cultivated fields adjoin a glacier. Above is an extensive glacier, situated at southern foot, of the great Nanga Parbat or Deamir mountain, about 30 miles in length to the head of the valley, where are two passes, Thosho 17,910 feet and Masena 17,000 feet, across which the Chilas tribes from Bunar used to raid into the Astor valley.

XLVIIIb GURAIS to ASTOR by KAMRI or BURJI PASS.—

5	Gurais P. O., T. O., B., E.— Bangla	...	...	73	4	Fair hill track passable for laden mules and ponies, often used by traders on their return journey to Kashmir, as there is good pasturage and some wood in the Kamri valley. The final ascent to the pass is stony, and the ground on top very spongy; the descent by a sharp zigzag is steep and muddy for 1,000 feet.	Up Barzil valley.	Kishenganga bridge.	7800	S. G. F. W. and T. plentiful.	Fort situated between 2 villages, Daner and Mankoot with bazars.
6	Gurikot of Gurais E.—	13	4	87	...				9200	S. F. and T. scarce, G. W. plentiful.	Small village.
	Thandapani	...	...	89	...				11000	F. and W. procurable.	Halting place.
				95	...		Kamri or Burji pass.		13400		
7	Kalapani E.—	12	...	99	...		Down Kamri valley.	Cross Kamri river several times by snow bridges.	......	S. and T. nil, G. F. W. plentiful.	Ditto.
8	Lohin Hadol	14	...	113	...		Down Guraigah valley.	Lohin Hadol bridge.	9600	Ditto.	Ditto.
	Marnai	...	...	116	4						
	Shankarpot or Dirli	...	...	119	4			Dirli bed.			
9	Pukarkot	10	...	123	...			......	......	S. and T. scanty, G. F. W. procurable.	Small village.

XLVIIIb ROUTE—contd.

No. of Marches	Names of Stages	Intermediate m. f.	Total m. f.	Nature of Route	Main Valleys and Mountain Passes	River crossings and Lakes	Altitude above Sea Level in Feet	Supplies and Transport at Stages	Remarks
	Rattu	...	123						
10	Chagam E.—	12	132	Mirmalik route joins here.	......	Mirmalik bridge.	8284	S. and T. scanty, F. and T. procurable, W. plentiful.	Village.
			135		Down Astor valley	Rupal bridge. Astor ,,	......	Ditto	Ditto.
11	Gurikot of Astor E.—	10 4	140	Joins highway from Srinagar to Gilgit.	......	Astor ,,	7800		
			145						
12	Astor (Idgah) or Hasora. P. O., T. O., B., E.—	7	152		......	......	7838	S. and G. procurable, W. and F. plentiful, T. moderate.	Village, fort, bazar and residence of Raja of Hasora.

On ascending from Gurikot, a high spur 12,438 feet is passed, then Gotomun at the head of one of the branches of the Jeshat stream, where bad avalanches of snow occur, and a stony rise to the Burji pass 13,400 feet across an old moraine. Encamp at mouth of east side stream about 4 miles down from the pass. Kalapani is the name given to the upper part of the Kamri valley, well grassed and some shrubs. This route is closed by snow from middle of November to end of May. It used to be called shorter than the Dorikun pass route, but is in reality about 3½ miles longer. Avalanches of snow are frequent on both sides of the pass and down the Kamri valley, forming snow bridges over river.

XLVIIIc GURAIS to DRAS by TILAIL VALLEY—

No. of Marches	Names of Stages	Intermediate m. f.	Total m. f.	Nature of Route	Main Valleys and Mountain Passes	River crossings and Lakes	Altitude above Sea Level in Feet	Supplies and Transport at Stages	Remarks
5	Gurais P. O., T. O., B., E.—	...	73 4	......	......	Kishenganga bridge.	7800	S. G. F. W. and T. plentiful.	Fort between 2 villages, Dauer and Mankoot with bazars and thana or tehsil.
	Churanan	...	77 4	Ascent very steep and slippery, right bank Lorlo-	......	Burzil bridge.			
			82	Chaklai ridge		......	11000		

No.	Stage	Dist.		Total		Road	Bridge or ford	Direction	Elevation	Supplies	Description
6	Lorloken *B.—*	11	::	84	4	way nala through Pultun nar valley, descent steep and slippery 2,000 feet to Lorloken, which is 100ft. above Kushpat Uri stream and 1,000ft. above Ki-	......	Up Kishen-gunga or Tilail valley right bank.	......	S. and T. nil, G. F. W. procurable.	Small grass plain on edge of birch forest.
	Bursai	::	::	86	::	shengunga river.	Kushpat Uri bridge.	...	......		
	Zadgai	::	::	88	::	Good road passable for laden animals through to Dras.	Kila Shay bridge.	...	......		
	Purana Tilail	::	::	90	::		Satani bridge	...	......	......	Large village.
7	Badagam	10	::	94	4		Nirilgah „ 8950	......	8950	S. G. F. W. and T. plentiful.	Ditto and thana.
8	Bodal	9	::	96	::		Gratinar „	......		S. G. F. W. and T. moderate.	Village and thana.
				103	4		Bodab „	......	......		
9	*Gujrind*	::	::	109	::	Rocky ascent of easy gradient and gradual descent.	Kishengunga bridge or ford.	......	......	S. and T. precarious, G. F. W. available.	Hamlet.
	Abdulhun *E.—*	7	4	111	::						
10	Koradgai *E.—*	16	::	119	::	The road passes through a wide open valley, barley chief culti-vation, numerous hamlets.	Koombal pass	Down Mushki val-ley left bank.	13000.	S. and T. nil, G. F. W. procurable.	Grass plain.
				127	::		......			S. and T. precarious, G. F. W. procurable.	
11	Haobal *E.—*	12	::	139	::		......	......	......		Hamlet.
12	Mushki *E.—*	9	::	148	::		......	......	......	S. G. F. W. and T. moderate.	Village.
13	Dras *P. O., B., C., E.—*	7	::	155	::	Join Srinagar and Leh road.	......	......	......	Ditto	Series of small vil-lages, fort and thana.

This road opens 15th June and closes in November on first fall of snow.

From Badagam there is a track fit for laden ponies up the Gratinar valley, which crosses the Bobal and another pass, and descends to the Nagai river, where it joins the road going from Minimarg eastwards to the Shingo river and to Kargil. Another track from Bodal or Batwhal goes up the Bodal ravine and crossing the pass at its head joins the foregoing route at the second march.

Badagam 94 miles 4 furlongs, Bobal or Boda 104 miles, Haddar Bal Maidan or Harrai 113 miles, Tarzi Bir or Danyih Bir 122 miles, Gultarri on Shingo river 131 miles. No supplies and no transport. G. F. W. procurable throughout. Hence a path crosses the river, when fordable, strikes up the Shingo valley left bank, and crossing an intervening ridge emerges on the Deosai plains and joins the main route from Burzil Choki to Skardu about the 124 miles of Route XLIX. There are no bridges on the Shingo river, and it is unfordable after heavy rain and during the melting of the snow.

For paths connecting the Tilail with the Sindh valley, see Routes La and Lb.

XLVIIId GODHAI to SKARDU by ALUMPI LA—

Number of Marches.	Names of Stages.	Distance in miles and furlongs. Intermediate. m. f.	Total. m. f.	Nature of Route.	Main Valleys and Mountain Passes.	River crossings and Lakes.	Altitude above Sea Level in feet.	Supplies and Transport at Stages.	Remarks.
9	Godhai B., E.—	...	131 4	Rough hill path for men on foot only. Riding ponies may be led over the worst places with care.	Up Ditchell valley.	Bubind bridge	9100	S. and T. precarious, G. F. W. available.	Small village.
10	Bubind E.—	11 ...	142 4		......	......	......	S. and T. nil, G. F. W. procurable.	Village.
			151 4		......	......	......	......	Foot of pass.
11	Ringmo Chani ...	15 4	155 4	Ascent and descent of pass extremely steep and rocky with snow slopes. This route was selected by Raja Sir Ram Singh, K.C.B., on his return from Gilgit in 1891 in preference to the Banok La, his ponies and those of his staff got through.	Alumpi La.	......	15200.	Ditto	Halting place.
	Tdashing Spung	...	158 ...		Down Shikarthang valley.	......	......		
		...	164 ...						
12	Shikarthang E.—	11 ...	169 ...		......	The river is crossed several times by bridges.	......	S. and T. nil, G. scarce, W. F. procurable.	Ditto.
13	Stakchun E.—	6 ...	175 ...		......		......	Ditto	Hamlet.
14	Kutsura E.—	13 ...	188 ...	Good road along sandy plain.	Up Indus valley left bank.	......	......	S. F. and coolies scanty, G. and W. procurable.	Village.

No.	Name		Total	Nature of road	Route	Bridge	Elevation	Supplies	Remarks
15	Pukora E.—	10	198	...	......	......	......	Ditto	Ditto.
16	Skardu P.O., T.O., C., E.—	10	208	...	......	......	7400	S. G. F. W. plentiful.	Cluster of villages, fort and capital of Baltistan.

From Shikarthang 168 miles a route branches off S. E. up the Dora Loomba over the Dori La to Boogival 191 miles, thence N. E. over the Burji La 15.697 feet descending down the Karpitu nala to Sarpitu 205 miles, and Skardu 209 miles.

From Astor 149 miles another track south-eastwards joins this route at Thlashing Spung, the junction of the two streams from either pass, ascending the Parishing valley to Popui 159 miles, camp at foot of Banok La 177 miles, cross the Banok La 15,500 feet, and down a ravine to Thlashing Spung 196 miles, and to Shikarthang 201 miles, whence there is a choice of two routes to Skardu as above, that by Katsura is the easier, passing through more cultivation.

The Banok La is seldom used, as this pass is closed earlier than the Alumpi La, and there are 2 small glaciers to cross. Both the passes are open from 1st July to the first fall of snow, and travellers are liable to suffer from the rarity of the air in crossing.

XLVIIIe ASTOR to RONDU by TRONGO PIR—

No.	Name	Stage	Total	Nature of road	Route	Bridge	Elevation	Supplies	Remarks
10	Astor or Hasora P. O., T. O., B., E.—	...	149	Rough hill path for men on foot only.	Up Parishing valley right bank.	Astor bridge	7838	S. G. F. W. and T. available.	Fort, village, bazar and tehsil.
		...	153			Parishing bridge.			
11	Popul	10	159	Gradual ascent to top of pass and steep descent.	......	......	......	S. and T. nil, G. F. W. procurable.	Small village.
12	Deorwhey	8	167	Road open for 3 months, July to October inclusive.	Up Deorwhey ravine. Trongo Pir.	......	15637	Ditto	Halting place.
13	Chutabar	13	180	......	Down Tukchun valley right bank.	Tukchun bridge.	......	Ditto	Hamlet.
	Harpo	...	185						

NUMBER OF MARCHES.	NAMES OF STAGES.	DISTANCE OF MILES AND FURLONGS — INTERMEDIATE. m. f.	DISTANCE — TOTAL. m. f.	NATURE OF ROUTE.	MAIN VALLEYS AND MOUNTAIN PASSES.	RIVER CROSSINGS AND LAKES.	ALTITUDE ABOVE SEA-LEVEL IN FEET.	SUPPLIES AND TRANSPORT AT STAGES.	REMARKS.
	XLVIIIc ROUTE—contd	... ...	185 ...						
14	Rondu (Mendi) ...	14 ...	194 ...	Steep descent to Indus river.	Indus valley	......	6050	S. G. F. W. and T. moderate.	Cluster of villages, residence of Raja.

There is an alternative track by Hurpo La 16,785 feet, where a mile of glacier has to be crossed. Astor 149 miles, Popul 159 miles, Camp at foot of pass, 170 miles 4 furlongs, Hurpo La 173 miles, down the Tukehnu valley to Papothang 182 miles, Hurpo 192 miles, and Memli or Kondu 200 miles. This road is not open until much later in July. Unladen ponies are crossed over.

From Dashkin 163 miles 4 furlongs the Indian Atlas sheet shows a path up the Dichil valley from the right bank of the Astor river to a high pass over the dividing range ; thence after crossing the head of the Sapser nala and a spur, the path descends down the Kurubar nala to Fulchurch on the left bank of the Indus river, a distance probably of 30 miles. Fulchurch is 15 miles west of Rondu, and on the right bank of the Indus river opposite are two tracks leading to Skardu, see Route XLV.

XLIX SRINAGAR to SKARDU by GURAIS and DEOSAI PLAINS—

NUMBER OF MARCHES.	NAMES OF STAGES.	DISTANCE — INTERMEDIATE. m. f.	DISTANCE — TOTAL. m. f.	NATURE OF ROUTE.	MAIN VALLEYS AND MOUNTAIN PASSES.	RIVER CROSSINGS AND LAKES.	ALTITUDE ABOVE SEA-LEVEL IN FEET.	SUPPLIES AND TRANSPORT AT STAGES.	REMARKS.
1	**Srinagar** P. O., T. O., C. E.—	... ...	0 ...	Carriage road for 6 miles and thence 10 ft. road passable for all laden animals through to Burzil Choki.	Down Jhelum valley left bank.	......	5235	S. G. F. W. and T. abundant.	Capital of Kashmir State. Large town, bazar and Hari Parbat fort.
	Shadipur ...	... ...	11 4		Do. right bank.	Noru bridge. Jhelum			
	Sumbhul	15 4	15 4		Along Eastern shore of Woolar Lake.	Jhelum "	.....	S.G.F.W. procurable, T. after notice.	Village and shops.
	E.— Ajas ...	... ...	23 4	Road from Sumbhul skirts northern shore of Manus					
		... ...	33 4	shore of Manus		Erin "			

No.	Stage	Inter.		Total		Road	Crossing / Pass	Elevation	Supplies	Remarks
2	**Bundipura** P. O., T. O., E.—	19	..	34	4	Bal Lake and the eastern shore of Woolar Lake, nearly level to Bundipura with a few ups and downs over spurs.	..	5200	S. G. F. W. and T. plentiful.	Large village and bazar.
3	**Tragbal** B. E.—, B. E. C.—	11	4	46	..		Tragbal spur	9160	S. and T. nil, W. scarce, G. F. plentiful.	Halting place in forest of pine trees.
	Safed Pattar	..	..	51	..		Rajdiangan pass.	11950	S. and T. nil, W. plentiful.	
4	**Gorai** B. E.—, *Kanzilwan*	12	4	53	4	Hence sharp zigzag ascent of 1 in 7 gradient to Tragbal and top of hill, then 2 miles easy gradient on both sides of pass, then sharp zigzag descent for 3 miles and gradient of 1 in 10 falls to Kishenganga, and easy rise up this and Burzil valley.	Down Zudkusu valley.	7400	S. and T. nil, W. from river, G. F. plentiful.	Small maidan.
				58	4					
		..	..	62	..		Kishengunga bridge. Up Kishenganga valley.	7800	S. G. F. W. and T. plentiful.	Town and tehsil or thana, bazars in vicinity.
5	**Gurais** P. O., T. O., B. E.—	15	..	73	4		Kishengunga bridge. Up Burzil valley.			Hamlet.
6	**Peshwari** B. E.—, *Minimarg*, T. O.—	14	4	88	..		Cross Burzil twice by bridges.		S. and T. nil, G. F. W. available.	Small village.
		..	..	93	..			9700	......	
7	**Burzil Choki** B. E.—	11	..	99	..		Barzil bridge Stakpita pass	10740	Ditto	Maidan and forest patches.
				102	4			12900		
				104	4	From Burzil Choki the road turns off N. E. to the Deosai or Devil's plains which are stony and barren, devoid of vegetation, the home of marmots and mosquitoes, early in the season, when the snow	Head Shingo ford. Sarsingar pass			
				107	..			13860		
				107	4		2 small lakes.			
8	**Sikhbach** E.—	15	..	114	..		Jerbarcho Lake 3 miles distant N. W.	13160	S. G. F. T. nil, W. plentiful.	Halting place.
				117	..					
	Chunda kut	..	..	120	4		Kinawai ford. Barwai			
				124	..					

Number of Marches.	Names of Stages.	Distance in miles and furlongs. Inter-mediate. m. f.	Distance in miles and furlongs. Total. m. f.	Nature of Route.	Main Valleys and Mountain Passes.	River Crossings and Lakes.	Altitude above Sea Level in Feet.	Supplies and Transport at Stages.	Remarks.
XLIX	ROUTE—contd.	...	124						
9	Lalpani *E.—* *Ali Malik Marhi*	13	127 / 129 / 132	is melting, the rivers are full and deep, and fording is difficult.	...... / ...... /	Lamalung ford / Pialung " /	12500 / 13330	S. F. T. nil, G. poor, W. plentiful.	Halting place.
10	Usar Mar *E.—*	12	139 / 143	Laden mules can be taken by this route, though there are places where the loads must be taken off and carried by men over the difficulty.	Burji La	...... /	13970 / 15700	Ditto	Ditto.
11	Karpitu *E.—*	16	155 / 157 4	From Burji La is a fair road to the Indus river.	......	...... / Satpar ford.	7636	Ditto	Village.
12	Skardu *P. O., T. O., C. E.—*	3 4	158 4	Indus river.	Indus valley	......	7400	S. G. F. W. and T. plentiful.	Cluster of villages. Fort, Waziri Wusarat, Capital of Baltistan.

At 117 miles, a track N. W. to the Jerbareho or Cherosar Lake 3 miles distant, skirts the Northern shore, crosses the Chuchor La and descends down a ravine, which falls into the Burzil river at the 118 miles 4 furlongs of Route XLVIII. The total distance apart being 17 miles. The Deosai plains are in reality a basin of 12,000 to 13,000 ft. elevation surrounded by high mountains with a single outlet to the S. E. the Shigar river, which flows into the Shingo river shortly before the latter falls into the Dras river. This plateau is not safe to cross before July or after September, as the snow lies deep and the high winds cause snow-drifts. There is little or no wood, occasional juniper roots serve as fuel. There is no vegetation except in the narrow valleys, and that is scanty. Through supplies and transport are indispensable, and can be obtained at Gurais and Skardu. This is the shortest and most direct route from Kashmir to Skardu, and is frequented by travellers, notwithstanding its many drawbacks.

At Ali Malik Marhi 132 miles another track turns off eastwards, and crossing the shoulder of the intervening mountain goes down the parallel Sutpur Loongma valley to Skardu. There are 3 marches from Lalpani 127 m., junction of 2 streams on the Sutpur Cho 140 miles, on the eastern shore of the Sutpur Tso or Lake 152 miles, and Skardu 163 miles.

XLIXa SKARDU to MUSTAGH PASS—

No.	Name	Intermediate	Total	Remarks (road)	Direction	Water	Elevation	Supplies	Description
12	**Skardu**	...	158 4	Fair road over well cultivated plain, dotted with villages, gardens and orchards of fruit trees, chiefly apricots.	Up Shigar valley left bank.	Indus ferry	7400	S. G. F. W. and T. plentiful.	Cluster of villages, Fort and Capital of Baltistan.
13	**Shigar**	13 4	172 4		......	......	7600	Ditto	Town and Fort.
14	**Khutti**	6	178	......	......	......	......	S. and T. precarious, G. F. W. procurable.	Small village.
15	**Kashimul**	13	191	......	......	......	......	Ditto	Ditto.
16	**Dusso**	15	206	Above the junction of the two rivers, Braldu and Basho, path fit for men on foot only.	Up Braldu valley.	Braldu river	......	Ditto	Ditto.
	Gund	...	211			"			
17	**Foljo**	12	218	From Foljo, path becomes rough and difficult with many ascents and descents over loose surface of mountain side.		3 hot springs sulphur.	......	Ditto G. scarce	Ditto.
18	**Hoto**	16	234			......	......	Ditto	Ditto.
19	**Askole**	12	246			Braldu bridge	......	S. G. F. W. and T. moderate.	Village.

Hence there used formerly to be two routes leading over the high Mustagh range towards Yarkund, the two passes being about 12 miles apart. Both have been disused for 30 years, partly owing to changes in the glaciers and to fear of robbers on the Northern side of the range. The route recorded by Major Godwin Austen in 1863 is as under :—

Number of Marches.	Names of Stages.	Distance in Miles and Furlongs. Intermediate. m. f.	Total. m. f.	Nature of Route.	Main Valleys and Mountain Passes.	River crossings and Lakes.	Altitude above Sea Level in Feet.	Supplies and Transport at Stages.	Remarks.
20	Korophon	8 ...	254 ...	...	Up Punmah valley right bank.	Biafo glacier	10145	S. and T. nil, G. F. W. procurable.	Halting place.
	Dusordo	...	262 ...						
21	Tsok	16 ...	270 ...	Path along bed of torrent over boulders.	...	...		Ditto	Ditto.
22	Punmah	6 ...	276 ...	Path along edge of glacier on right bank.	...	Punmah glacier.	10318	S. G. F. T. nil, W. melted snow.	Ditto.
23	Chongralter	8 ...	284 ...	...	Cross glacier to left bank.	...		Ditto	Ditto.
24	Shingchakpi	8 ...	292 ...	...	...	...		Ditto	Ditto.
25	Skeenmang	6 ...	298 ...	Rough and tedious way up, the glacier, making detours to avoid crevices.	Up Chiring valley.	Mouth of Nobundi Sobundi glacier.		S. F. T. nil, G. moderate, W. melted snow.	Grassy level space.
26	Tsokar	6 ...	304 ...	...	...				
27	Chiring	6 ...	310 ...	...				Ditto	Halting place at end of spur.

Mustagh pass	...	14	...	324	...	......	......	Mustagh or Karakoram range of mountains.	......	18400 } 19003 {	Western pass. Eastern pass.

On the northern side, this route, as explored by Lieutenant F. E. Younghusband in 1887, descended down a glacier and after joining the route from the other Mustagh pass at Parong and another path from the Shimshal pass (due west which leads into Hunza) at Saget jangal, came to the Shaksgam or Oprang valley and thence reached the Yarkund river either at Gil or at Dora by crossing the Aghil Dawan pass 16,500 feet in to Raskum.

There is no path yet known onwards down the Yarkund valley, owing it is said to high cliffs which border the river. From Dora, this route goes eastwards up the Yarkund valley to Chiragh Saldi, and thence northwards over the Chiragh Saldi and Tashkurgan passes by Kugiar and Kargalik to Yarkund. Another route from Skardu towards Yarkund formerly existed up the Shayok valley to Khapalu, thence up the Saltoro valley and the Bilafun glacier to a high pass over the Mustagh range. This route has long been abandoned for similar reasons.

The natural difficulties to be met with in crossing the lofty Mustagh chain of mountains are so serious as to render it improbable that traffic between Kashmir and Yarkund will ever take this direction. If Gilgit could become a trade centre like Leh, traffic would be more likely to seek a passage this way; now that the passes above Hunza are open and that a stop has been put to Hunza raids.

From Khutti 178 miles there is a shorter path up the Skoro valley over the Skoro La 16,644 feet to Askole which is open in summer, by Kutzah, 12,553 feet, Nangbrok 190 miles, over pass and glacier 6 miles long to Thlabrok 204 miles, and Askole 208 miles, crossing the Braldu river by a bridge of large span, 270 feet, at Askole.

From Punmah upwards for 6 marches, the way is either alongside the moraine shed from the glacier, crossing the tributary side glaciers or upon the main glacier, avoiding rock ridges and large crevasses. Though some of these marches may appear short, the way is very devious to avoid obstructions. There is difficulty in finding a proper path, while at that high elevation the rarified air induces quick respiration and any exertion is followed by great fatigue. Many persons suffer greatly.

From Askole upwards in a direct course, the distance over the glaciers would not exceed 80 miles rising 9,000 feet to the top of the Mustagh pass; the average gradient of the glaciers seems therefore fairly easy.

On the north side of the Mustagh pass, the way is down a similar extensive glacier so that for at least 10 marches travellers must carry grass and wood fuel, besides supplies for men and animals.

I. SRINAGAR to SKARDU by DRAS—

Srinagar P. O., T. O., C., E.—	...	...	0	...	This first stage by land or water along good road or by boat across	Jhelum valley.	......	5235	S. G. F. W. and T. abundant.	Capital of Kashmir State, large town, bazars, Hari Parbat Fort.

Number of Marches	Names of Stages	Distance in Miles and Furlongs — Intermediate m. f.	Distance in Miles and Furlongs — Total m. f.	Nature of Route	Main Valleys and Mountain Passes	River Crossings and Lakes	Altitude above Sea Level in Feet	Supplies and Transport at Stages	Remarks
L	ROUTE—contd.	...	0						
1	Gunderbul E.—	14 2	14 2	Anchar Lake or down Jhelum river to Shadipur and up Sindh river.	Up Sindh valley left bank.	Sindh bridge.	5230	S. G. F. and coolies available, W. plentiful.	Village.
			22 4			Ditto.			
2	Khangan E.— Haiyan	11 3	25 5	Hence a good road up Sindh valley passable for laden animals.	Right bank	Ditto	6000	Ditto	Ditto.
			30						
3	Gund E.— Kulan, E. confned—	13 6	39 3	Road rough and rocky, but passable for horses.		Cross Sindh river several times according to present state of bridges.	6700	Ditto	Ditto.
4	Gugangnir E.—	8	43 3				7400	S. nil, G. and T. moderate, F. and W. plentiful.	Small village.
			47 3	Road good	Left bank Right ,,	Sindh bridge. Ditto			
5	Sonamarg P. O., T. O., E., some old log huts—	7 2	51 3				8650	S. scarce, T. moderate, G. F. W. plentiful.	Sanitarium on grassy downs.
			54 5						
6	Baltal E.—	9	63 5	Steep ascent for about 2,000 feet, and very gradual descent on north side.	...	Ditto	9000	S. and T. nil, G. F. W. procurable.	Huts.
			69 4		Zoji La	......	11300		

No.	Stage	Dist.	Total	March	Road	Bank	Bridge	Elevation	Supplies	Remarks
7	**Matayan** B., E.— Pandras	15	78	5	......	Down Goomber or Dras valley left bank.	......	11000	S. nil, F. T. moderate, G. W. procurable.	Hamlets.
8	**Dras** P. O., T.O., B., C., E.	12	84	4	Road of easy gradient over stony ground, pass three stone pillars.	......	Mushki bridge. Marpoebu bridge.	9825	S. G. F. W. and T. moderate.	Series of small villages, fort and thana.
9	**Tashgam** B. E. Kharbu E.—	15	90	4	Narrow passage round rock at bridge, valley narrow and barren.	Right bank	Dras bridge	9390	Ditto	Village and thana.
	Kuksar opposite bank		91	4				......	......	Mouth of Shingo Shigar river.
10	**Karkitchu** E.—	14	106	4	Road difficult in places.	Left bank	Dras bridge	......	Ditto	Small village.
			113	...				......	......	Junction of Saru river.
			115	...				......	......	Ditto.
11	**Gangani** E.—	10	120	4	Ditto along precipices in narrow valley.	......	Dras bridge	......	S. scarce, ditto	Ditto.
			126	4			......	......		
12	**Olthingthang** E.—	12	130	4	Rugged path over scaffolding in places.	Down Indus valley left bank.	Bamachan-cho bridge.	......	Ditto	Ditto.
			141	4			......	......		Junction of Dras and Indus rivers.
			143	4			......	......	......	
13	**Tarkuti** E.— Shirating	14	147	...	Hard march with long climb half way to Kartaksho.	......	......	7800	Ditto	Small village.
			156	4			Torgooncho	......		
			160	4			......			
			165	...			Gidiaxdoocho.			

12

Number of Marches.	Names of Stages.	Distance in Miles and Furlongs.		Nature of Route.	Main Valleys and Mountain Passes.	River crossings and Lakes.	Altitude above Sea Level in Feet.	Supplies and Transport and Stages.	Remarks.
		Inter-mediate. m. f.	Total. m. f.						
L	*ROUTE—contd.*	...	165 ...						
14	**Kartaksho or Kharmang.** E.—	1. ...	173 4	Fair road on right bank, while that on left bank crosses over high stony ridge, then fairly level along river. From Tolti	Down Indus valley left bank.	Indus rope bridge.	......	S. G. F. W. and T. available.	Fort and large village on right bank of Indus river.
			178 4		...	Ingotcho.			
15	**Tolti** E.— *Shadool*	12 ...	185 4	steep ascent over high cliffs and easy descent to level ground and cultivation.	...	Ditto. Kusuracho. Dumsumcho.	......	S. G. F. W. and T. moderate.	Village and fort on left bank.
			194 ...		...				
16	**Parkuta** E.— *Sermi*	14 ...	199 4	From Parkuta fair road, crossing several rock stairs with long strips of cultivation.	......	Katicho.	......	S. G. F. W. and T. plentiful.	Large village and fort.
			204 7			Murkocho.			
17	**Gol** E.—	12 4	212 .	From Gol level road, crossing several rocky spurs and stony.		Gudcho.	...	S. G. F. T. moderate, W. plentiful.	Village.
18	**Kepchung** E.— *Gorpa*	17 ...	229 ...	From Kepchung, road very good and level.		......	...	Ditto	Ditto.
		...	230 ...	......		Kepchungcho.			

19	**Skardu** *P. O., T. O., C., E.—*	4	...	233	...	......	......	7400	S. G. F. W. and T. plentiful.	Capital of Baltistan. Cluster of villages, fort, tehsil or thana.

This road is usually open from June to November inclusive.

Dr. A. Neve states that there is a direct mountain path from the Shalimar bagh on the N. E. corner of Dal Lake at Srinagar in a northerly direction over a ridge above 9,000 feet high and descending through the forest to Haiyan in the Sindh valley about 15 miles in length. From Haiyan the traveller could go to Kulan and the next day to Sonamarg.

From the Sindh river bridge 22 miles 4 furlongs, there is a road down the right bank of the river past Maugam 26 miles, to the Maunshal Lake 36 miles, along an old irrigation canal from the Sindh river and joins the Gilgit road near Sufferpur 38 miles at the N. E. corner of the Lake. In returning from the Sindh valley, travellers often take this route down to Maunshal. On the south side of the lake are the limestone quarries which supply the City of Srinagar.

From Parkuta 199 miles 4 furlongs, a track goes westwards up the Katichu valley by Soomba and Dhuppa over the Katichu La 15,053 feet, and goes across the head of the Sutpur Chu to Ali Malik-ke-mur on the Deosai plains, the distance is 40 miles, and is passable for ponies.

From Sermi 204 miles 4 furlongs, a path goes westwards up the Marko Loomba, and crossing the Gonnathang Migo pass, it turns northwards down the Kepchung nala to Grapi at mile 230 of the main road. The distance by this pass is about the same.

From Gol 212 miles another path goes westwards up this nala over the Thurigo pass, and turns northwards down the Kepchung nala to Grapi at mile 230 of main road. The distance by this pass also is about the same.

L₂ SINDH VALLEY to TILAIL VALLEY by GUNGABUL NAG—under HARAMOOK PEAK—

1	**Srinagar** *P. O., T. O., C., E.—*	...	...	0	...	By good road or by boat to Gunderbol.	......	5235	S. G. F. W. and T. abundant.	Capital of Kashmir State.
	Gunderbul *E.—* *Nagar*	14	2	14	2	Good road to the Sindh bridge and fair path to Wangut.	Up Sindh valley.	5230	S. G. F. and coolies available, W. plentiful.	Village.
		...	...	17	2	......	Sindh bridge.	......		
		...	...	22	4	......				
2	**Drogdun or Pron** *E.—* *Kachanwhol*	10	...	24	2	......	Up Kankwai valley right bank.	......	S. nil, G. F. W. plentiful, few coolies.	Small village.
		...	...	27	2					

Number of Marches	Names of Stages	Distance of Miles and Furlongs — Intermediate m. / f.	Distance of Miles and Furlongs — Total m. / f.	Nature of Route	Main Valleys and Mountain Passes	River Crossings and Lakes	Altitude above Sea Level, in feet	Supplies and Transport at Stages	Remarks
La	ROUTE—contd.	... ...	27 2	.....	......	......	......	......	......
3	Wangut E.—	8 2	32 4	.....	......	......	6800	S. and T. nil, G. F. W. procurable.	Small village.
	Temple ruins	... ...	35 ...			Nagbul spring	......		Rajdaibul and Nagbul temples.
4	Tronkul E.—	8 4	41 ...	From Nagbul, the path rises up the mountain side by a steep zig-zag to the birch forest at Tronkul—hence gradual descent over undulating grassy slopes to Gungabul. Easy ascent to pass and gradual descent to Migadol Nag.	......	......	10000	Ditto	Limit of birch forest.
5	Gungabul Nag E.—	6 4	47 4		......	......	11800	S. F. T. nil, G. W. available.	Sacred Lake.
6	Migadol Nag E.—	6 ...	50 ...		Sat Saran pass, Down Shah and Nai glen.	......	......	Ditto	Lake.
7	Gadasir E.—	6 ...	53 4		Renino ridge.	Gadasir nala	......	S. and T. nil, G. F. W. procurable.	On river bank.
8	Lahun-i-thul E.—	9 ...	59 4	Rough path onwards across 2 valleys and 2 spurs to Tilail.	......	Lahun-i-thul nala.	......	Ditto	Ditto.
	Wazri Thal	... ...	73 4	......	Cross spur.				

9	Badagam E.—	...	6	4	75	...	Tilail valley	Kishengunga bridge.	8250	S. G. F. W. and T. available.	Large village and thana on right bank Kishengunga.

There are several lakes in the vicinity of Gungabul nag north of Haramook Peak 16,903 feet, and the northern glacier from the latter comes right down to the Gungabul lake.

This is a great place of pilgrimage, and is said to be one of the sources of the Ganges. Passing westwards between Gungabul nag and Loolgool nag and crossing an intervening ridge, Sirbal nag or Kola Sar is reached about 4 miles distant, hence there is a path which crosses another ridge 14,000 feet, and drops steeply and westerly down the Erin nala to Kodoora 7,000 feet, and 9 miles, and to Bandipura 5,200 feet, and 13 miles. Total distance from Gungabul to Bandipura 26 miles.

The ascent of the Haramook Peak is usually made from Sirbal nag.

There is another approach to Gungabul nag from the Sindh valley by the Chittengool nala and the Brahimsar pass, crossing the head of the Kankwai valley. The same route is followed to the Sindh bridge 22 miles 4 furlongs, whence road turns off due north to Chittengool 25 miles 4 furlongs, Brahimsar nag 34 miles 4 furlongs, pass 36 miles, Gungabul nag 44 miles.

This road is traversed by laden ponies and mules from June until the first fall of snow in November.

15 SONAMARG to TILAIL VALLEY—*Bates No. 73.*

5	Sonamarg P.O., T.O., E.—	...	...	54	5	Good hill path through grassy valley with patches of birch forest.	Up Nichinai valley.	......	8650	S. scarce, T. moderate, G. F. W. plentiful.	Sanitarium.
	Saribal	...	...	56	...			Sindh Mair bridge.	......	......	Marg.
				59	...						
6	Nichinai E.—	...	7	...	61	5	Steep ascent and easy descent over snow.	......	......	13500	S. and T. nil, G. F. W. procurable.	Halting place.
				63	4		Nichinai Suga.	Vishan Sar.			
				65	...		Across head of Raman Sind.				
7	Krishan Sar E.—	...	8	...	69	5		......	Krishan Sar	12000	S. and T. nil, F. scarce, G. W. plentiful.	Ditto.

Number of Marches.	Names of Stages.	Distance in miles and furlongs. Intermediate. m. f.	Total. m. f.	Nature of Route.	Main Valleys and Mountain Passes.	River crossings and Lakes.	Altitude above Sea Level in Feet.	Supplies and Transport at Stages.	Remarks.
Lb	ROUTE—contd. ...	8	69 5	Steep zig-zag ascent and steep descent by a fair path and easy march down valley. From Mushdi Nar path lies up a narrow gorge steep and slippery, crosses ridge and descends down another rocky gorge.	Cross ridge.	......	13000		
8	Mushdi Nar E.—	...	71 ...		Down Gadasir valley.	Gadasir nag.	10000	S. and T. nil, G. F. W. plentiful.	Halting place.
		...	73 ...		......	......	13000		
		8	77 5		Renino ridge				
9	Lohun-i-Thul or Dokolla Bal E. small.—	5	82 5	After crossing Lohun-i-Thul nala steep ascent of mountain and descent along ridge, then drop down spur through forest to Wazri Thul opposite Badagam.	Across Lohun-i-Thul valley	Lohun-i-Thul nala.	9000	Ditto	Ditto.
	Wazri Thul ...	...	88 4		Cross spur	......	11500		
10	Badagam P. O., E.—	7 3	90 ...		Tilail valley	Kishenganga bridge.	8250	S. G. and T. moderate, W. plentiful.	Large village and thana on right bank Kishenganga.

Some of these distances given in the route book appear too short.

There is another path from Siribal marg, which after crossing the Nichinai range follows down the Raman valley, when the river is fordable, and leads to the village of Botal in the Tilail valley, crossing the Kishenganga by the Anaikot bridge, the total distance from Sonamarg being about 50 miles.

Another path from Sonamarg, after crossing the Sind bridge east, goes northwards up the Niligar ravine, crosses a high pass and glacier and descends down the Nilinai nala to the point where it falls into the Koraigai or Mushki river, and joins the road from the Tilail valley to Dras. See Route XLVIIIc, at the eastern foot of the Kwambul pass, the whole distance being about 25 miles.

Lc DRAS to GURAIS by SHINGO VALLEY:—

	Station					Road remarks	Direction	Height	Supplies	Description
	Dras P. O., T. O., B., C., E.	...	...	91	4	Rough and rugged path, over high spurs and along river, passable for footmen.	Up Marpo Chu.	......	S. G. F. W. and T. moderate.	Series of small villages, fort and thana.
				103	0	......	......	......		
1	Marpo E.—	11	4	105	...		Marpo La down Moonli valley.	9825	S. and T. nil, G. F. W. procurable.	Halting place.
2	Sumalo E.—	18	...	121	...	Fair path along the valley broken by many ups and downs.	Up Shingo valley right bank.	......	Ditto	Hamlet.
3	Gultar E.—	5	...	126	...	......	......	......	S. precarious, G. F. W. available, few coolies.	Small village.
4	Camp E.—	10	...	136	...	......	......	......	S. and T. nil, G. F. W. procurable.	Halting place.
5	Dumel E.—	10	...	146	...	Easy ascent and descent over the intervening ridges	......	......	Ditto	Ditto.
				153	...		Cross ridge down Nagai glen.			
6	Nagai E.—	11	...	157	...	......	......	......	Ditto	Ditto.

Number of Marches.	Names of Stages.	Distance in miles and furlongs. Intermediate. m. f.	Total. m. f.	Nature of Route.	Main Valleys and Mountain Passes.	River crossings and Lakes.	Altitude above Sea Level is Feet.	Supplies and Transport at Stages.	Remarks.
L6	ROUTE—contd. ...	...	157 ...						
	Minimarg ...	11 ...	167 ...	Join Gilgit road 93 miles between Gurais and Astor.	Down Burzil valley.	Burzil	......	...	Hamlet on Gilgit road.
7	Peshwari E.— ...	15 ...	172 ...	......	......	......	......	S. G. F. W. and T. moderate.	Hamlet.
8	Gurais P. O., T.O., B., E.— ...	14 4	186 4	......	Kishenganga valley.	Kishenganga bridge.	7800	S. G. F. W. and T. plentiful.	Fort and thana situated between villages Daner and Mankoot with small bazars.

This route is seldom used as there are no supplies and no coolies available. It is passable from July to October inclusive.

From Gultar 126 miles, a path westwards leads both to Bodial and Badagam in Tilail valley.

From Dumel 146 miles, a track crosses the Shingo river when fordable and continues up the left bank for 20 miles to the head of the valley, where it joins mile 104 of Route XLIX, Srinagar to Skardu between the Stakpita and Sarsingar passes.

From Nagai 157 miles, another path southwards over the Bobal pass and down the Gratinar ravine to Badagam in the Tilail valley.

From Dras 91 miles 4 furlongs, there is a loop route to Sumalo down left bank Dras valley to Tashgam 106 miles 4 furlongs, and Kuksar at junction of Shingo river 115 miles; thence up Shingo valley right bank to Thatanot 125 miles, Kunar 135 miles, Fransart 144 miles, here it crosses the Shingo river to left bank and continues to Chamalong 151 miles, whence it either re-crosses the same river to Sumalo 157 miles, or continues up the left bank of the Shingo valley for 50 miles to its head at the eastern foot of the Stakpita pass.

L_d KARGIL or KARKITCHU to ASTOR by SHIGAR VALLEY and DEOSAI PLAINS—

	Name	Stage	Total miles	Road remarks	Direction	Feature	Elevation	Supplies	Remarks
	Kargil (P. O., T. O., C., E—)	...	...						
1	Karkitchu (E.—)	11	120 / 125	Along Leh road to Chunagund 8 miles and cross Dras river to Karkitchu.	Up Dras valley. Up Shigar valley left bank.	Dras bridge	9390	S. G. F. W. and T. moderate.	Small village.
2	Dring	10	131 / 134 / 138	Rough and rugged path, very difficult in places for laden animals.		Phultukswai. Junction of Shingo and Shigar rivers.	.....	S. and T. scanty, G. F. W. procurable.	Ditto.
3	Ruia	9	140			Karpachu	.....	Ditto	Ditto.
4	Mutial or Gunial	10	150				.....	Ditto	Ditto.
5	Das	13	163	Path improves as valley widens out and emerges on to Deosai plains.			.....	S. and T. nil, G. F. scanty, W. plentiful.	Hamlet.
6	Katasiri	18	181 / 185			Shigar ford.	.....	Ditto	Halting place.
7	Chumda Kut	16	197	Crosses road from Srinagar to Skardu at 120 miles, Route XLIX.	Deosai plains		.....	Ditto	Ditto.
8	Cherosar	9	206 / 207		Chachor La.	Jerharcho lake.	.....	Ditto	Ditto.

Number of Marches.	Names of Stages.	Distance in miles and furlongs. Inter-mediate. m. f.	Total. m. f.	Nature of Route.	Main Valleys and Mountain Passes.	River crossings and Lakes.	Altitude above Sea Level, is Feet.	Supplies and Transport at Stages.	Remarks.
Ld	ROUTE—contd.	...	207 4	.....	Down Chor Chu.	.....	......		
			216 ...	Join Gilgit road at mile 119 of Route XLVIII.					
9	Das	13 ...	219 ...		Down Barzil valley.	......	......	S. and T. nil, G. F. W. available.	Small village.
10	Godhai E. Gardot	10 4	229 4	.....	.....	......	......	Ditto	Ditto.
		... ...	240 ...	.....	Down Astor valley.	Astor bridge	7800		
11	Astor P.O., T.O., B., E.—	17 4	247 4	.....	.....	......	7800	S. G. F. W. and T. moderate.	Fort and thana, residence of Raja of Hasora.

From Mutial 149 miles, a path branches off up to the head of the Karpochu valley and crossing the Bari La, 178 miles, descends down the Prinkiting Chu valley to its junction with the Upper Shigar river, and crossing the latter 204 miles, it joins at 205 miles the Srinagar and Skardu route XLIX at the crossing of the Pialungwai, 128 miles 4 furlongs between Kalapani and Ali Malikke Mur on the Deosai plains.

L: KARKITCHU to PARKUTA by KHORABORIGO LA -

10	Karkitchu	... ...	120 4	Rough and rugged path, very diffi-cult in places for laden animals.	Up Shigar valley left bank.	......	......	S. G. F. W. and T. moderate.	Small village.
		... ...	125 ...						

No.	Name		Dist.		Total		Road / Direction			Supplies	Character
11	Dring	...	10	4	131	...	......	......	......	S. and T. scanty, G. F. W. procurable.	Ditto.
					134	...					
12	Auril	...	9	...	140	...	Up Phultukswai valley.	......	......	S. G. F. T. moderate, W. plentiful.	Ditto.
13	Phultuks	...	7	...	147	...	......	......	......	Ditto	Village.
					152	4	Path branches off to Torgoon La.				
14	Phultuks Tso	...	11	...	158	...	Khoraborigo La.	Lake	......	S. and T. nil, G. F. W. procurable.	Halting place.
					164	...					
15	Rongul	...	20	...	178	...	Down Genial valley.	......	......	Ditto	Hamlet.
16	Shadoek	...	9	...	187	...	Join the Skardu road at mile 194 and continue to Parkuta, mile 199½.	Indus valley left bank.	Dunsumchu	S. and T. scanty, G. F. W. procurable.	Small village.
17	Parkuta	...	5	4	192	4	Indus valley	......	......	S. G. F. W. and T. plentiful.	Large village and fort.

This route is more direct and 7 miles shorter than the main road down the Suru and Indus valleys.

From mile 152½ about half-way between Phultuka and the Lake, a path turns eastwards 30 miles long over the Torgoon La, and down the Torgoon Chu by Dado Niril to Shirting at mile 160 of the main road l.

From the same point following the same path over the Torgoon La for the first 10 miles, another track diverges northwards across the heads of the two valleys, Torgoon and Gidiaxdo Lxoongma, and the intervening spur between by the Kimunay La, it drops down the Kusura Lxoongma by Thasing to Tolti at mile 183¼ of the main road. The total distance of this transmontane route from Phultuks to Tolti is 40 miles.

LI SRINAGAR to LEH by DRAS—

Number of Marches	Names of Stages	Distance in miles and furlongs — Intermediate m. f.	Distance in miles and furlongs — Total m. f.	Nature of Route	Main Valleys and Mountain Passes	River crossings and Lakes	Altitude above Sea Level in Feet	Supplies and Transport and Stages	Remarks
	Srinagar P. O., T. O., C., E.—	...	0	The first stage by road or by boat, either across Anchar lake or down Jhelum river to Shadipur and up Sindh river to Gunderbul.	Jhelum valley	...	5235	S. G. F. W. and T. abundant.	Capital of Kashmir State, large town, bazars, Hari Parbat fort.
1	Gunderbul E.—	14 2	14 2	Hence a good road up Sindh valley, passable for laden animals.	Up Sindh valley left bank.	Sindh bridge	5230	S. G. F. and coolies available, W. plentiful.	Village
		3	22 4			Ditto.			
2	Khangan E.—	11 3	25 5	......	Right bank	Ditto	6000	Ditto	Ditto.
	Haigan	...	30 ...	......	......	Cross Sindh river several times according to present state of bridges.			
	Surphrar	...	35 ...	......					
3	Gund E.—	13 6	39 3	......	......		6700	Ditto	Ditto.
	Kulan E. confined—		43						

No.	Name of stage	m.	f.	Total	f.	Nature of road	Bank of river	Bridge	Height	Supplies	Remarks
4	Gugangair E.—	8	...	47	3	Road rough and rocky but passable for horses.	......	......	7400	S. nil, G. and T. moderate, F. and W. plentiful.	Small village.
5	Sonamarg P.O., T.O., B., E. some old log huts	7	2	51	3	Road good	Left bank	Sindh bridge.	8650	S. scarce, T. moderate, G. F. and W. plentiful.	Sanitarium on grassy downs.
				54	5	......	Right bank	Ditto.			
6	Baltal E.—	9	...	55	5	Steep ascent for about 2,000 feet and very gradual descent on north side.	Zoji La	......	9900	S. and T. nil, G. F. W. procurable.	Huts.
				63	5				11300		
7	Matayan B., E.—	15	...	69	4		Down Goomber or Dras valley left bank.	......	11000	S. nil, F. T. moderate, G. W. procurable.	Hamlets.
	Pandras			78	5	......	......	Mushkibridge.			
				84	4						
8	Dras P.O., T.O., B., C., E.	13	7	90	4	Rough and stony road.	......	Marpochu „	9825	S. G. F. W. and T. moderate.	Series of small villages, fort and thana, 3 stone pillars.
				91	4						Village and thana.
9	Tashgam B., E.— Kharbu E.	15	...	106	4	......	Right bank	Dras bridge	9390	Ditto	Police station.
				113	:		......	......	......		
10	Chunagund E.—	15	...	121	4	Road rough and broken.	......	......	8675	S. and T. nil, G. F. W. procurable.	Small village.
				123	4						
11	Kargil P.O., T.O., B., E.—	6	...	127	4	Road over sandy plateau.	Up Suru valley left bank.	Junction of Suru and Dras rivers. Suru bridge	8787	S. G. F. W. and T. plentiful.	Capital of Parik, fort and thana.
	Pashkim E.			133	:	......	Up Wakachu valley left bank.	Wakka bridge	......	......	Large village and fort.

Number of Marches	Names of Stages	Distance in miles and furlongs — Inter-mediate (m. f.)	Distance — Total (m. f.)	Nature of Route	Main Valleys and Mountain Passes	River crossings and Lakes	Altitude above Sea Level in Feet	Supplies and Transport at Stages	Remarks
LI	ROUTE—contd.	......	133 ...						
12	Shergol B., E.—	18 6	146 2	Road good	......	......	10290	S. G. F. W. and T. available.	Village and Buddhist monastery.
	Mulbeck	......	149 ...	Easy ascent and descent.	Namika La	...	13000	......	Large monastery and colossal figure cut out of rock.
		......	158 ...						
13	Kharbu	19	165 2	......	Up Sasse (Coena valley.)	......	10590	Ditto	Group of villages.
	Hiniskoot	......	172 4						
14	Lamayuru B., E.—	......	176 ...	Easy ascent and descent.	Photu La	......	13300	S. G. F. W. and T. moderate.	Large Monastery. Fort.
	Khalsi	15 2	180 4	Road crosses torrent several times.	Up Indus valley right bank	Indus bridge	11400	Ditto	Village.
		......	190 4	Good road	......	......	10000	Ditto	Ditto.
15	Nurla B., E.—	......	19: ...	Road rough over granite boulders.	......	Phodru Drokpo bridge.	......	S. and T. nil, G. F. W. available.	Small village.
		18 2	198 6						
16	Saspul B., E.—	14 6	213 4	Road better, crossing plateau.	......	Saspul Drokpo bridge.	......	S. G. F. W. and T. procurable.	Large village.
	Bazgo	......	221 ...			Bazgo Drokpo bridge.			

No.	Place	m	f	Total m	f	Bridge	Elevation	Road	S. G. F. W. and T.	Remarks
17	**Nimu** B., E.—	11	4	225	...	Sucuo Drokpo bridge.	......	Road over rough ground and barren plateau.	S. G. F. W. and T. moderate.	Small village.
	Phagrag B.	...	...	236	...	Lunachuo Fao bridge.	......			
	Pitak	...	...	239	...	......	10500	Good road hence over gravelly slope to Leh.	S. and T. nil, G. F. W. procurable.	Village and monastery.
18	**Leh** P. O., B., C., E.—	18	2	243	2	......	11400		S. G. F. W. and T. abundant.	Large town and fort, capital of Ladak.

This road is usually open from the middle of June to middle of November, though snow may be met with on top of Zoji La to end of June. It is the chief trade route between Kashmir and Yarkand.

From Kargil, 127 miles 4 furlongs, a path goes eastwards over the Hamothing La to Dungol on the Indus by Apatithung 136 miles, Hamothing La 140 miles, Lato 144 miles, Dungul 151 miles.

For southern route from Kargil 127 miles 4 furlongs by Sankhu 9,970 feet, opposite Kurtse, to Suru 171 miles 4 furlongs, see Route XVI.

From Shergol a track goes westwards over the Naktul La by Yogmagil 12 miles to Chatiakot on the Suru river 15 miles. Total 27 miles.

From Mulbeck an alternative track south-eastwards crosses over the Sirwastan La to Kharlon, being about the same distance as by the main road over Namika La.

From Hiniskoot 172 miles, a path goes south-westwards up the Kangi ravine by Kilchu 13 miles, crosses the Kangi La 12 miles, to Ringdom Monastery 15 miles on the Suru or Sankpo river. Total length 40 miles.

From Nurla, 198 miles 6 furlongs, there is an alternative route to Bazgo, which branches off a little beyond the village of Nurla, turns up a ravine northwards to Timisgam 203 miles, rising about 1,500 feet. It then goes eastwards to Hemis Shukpa, where there is a grove of pencil cedars and the ruins of an old tower 210 miles, and continuing along the high plateau broken by occasional ravines, Taratse 220 miles is reached, and then Bazgo 226 miles. If this upper route be taken, the stages from Nurla would become Hemis, Bazgo, Phayang and Leh.

LIa SINDH VALLEY to LIDAR VALLEY by JAJIMARG and DACHINPARA—

No.	Place	m	f	Total m	f	Feature	Elevation	Road	S. G. F. W. and T.	Remarks
	Kulan	...	...	43	3	Sindh bridge.	......	Road from Kulan to Lidarwat not safe for laden ponies, very slippery and dangerous in wet weather.	S. G. F. W. and T. moderate.	Small village.
	E. roobuai—	...	...	47	4					
	Zuerind E.	...	...	51	4					
	Yeuna Nag E.	...	...	54	4	Basnai range Plateau called Jajimarg.				
1	**Sekiwas in Jaji-marg.** E.—	11	7	57	7	Lake.	14000		S. and T. nil, G. W. plentiful, P. dwarf Juniper.	Halting place.

Number of Marches	Names of Stages	Distance in Miles and Furlongs — Intermediate m. f.	Total m. f.	Nature of Route	Main Valleys and Mountain Passes	River crossings and Lakes	Altitude above Sea Level in Feet	Supplies and Transport at Stages	Remarks
LIa	ROUTE—contd.	...	...						
2	Lidarwat E.—	14 4	57 7	Hence a fair road passable for laden ponies and mules.	Down Lidar valley left bank. This valley is called Dachinpara.	Lidar bridge	......	S. and T. nil. G. F. W. available.	Halting place.
3	Aru E.—	9 1	67 ...	......	......	......	......	Ditto	Hamlet.
4	Pahlgam E.—	9 ...	76 ...	Good road passable for laden animals.	......	......	8500	S. G. F. W. plentiful, T. available.	Chief place in Dachinpara, cluster of villages.
	Ganeshbal	9 ...	85 ...	......	......	......	......	......	Chief stage of pilgrimage.
	Batkot	... ...	... ...	......	......	......	......	......	Village.
5	Eishmakam E.—	14 ...	99 ...		......	......	......	Ditto	Mahomedan shrine, old copper mine at Harjat Nag.
6	Bawan E.—	10 ...	109 ...		......	......	......	Ditto	Beautiful spring, temple and caves.
7	Islamabad or Anant Nag. P.O., T.O., B., C., E.	4 4	113 4	......	......	Sulphurous hot springs.	5450	S. G. F. W. abundant, T. ample.	Town and bazar, head-quarters of district.

There are tracks from two places in the Sindh valley to Jajimarg, *viz.*, Surphrar 35 miles, and Kulan 43 miles 3 furlongs. The former is seldom used. Most travellers go first to Sonamarg, and on their return branch off from Kulan. If coming the other way, they take the Kulan route as the nearest to Sonamarg. From Kulan after crossing the Sindh river the road ascends a spur through pine forest for 5 miles, then through birch trees, and ascends the grassy sides of the hill to Yemsa Nag and upwards to the summit, whence an easy descent to Sekiwas. From Jajimarg are paths to the seven lakes, through Nag Baran to Srinagar, through Arphal to Panjær, and through Trahal to Awantipur.

Lb. BALTAL to AMARANATH—

No.	Stage					Remarks	Direction	Feature	Feet	Supplies	Remarks
6	Baltal	...	...	63	5	This track is only practicable while the snow bridges across the river are able to bear weight.	Up the Sangam Kol or Upper Sindh valley.	......	9000	S. and T. nil, G. F. W. procurable.	Huts.
7	Panjitarni	8	...	71	5			......	......	S. and T. nil, G. W. available, F. Juniper bushes.	Halting place.
8	Amaranath Cave	5	.	76	5	There is no regular path; closed after June.	......	Cave in the gypsum rock.	13000	Nil.	Celebrated place of pilgrimage sacred to Siva.

Lc. DRAS to ZANSKAR by SURU—

No.	Stage					Remarks	Direction	Feature	Feet	Supplies	Remarks
	Dras. *P. O., T. O., B., C., E.*	...	...	91	4	Rough road for laden animals.	......	Dras river	9825	S. G. F. W. and T. moderate.	Series of small villages, fort and thana.
	Pranwari	...	...	97	...	Steep ascent and easy descent.	Lamagoos La.				
				100	...	Gentle ascent and steep descent.	Umba La.				
1	Umba. *E.—*	15	4	104	...	......	Down Nakpo chu valley.			Ditto	Village.
				107	...						
2	Sankhu	9	...	116	...	Fair hill road	Up Sora valley left bank.	......	9070	S. G. F. W. and T. procurable.	Junction of Phulangna or Kurtse river.

Number of Marches.	Names of Stages.	Distance in Miles and Furlongs. Inter- mediate. m. f.	Distance in Miles and Furlongs. Total. m. f.	Nature of Route.	Main Valleys and Mountain Passes.	River Crossings and Lakes.	Altitude above Sea Level in Feet.	Supplies and Transport at Stages.	Remarks.
Llc	ROUTE—contd.	...	116 ...						
3	Suru E.—	9 ... / 18	134 ...	Hence steep ascent and descent over Parkutse spur or go round latter along right bank of Sankpo river about 12 miles.	Up Sankpo valley right bank. Parkutse La.	Suru bridge	10624	S. G. F. T. moderate, W. plentiful.	Fort and village.
4	Parkutse	6	137 ... / 140 ...		Up Sankpo valley right bank.	......	......	S. and T. nil, G. F. W. available.	Small village.
5	Gulmatongo	12	152 ...	Easy road passable for laden animals.	......	......	......	Ditto	Huts.
6	Ringdom or Gonpa Lama serai E.—	17	169 ...	......	......	Kungi ford	......	S. and T. precarious, F. G. W. available.	Lama monastery.
	Tari Tongus	...	171 4			Paller Brokhpo.			
7	Randun Sankpo E.—	13	182 ...	On both approaches to this pass, several spurs have to be crossed which break up the road, but the general gradient is easy.	......	......	......	S. F. G. T. nil, W. plentiful.	Junction of Maroo or Petgam road at foot of Pensi La. Cross glacier.
		...	192 ...		Pensi La	......	14400	......	
8	Chumkurmoo	20	202 ...		Down Doda or Zanskar valley left bank.	......	......	S. and T. nil, G. F. scanty, W. plentiful.	Halting place.

9	Abring or Rooshool E.—	16	...	218	...	Rough road but passable.	......	......	......	Ditto	Hamlet.
10	Phe E.—	12	...	230	...	Fair hill track passable for laden animals.	......	......	12000	S. G. F. W. procurable, few coolies.	Village nearly opposite Ating on right bank.
	Tungring	...	...	238	...	......	Doda bridge.	Right bank			
11	Seni Gonpa E.—	11	...	241	...	......	Seni Tokpho bridge.	...	11560	Ditto	Village and temple.
				243	...	......	Tissrap Lingti Chu or Sindu.	...			
12	Padam E.—	9	...	250	...	......	......	...	11373	S. G. F. W. and T. procurable.	Former capital of Zanskar, village and fort.

From Sankhu 116 miles after crossing the Suru river there is a road eastwards up the Phulangma or Kurtse river to Kurtse 119 miles, a small town, and Itchu 137 miles, whence there is said to be a difficult footpath up the Hang ravine south-east over the high range to Ringdom monastery 161 miles.

From Ringdom 169 miles there is a difficult footpath over the Lima Lorsa La 184 miles, across the head of the Omachu valley to Kesi La 206 miles, across the head of the Lanung Chu valley to Huboona La 214 miles and 15,453 feet, down Tchelong Chu valley to its junction with the Omachu 222 miles, crossing the spur on both sides of this river, up the left bank of the Zanskar river by Hanomil 234 miles, Padum 240 miles, Zozar 252 miles and 11,583 feet, where there is a rope bridge over the Doda or Zanskar river and along the right bank to Thonde 250 miles, and to Padam 270 miles.

At Tungring, join road from Umasi La, see Route XVII.

LII SRINAGAR to LEH by SURU—

THERE ARE SEVERAL POSSIBLE ROUTES ACROSS THE HILL COUNTRY AS SHOWN IN THE FOLLOWING TABLE.
FIRSTLY, OF PASSES BETWEEN THE JHELUM, DACHINPARA OR LIDAR AND THE MAROO OR WURDWAN VALLEYS.

SUNASUR NAG.

Miles		Place
0		Srinagar 5,235ft.
3		Takt-i-Suliman 6,263ft.
4		Gupcar
7		Nisbut Bagh
9	9	Shalimar
11		Harwan *Bund of Water works,*
17	8	Dajgaon
30	13	Nagbaran
0		Srinagar
8	8	Pampur
11		Wean *Iron mines.*
14	6	Shar
17		Westerwan ridge
19		Pustuni

KISSLIN GULLI OR DIDOOF NAG.

Miles		Place
0		Srinagar
8		Pampur
18	18	Awantipur
25	7	Trahal *Up Patarkool valley. (Sotoor for Nag-baran.)*
33	11	Bhogmoor pass 9,100ft.
37	12	Wallarhama
0		Wallarhama
8		Danhut
51	14	Luangni valley
54		Doodschur Nag nala

HAIBBUL GULLI.

Miles		Place
0		Srinagar
8		Pampur
18	18	Awantipur
29	11	Bij Behara *Cross mouth of Lidar valley.*
43	14	Salee
47½		Veil
49		Mesaj pass
51	8	Gowrun *Up Antihar valley*
54		Rishpura

NILTOPA GULLI OR CHOR NAG.

Miles		Place
0		Srinagar
8		Pampur
18	18	Awantipur
29	11	Bij Behara *Across Dachinpara*
43	14	Salee
47½		Veil
49		Mesaj pass
51	8	Gowrun *Across Antihar valley.*
		……
54		Rishpura

MARGAN PASS OR SHILSAR PASS.

Miles		Place
0		Srinagar
8	8	Pampur
18	18	Awantipur
29		Bij Behara
35	17	Islamabad
41		Achibal
46	11	Shangus
49		Shangus
51	8	Hurrikun gulli
52		Karpoor
58	12	Nowboog *Up Nowboog valley.*

HOKSAR PASS.

Miles		Place
0		Srinagar
8		Pampur
18	18	Awantipur
29		Bij Behara
35	17	Islamabad *Up Brinagh valley.*
48	13	Sagam
54		Wangam
55	8	Gohoon *Up Nowboog valley and Brinwar ravine.*

Arphal ... *In Patarkool valley.*	...	21	......	...	...	**Dardpoora** ...	...	55	**Kimrun** ...	7½	58½	**Gooran** ...	9	67	**Doos**	...	63
Sotoor	9	23	**Kisslin gulli**	...	58	**Hairbul Nag**	10	61	**Niltopa gulli**	...	64½	**Margan pass** 11,600 ft.	...	73	**Rajparan** ...	14	70
Tamnag ridge	..	31	**Kisslin** ...	13	64	**Ditto Gulli** ...	...	62	**Zamkut** ...	9	67½	**Inshin** ..	16	83	**Hoksar pass** 13,315 ft. *Down Sutgul valley.*	...	74½
Nagbaran	10	33	**Suknis**	12	76	**Jajmarg** ... *Down Choi Draman Nai.*	...	63	**Suidraman** ...	7½	75	**Baswan** ...	...	91			
									Baswan	...	80						
Nagbaran ...	...	33	**Wallarhama**	...	37	......	...	...	**Suknis** ...	13	88	**Suknis** ...	16	99			
Cross high ridge	...	36	**Eishmakan** ...	...	43	......	...	...	**Bij Behara** ...	...	29	**Shangus** ... *In Arpat or Kutihar valley.*	...	46	**Phamber** ...	13	83
Tar Sar	...	37	**Lokutpoora springs.**	...	45	**Suidraman** ... *In Wurdwan valley.*	11	72	**Islamabad** ...	6	35	......	...	...	**Dolwas ridge** ...	...	86
									Martund ... *Ancient temples.*	6	41						
Lidar Wat ... *In Dachinpara valley.*	12	45	**Harpat Nag** *Old Copper mine.*	14	51	......	...	...	**Renipura** ... *Across Arpat valley.*	..	45½	**Wutrus** ...	...	47½	**Maroo or Pet-gam.** *In Wurdwan valley.*	14	97
Aru ...	9	54	**Goguldar** ...	...	55	**Baswan** ...	..	77	**Watrus** ...	8½	49½	**Halkun gulli**	...	52			
									Metmoo ...	...	53						
Pailgam	9	63	**Liwapatur pass** ...	..	57½	**Suknis**	13	85	**Saogam** ...	7½	57	**Nowboog** ...	10	56			
Tanin ...	10	73	**Lungni valley**	8	59	......	...	...	**Chor Nag gulli**	...	69	**Gooran** ...	9	65			
Zoijpul ..	...	78	**Didoof Nag and gulli.**	...	62		...	...	**Hirmai** ...	16	73	**Shilsar pass**	...	72½			
Sunasur Nag	8	81															
Ditto Gulli	...	83	**Baswan** ... *In Wurdwan valley.*	13	72	......	...	...	**Inshin** ... *In Wurdwan valley.*	8	81	**Pasur Nai** ...	16	81			
									Baswan ..	...	89	**Maroo or Pet-gam.** *In Wurdwan valley.*	12	93			
Suknis *In Wurdwan valley.*	10	91	**Suknis** ...	8	80	......	...	...	**Suknis** ...	16	97						

SECONDLY, OF PASSES BETWEEN THE WURDWAN AND SURU VALLEYS—

BHUTKHOL PASS KWAJ KUR ROUTE.		BHUTKHOL PASS RANGMARG ROUTE.		CHILUNG PASS.		REMARKS.
	Miles.		Miles.		Miles.	
Suknis ...	76	Suknis ...	80	Maroo or Petgam. ...	93	All the foregoing routes between the Jhelum, Dachinpara and Wurdwan valleys are comparatively easy with the exception of the high snow passes, which are all difficult. The Sunasur Nag, Hairbol, Niltopa and Chor Nag are the worst passes with bad approaches.
Dumhoi ...	9 / 85	Dumhoi ...	9 / 89	Zubban *Hot Springs.* ...	101	
Morsekhol ...	12 / 97	Pajahoi ...	94	Metwan ...	14 / 107	
Bhutkhol pass 14,370 ft.	107	Kanital ...	15 / 104	Maharran ...	10 / 117	
Dunore ...	20 / 117	Bhutkhol pass ...	114	Kailgan rocks ...	12 / 129	Between the Wurdwan and Suru valleys both the Bhutkhol and Chilung passes are most trying, the Chilung pass is the worst over 10 miles of glacier.
		Jalahoi ...	16 / 120	Camp *west foot of glacier.* ...	12 / 141	
Suru ...	10 / 127	Suru ...	15 / 135	Chilung pass *East foot of glacier* ...	146	There are two ways over the Bhutkhol pass dependent upon the state of the snow. When the latter is hard, the Rangmarg route is preferred, as it is longer and of easier gradient. Afterwards the Kwaj Kur route, which is steeper, is taken.
Parkutse ...	6 / 133	Parkutse ...	6 / 141	Ramdun Sankpo. ...	151	
Gulmatongo ...	12 / 145	Gulmatongo ...	12 / 153	*Junction of road from Pensi La.* ...	20 / 161	
Ringdom *Lama Monastery* ...	17 / 162	Ringdom *Lama Monastery.* ...	17 / 170	Ringdom *Lama Monastery.* ...	13 / 174	

THIRDLY, OF PASSES BETWEEN THE SURU AND INDUS VALLEYS—

	KUNGI LA AND PHOTU LA.	KUNGI LA AND CHOMO-THANG LA.	KUNGI LA, CHOMOTHANG LA, AND CHOKE LA.		KUNGI LA, CHOMOTHANG LA, CHOKE LA AND KUNDE LA.	REMARKS.
	Miles.	Miles.	Miles.		Miles.	
Ringdom	... 162					Between the Suru and Indus valleys, both roads over the Kungi La to Lamayuru are fairly passable. At Lamayuru, the main road from Srinagar to Leh Route LI is joined.
West foot of pass...	12 174					
Kungi La	... 177					
Down Haman valley.						
Kilchu	15 180	Kilchu ... 189				
Kangi	... 192	Kangi ... 192				
Hiniskut	13 202	Domboom ... 6 195				
		Chomothang La. ... 200				
		Down Shilla Kong valley.				
Photu La	... 206½	Shilla 19 214	Shilla ... 214			
			Up Kopchar valley.			
		Prinkitil La ... 217	Phanjila 7 221			On the Choke La route there is no bridge over the Indus at Nimu.
Lamayuru	9 211	Lamayuru ... 6 229	Hinjoo 9 230			
Join Leh road over Zojila.		*Join Leh road.*	Choke La ... 234½			
			13,513 ft.			
			Down Sumdahjoo.			
Khalsi	... 221	Khalsi ... 239	Drogulika 10 239			
Indus bridge.		*Indus bridge.*				

THIRDLY—(*continued.*)

KUNGI LA AND PHOTU LA.	Miles.		KUNGI LA AND CHOMOTHANG LA.	Miles.		KUNGI LA, CHOMOTHANG LA AND CHOKE LA.	Miles.		KUNGI LA, CHOMOTHANG LA, CHOKE LA AND KUNDU LA.	Miles.		REMARKS.
Nurla ...	18¼	239¼	**Nurla** ...	18¼	238¼	**Ezas** ... *Down Zanskar river.*	9	249	**Ezas** ... *Up Zanskar river.*	...	249	
Saspul	14¾	244	**Saspul** ...	14¾	253	...... *Cross Indus river*	...	264	**Chiling** ... *Up Markha river.*	8	257	On the Kunda La route there is a bridge over the Indus at Shushot, but the road about Chiling on the Zanskar river and up the Markha river is a mere footpath.
Nimu	11½	255½	**Nimu** ...	11½	264½	**Nimu** ... *Join Leh road.*	16	265	**Skio** ...	9	266	
									Kunda La ... 16,211 ft.	...	275	
Leh ... 11,500 *feet.*	18¼	273¾	**Leh** ...	18¼	282¾	**Leh** ...	18¼	283¼	**Urucha** ...	12	278	
									Khawuch ...	16	294	
									Shushot, Indus bridge. 10,560 ft.	...	299	
									Leh ... 11,500 ft.	10	304	

LIII   SRINAGAR to INSHIN in WURDWAN by the MARGAN or IKPATRAN PASS—

NUMBER OF MARCHES	NAMES OF STAGES.	DISTANCE IN MILES AND FURLONGS. Inter- mediate. m. f.	Total. m. f.	NATURE OF ROUTE.	MAIN VALLEYS AND MOUNTAIN PASSES.	RIVER CROSSINGS AND LAKES.	ALTITUDE ABOVE SEA LEVEL IN FEET.	SUPPLIES AND TRANSPORT AT STAGES.	REMARKS.
	Srinagar P. O., T. O., C., E.—	...	0	By road or by boat up the river Jhelum to Kanabul, 50 miles by water.	Up Jhelum valley on right bank.	....	5235	S. F. G. W. and T. abundant.	Capital of Kashmir. Hari Parbat fort. Large town and bazars.
	Pandrethan	...	4	......		......	......	......	Ancient capital and temple in ruins.
	Pampur E.	...	8			......	......		
1	**Awantipur** E.—	18	18	......		......	5300	S. and T. nil, F. G. W. plentiful.	Two ancient temples in ruins.
	Bij Behara	...	29	......		......	......	......	Town and temples.
	Kanabul B.	...	4	......		......	5400	......	Terminus of river navigation.
2	**Islamabad** P. O., T. O., C., E.—	17	35	Good road passable for laden animals to Nowboog.	Cross mouth of Arpat valley, then ascend Kuti- har to Shangus along left bank.	Sulphurous springs.	5450	S. F. G. W. and T. ample.	Town, bazar and head-quarters of zillah.
	Achbal B.	...	36	......		Arpat bridge	......	......	Old Imperial garden and famous spring.
			41						
3	**Shangus** E.—	11	46	......		......	......	Ditto	Large village.

Number of Marches	Names of Stages	Distance in miles and furlongs. Inter-mediate. m. f.	Total. m. f.	Nature of Route.	Main Valleys and Mountain Passes.	River Crossings and Lakes.	Altitude above Sea Level in Feet.	Supplies and Transport at Stages.	Remarks.
LIII	*ROUTE—contd.*	...	...						
	Karpur E.	11	46	......	Cross Karpur range by Hurrikun or Hulkun gulli.	......	......	S. G. F. W. and T. moderate.	Village on high ground.
		...	52						
4	**Nowboog** *E.—*	12	58	Hence road becomes rough but is passable for laden animals to Inshin.	Up Nowboog valley.	......	......	S. G. F. W. plentiful, T. available.	Large village.
5	**Gooran**	9	67		......	Nowboog bridge.	......	Ditto	Small village.
		...	73	Road over pass of easy gradient but rocky on both sides, level plain for 2 miles on top of pass, fine views eastwards and westwards.	Margan pass or Ikpatran.	...	11600	......	Pir Punjal range.
6	**Inshin in Wurd-wan.** *E.—*	16	83			Wurdwan bridge.	8143	S. and T. precarious, F. G. W. plentiful.	Village and capital of Wurdwan.

The alternative route by Halkun gulli from Shangus to Nowboog is 2 miles shorter, but not so good.

There is another route from Islamabad 35 miles, by Martand 41 miles, where are the ancient temples of the Sun, cross the Arpat or Kutihar valley to Watrus 49½ miles and ascend left bank and ravine to Saogam 57 miles, thence ascend the Palapat spur of the main range Pir Punjal to the Chor Nag and gulli 63 miles and descend down the Hirnai ravine and cross the Wurdwan river by bridge to Inshin 81 miles. The approaches to the Chor Nag pass on both sides are very steep and rocky.

LIV SRINAGAR to HANLE by ZANSKAR—

No.	Stage	Dist. between	Total dist.	Road	Route	Remarks	Elevation (feet)	Supplies	Description
	Srinagar P. O., T. O., C., E.—	...	0	By road or by boat up the river Jhelum to Karabul, 50 miles by water.	Up Jhelum valley, on right bank.	......	5235	S. F. G. W. and T. abundant.	Capital of Kashmir. Hari Parbat fort. Large city and bazars.
	Pandrethan E.—	...	4	......	......	......	......	......	Ancient capital and temple in ruins.
	Pampur E.	...	8						
1	Awantipur E.—	18	18	......	......	......	5290	S. and T. nil. F. G. W. plentiful.	Two ancient temples in ruins.
	Bij Behara								
	Kanabul B.	...	23¾				5400	......	Terminus of river navigation.
2	Islamabad P. O., T. O., C., E.—	17	25	Good road passable for laden animals to Doos.	Up Bringh valley.	Sulphurous springs. Aryat bridge.	5450	S. F. G. W. and T. plentiful.	Large town, bazar and head-quarters of zillah.
3	Sagam E.—	13	36	......	......	......	......	S. F. G. W. and T. available.	Large village.
	Wangam E.	...	48						
4	Gohoon E.—	8	54	......	Up Nowboog valley and Brihwar ravine.	...	......	S. and T. nil, F. G. and W. procurable.	Small village.
	Doos E.—	...	63	Hence road is very difficult in places for laden animals.	......	......	...	S. F. G. W. and T. available.	Large village.
5	Rajparan E.—	14	70	......	......	......	......	S. and T. nil, G. F. W. plentiful.	Halting place.

Number of Marches.	Names of Stages.	Distance in miles and furlongs. Intermediate. m. f.	Total. m. f.	Nature of Route	Main Valleys and Mountain Passes.	River crossings and Lakes.	Altitude above Sea Level in feet.	Supplies and Transport at Stages.	Remarks.
LIV	ROUTE—contd.	...	70 ...			......			
6	Phamber E.—	14	74 4	Approaches on both sides rough, steep and stony.	Hoksar pass down Sutgul ravine.	......	13315	S. and T. nil, G. F. W. plentiful.	Halting place.
		13	83 ...	......	Dolwas spur	......	...		
7	Maroo or Petgam in Wurdwan. E.—	14	97 ...	Path rough and rugged and very difficult in places for ponies.	Up Furriabad valley right bank.	Wurdwan bridge.	......	S. F. G. W. and T. moderate.	Village and custom house.
	Zebban E.	..	105 ...	......	......	......	......	......	Hot springs.
8	Metwan E.—	14	111 ...	......	......	......	......	S. and T. precarious, G. F. W. moderate.	Small village.
9	Maharran E.—	10	121 ...	......	......	......	......	Ditto	Ditto.
10	Kailgang rocks E.—	12	133 ...	......	......	......	......	S. and T. nil, G. F. W. moderate.	Halting place.
11	Camp west foot of glacier	12	145 ...	......	......	......	......	S. and T. nil, G. F. scanty, W. plentiful.	Ditto.
		..	150 ...	Glacier 10 miles long.	Chilung pass.	......	......		

No.	Name of place	Distance	Total	Nature of road	Direction	Bridges	Height (feet)	Supplies	Remarks
	East foot of glacier ...	:	155	...	......	......	...	S. F. G. T. nil, W. plentiful	Cross glacier.
12	Ramdun Sank-po	20	165	Junction of 2 roads, down valley to Surn, and up to Padam by Pensi La.	Pensi La	......	14400	......	Halting place.
13	Chumkurmoo	20	185	Easy gradient crossing spurs on both sides of pass.	Down Doda or Zanskar valley left bank.	......	...	S. and T. nil, F. G. scanty, W. plentiful.	Hamlet.
14	Abring or Roos-hool	16	201	Rough road bot passable.	......	......	...	Ditto	
15	Phe	12	213	Fair hill track, passable for laden animals, junction of road from Kishtwar over Umasi La.	......	Dola bridge.	12000	S. F. G. T. procurable, few coolies.	Village nearly opposite Ating on right bank.
	Tungring	:	:	......	Right bank	......	...		
16	Seni Gonpa E.—	11	224	......	......	Seni Tokpho bridge.	11560	Ditto	Ditto and temple.
17	Padam E.—	9	233	......	......	Tsarap Lingti Chu bridge.	11873	S. G. F. W. and T. procurable.	Former capital of Zanskar, village and fort.

Hence there are two routes to Hanle, one by Thonde, Shadi, Sloon and Lachalung to the Tso Morari Lake and the other up the Tsarap Lingti Chu across a corner of the British territory to the same Lake.

No.	Name of place	Distance	Total	Nature of road	Direction	Bridges	Height (feet)	Supplies	Remarks
18	Thonde E.—	9	242	Rough hill track, very difficult in places for laden animals.	Thonde La down Shingri Chu.	......	11450		
		:	248				16700		

Number of Marches	Names of Stages	Distance in miles and furlongs		Nature of Route	Main Valleys and Mountain Passes	River crossings and Lakes	Altitude above Sea Level in Feet	Supplies and Transport at Stages	Remarks
		Intermediate m. f.	Total m. f.						
LIV	*ROUTE—contd.*	...	...				...		
19	**Soulantakakh**	...	248	Instead of following river, spar opposite junction may be crossed by Shingri La.	...	Cross Shingri Chu several fords.	...	S. F. G. T. nil, W. procurable.	Junction of Niri Chu.
	Malla Samda	14	256	...	Down Niri Chu left bank.	...	...	......	One mile to Shadi Monastery.
	Shalipo	...	263	...	Right bank	Niri bridge	...	S. and T. scanty, F. G. W. available.	
		...	266 4				...		
20	**Tontak Gonpa**	16	270			Ditto.	...		
	E:—	...	272	From Bokung another path follows down the right bank of Niri Chu to its junction with	Malo Kontse La.		...		
	Bokung	...	276 4		Gotunta La	...	16870.		
		...	278		Up Shoon valley right bank.		...		
		...	284	Shoon river and up the right bank of latter to Karmoch, thus avoiding the two passes, distance about the same.		...	...		
21	**Karmoch**	16	288		Up Shoon valley right bank.	...	...	Ditto	Small village.
	Mane Leh	...	295			...	...		
22	**Sutak**	14	302	...	...	...	...	Ditto	Hamlet.
23	**Takh**	9	311	...	...	Hot spring.	...	S. and T. precarious, F. G. W. procurable.	Small village.
		...	317						

No.	Station	Miles	Total	Road notes	Pass / Valley	Position	Height	Supplies	Remarks
24	Juktak	13	324	Join main road Lahoul to Leh passable for baden animals to 380 miles.	Up Gata ravine.	...	...	S. F. G. T. nil, W. procurable.	...
25	Sumdo *B.E.—*	8	332	......		...	......	Ditto.	Ditto.
	Piabogokma	...	334		Lachalung La.	......	16630.		Hamlet.
			340						
26	Sum Gal *E.—*	18	350	Khiangchu maidan, good road.	Up Sum kheyl Loombo.	...	...	S. and T. precarious, F. G. W. procurable.	
27	Tractagol	16	393	Rough and rugged path.		...	...	S. F. G. T. nil, W. scanty.	
			370	......	Telekon La down Phirse valley.				
28	Huahl	12	378	Junction of road from Lanyer La.		...	...	S. and T. nil, F. G. W. scanty.	
29	Manechan *E.—*	14	392	Junction of road from Pangpo La.	...	...	...	S. and T. nil, F. G. W. scanty.	
30	Khulmoche *E.—*	11	403	......	...	...	...	S. and T. nil, F. G. W. scanty.	Halting place.
34	Kiangdom *E.—*	11	414	Rough track passable for baden animals.		South end of Tso Morari Lake.	14900	S. F. T. nil, G. W. scanty.	Ditto.
			422	......	Narboo La.	Lake			Plain, Lake water brackish.
35	Lam Tso *E.—*	20	434	......	Across head of Parechu valley.	...	...	S. and T. nil, F. G. W. procurable.	Halting place.
			443	......		...	...		Ditto.
36	Dongam Le *E.—*	9	447	......	Lenak La.	...	...	S. and T. nil, F. G. W. procurable.	Two tracks over this pass.

Number of Marches.	Names of Stages.	Distance in miles and furlongs.		Nature of Route.	Main Valleys and Mountain Passes.	River Crossings and Lakes.	Altitude above Sea Level in feet.	Supplies and Transport at Stages.	Remarks.
		Intermediate. m. f.	Total. m. f.						
LIV	ROUTE—contd.	... ...	447 ...				......		
37	Gongra Le E.—	11 ...	454 ...	......	......	......	......	S. and T. nil, F. G. W. procurable.	Halting place.
38	Hanle E.—	20 ...	474 ...	Across Thungangeri plain.	......	On left bank of Hanle river.	14270	S. F. G. W. and T. moderate.	Village and large monastery and thana.

From Huahl 378 miles, there is a path eastwards over the Lanyer La 385 miles, and down the Kingha Sharma ravine to 392 miles, whence another path turns off south-east over the Karzok La 399 miles, and down the Karzokfoo to Karzok monastery 408 miles, and 14,960 feet on the western bank of the Tso Morari Lake. Thence going southwards along this same shore Kharlung is reached at 414 miles and Kiangdom at 426 miles.

Or continuing from the Kingha Sharma camp at 392 miles down this ravine eastwards, Shakshang 404 miles, is met on a plain, in which the Tso Kiagr Lake is situated; thence southward, along the same stream which flows into the north end of the Tso Morari at Peldo, Deldo Le, 413 miles is reached. Following the eastern shore of this Lake to Lunkserma Le 425 miles, the road strikes off eastwards over the Chagarchau La 436 miles, to Ooti 341 miles, and southwards to Lam Tso 444 miles.

LIVa ZANSKAR to TSO MORARI LAKE by TSARAP LINGTI CHU—

Number of Marches.	Names of Stages.	Distance in miles and furlongs.		Nature of Route.	Main Valleys and Mountain Passes.	River Crossings and Lakes.	Altitude above Sea Level in feet.	Supplies and Transport at Stages.	Remarks.
		Intermediate. m. f.	Total. m. f.						
17	Padam E.— Bardun Gompa or Pigchu.	... ...	233 ...	Fair road, passable for laden animals.	Up Tsarap Lingti valley left bank.	......	11373	S. F. G. W. and T. procurable.	Former capital of Zanskar, village and fort.
		... ...	239 ...						

No.	Name	Miles	Total	Road	Valley / Direction	River / Bridge	Elevation	Supply	Remarks
18	Reru E.—	15	243	Junction of road from Poat La down Tema-Tokpho road rough.	......	Chemchekora bridge. Reru Tokpho bridge.	......	S. and T. precarious, F. G. W. procurable.	Hamlet.
			248		......		......		
19	Sar Leh E.— Char	13	261	......	......	......	......	Ditto	Ditto.
		..	263	......	Junction of Niri Chu river.	Char bridge	12800	......	On right bank.
20	Tetha E.—	9	270	Good road	......	......	......	Ditto	Hamlet.
21	Kargyah E.—	11	278	Hence a road over the Phirtse La to Chumikmarpo 15 miles.	......	......	13670	S. F. G. W. and T. procurable.	Village.
			281						
			287						
22	Chumikmarpo	13	294	......	Surichan La, down Lingti Chu valley.	Two small glaciers. Cross several ravines. Yunan river.	......	S. G. F. T. nil, W. procurable.	Junction of Yunan river.
			311				......		
23	Lingti Sarchu E.—	19	313	Boundary of Kashmir, cross border into British territory to Pankpo La	Up Tsarap or Maling valley.	Sarchu river	......	S. F. T. nil, G. W. available.	Junction of Sarchu and Lingti rivers.
24	Lama Guru	17	330	Road good as far as Lama Guru, hence difficult in places.	......	......	......	S. F. T. nil, G. scanty, W. available.	Halting place.
25	Thung Chung Chiri.	12	342	Fairly easy ascent and descent, but slippery over snow slopes.	......	Maling ford	......	Ditto	Ditto.
			356				17500		
26	Tso Kum	18	360		Paukpo La down Lankpol valley right bank.	Lake.	......	Ditto	Ditto.

14

Number of Marches	Names of Stages	Distance in miles and furlongs. Intermediate m. f.	Total. m. f.	Nature of Route.	Main Valleys and Mountain Passes.	River crossings and Lakes.	Altitude above Sea Level in feet.	Supplies and Transport at Stages.	Remarks.
LIV*a*	ROUTE—*contd.*								
27	Khiang Shisa	18 ...	360 ...				......	......	Hamlet.
		11 ...	371 ...	Good road onwards down Lankpol and Phirsefoo to Kiangdom.	...	Kurgiepl nala.			
			372 ...						
28	Manechan E.—	8 ...	379 ..	Join direct road from Thonde to Tso Morari.	...	......	......	S. and T. nil, F. G. W. scanty.	Halting place, junction of Phirse river.
29	Khalmoche E.—	11 ...	390 ...	......	...	......	......	Ditto	Halting place.
30	Kiangdom E.—	11 ...	401 ...	......	...	South end of Tso Morari.	14900	S. F. T. nil, G. W. scanty.	Plain, Lake water brackish.

This route is open from about middle of July to middle of October.

From Char bridge 253 miles, a road north-east by Char 264 miles up the right bank of the Niri Chu to Phooktal Gonpa 268 miles, and onwards to Bokung bridge 278 miles, where it joins the Thonde and Tso Morari road at mile 276½ between Tontak Gonpa and Karnoch.

From Lingti Sarchu 313 miles, there is a road due north along the Tsarap valley to Juktak 324 miles, where it joins the Thonde and Tso Morari road at mile 324, one march from the Lachalung pass.

The two alternative Routes LIV and LIVa are therefore equal in length as far as Juktak.

There is not much difference in the length of these two routes between Padam and Kiangdom, the Thonde and Lachalung pass route is perhaps the easier of the two, as crossing the snow over the Pankpo La is a difficulty.

LV   SRINAGAR to SIMLA and UMBALLA by KISHTWAR and KULU—

No.	Station	Intermed.	Total	Road	Route	River / Springs / Bridge	Elevation	Supplies	Remarks
	Srinagar P. O., T. O., C., E.— Pampar E.	...	0	By road or by boat up the river Jhelum to Kanabul 50 miles by water.	Up Jhelum valley right bank.	......	5235	S. F. G. W. and T. abundant.	Capital of Kashmir, Hari Parbat fort, large city and bazars.
1	**Awantipur** E.— Bij Behara, Kanabal B.	18	8 18	......	Left bank.	Jhelum bridge Ditto	5300 5400	S. and T. nil, F. G. W. plentiful.	Two ancient temples in ruins. Terminus river navigation.
2	**Islamabad** P. O., T. O., C., E.,— Achibal B., E.—	17	29 ...... 33·4 35 ...... 41	Good road, passable for laden animals, which cannot cross the Chenab and Wardwan rope bridges near Kishtwar.	Up Bringh valley.	Sulphurous springs.	5450	S. F. G. W. and T. plentiful.	Large town, bazar and head-quarters of zillah.
3	**Harhama** E.— Sagam	11	46 ...... 49	......	......	......	......	S. F. G. W. and T. moderate.	Village.
4	**Wyl** E.— Prowo	9	55·4 60	......	......	Bringh bridge	......	S. and T. nil, F. G. and W. procurable.	Junction of Nowboog river.
5	**Wankringi or Karbodaram** E.—	9	64·4 67	Road good, but steep ascent and descent over pass. Road very fair.	Up Marbal ravine.	......	11550	S. and T. nil, F. G. and W. plentiful.	Hamlet.
6	**Singpur** E.— Chatru	9	73 78	Marbal pass down Kashot Khol valley.	Marbal pass down Kashot Khol valley.	......	......	S. and T. nil, F. G. and W. procurable.	Small village.
7	**Moghul Maidan** E.—	10	83·4 90 91·4	Road fair with exception of crossing the two rope bridges to Kishtwar.	......	Wardwan bridge. Chenab do.	......	S. and T. scarce, F. G. and W. procurable.	Junction of Sinchun Khol. Small village.

Number of Marches.	Names of Stages.	Distance in miles and Furlongs. Inter- mediate. m. f.	Total. m. f.	Nature of Route.	Main Valleys and Mountain Passes.	River Crossings and Lakes.	Altitude above Sea Level in Feet.	Supplies and Transport at Stages.	Remarks.
LV	ROUTE—contd.	... ...	91 4						
8	Kishtwar P. O., E.—	11 4	95 ...	Good road from Kishtwar except in two places.	Chenab valley	......	5000	S. G. F. W. and T. plentiful.	Small town and fort on high plateau above junction of Wurdwan and Chenab rivers.

From Wyl 55 m, 4f, at the entrance of the Nowhoog valley, there is a loop route up the latter and the Brinwar ravine to Doosu, 62 miles, hence over the Chingam pass, 70 miles, and down the Dangur Nar to Chingam 80 miles, and following the Sinchun Khol to its junction with the Kasher Khol at Chatru, 86 miles. There is a good road on the western side to the foot of the Chingam pass : both the ascent and descent are precipitous and rugged over much snow and ice ; from the foot of pass on eastern side to Chingam the track is fair and hence to Chatru good.

9	Bagni	13 ...	108 ...	Hence road bad along the wooded hills overhanging the Chenab with many ups and downs and along precipices to Siri.	Up Chandra Bhaga valley left bank.	......	6150	S. and T. precarious, F. G. and W. plentiful.	Hamlet.
10	Pyas	10 ...	118 ...	Road fair to Atholi through cultivation.	......	......	6320	S. and T. nil, F. G. and W. procurable.	Ditto.
11	Siri E.— Jhar	9 4	127 4		......	......	8700	S. and T. nil, F. G. and W. procurable.	Halting place 2000 ft. above Chenab. Path southwards over Panji pass into Karney Gad valley.
		... ...	137 ...				......	......	

No.	Name		Miles		Remarks on road	Cross to right bank	Chanura Bhaga bridge	Elevation	Supplies	Remarks
12	Atholi E.—	14	141	4	Junction of Padar and Chenab rivers. Road fair.	...	Chanura Bhaga bridge.	6360	S. F. G. W. and T. procurable after notice.	Village on left bank, Golabgurh fort, chief place of Padar, opposite on right bank.
13	Sol E.—	8	149	4	Road very difficult in 2 places.	...	Sheadi bridge.	......	S. F. G. W. and T. moderate.	Village on right bank.
14	Ashdari E.—	10	151 159	4 4	Road fair	......	Oobiar ,,	......	S. and T. nil, F. G. and W. procurable.	Hamlet.
	Kashmir and Chamba border.									
15	Darwas C., E.—	10	165 169 170	4 4	Junction of road eastwards over Sursunk and Poat La to Reru in Zanskar. Fair road.	... .	Bilon ,, Sursunk ,,	8499	S. F. G. W. and T. available.	Large village.
16	Kilar E.—	6	175	4	Junction of road south westwards over Sachi pass by Tisa to Chamba.	......	......	8411	S. F. G. W. and T. procurable.	Village.
17	Sauch E.—	8	184 185	4	Junction of road south westwards over Chini pass to Tisa and Chamba.	......	Tuan ,,	7886	S. F. G. W. and T. moderate.	Ditto.
18	Majrao	7	191	...	Rough and rugged road, very difficult in many places from Sauch to Saor.	......	... ,,	......	S. and T. nil, F. G. W. procurable.	Hamlet.

Number of Marches	Names of Stages	Distance in miles and furlongs — Intermediate m. f.	Distance in miles and furlongs — Total m. f.	Nature of Route.	Main Valleys and Mountain Passes.	River Crossings and Lakes.	Altitude above Sea Level in Feet.	Supplies and Transport at Stages.	Remarks.
LV	ROUTE.—contd.	...	...				......		
19	Saor	7	191	...			......	S. and T. nil, F. G. W. procurable.	Hamlet.
		8	199	...	Cross to left bank.	Chandra Bhaga bridge.	......		
20	Tindi		200	Junction of 2 roads westwards over the Charg and Drali passes into Chamba.			......	S. F. G. W. and T. moderate.	Village on left bank Chandra Bhaga.
		14	213	...	Cross to right bank.	Ditto.	......		
			219	...			......		
21	Margraon	16	229	......		Bendi bridge.	......	S. and T. nil, F. G. and W. procurable.	Hamlet on right bank.
	Odapur		233		Cross to left bank.		......		
			236			Chandra Bhaga bridge.	......		
22	Triloknath E.—	9	237 4	Junction of road westwards over Kalicha pass 15,960 feet to Chamba.			9366	S. F. G. W. and T. plentiful.	Several villages on left bank. Hindu temple frequented by pilgrims.

From Sauch to Odapur there is another route inland over the Gurdhar pass, 17,000 feet, which is taken when the river route is dangerous. There are 2 tracks over the Gurdhar pass between Bataor and Miyar, both very bad and arduous, grass shoes and ice axes necessary. The longer route goes from Bataor to Leias 6 miles at foot of pass, to Chirpat 15 miles crossing pass and to Miyar 3 miles.

No.	Name			Miles	Road	Pass / Valley	Bridge	Elevation	Supplies	Remarks
17	Sauch	...	...	184		Up Tnan valley.	......	7886	......	Hamlet.
18	Saichu	12	...	196	Ditto	......	Tnan bridge	8412	S. and T. precarious, F. G. and W. procurable.	Ditto.
19	Bataor	9	...	205, 214	Very bad ascent, cross long snow field, cutting steps, and more difficult descent.	Gurdhar pass down Bendi valley to Odapur.	......	11633, 17000	S. and T. nil, F. G. W. procurable.	There are 2 routes both over Gurdhar pass both very bad, the other by Leias and Chiryat. Hamlet.
20	Miyar	16	...	221, 227	Road fair down valley, but difficult near Odapur.	......	Bendi bridge	10215	S. and T. precarious, F. G. and W. procurable.	Village and Hindu Temple.
21	Odapur	12	...	233, 236	Road good	Cross to left bank.	Bendi „ ; Chandra Bhaga bridge.	......	S. F. G. and T. scanty, W. plentiful.	Village and Hindu Temple.
22	Triloknath	4	4	237, 239	Road easy	Cross to right bank.	Chandra Bhaga bridge. Ditto.	9566	S. F. G. W. and T. plentiful.	Cluster of villages on left bank Chenab, Hindu temple frequented by pilgrims.
	Bamankoti *Chamba boundary, enter Kulu or British territory.*	...	...	243	Junction of road over Chobia pass to Chamba.					
23	Jarna *Perpeh on left bank Lota*	14	...	252, 254, 262	Road fair ... Junction of road over Kukti pass 17000 feet to Chamba.	......	Ditto	......	S. F. G. W. and T. plentiful.	Village on right bank Chenab river.

Number of Marches.	Names of Stages.	Distance in miles and furlongs.		Nature of Route.	Main Valleys and Mountain Passes.	River Crossings and Lakes.	Altitude above Sea Level, in Feet.	Supplies and Transport at Stages.	Remarks.
		Intermediate. m. f.	Total. m. f.						
	ROUTE—contd.	...	...						
LV 24	Tandi	...	262 ...	Good road	...	......	......	S. F. G. W. and T. available.	Village at confluence of Bhaga and Chandra rivers.
		14	266						
25	Kailing	...	270 ...	Bagha valley well cultivated. Road easy with exception of narrow part round rocks.	Cross Bagha valley at its mouth.	Bhaga bridge	10100	S. F. G. W. and T. moderate.	Capital of Lahoul, Moravian Mission.
	Kardang E.	4	271 ...						
26	Gundla	...	282 ...	Junction of road westwards over Kara Baghal pass to Chamba and Kulu. Opposite Gundla a remarkable precipice.	......	Cross 2 large hill torrents bridged.	10300	S. F. G. W. and T. available.	Village on cultivated terrace.
		12							
27	Sissu	...	291	Road bad in places, many ups and downs, wild scenery.	...	Sisu " 5 hill torrents crossed by bridges.	9938	S. F. and T. scarce, G. and W. procurable.	Small village.
	E.—	9							
	New Koksar	...	301 ...	......	...	......	......	S. F. and T. scanty, G. and W. plentiful.	G. Village.
			304 ...	......	......	Chandra			

No.	Stage	m.	Total	Remarks	Route	Bridge	Elevation	Supplies	Rest house.
28	Koksur *B. C. E.—*	14	305	Ascent and descent of pass very steep. Cross this pass very early in morning owing to high wind after 9 A.M.	Rotang pass down Beas valley right bank.	......	10260	S. and T. nil, F. G. W. available.	Hamlet.
			311				13500		
29	Rahla *E.—*	10	315	Good road through lovely scenery, all the way to Sultanpur.		......	9000	......	Good sport up Solung nala. Snake temple.
	Pulchan		318			Solang or	......		S. and T. available.
	Barwa		320			Sarahi bridge			On upward journey take supplies at Burwa.
			321			Chenag ,,			
			322			Kshal ,,			
30	Manali *E.—* *Baran*	10	325			Manali ,,	......	S. F. G. W. and T. procurable.	Chikor shooting. Village.
			330			Kush ,,			Rel bears round Shegli.
			334						
31	Dwara or Katrain *B., E.—*	13	338		Down Beas valley.	Doli ,,	4723	S. F. G. W. and T. available.	Dwara small town, Katrain bungalow.
			342			Raison bridge			
			344			Bandrol ,,			
32	Sultanpur *P. O., D. B., E.—*	12	350			Beas bridge.	4002	S. F. G. W. and T. plentiful.	Capital of Kulu, town, tazar, tehsil and police thana on right bank of Beas.

From Rahla, 315 miles, there is another route along the left bank of the Beas river to Sultanpur and Bajaora.

No.	Stage	m.	Total	Remarks	Route	Bridge	Elevation	Supplies	Rest house.
29	Rahla *E.—*	...	315	......	Head of Beas valley.	......	9000	S. and T. nil, G. F. W. available.	Hamlet.

Number of Marches	Names of Stages	Distances in miles and furlongs		Nature of Route.	Main Valleys and Mountain Passes.	River crossings and Lakes.	Altitude above Sea Level, in feet.	Supplies and Transport at Stages.	Remarks.
		Inter-mediate m. f.	Total. m. f.						
LV	*ROUTE—contd.*								
	Burwa, E. ...	...	315	Fine plain ...	Down left bank.	...	...	S. and T. available.	On upward journey take S. and T. here for crossing Rotang pass.
30	**Bashist** *E.—*	...	320	......	......	Hot springs.	6683	Ditto	Small village.
		7	322	......	......	Beas bridge.			
		...	324	Junction of road eastwards over Hamta pass 14,000ft. to Spiti.	......	Hamta „		......	Good sport up nala.
			326						
31	**Jagatsuk** *E.—*	...	328	......	......	Doagru „	5985	S. F. G. W. and T. moderate.	Small village.
	Gojra	6	327	Good road through beautiful scenery.	......	Splendid cascade.			
32	**Nagar** *E.—*	...	337	......	...	Beas bridge	5780	S. F. G. W. and T. ample.	Small civil station on left bank of Beas.
	Kóts	9	342	......	......	Raogi „		......	Fair sport up nala.
		...	345	......	......	Kóts „			

No.	Stage	Miles	Total	Nature of road	Rivers crossed	Bridge or Ferry	Elevation (feet)	Supplies	Remarks
33	Sultanpur P. O., D. B., E.—	13	350		......	Beas bridge	4092	S. F. G. W. and T. plentiful.	Capital of Kulu, town, bazar, tehsil and police thana on right bank of Beas.
			350	Road branches off westwards over Babu pass 10,000 ft. to Palampur, Kangra and Pathankot 141 miles.	......	Sorbari "		......	Called Duff bridge.
			355	Road branches off eastwards up Parbati Nala to Manikarn hot springs, 5,587 ft.	......	Beas bridge			
34	Bajaora B., E.—	9	359	Road branches off westwards over Dulchi pass 6,000 ft. to Mandi.	......	Kandi "	3573	S. F. G. W. and T. procurable.	Small bazar and old ruined fort on right bank of Beas. Good sport around.
	Badool		362	Bridle road made and bridged throughout in good order and passable for laden animals to Nag-konda.		Beas "		Ditto after notice.	
35	Larji B., E.—	12	371		Up Chata valley.	Synj "	3710	S. F. G. W. and T. moderate.	Hamlet on left bank of Synj river at junction with Chata river.
			373		Cross to left bank.	Chata "		......	Small village.
36	Manglaor B., E.—	8	379		Right bank.	Ditto			Large village, tehsil and police thana.
37	Plach P. O.	9	381			Ditto	5718		
	Jibi		382				5860		Small village.
			388	Ascent through pine forest and by steep zigzags to top of pass and descent gradual.			10000	Ditto after notice.	
			395	Fine scenery	Jalaori pass down Arni valley.				
38	Kot B.—	11	399				7750	S. F. G. W. and T. moderate after notice.	Ditto.
39	Choni B.—	9	408	Road leaves the valley and ascends a spur.	Cross spur and descend into Sutlej valley.	Arni bridge	6162	S. F. G. W. and T. plentiful.	Cluster of villages.

Number of Marches.	Names of Stages.	Distance in miles and furlongs.		Nature of Route.	Main Valleys and Mountain Passes.	River Crossings and Lakes.	Altitude above Sea Level, in feet.	Supplies and Transport at Stages.	Remarks.
		Inter-mediate. m. f.	Total. m. f.						
LV	ROUTE—contd.	9 ...	408 ...		.....	.....	.....		
40	Dularsh B.—	8 ...	416 ...	Continuous descent, very steep in places to Sutlej river and after crossing, very steep ascent by zigzags.	.....	.....	.....	S. F. G. W. and T. moderate after notice.	Village.
			421 ...		.....	Sutlej bridge	.....	.....	Called Lori.
41	Komarsen B.—	9 ...	425 ...	Continuous ascent up spur, steep in places, to Nagkunda where join Hindustan and Thibet road.	.....	.....	.....	Ditto	Large village.
42	Nagkunda P. O., D. B.	7 ...	432 ...		......	......	8800	S. F. G. and T. moderate, W. scarce.	Small bazar.

From Hamta 326 miles, there is a track eastwards up the Raini or Hamta valley by Chika 11 miles over the Hamta pass 14,000 feet to Chaktru 20 miles, on the Chandra river left bank (opposite the site of old Koksar) on the road to Spiti.

From the Duff bridge over the Beas at 355 miles, there is a track north-eastwards up the Parbati valley to Chang 7 miles, Jherri F. B. 15 miles, Manikarn R. 5,587 feet 23 miles, where there are hot springs, Phaiga F. B. 31 miles, and to another hot spring at 34 miles.

This nala is preserved and the hot springs are much resorted to.

There is another route from Mandlaor 379 miles by Rampur, and Kotgurh to Nagkunda, which is passable for laden animals as far as the Sutlej rope bridge at Rampur, where join Hindustan and Thibet road.

No.	Stage	Dist.	Total	Road	Valley notes	Bridge	Elev.	Supplies	Remarks
36	Manglaor B. E.—		379	Gradual ascent through cultivation and forest.	Up eastern Chata valley.	Chata bridge	.....	S. F. G. W. and T. moderate.	Small village.
	Plach P. O.		381		.....	.....	5718	.....	Large village, tehsil and police thana.
			382		.....	Chata bridge.			
37	Tung or Bathad B.—	12	391	Sharp rise and over undulating grass plain to pass, the descent very steep in zig-zags, to the fine level and grassy plateau of Surone.	.....	.....	.....	S. and T. nil, G. F. W. procurable.	Hamlet.
38	Suron B.—	9	397		Dhol pass down Kurpan valley.	.....	6000	S. and T. moderate, F. G. W. procurable.	Village in Seoraj.
			400			Kurpan bridge.			
			404		.....	.....			
39	Ursua Jagatkhana B.	9	409	Gentle rise, pass through forests and sharp descent down steep hill by zig-zags to Rampur rope bridge.	Road leaves valley and crosses Dhaor spur into Sutlej valley.	.....	.....	Ditto	Ditto.
			414						
40	Rampur P. O., D. B., C., E.—	7	416	Good road down valley.	Down Sutlej valley left bank to Kot-gurh.	Sutlej bridge.	3700	S. F. G. W. and T. plentiful.	Capital of Bisahir, residence of Raja. Town and bazar.
			422		.....	Nogri „	3462		
			427			Muchara „			
41	Nirit B.—	13	429		.....	.....	3600	S. and T. scanty, F. G. W. procurable.	Small village on left bank of Sutlej river.
			431		...	Berakhad „	3400		
42	Kotgurh P. O., D. B.—	10	439	Continuous ascent up a spur of Hatu Pir mountain to Nagkunda, good road.	.....	.....	(5600)(7215)	S. G. F. W. and T. procurable.	Village, Mission, tehsil, and tea garden.
			441		.....	.....	.....		Bareri, tea garden.

Number of Marches.	Names of Stages.	Distance in Miles and Furlongs.		Nature of Route.	Main Valleys and Mountain Passes.	River Crossings and Lakes.	Altitude above Sea Level in Feet.	Supplies and Transport at Stages.	Remarks.
		Intermediate. m. f.	Total. m. f.						
LV	ROUTE—contd.								
43	Nagkunda D. B.—	... ...	441 ...	Road in excellent order along the mountain ridge to Simla.	......	......	8700	S. G. F. and T. moderate, W. scarce.	Small bazar.
	Narari	10 ...	449 ...						
		... ...	454 4						
43	Mattiana D. B.—	11 ...	460 ...	......	......	......	7600	S. scanty, F. G. W. and T. available.	Village.
44	Theog D. B.—	11 2	472 ...		......	......	7420	S. F. G. T. procurable, W. scanty.	Hamlet.
45	Phagu D. B.—	5 6	477 ...	Roads to Masuri and Chor peak branch off here.	......	......	8170	S. F. G. W. and T. moderate.	Ditto.
	Mahasu	... ...	481 ...	Descent to Simla.		......	8328	......	Bazar.
	Sanjoli	... ...	483 ...	Road to Mashobra	Tunnel 500 ft.	......	......	......	Toll bar.
		... ...	486 ...	......			......		Bazar.
		... ...	487 ...						
46	Simla P. O., T. O., Hotels C.	12 ...	489 ...	Carriage road made and bridged throughout, Tonga service to Kalka.	This road follows generally the watershed spur, which separates the drainage of	......	7200	S. F. G. W. and T. abundant.	Summer capital of India, sanitarium, town, large bazar, Palace of His Excellency the Viceroy and Governor-General of India.

No.	Place		Miles		Remarks on road		Height (feet)	Supplies	Remarks
47	Kiari Ghat, *D. B.—*	16	505	......		the Sutlej from that of the Giri river.	5427	S. and T. nil, F. G. W. moderate.	Three shops.
	Kasda ghat	...	510 4	Road branches eastwards to Chail, palace of H. H. Maharaja of Patiala.	......		4650.		
48	Solon *P. O., T. O., D. B., C. E. small.*	15	520	......		......	5000	S. F. G. W. and T. available.	Village and bazar small cantonment and brewery.
	Baro ghat	...	525	......		......	5868		
			530						
49	Dharampur *D. B., E. very small.*	12	532	Cart-road 2½ miles to Dagshai cantonment. Cart-road branches to Sunawar Lawrence Asylum and Kasauli 7 miles. Great landslip 7 miles from Kalka.	......		4900	S. F. G. W. and T. procurable.	Toll bar.
			540						
50	Kalka *P. O., T. O. Hotel, C. E.—*	15	547	......		......	2200	S. F. G. W. and T. plentiful.	Large village and terminus of branch railway from Delhi and Umballa.

From Negri bridge 422 miles there is a road up to Bahil R. 427 miles on the Hindustan and Thibet road, and along latter by Suagri R 8,400 feet 439 miles, at the head of the Pabar valley, Kudrala F. R. 9,400 feet; 449 miles, Bagi D. R. 8,900 feet 457 miles, at the head of the Giri valley, through forest to Nagkupda D. R. 8,700 feet 469 miles. Another bridle road also branches off from 532 miles to Subathu At 521 miles there is a road good for riding to Subathu cantonment 529 miles. 542 miles. Umballa is 39 miles distant from Kalka by rail.

LVa SIMLA to KALKA by OLD ROAD—

Number of Marches	Names of Stages	Distance in Miles and Furlongs — Intermediate m. f.	Total m. f.	Nature of Route.	Main Valleys and Mountain Passes.	River Crossings and Lakes.	Altitude above Sea Level in Feet.	Supplies and Transport at Stages.	Remarks.
46	Simla	...	489 ...	......	......	......	7200	S. F. G. W. and T. abundant.	Summer capital of India and sanitarium, town and large bazar.
	Batori ghat	...	493 ...	Road to Jutogh and Bilaspur 38½ miles.	......	......			
47	Sairi *Hotel, E. very small*	13 ...	502 ...	Good bridle road the whole way from Simla to Kalka.	......	......	4950	S. F. G. W. and T. procurable.	Small bazar.
	Haripur	...	507 ...			Blini bridge.	2717		
		...	508 ...			Gumber „			
48	Kakar hatti *Hotel, E. small*	7 ...	509 ...	......	......		3600	Ditto	Small village.
	Subathu P. O.—		511 ...	Cart road to Dharampur 10 miles.	......		4250		
			515 ...			Kutiar nala	3500		
49	Kasauli *P. O., D. B. hotel—*	13 ...	522 ...	Ditto and bridle road to Sunawar Lawrence Asylum 3 miles.	......	......	6300	S. F. G. W. and T. plentiful.	Convalescent depot and small civil station, bazar.
50	Kalka *P. O., T. O., D. B. hotel, C. E.—*	9 ...	531 ...	......	......	......	2200	Ditto	Bazar and thana. Terminus of branch railway from Delhi and Umballa.

LVb SOLON to HARDWAR by NAHAN in SIRMUR and DEHRA—

No.	Name of stage				Condition of road	Description of country	Fords, &c.	Elevation	Supplies	Remarks
48	**Solon**	...	...	520	Footpath down hill	Descent down flank of hill to Teleri mba, then rise up the	......	5000	S. F. G. W. and T. available.	Small cantonment and bazar.
	Teleri	...	.	527	At Teleri ghat, join the bridle road from Dagshai 4 miles distant.		Teleri ford	4000		
	Saadawa ghat	...	...	529		Naini spur and along	......	4600		
49	**Naini bazar** B.—	10	...	530	......	flank of mountain	......	4900	S. F. G. W. and T. moderate.	Two shops.
	Charani ghat	...	...	534	Good 10 feet road of easy gradient made and bridged throughout.	ridge to Charani ghat, hence keep	......	5000		
50	**Surahan** B.—	12	2	542	There is very little space anywhere for pitching tents, and water is very scanty.	along top of ridge to Baneti, descend down flank of hill	......	5250	S. F. G. W. and T. procurable.	Village, shops and tehsil.
51	**Baneti** B.—	14	3	536		to Banog and rise up to Nahan.	......	4400	Ditto	One shop.
	Banog	...	...	568	......		......	2500		
52	**Nahan** P. O., T. O., D. B., C.	13	3	569	Rough cart-road unbridged from Nahan down to Khadir-ke Bagh and up the Markunda valley to Kolar; thence through the Kyarda Dun to the Jumna river.	Up Markunda valley.	......	3000	S. F. G. W. and T. ample	Town and residence of Raja of Sirmur. Military Cantonment, large bazar, iron workshop.
	Khadir-ke Bagh	...	...	573		......	Cross Markunda fords several times.	1450		
	Kolar	...	...	581		Down Bhatta valley.				
53	**Majra** B., E.—	20	...	589	......		} Cross Bhatta ford twice.	......	S. F. G. W. and T. available.	Bazar and thana.
			...	591						Ditto.
			...	593		......				
			...	596		Across				
	Ponta		.	589	......	Jumna valley.	Jumna ferry	1250		

Number of Marches	Names of Stages	Intermediate m. f.	Total m. f.	Nature of Route	Main Valleys and Mountain Passes	River Crossings and Lakes	Altitude above Sea Level, in feet	Supplies and Transport at Stages	Remarks
LV6	ROUTE—contd.								
54	Rampur Mundi B., E.—	...	589	Earthen cart-road unbridged to Jhajra, whence bridged and metalled to Dehra.	Across drainage of Himalayas into Asun river.	......	1334	S. F. G. W. and T. procurable.	Village.
	Fattehpur E.—	12	601			......	1433	......	Cross Chakrata and Timli pass road.
		...	604	......					
		4	607			Sittarao.			
55	Sahanspur P. O., B., E.—	9	610	......			1621	Ditto	Village and thana
	Jhajra	...	613			Suarnarao.			
		...	618	......					
56	Dehra P. O., T. O., Hotel, C., E.—	...	621	Rough earthen cart-road, unbridged from Dehra to Hardwar.	......	Tous bridge.		S. G. F. W. and T. abundant.	Military Cantonment, Civil station, town and bazar.
		17	627				2229		
		4	629		Across drainage of Himalayas into Suswa river.	Rispanarao.			
57	Lachiwala E.—	10	637	......		......	1680	S. G. F. scarce, T. nil, W. plentiful.	Small village on right bank Song river.
58	Kunsrao C., E.—	6	645	......	......	......	1380	Ditto	Small village on right bank Suswa river.
		.	645			Suswa river.			
	Raiwala	8	652	......	......	......	......	......	On right bank Ganges, good fishing.
		...	654			Moticbur nala.			

59	Hardwar P. O., T. O., D. B., C., E.—	12	...	657	6	......	......	1050	S. G. F. W. and T. abundant.	Small town and bazar; celebrated bathing ghat on Ganges River.

From Rampur 416 miles, a road goes southwards by Balli, B., Sungri, B., where it crosses the high range dividing the Sutlej and Tonse valleys, Roru on the Pabar river and down this valley, along the right bank, by Rajengarh, Simlna or Arakot and Baig or Tuni bridge F. B, below the junction of the Pabar and Tonse rivers at miles 32? of Route XIX between Simla and Masuri.

From Simla 489 miles, there is a rough path down the Giri valley frequented by fishermen, by Dogra, 4,300 feet (under Junga 5,300 feet, capital of Kuenthal State) 8 miles, Khargann 3,100 feet 22 miles, Newar 33 miles, Seeon 42½ miles, Satibagh 52½ miles near Rauka Lake, Konilla 60½ miles, Sattawan 69½ miles, Rajghat 80½ miles, at junction of the Giri and Jumna rivers, Jumna ferry 82½ miles; Khargann is about 10 miles below Solon, and Satibagh 18 miles from Nahau.

From Kolar a road branches southwards over the Baila Pass of the Siwalik Range to Bilaspur 20 miles, and Jagadhri railway station 15 miles; total 35 miles.

From Nahan there is a cart-road down the hill to Kala Amb 11 miles, whence there are cart-roads to Umballa 30 miles and to Sadhaura 8 miles.
From Sadhaura there are two cart-roads to the N. W. Railway, at Barara 16 miles, and at Jagadhri 18 miles.

LVI SRINAGAR to SIMLA and UMBALLA by CHAMBA and KANGRA—

	Srinagar : : :		0 ...	By road or by boat up the river Jhelum to Kanatnul 50 miles by water.	Up Jhelum valley right bank.	......	5235	S. F. G. W. and T. abundant.	Capital of Kashmir, Hari Parbat fort.
	Pampar : :		8 ...				5300		Large city and bazar.
1	Awantipur E.—	18 ...	18 ·	......				S. and T. nil. F. G. W. plentiful.	Two ancient temples in ruins.
	Bij Belara		29 ...	......	Left bank	Jhelum bridge	5400	......	Terminus river navigation.
	Kanabal, B.		33 ... 4	......	Right bank	Ditto			
2	Islamabad P. O., T. O., C., E.—	17 ...	35 ...	Good road passable for laden animals.	......	......	5450	S. F. G. W. and T. plentiful.	Large town, bazar and head-quarters of zillah.

Hence there are two routes to Budrawar, one by the Marbul pass and Kishtwar, see Route LV, marches 2 to 8, and Route XVII, marches 12 to 8, the other as under:—
Travellers in Budrawar are advised to apply for a purwanah for supplies and transport to Raja Sir Amar Sing, K.C.S.I., at Jammu.

Number of Marches.	Names of Stages.	Distance in miles and furlongs.		Nature of Route.	Main Valleys and Mountain Passes.	River Crossings and Lakes.	Altitude above Sea Level, in feet.	Supplies and Transport at Stages.	Remarks.
		Inter-mediate. m. f.	Total. m. f.						
LVI	ROUTE—contd.	...	...						
3	Vering P. O., T. O., B., E.—	...	35 ...	......	Up Sandrin valley.	Bringh bridge Sandrin ,,	6000	S. F. G. W. plentiful, T. available.	Large village and tehsil. Copious spring and ruins. Customs post.
4	Chaon	16 2	51 2	......	......	Ditto.	......	Ditto.	
5	Camp—Southern foot of pass.	10 ...	57 61 69 2 2 2	Steep ascent and descent.	Brarihal pass. Down Linder Khol valley.	......	......	S. and T. nil, F. G. W. plentiful.	Halting place.
6	Gayi	13 ...	74 2	......	......	......	......	S. F. G. W. and T. available.	Small village.
7	Bhagwan	7 ...	81 2	Rough and stony road.	......	......	......	Ditto	Ditto.
8	Doda	9 ..	90 94 2	......	Up Chenab right bank.	......	......	S. F. G. W. and T. plentiful.	Large village and thana.
9	Kalen	7 ..	97 2	Good road passable for laden animals.	Across Chenab valley. Up Neroo valley left bank.	Chandra Bhaga or Chenab rope bridge.	......	S. F. G. W. and T. available.	Small village.
10	Budrawar	10 ..	107 118 2 2	Fair road passable for laden animals.	......	......	5427	S. F. G. W. and T. ample.	Capital of Bodrawar, Jaghir of Raja Sir Amar Singh, K.C.S.I. Iron mines.
11	Thenala	8 ...	126 2	Long ascent to pass and steep descent	......	......	......	S. and T. nil, F. G. W. plentiful.	

No.	Name	Dist.	Total	Road	Padri pass / valley	River	Elev.	Supplies & water	Remarks
12	Langera.—*Encamp on roof of huts.*	14	128	down stony bed of stream.	Padri pass down Kandi Mari valley. Down Shoon valley.	.....	9000	.....	Border of Kashmir and Chamba.
13	Bhandal *Dugi*	6 / 12	141 / 153 / 157	Road fair	.....	Shoon ferry	5982 / 5679	Ditto / S. F. G. W. and T. available.	Hamlet. Large village. Ditto.
14	Manjiri R.—	14	167 / 168	Road hilly and stony.	Across Sachin valley.	.....	.....	Ditto	Ditto.
15	Chamba P. O., T. O., D. B., C., E.—	16	163	Rough and stony road.	.....	Sachi bridge. Ravi ..	3000	S. F. G. W. and T. abundant	Capital of Chamba, residence of Raja. Large town and bazar.

From Chamba, a route goes northwards over the Sachi pass and across the Chaula Bagha river to Kilar in Paugi at miles 175½ of Route LV; the marches from Chaula are, to Masruud 12 miles, Kaht 9 miles, Alwas 12 miles, crossing Sachi pass and Chandra Bhaga river to Kilar 2½ miles.—Total 89 miles.

From Tisa a path branches eastwards over the Chaini pass and Chandra Bhaga river to Sanch at miles 184 of Route LV.

From Chamba are two paths north-eastwards by Chanju over the Chara and Drali passes to Tindi on the Chandra Bhaga river at mile 213 of Route LV; also a third path over the Kalichu pass to Trilokuath, and a fourth path over the Chobia pass and Chandra Bhaga river to Bamankoti at mile 243 of Route LV.

From Chamba, there are two routes eastwards up the valley of the Ravi and over the Kukti and Bara Baghal passes and across the Chandra Bhaga river to Tundi in Lahoul, see Route XVIII, marches 11 to 19.

From Chamba to Dalhousie 6,744 feet are two roads, the Upper to Khajiar 7 miles, where there is a Dak Bungalow 6,000 feet at the end of a level and grass valley surrounded by fine deodars, and thence to Dalhousie 10½ miles.—Total 17½ miles. The lower road is longer but more level, to Chil, B., 9 miles, and to Dalhousie 12 miles.—Total 21 miles. Through transport necessary.

From Chamba to Pathankot, there are three roads, one down the Ravi valley to Batri 14½ miles, Sindhara 12½ miles, Plaondgota 10 miles, Shalpur 11½ miles, Pathankot 8 miles.—Total 56½ miles. The second through Dalhousie 17½ miles, Nynee Khud 13 miles, Daneira 10 miles, Dhar 11 miles, Shahpur 12 miles, Pathankot 8 miles.—Total 71½ miles. The third through Chuari 17¾ miles, Nurpur 16 miles, Puthankot 16 miles.—Total 49¾ miles.

From Chamba to Dharmsala 6,111 feet in Kangra are two routes, one eastwards up the Ravi valley to Rakh 12 miles, Chitrali 10 miles; thence south-eastwards by Koti 4 miles, Chanota 8 miles; hence southwards by Kanar-i 9 miles, crossing Andrar pass 14,100 feet over the Dhaoli Dhar range to Dharmsala D. R. 6,111 feet 11 miles, and Kangra 2,400 feet 10½ miles.—Total 64½ miles. The second route from Chamba south-eastwards by Rareri 6 miles, crossing pass with steep descent of 5 miles to Chuari 12 miles, Rapir 7 miles, Sihunta 9 miles, Rithloo 12 miles 3,184 feet; hence either to Dharmsala 11 miles.—Total 57 miles, or by Chytroo to Kangra 13 miles.—Total 59 miles. This is a rough and bad road for ponies.

Number of Marches	Names of Stages	Distance in Miles and Furlongs — Intermediate m. f.	Distance in Miles and Furlongs — Total m. f.	Nature of Route	Main Valleys and Mountain Passes	River crossings and Lakes	Altitude above Sea Level in Feet	Supplies and Transport at Stages	Remarks
LVI	ROUTE—contd.								
16	Rareri	16 ...	183 ...	......	......	...	......	S. F. G. W. and T. procurable.	Village.
	Mankot	6 ...	189 ...	Steep descent from pass for 5 miles.	Mankot gully.	......	......		
17	Chuari	12 ...	201 ...	......	......	......	......	Ditto	Customs post.
	Jajra	...	207 ...	... ...	......	Chukki ford.	......		
18	Nurpur P. O., D. B., C. E.—	16 ...	217 ...	Join cart-road from Puthankot up the Kangra valley to Palampur 71 miles, bridged throughout with the exception of 7 causeways over rao crossings and partially metalled.	Across drainage of Himalayas, Dhaoli Dhar range, falling southwards into Beas river.	......	2000	S. F. G. W. and T. ample.	Ancient fort and town, large bazar and tehsil.
	Jonteh	...	226 ...	......	......	......	2200	......	Cultivated plateau.
19	Kotla P. O., D. B., E.—	13 ...	230 ...	......	......	Dehri bridge wooden arch 200ft. span.	1700	S. F. G. W. and T. available.	Large village and thana.
	Mundigram	...	239 ...	......	......	......	2740	......	Tea gardens.
20	Shahpur P. O., D. B., E.—	10 5	240 5	......	......	......	2500	Ditto	Bazar and plateau.
			244 2	......	......	Chumbi bridge.	2330	......	
			247 ...	......	......	Guj bridge.	2400	......	Road branches to Dharmsala.

No.	Place			Miles		Road remarks	River remarks	Bridge	Height (feet)	Supplies	Description
21	Gurkhari, 2½ miles south to Kangra and 8 miles north to Dharmsala by cart-road.	10	4	248	4	......	......	Maji "	2450	S. F. G. W. and T. plentiful at Kangra and Dharmsala.	Kangra, ancient fort, large town and bazar, celebrated Devi temple frequented by pilgrims.
		1		251	1	......	......	Mamuni "	2450	......	Dharmsala, convalescent depot, small military cantonment, and civil station, town.
22	Nugroteh	7		255	4	......	......	Panera bridge	2450	......	Bazar.
	Malan bazar			258		......			2850	S. F. G. W. and T. available.	Several tea gardens on Patahar range.
				261		......			3000	......	
23	Palampur P. O., D. B., C., E.—	14	4	265	2	Cart-road under construction from Palampur to Mandi.	......	Nogul bridge	3070		
				272		......	......	......	4050	S. F. G. W. and T. plentiful.	Large bazar and centre of Tea gardens
24	Baijnath D. B., C., E.—	9	4	281	4	Near border of Mandi State.	Across head of Rana drainage.	Jimmu bridge	3300	S. F. G. W. and T. procurable after notice.	Hindu ancient temples, place of pilgrimage, cluster of villages.
25	Dholu in Mandi B., F.,— Ginua	12		293	4	Cart-road southwards from Ginua to Mandi and bridle road eastwards from Ginua to Kulu.	Down Rana valley keeping along ridge of spur separating the Rana and Ool valleys.	......	...	S. F. G. W. and T. available.	Village.
				300		......		......	5100	......	Salt mines.
26	Hurla in Mandi B.—	13		306	4	......		......	4740	Ditto	Village.
27	Drung in Mandi R., E.—	12		318	4	......		......	3500	Ditto	Salt mines.

Number of Marches	Names of Stages	Distance in Miles and Furlongs — Intermediate m. f.	Total m. f.	Nature of Route	Main Valleys and Mountain Passes	River Crossings and Lakes	Altitude above Sea Level, in Feet.	Supplies and Transport at Stages.	Remarks.
LVI	ROUTE—contd.	... ...	318 4						
28	Mandi P. O., D. B., C., E. —	11 4	330 ...	Good road passable for laden animals.	Up Sukaty valley.	Beas bridge, iron suspension 240 feet span.	2991	S. F. G. W. and T. abundant.	Capital of Mandi State, residence of Raja. Large town and bazar.
29	Suket P. O., E. —	16 ...	338 ...	Flat and level road	Down Sutlej valley.	Sukaty bridge.	2965	S. F. G. W. and T. plentiful.	Capital of Suket State, or Bened. Town and bazar.
		...	346 ...	... ...					

From Dharmsala there is an upper bridle road bridged throughout, 11 miles to Dadh D. B., 3,500 feet and 10 miles to Palampar D. B., passing by the Kuniara Slate quarries at 3½ miles from Dharmsala. It is dotted with tea gardens.

From Kangra there is a road by Ranital, Jiuala Mukhi 1,883 feet, Nadaun, where cross Beas river to Behaspur and Simla, which is described in Route XIX, marches 11 to 21.

From Palampur 272 miles there is a track northwards over the Dhaoli Dhar range by Bumsoru 3 miles, Klaj pass 14,400 feet 18 miles, to Chamir 30 miles, on the left bank of the Ravi river in Chamba at mile 166 of Route XVIII between Chamba and the Bara Baghal pass.

From Guma 300 miles the Kulu road eastwards continues to Jhatingri B., 6,000 feet, in Mandi 204 miles 4 furlongs, crosses Ool bridge, Badwani B., 6,700 feet, in Mandi 317 miles 2 furlongs, cross Butan pass 9,060 feet, Karann B., in Kulu 227 miles 2 furlongs, Sultanpur 335 miles 2 furlongs, D. B., 4,043 feet, tehsil, chief town in Kulu. This route is closed in winter.

From Drung 318 miles 4 furlongs, in Mandi another route goes eastwards to Kulu, which is open in winter, by Kataula B., in Mandi 330 miles 4 furlongs, cross Dulchi pass 6,700 feet, 338 miles 4 furlongs, Kandi B., 339 miles 4 furlongs, Bajaora D. B., in Kulu 3,573 feet 348 miles, Sultanpur 357 miles.

From Bajaora is the Kulu route to Simla by Plach and Kotgarh which is described in Route LV, marches 36 to 46.

From Mandi 330 miles eastwards to Kataula is 13 miles.

No.	Name	Stage	Total	Road		Sutlej crossing	Elevation	Supplies	Remarks
30	**Dihar** P. O., B.—	12	358, 364	...	Ditto left bank.	Sutlej ferry Ullay bridge.	...	S. F. G. W. available, T. nil.	Large village on right bank Sutlej.
31	**Bilaspur** P.O., B., E. extensive	11	369, 372	Road fair passable for laden animals.	...	Gumrola bridge. Gumber bridge.	1600	S. F. G. W. and T. ample.	Capital of Bilaspur or Kahlur State, residence of Raja. Large town and bazar.
	Nairi	...	374	...	...	...	...	...	
32	**Kundulu**	16	379, 385	Stony ascent and descent.	Chamba range. Across drainage of Chamba range, up Buijar Dun.	...	...	S. F. G. W. and T. procurable.	Village 2 miles from Hindur.
33	**Nalagurh** P. O., B., E.—	14	399	Good road but steep.	Up Sirsa valley in Pinjor Dun.	...	...	S. F. G. W. and T. plentiful.	Capital of Hindur State. Town and bazar.
34	**Badi** B., E. limited—	12	411	Ditto	...	...	...	S. and T. after notice, F. G. W. available.	Small village.
	Karaupur	...	418	Ditto	...	...	...	...	Ditto.
35	**Kalka,** terminus of branch railway from Umballa. P. O., T. O., Hotel, C., E. confined and stony.	13	424	By Railway	...	...	2200	S. F. G. W. and T. ample.	Large village situated at foot of Himalayas, whence two roads to Simla.
36	**Umballa** by rail	39	463	...	...	...	...	...	

From Bilaspur there are two roads eastwards to Simla, of which the southerly one up the Gumroda valley is described in Route XIX, marches 18 to 21, the northerly one runs thus: Bilaspur 369 miles, Namuli B, 381 miles, Erki B, 395 miles, Jutogh 411 miles, Simla 417 miles.

From Nalagurh is a road westwards to Rupar 1,150 feet and 16 miles, a town on the left bank of the Sutlej river, where it issues from the Himalayan hills, and at the head of the Sirhind Canal. A branch tramway, formerly extended from Nalagurh by Rupar and Machiwara to Doraha on the N.-W. Railway, to serve for the construction of the head works of the Sirhind Canal and it has since been taken up.

LVIa BUDRAWAR to JALANDHAR and AMRITSAR by PUTHANKOT—

Number of Marches.	Names of Stages.	Distance in miles and furlongs. Intermediate. m. f.	Total. m. f.	Nature of Route.	Main Valleys and Mountain Passes.	River Crossings and Lakes.	Altitude above Sea Level in Feet.	Supplies and Transport at Stages.	Remarks.
10	Budrawar	...	118 2	Fair road passable for laden animals runs almost due south to Puthankot and Jalandhar.	Up Halun valley.	......	5427	S. F. G. W. and T. abundant.	Capital of Budrawar and Jaghir of Raja Sir Amar Singh, K.C.S.I. Large town, bazar and fort.
			132		Chatardhar pass.	......	10100		Halting place.
11	Camp at southern foot of pass.	14 6	132	......	Down Jalar valley left bank.	......	...	S. and T. nil. F. G. W. plentiful.	
12	Loang	15	148	......	Down Siowa valley.	......	...	S. F. G. W. and T. procurable.	Small village.
13	Hartli (Oojow)	8	156	......	Banjil pasa over Ramruchun or Chara ridge	Siowa bridge.	...	S. F. G. W. and T. available.	Village.
			158						
			160						
14	Pood	14	170	......	Down Chil valley.	......	...	Ditto	Ditto.
15	Basuoli P. O. C. E.—	13	183	......	Down Ravi valley right bank.	......	2170	S. F. G. W. and T. plentiful.	Town, fort, and bazar on right bank of Ravi river.

No.	Stage		Dist.	Description of road		River crossing	Elev.	Supplies	Remarks
16	Thain	12	195	......	Cross to left bank.	Ravi ferry	......	Ditto	Village and fort,
17	Madhopur P. O., D. B., E.—	15	210	Cart-road hence to Puthankot.	......	......	1137	Ditto	Bazar and canal workshop.
18	Puthankot P. O., T. O., Hotel, C., E.—	10	220	......	......	......	950	Ditto	Town and bazar. Terminus of branch railway.

Hence there is a branch railway by Gurdaspur 23 miles and Batala 43 miles, to Amritsar 67 miles in length.

From Puthankot there are two routes to Jalandhar, one direct by Mokerian and the other through Kangra and Hoshiarpur.

No.	Stage		Dist.	Description of road		River crossing	Elev.	Supplies	Remarks
19	Mirthal	12	222 232	Earthen unbridged road, stony in places, crossing many ravines.	Down Beas valley.	Chukki ford. Beas ferry	......	S. F. G. W. and T. procurable after notice	Small village on right bank Beas
20	Mokerian P. O., B., E. good—	12	245	......	......	......	915	S. F. G. and T available, W. plentiful.	Small town and fort.
21	Dasoha P. O., C., E. good—	9	254	Good road from Da-oha to Jalandhar.	......	......	......	Ditto	Village.
22	Tanda P. O., D. B., E. good	10	264 272 275 277	......	......	Veyn bridge Ditto.	......	Ditto	Ditto.
23	Kala Bakru E. good—	13	...	......	......	......	......	S. F. G. W. and T. procurable after notice	Small village.
24	Jalandhar P. O., T. O., D. B., C., E.—	14	291	......	......	......	778	S. F. G. W. and T. abundant.	Station N.-W. Railway, civil station and military cantonment. Headquarters of Commissioner large city and bazar.

The other route by Kangra and Hoshiarpur is as under:—

Number of Marches.	Names of Stages.	Distance in miles and furlongs. Intermediate. m. f.	Total. m. f.	Nature of Route.	Main Valleys and Mountain Passes.	River crossings and lakes.	Altitude above Sea Level in feet.	Supplies and Transport at Stages.	Remarks.
18	**Puthankot** P. O., T. O., Hotel, C., E.—	...	220	Cart-road bridged throughout, with exception of causeways between the Lyall Viaduct and Kotla. It is partially metalled, and the soil being gravelly, tongas and ekkas can travel at a good speed. Ground undulating throughout.	Across drainage of Himalayan range, Dhaoli Dhar, which falls southwards into the Beas river.	...	950	S. F. G. W. and T. plentiful.	Terminus of branch railway, town and bazar.
19	**Lyall Viaduct** E.—	7	227	...	...	Bridge over Chakki river, 28 spans of 40 ft. stone arches.	1300	S. and T. nil, G. F. W. plentiful.	Halting place.
	Banda	2	229	...	...	...	...	......	......
	Bodki	2	233	...	...	...	...		Shops.
20	**Noorpur** P. O., D. B., C., E.—	9	236	...	...	...	2050	S. F. G. W. and T. ample	Ancient fort, tehsil, large town and bazar.
	Jaugh	...	245	...	...	...	2200		
21	**Kotla** P. O., D. B., E.—	13	249	...	...	Dehri bridge wooden arch 200 ft. span.	1700	S. F. G. W. and T. available.	Large village and thana.
	Parki	...	253	...	...	...	2740	......	Shops.
	Mandigram	...	258	...	...	...	2740	......	Tea gardens.
22	**Shahpur** P. O., D. B., E.—	10 5	259 260	...	...	Koli bridge.	2500	Ditto	Bazar and plateau.
	Nerti	...	263	...	...	Chumbi ,,	2230	...	Road branches to Dharmsala.

No.	Stage	m.	f.	Total	Road	Feature crossed	River / Bridge	Elevation	Supplies	Remarks
	Gurkhari	...	...	266	.....	.....	Guj „	2390	.....	Cart-road to Palampur.
			4	267	.....	.....	Maji „	2450	.....	
23	**Kangra** P. O., D. B., E.—	13	1	270	.....	.....	Mamuni bridge.	2450	S. F. G. W. and T. plentiful.	Ancient fort on high rock above Kangunga. Celebrated Devi temple in Bhawani. Large bazar.
			3	273	Hence bridle road passable for laden animals to Hoshiarpur.	.....	.....	2400		
	Daulatpur		4	274	.....	.....	Bangunga bridge.			
			4	278	.....	.....	Ditto.	4100	.....	
24	**Ranital** B., E.—	11	4	282	.....	.....	.....			
				284	.....	Bhagrot saddle.	.....	2000	S. F. G. W. procurable. T. nil.	Small village, cross-es road from Hurripur to Juala Mukhi.
				287	.....	.....	.....			
25	**Gopipur Dehra** P. O., D. B., E.—	13		297	.....	Across Beas valley.	Beas bridge of boats or ferry in rains. Gopipur Rao.	1400	S. F. G. W. and T. available.	Town, lazar, tehsil and schools.
				300	.....	.....	.....			
26	**Bharwain** D. B.—	11	4	308	Crosses wide raos in Jeswunt Doon, which are very sandy and heavy.	Summit of Siwalik range.	.....	3000	Ditto after notice. W. scanty.	Small village.
	Kirno		4	311	.....	.....	Sohan feed	2400	.....	Road 3 miles east to Unah. Hamlet.
27	**Gagret** B., E.—	13	4	319	.....	.....	.....	.....	Ditto	
			4	321	.....	Nain pass.	.....	.....		
				324	.....	.....	.....			
28	**Manguwal** B., E.—	7	4	328	.....	Southern base of Siwalik hills	.....	.....	S. and T nil. F. G. W. procurable.	Halting stage.
				331	.....	.....	Maskara Rao.			

Number of Marches.	Names of Stages.	Distance in miles and furlongs. Intermediate. m. f.	Distance in miles and furlongs. Total. m. f.	Nature of Route.	Main Valleys and Mountain Passes.	River crossings and Lakes.	Altitude above Sea Level, in feet.	Supplies and Transport at Stages.	Remarks.
LVIa	ROUTE—contd.	...	331						
29	Hoshiarpur P. O., D. B., C., E. continued—	8 4	337	Hence - cart road bridged and metalled to Jalandhar, where dak gharis procurable.	......	Choca Rao	1055	S. F. G. W. and T. ample.	Small civil station, town and bazar.
30	Adumpur	14	351	......	......	......	880	Ditto after notice	Small village.
	Nasrola	...	358 4	...	......	Nasrala Rao.			
31	Jalandhar P. O., T. O., D. B., C., E.—	11	362	......	......	......	778	S. F. G. W. and T. abundant.	Station on N.-W. railway, civil station and military cantonment. Large city and bazas. Head-quarters of Commissioner of Jalandhar.

From Hoshiarpur there is a good road eastwards to Mandi thus:—

Hoshiarpur D. B., 1,055 feet, across Panda Gala of outer Siwalik range 14 miles, across Sohan river in the Jeswant Dun to Oonuh B., 1,329 feet 26 miles, across two ranges of the inner Siwalik hills 29 to 39 miles, to Barsar B., 42 miles, across Jaroli pass of Hamirpur range 52 miles, to Aghar B., 54 miles, across Lundrar pass of another range 60 miles, across Sher Khud river 68 miles, to Pamla B., 3,308 feet, in Mandi 70 miles, across another range 76 miles, to Galma R., 3,004 feet 82 miles, and down Sukaty valley to Mandi D. B., 3,000 feet 95 miles.

LVII   GILGIT to SRINAGAR—*See Route* XLVI.   Srinagar to Chilas by Karnakduri pass, 15,008 feet.
                                  XLVII.   Srinagar to Astor by Shontar pass, 15,052 feet.
                                  XLVIII.   Srinagar to Gilgit by Burzil Dorikun pass, 13,900 feet.

LVIII   GILGIT to SRINAGAR by SKARDU—*Old Route, Map.*

	Place	Dist.	Total	Road	Valley / Route	River	Elevation	Supplies	Remarks
	Gilgit or Gilit P.O., T.O., E.—	0	...	Road fair, mostly over maidan, fit for pony traffic in winter. Closed in summer owing to want of bridges.	Down Gilit valley left bank.	Gilgit river	4890	S. F. G. and T. moderate, W. plentiful.	Military Cantonment, town and bazar.
	Dainyor	4	...		...	Hunza "	......	...	Residence of Political Agent, headquarters of province.
	Ushkhau	12	...		...	Bagrot "			
1	Chamogah E.—	17	17	Three bad parris or cliffs in this march.	......	Batakor nala	......	S. and T. nil, G. F. W. available.	
2	Boogun	26	14	......	Up Indus valley right bank.	...	......	Ditto F. scarce.	Junction of Gilgit and Indus rivers.
	Shuta	31		Very rough road, 3 bad cliffs to cross impassable for ponies.	The river flows through a succession of	Shuta nala.			
		33				Hanwehal "			
		37				khaltar "			
		38							
3	Sasil (Haramosh) E.—	40	9	Road very bad over rock cliffs, ladders used in several places, one steep ascent and descent.	deep gorges with high precipitous cliffs on both sides.	Dach "		S. and T. scarce, G. F. W. plentiful.	Jhula bridge over Indus river 260ft. span.
	Shabtot	43				Shabtot "			
4	Borungdoi	48	8	Hard work, steep ascent and descent of 4,000 and 5,000 feet.	Shingos spur of Haramo-h south peak.	Borungdoi " Hot springs		S. and T. nil, G. F. scarce, W. available.	
		50							
		53				......	10500		

Number of Marches.	Names of Stages.	Distance in miles and furlongs.		Nature of Route.	Main Valleys and Mountain Passes.	River Crossings and Lakes.	Altitude above Sea Level in Feet.	Supplies and Transport at Stages.	Remarks.
		Intermediate. m. f.	Total. m. f.						
LVIII 5	ROUTE—contd. Shingos ...	... ...	53 ...	Half march good and half march bad along the face of cliffs.	...	Gorosil nala	......	S. and T. very scanty. G. F. W. plentiful.	Hamlet opposite Sapser on left bank Indus.
	Buleha B.,— ...	11 ...	59 ...		...	......	......	S. and T. very scanty.	Hamlet.
		...	68 ...						
6	Shutroon ...	13 ...	72 ...	Road fair with exception of 3 bad cliffs.	...	....	......	S. and T. nil. F. G. W. available.	
7	Stak E.,— ...	6 ...	78 ...		...	Stak bridge	......	S. F. G. W. and T. plentiful.	Village and fort opposite Fulchurch on left bank Indus.
8	Steriko E.,— ...	10 ...	88 ...	Better road fit for riding ponies, though cliff crossings prevent use of laden ponies.	Up Indus valley right bank.	......	......	S. F. G. W. and T. plentiful.	Village.

Between Gilgit and Stak there are no supplies and no transport, grass and wood fuel are scarce.

From Stak there is a loop route N. E. up the Stak valley, passing several small villages to Kurchung 86 miles, over Stak I a 98 miles, crossing a small glacier, and S. E. down the Tormik valley by Dunsah 104 miles, Hurimul 113 miles, Kashipa or Bazgran 116 miles, to Dusu 120 miles, on right bank of the Indus river.

From Hurimul a path goes westwards over the Ganto La 15,110 feet 119 miles, and down the Boltoro Losmla to Chutrun hot springs 116 mile, on the right bank of the Basha river.

From Bazgan 3 miles below Hurimul, in the Tormik valley, another path westwards crosses the Munbluk pass and goes down the southern slope of the Bokdar spur to the junction of the Basha and Braldu rivers 8,227 feet, which united form the Shigar river.

The regular route down the Indus valley on right bank continues from Stak as under :

No.	Name	Miles	Total	Road	Crossing	Feature	Elevation	Supplies	Remarks
9	Twar *E.—*	...	94	Road good with exception of 3 cliffs.	......	......	......	Ditto	Large village—Jhula 110 ft. span over Indus to Roudu (Mendi) on left bank.
10	Dusu *E.—* *Buicha*	10	104 4	Road fair	Cross spur.	Tormik bridge.	......	S. and T. scarce, F. G. W. plentiful.	Village at mouth of Tormik valley.
			106	......		Hontara ,,			
			108	......					
11	Tungus	9	113	Ditto	......	Tungus nala.	......	S. F. T. scarce, G. W. plentiful.	Hamlet.
12	Tsarri	10	123	Ditto	......	......	......	S. and T. scarce, F. G. W. plentiful.	Ditto.
13	Komru *E.—* *Khergron*	9	132	Road good and level over wide sandy plain.	Indus valley widens out.	Kuardo nala.	......	S. F. G. W. and T. plentiful.	Large village.
			138	......					
14	Skardu *P. O., T. O., C., E.—*	12	144	......	Cross to left bank.	Indus ferry	7400	S. F. G. W. and T. abundant.	Capital of Balistan. Cluster of villages, fort, tehsil,thana, headquarters of Wazir.

For the road onwards from Skardu to Srinagar, see Routes :

XLIX by Deosai plains and Gurais 155 miles 4 furlongs, open only from July to September inclusive.—Total 299½ miles,

L by Dras and Sindh valleys 233 miles, open from June to November inclusive. Total 374 miles.

The route Gilgit to Skardu is open to footmen all the year, except when the rivers are in flood.—Travellers had better take all their provisions and supplies through from Gilgit or Skardu, and through transport also, changing a few coolies only on the road.

From Sasli Haramosh, after crossing the Indus rope bridge, there is a difficult path down left bank by Sinjak Brangsa 12 miles, to Bunji 12 miles. Total 24 miles.

From Sapser on left bank of the Indus opposite Bulchu 68 miles, a path goes southwards over the Lokam pass of the dividing range and descends down the Dichil nala to the Astor river opposite Dashkin at 163½ miles of Route XLVII].

From Fulchurch on left bank of the Indus opposite Stak 78 miles, a track ascends the Pimdas nala southwards to Sitter which joins the foregoing path at the northern foot of the Lokam pass.

From Roudu (Mendi) on the left bank of the Indus, opposite Twar 94 miles, a track ascends the Tuekchun valley southwards to Chutabar, whence it forks out by two paths over the Trongo Pir and Hurpo La of the dividing range, which uniting again in the Parishing valley, continues westwards to Astor, see Route XLVIIIe and foot-note.

LIX GILGIT to JAMMU by KISHENGUNGA VALLEY and KOTLI, 431 miles—See Route X.

LX GILGIT to RAWUL PINDI by BARAI PASS and MOZUFFERABAD—Map. Weightman.

Number of Marches.	Names of Stages.	Distance in miles and furlongs. Intermediate. m. f.	Total. m. f.	Nature of Route.	Main Valleys and Mountain Passes.	River crossings and Lakes.	Altitude above Sea Level in Feet.	Supplies and Transport at Stages.	Remarks.
	Gilgit or Gilit P. O., T. O., E.—	0 ..	..	Made road towards Srinagar as far as Ramghat, bridged and passable throughout for laden animals.	Down Gilgit valley light bank.	.....	4800 / 5025	S. F. G. T. moderate, W. plentiful.	Military Cantonment, fort, town, bazar, residence of Political Agent, head-quarters of province.
1	Minawar B. E.—	9 ..	9 ..	....	.....	......	4000	S. and T. nil, F. W. available, G. scarce.	Small village.
2	Safed Pari B. E.—	10 ..	19 ..	Ascent and descent of easy gradient.	.....	.....	.....	S. F. G. T. nil, W. from river.	Cliff.
	Pertab pul C.	...	20 ..	....	Down Indus valley left bank.	Indus bridge wire rope suspension 330 ft. span.	3830	Ditto	Serai on left bank Indus.
3	Bawanji or Bunji P. O., T. O., B. E.—	17 ..	36 ..	.....			4631	S. G. W. and T. moderate, F. scarce.	Fort and bazar.
	Ramghat	...	43 4	Hence turn westwards from Sri-	.....	Astor bridge.	3700	......	Military post.

No.	Station		Dist.	Total	Remarks on road	Valley	Intermediate	Elevation	Water and supplies	Remarks
4	Leechar	...	13	49 / 51 / 52	nagar road down left bank Indus valley. The hill slopes along base of Hatu Pir between Ramghat and Jaliper are exposed to shale slides; 6 feet road recently opened out and bridged to Bagtogah.	......	Leechar „ Raikhest „ Phungatori „	......	S. and T. nil, F. G. scarce, W. from river.	Site of great mountain slip from Hatu Pir into Indus in 1841, which blocked the river.
5	Jaliper	...	14	63 / 67 / 69		......	Jaliper „ Ganalo „ Goar „	......	Ditto	Halting place.
6	Bagtogah *E.—* *Diamirai*	...	15	78	Turn southwards and ascend Bunar valley by a rough and stony path.	Up Bunar valley.	Bunar „	......	Ditto	Opposite Ges on right bank Indus.
7	Bunar *E.—*	...	12	86	......	......	......	......	S. F. G. W. and T. moderate.	Fort and village.
8	Paloi	...	11	90	......	......	......	......	S. and T. scanty, F. G. W. available.	Hamlet.
9	Bunar Dumel	...	12	101 / 113	Very rough path on ascent and descent from pass—steep on both sides.	Barai pass down Barai ravine.	......	14000.	S. and T. nil, F. G. scanty, G. W. available.	North foot of pass.
10	Kalan *Mori*	...	18	122 / 124 / 131	......	......	......	......	Ditto	South foot of pass.
11	Dumel Pain *E.—*	...	12	137 / 143	Join the Astor and Kishengunga road, passable for laden animals.	Down Kiel valley.	......	7300	S. and T. nil, F. G. W. plentiful.	Hamlet.

Number of Branches.	Names of Stages.	Distance in miles and furlongs. Inter- mediate. m. f.	Total. m. f.	Nature of Route.	Main Valleys and Mountain Passes.	River Crossings and Lakes.	Altitude above Sea Level in Feet.	Supplies and Transport at Stages.	Remarks.
LX	*ROUTE—contd.*	...	...						
12	**Khel** E.—	...	143	Between Khel and Shardi, 13 miles of the road are difficult for laden ponies.	Down Kishenganga valley right bank.	......	6250	S. and T. scanty, F. G. W. plentiful.	Village.
13	**Seri** E.—	8	151 ...	......	......	......	6000	S. T. nil, F. G. W. plentiful.	Small village.
		8	159 ...	......	......	Kankatori bridge.			
14	**Shardi or Kurigam** *P. O., E.—*	...	165 ...	Road chiefly through fields with many ups and downs over spurs.	......	Kishenganga bridge. Kurigam „	5850	S. and T. available, F. G. W. plentiful.	Shardi fort on left bank, Kurigam on right bank.
		9	168 ...						
15	**Dudnial** E.—	9	177 ...	Difficult path over precipitous cliffs.	......	Kishenganga bridge.	5050	Ditto, T. nil.	Hamlet.
	Changa	...	179 ...	......	......	Badore „			
16	**Doarian** E.—	7	184 ...	Road rough and stony, partly through fields, forest and grassy slopes.	......	Seri „ Oolari „ Babanka Katta bridge.	5050	S. F. G. W. and T. available.	Small village.
	Tali Lohat	...	185 ... 189 ... 191 ...						

No.	Stage	Dist.	Total		Remarks on road		Intermediate place	Elevation	Supplies	Remarks
17	**Karen** P. O., E.—	8	192	...	Road fair and level through forest and fields.	.....	Kishengunga bridge.	4650	S. F. G. W. and T. plentiful.	Karen fort on left bank, large village in Drawar.
	Lalla	...	198	...		.....		.....		
18	**Shahkot**	9	201	...	Road rough and stony, and crosses several high spurs and the Jagran valley.	.....	Katta „	4300	S. and T. nil, G. F. W. available.	Small village.
	Salkatla on left bank	—	202	4		.....	Kishengunga bridge.	.....	.....	
	Dooral	...	205	...		.....	Jagran „	.....	.....	Village.
19	**Jora**	10	211	...	Road rough and stony to Jora and thence ascends spur.	.....		.....	Ditto	Ditto.
	Baran	...	216	...		.....		3700	.....	Large village.
20	**Chowgali**	11	222	...	Road descends steeply through rocky gorge and along mountain side over spurs.	Chow gali		6000	S. and T. nil, F. G. W. available.	Dok.
21	**Balagran** E. small—	8	230	...	Road chiefly through fields.	.....		.....	S. and T. moderate, F. G. W. available.	Village.
	Jing	...	234	...		.....	Urshi bridge	.....		
22	**Pala** E.—	8	238	...	Ditto	.....		.....	S. F. G. W. and T. plentiful.	Large village.
	Mundelool	...	241	...		.....	Pakot „	.....		Village.
23	**Kuri** P. O., E.—	7	245	...	Road rough and stony to about half way, thence through patches of cultivation.	.....	Shalam „	.....	Ditto	Small town.

Number of Marches	Names of Stages	Distance of Miles and Furlongs		Nature of Route	Main Valleys and Mountain Passes.	River Crossings and Lakes.	Altitude above Sea Level in Feet.	Supplies and Transport at Stages.	Remarks.
		Intermediate m. f.	Total m. f.						
LX	ROUTE—contd.	...	245						
24	Mozufferabad P. O., C., E.—	9	251	...	.....	Kishenganga bridge.	2470	S. F. G. and W. plentiful, T. moderate.	Town and bazar, fort and head-quarters of zillah.
	Deewal P. O., T. O., D. B., E.	...	255	Join cart-road, bridged and metalled from Srinagar to Rawul Pindi; open all the year except when there is heavy snow at Murree in January and February.	Down Jhelum valley left bank.	Jhelum bridge.	2225		
25	Dulai D. B., E. confined—	11	265		......	......	2105	S. F. G. W. procurable, T. after notice.	Hamlet.
26	Kohala (Kashmir border) P. O., T. O., D. B., E. small—	12	277	......	Cross to right bank.	Jhelum bridge.	1916	Ditto	Small bazar and customs post.
28	Murree (Sunny Bank) P. O., T. O., Hotels, C., E.—	27 4	304	Road bridged and metalled, regular tonga service.	Kuklanha	......	6600	S. F. G. T. ample, W. from new supply.	Murree, head-quarters of Lieutenant-General Commanding Punjab Army. Civil and Military Sanitarium, town and large bazar.

| 31 | Rawul Pindi ... P. O., T. O., Hotels, D. B., C., E.— | 36 | 6 | 341 | 21 | ...... | ...... | ...... | 1700 | S. F. G. W. and T. abundant. | Large Military Cantonment and Civil Station, fort, city, head-quarters of district and division, and station on North-Western Railway. |

For description of route between Kohala and Rawul Pindi see Route XLII, marches 10 to 15.

From Shahkot 201 miles, or Dooral 205 miles, there is a shorter route to Pala by the Sarango or Sirsunga pass, up Jagran valley westwards to Kuttun 209 miles, southwards up ravine over the Sirsunga pass, to Jabbian Dok 217 miles, descending Urshi valley south westwards to Panjoor 226 miles, and to Pala 232 miles.

There are several cross routes over the dividing range between the Kishenganga and Khagan valleys, those chiefly used by traders are :—

From Kurigam or Doarian by Ratti gali to Burawai.
From Tali Lohat up Oolari valley by Jotari pass to Burawai.
From Karen up Babunka katta valley by Nagtora over Chirik gali, across Jagran valley and over Shikara gali to Manur.
From Shahkot or Dooral up the Jagran valley by the Tor gali to Ratta kund.
    Ditto   ditto   by the Shikara pass to Manur.
    Ditto   ditto   by the Bichla pass to Manur.
From Mundabal up the Pakot valley by the Bhadri gali to Bhunja.
From Kuri up the Shalam valley by Rajkot and Makra gali to Ghanul.
    Ditto   ditto   by Nur gali to Kalakot.
    Ditto   ditto   by Galoti gali to Kalakot, well frequented.
From Mozafferabad by Doob gali to Garhi Habibulla, regular road, 10 miles.
    Ditto   by Lohar gali to   ditto   ditto   12 miles, well frequented.

LXI GILGIT to HASSAN ABDAL or KALAKE SERAI by KHAGAN VALLEY and ABBOTTABAD—*Furr, Anderson.*

Between Gilgit and Chilas in a line due south are two high ranges of mountains over 15,000 feet high, with an intervening valley, the Sai or Buribasai (which flows into the Indus at Sai a short distance above Banji) and beyond the Indus river without bridge or ferry to cross. Difficult paths lead from Gilgit across the first range to Paiot 11,400 feet and Gashu 8,400 feet on the Sai river ; thence across the second range from Paiot over the Kimejut pass 14,000 feet down the Hodar valley by Hodar to the Indus, and over Bariben pass down the Khinar valley by Totambal, Dusi to Thalpen on right bank of the Indus opposite Chilas ; or from Gashu by the Malhat or Mtere passes, and down the valley of the same name to Gez, on right bank of the Indus, opposite Bunar.

The ordinary road from Gilgit by Bunji to Chilas should be followed as under :—

Number of Marches.	Names of Stages.	Distance in miles and furlongs. Intermediate. m. f.	Total. m. f.	Nature of Route.	Main Valleys and Mountain Passes.	River Crossings and Lakes.	Altitude above Sea Level in Feet.	Supplies and Transport and Stages.	Remarks.
	Gilgit P. O., T. O., E.—	...	0 ...	Made road towards Srinagar as far as Ramghat, bridged and passable throughout for laden animals.	Down Gilgit valley right bank.	......	4890 } 5025 }	S. F. G. T. moderate, W. plentiful.	Military Cantonment, fort, town, bazar, residence of Political Agent, head-quarters of province.
1	**Minawar** B., E.—	9 ...	9 ...	......	...	......	4000	S. and T. nil, F. W. available, G. scarce.	Small village.
2	**Safed Pari** B., E.—	10 ...	19 ...	Ascent and descent of easy gradient.	...	......	......	S. F. G. T. nil, W. from river.	Cliff.
	Pertabpul C.	...	29 ...	......	Down Indus valley left bank.	Indus bridge steel wire rope.	3850	Ditto	Serai on left bank Indus.
3	**Bunji** P. O., T. O., B., E.—	17 ...	36 ...	......	......	......	4631	S. G. W. and T. moderate, F. scarce.	Fort and bazar.
	Ramghat	...	43 4	Hence turn westwards down Indus valley, left bank to Chilas, 6 feet road made and mostly	......	Astor bridge	3700	......	Military post.
4	**Leechar**	13 ...	49 ...		......	Leechar „	......	S. and T. nil, F. G. scarce, W. from river.	Site of great mountain slip from Hatu Pir into Indus river in
		...	51 ...		......	Raikheot „			

No.	Station	Dist.	Total	Road	Direction	Intermediate stages	Elevation	Supplies	Remarks
5	**Jaliper**	... 14	52 ...	bridged. Hill slopes below Hatu Pir exposed to shale slides.	......	Phungatori „	......	Ditto	1841 which blocked up the river. Halting place.
		:::	63 :::		......	Jaliper „	......		Ditto
6	**Bagtogah** *E.—*	... 15	67 ...	Rest of road fairly easy.	......	Ganalo „	......		
		:::	69 :::	......	......	Gonar „	......	Ditto	Opposite Ges on right bank Indus.
		:::	78 :::	......	......	Bunar „	......		
		::	88 :	......	......	Khanogah „	......		
7	**Chilas** *P. O., B., E.—*	... 13	91 ...	Hence turn southwards and ascend Khanogah valley to Basia and up western Thak ravine to Babusar.	Up Khanogah valley.	......	......	S. T. W. moderate, F. G. scarce.	Fort, small cantonment, village and lazar.
	Datsa	:::	95 :::						
	Singal	:::	97 :						
	Basha	:::	99 :::			Niat bridge.			
		:::	101 :::						
8	**Thak** *E.—*	... 14	105 ::	Good road of easy gradient. Eastern Niat ravine leads to Kamakduri pass 15,000 feet and down to Kishengunga valley at Shardi.	......	Thak „	......	S. F. G. W. and T. moderate.	Village and fort on summit of high rock.
9	**Babusar** *E.—*	... 8	113 ...		...	Thak ravine crossed 4 times by bridges.	......	S. and T. nil. F. G. W. plentiful.	Hamlet.
		:::	117 ...	Ascent and descent of pass steep over easy ground.	Babusar pass down Khagan valley	......	13500		
10	**Gittidas**	... 6 4	119 4	......	......	Gittidas-ka katta.	12100	Ditto F. Juniper.	Halting place.

Number of Marches	Names of Stages	Distance in miles and furlongs — Intermediate m.	f.	Total m.	f.	Nature of Route	Main Valleys and Mountain Passes	River crossings and Lakes	Altitude above Sea Level in Feet	Supplies and Transport at Stages	Remarks
LXI	ROUTE—contd.										
	Lalusar Lake ...	...	...	119	4	Road recently re-made, passable throughout for pack animals, cliff passages improved and some bridges provided.	Down Gittidas ravine to Lake along left bank, thence down	Kunhar ford	11700	.....	Bridge will be built.
11	Basul E.— ...	10	...	126	4		Kunhar or Nainsook river, crossing to right bank at Basul and left bank at Burawai, and keeping along the left bank to Narang, whence good road along either bank to Khagan. Then along left bank to		11000	S. and T. nil, F. G. W. plentiful.	Halting place.
	Kotawai	...	...	129	4	......		......	.....	......	Junction of Furbidia-ka-katta.
	Seri	...	...	133	4	......		......	.....	......	Ditto Julkhud-ka-katta.
12	Bu awai ...	11	6	141	2			Kunhar bridge	9330	Ditto	Ditto Jora-katta.
13	Bhatta Kundi ...	8	2	149	4	Between Bhatta Kundi and Narang are some difficult cliffs.		Bhatta Kundi	.....	Ditto	Junction of Bhatta Kundi-ka-khatta.
	Sehock on right bank	...	...	153	...	......		......	.....	......	Sapal pass road from Yaghistan.
	Saiful Malik Lake 4½ miles east.	...	...	158	...			Saiful Malik Lake.	11000	......	Up rocky gorge east.
14	Narang ...	9	4	159	...	Between Narang and Khagan good road along either bank.		Kunhar bridge.	8275	S. F. G. W. and T. plentiful.	Highest village in Khagan valley. Food depot for Gujar herdsmen.
15	Khagan ...	14	4	173	4	Road difficult in places.		Ditto	6800	S. and T. scanty, F. G. W. plentiful.	Village on left bank.

No.	Name of place	Intermediate	Furlongs	Total miles	Description of road	Crossing	Bridges and fords	Elevation	Supplies	Remarks
16	*Diwan Bela*					Jared and Kawai to Balakot, where cross over to right bank.	Nainsook gorge.			Site of great battle in which Sikh Army was annihilated by mountain tribes.
	Manaur	10							Ditto	
	B.—									
	Bichla 3 miles up nala.		4	178			Bichla bridge.			
	Jared		4	183						
	Malkandi, F.B.		4	185				5135	Ditto	Village on left bank.
	Bhunja 3 miles up nala		4	187	Between **Bhunja** nala and **Paras** are some dangerous cliffs, where loads should be taken off animals and carried by men.		Bhunja bridge			
	Paras			191						
				195						
17	**Kawai**	14	4	198	Road fair, several steep ascents and descents, narrow in places.			5025	S. and T. moderate, F. G. W. plentiful.	Small village.
	B.—						Ghanal ,,			
	Ghanal 2 miles up nala			200						
18	**Balakot**	13		211	Road good and easy over pass. From Bisyan, the road continues down the valley to Garhi Habibulla 232 m. 3 fg. D. B. and joins the Kashmir road.		Kunhar ,,	3700	S. F. G. W. and T. plentiful.	Small town and thana on right bank.
	B.E.—			219		Dun gali				Pass of easy gradient on both approaches.
	Biayan			220						Small village.
19	**Jaba**	11		222	Joins the earthen and bridged cart-road to Abbottabad.				S. F. G. W. and T. moderate.	
	B.—			228						
20	**Mansera**	13		235			Bhatti bridge	3540	S. F. G. W. and T. plentiful.	Large village and tehsil.
	P.O., D.B., C., E.—									
21	**Abbottabad**	16		251	Good road metalled and bridged, excepting large rivers.			4005	S. F. G. W. and T. ample.	Military Cantonment, Civil Station, town, headquarters of district Hazara.
	P.O., T.O., D.B., C.E.						Dor ford			
	Sultanpur		4	259				2700		
	Chamba B.C., E.		4	261				2610	S. F. G. after notice, W. from well, T. nil.	Halting place.

Number of Marches	Names of Stages	Intermediate m. f.	Total m. f.	Nature of Route	Main Valleys and Mountain Passes	River Crossings and Lakes	Altitude above Sea Level in Feet	Supplies and Transport at Stages	Remarks
LXI 22	ROUTE—contd. Haripur P.O., T.O., B.B., C., E.	...	261 4	Tonga service to Hassan Abdal.	......	......	1730	S. F. G. W. and T. plentiful.	Town, lazar, tehsil.
	Hattar	23 2	274 2	......	......	......	......	S. F. G. after notice, W. from well, T. nil.	Halting place.
	Belartope	...	287 4	......	......	Haro ford	1600		
23	Kalake Serai P. O., T.O., D. B.,	21	295 4	......	......	......	1690	S. F. G. T. after notice, W. from well.	Small town and Station on N. W. Railway.
	Hassan Abdal or P. O., T. O., D.B., 1½ miles distant from Railway Station.	19	293 2	......	......	......	1400	S. F. G. W. and T. available.	Ditto.

Lay in supplies at Gilgit, Bunji, Chilas and Balakot—

From Chilas there is another more westerly route up the Botogah valley by Mati Shing and Philiat, and up the Philiat ravine over the Botogah pass to the Gittidas Creek and Lalusar Lake—about 6 miles longer than the Balusar route.

From the Kaghan valley there are several tracks over the dividing range or Kashmir border into the Kishengunga valley, those best known are :—

From Kotawai, up the Purbidia-ka-katta over the Siral gali and down this ravine into the Kankatori valley to Shardi on the Kishengunga.

From Seri, up the Julkhud-ka-katta over the Nari Nar pass and down this ravine to Surgan in the Kankatori valley.

From Burawai, a good path up the Jora-katta over the Chantari or Ratti gali and down the Oolari valley either to Kurigam or Doarian on the Kishengunga.

From Bhatta Kundi up this nala over the Tor gali into the Jagran valley and Drawar.

From Manaur are paths up this nala and its branches over the Shikara and Bichla passes into the Jagran valley and Drawar.

From Bhunja is a rough path over the Bhadri gali to Pala and Kuri.

From Ghanul another rough path over the Makra gali and down the Shalan valley to Kuri.

From Balakot is a road much used by traders over the Galoti gali into the Shalan valley to Kuri on the Kishengunga.

Balakot down Khagan valley by Bisyan to Garhi Habibulla is 12½ miles.

LXII GILGIT to DAREL.—Map.

No.	Name of place	Intermediate	Total	Nature of road	Direction	Rivers, fords	Elevation	Supplies	Remarks
	Gilgit	...	0	Good road to Naupur, where it turns westwards up the Kergah valley to its source. Very rough track to Jut.	...	...	4890 / 5025	S. F. G. T. moderate, W. plentiful.	Military Cantonment, fort, town, bazar, residence of Political Agent, capital of province.
	Naupur	...	3 / 4	......	Up Kergah valley.	Shuku ford. / Singaigah „ / Kergah bridge.	...	......	Small village.
		...	8						
		...	11						
1	**Jut**	16	16	Fair road through beautiful country with green sward and pine forests to the head of the valley, where vegetation ceases, and the rugged hill sides are covered with piles of splintered rock.	...	...	8900	S. and T. nil, F. G. W. plentiful.	Halting place.
	Shaiwase Harai	...	18				...	Ditto	Ditto.
2	**Maja Mazne**	7	23			...	...	Ditto	Ditto.
	Dati Harai	4	26						
3	**Takorbas**	7	30 / 34		Chonchar pass, across Khanbari valley.	......	14,000.	Ditto	Ditto.
4	**Kalichunji**	8	38	......	Kuli pass, down Karigah glen. Down Darel valley.	Khanbari ford.	...	Ditto F. scarce.	Ditto.
		...	46						
5	**Yahchot**	16	54	Rough road, difficult in places.	......	...	...	S. F. G. W. and T. moderate.	Small village and fort.
	Naukind	...	59						
	Bududarkot	...	63						

Number of Marches.	Names of Stages.	Distance in miles and Furlongs.		Nature of Route.	Main Valleys and Mountain Passes.	River Crossings and Lakes.	Altitude abo Sea Level in feet.	Supplies and Transport at Stages.	Remarks.
		Inter-mediate. m. f.	Total. m. f.						
LXII	ROUTE—contd.	... ...	63 ...	... ...	......	......	......		
6	**Samakial or Dudokot**	13 ...	67 ...	......	......	......	......	S. F. G. W and T. moderate.	Fort and chief place in Darel.
	Phogrj	... ...	70 ...						
	Gaiah	... ...	73 ...	......	......	......	......	Ditto	Village.
7	Indus river	9 ...	76 ...	Right bank of Indus river.					

From Kalichwuji 38 miles, there is a rough path down the Khanbari valley to the Indus river. In this valley are said to be minerals, which were once worked, hence the name.

There is another track to Darel from Singal at mile 32 of Route LXIII, which turns southwards up the Singal valley and the Patare ravine over the Dolar gali to Yalchot, in length about 40 miles from Singal.

LXIII GILGIT to CHITRAL by MASTUJ—*Beynon*.

	Names of Stages.	m. f.	m. f.	Nature of Route.	Main Valleys.	River Crossings.	Altitude.	Supplies.	Remarks.
	Gilgit or Gilit P. O., T. O., C. E.—	... ...	0 ...	Six feet made road from Gilgit to Gupis, open throughout the year and passable for pack animals.	Up Gilgit valley right bank.	......	4880 } 5025 }	S. F. G. and T. moderate, W. plentiful.	Military Canton-ment, fort, town, bazar, residence of Political Agent, and capital of pro-vince.
	Naspur	... ...	3 ...		......	Kergah bridge			
	Himal	... ...	9 ...		......	Heltar „	5150.		

No.	Stage	Miles	Total miles	Nature of country	Intermediate places		Elevation	Supplies	Remarks
1	**Sharot** E.—	18	18	It crosses fans of alluvial soil at the mouths of streams where small villages are situated with orchards, gardens and cultivation around.	Shikaiot „	......	6000	Ditto	Small village.
	Shikaiot		19						
	Gulapur		21		Yasin rope bridge.		......	......	Fort and capital of Punial.
	Cherkala on left bank		23						
			25	......	Dalmati „	Called Yasin valley upwards.	5800		
2	**Singal** E.—	14	32	......	Singal „	......	6200	S. and T. nil, G. F. W. procurable.	Small village and fort.
	Gulmati		35		Gulmati „				
	Gurjar		38						
3	**Gakuch** E. below village at 6,000 feet.	10	42	Between such it crosses hill spurs varying in ascent and descent.	......	......	7170	S.F.G.W. procurable, T. moderate.	Ditto.
	Aish		44						
	Hopar		47						
			51						
4	**Sumar** E.—	13	55	......	Yangan „ Sirogah bed.	......	......	S. G. T. nil, F. W. procurable.	Junction of Ishkoman and Yasin rivers.
	Roshan		62		Roshan bridge.				
			63						

Number of Marches.	Names of Stages.	Distance in miles and furlongs.		Nature of Route.	Main Valleys and Mountain Passes.	River crossings and Lakes.	Altitude above Sea Level in Feet.	Supplies and Transport at Stages.	Remarks.
		Inter-mediate. m. f.	Total. m. f.						
XLIII	ROUTE—contd.	...	...						
5	Gupis E.—	...	63 ...	From Gupis country road improved and rendered passable for laden animals to Chitral.	Called Ghizar valley upwards.	Injarot bed.	7400	S.G. F.W. procurable, T. moderate.	Small village and fort at junction of Ghizar and Warshigan rivers.
		13 ...	68 ...			Khogah „			
			73 ...						
			78 ...						
6	Dahimal	17 ...	85 ...	......	......	Dahimal rope bridge.	8260	S. G. T. nil, F. W. procurable.	Small village.
			88 ...			Kachun bridge			
			90 ...	Bad pari & gallery					
			92 ...						
7	Pingal E.—	10 ...	95 ...	Road from Pingal to Gasht always bad from snow between 15th December and 15th March; and the Shandur pass is usually closed for one month during this period.	Up Ghizar valley right bank.	Sozat „	9000	S. and T. nil, F. G. W. procurable.	Small village.
	Darband	...	98 ...	......	......				
8	Chashi	...	104 ...		... ...	Chashi bridge and fort.	9600	Ditto	Ditto.
		10 ...	105 ...		......	Bandar Lake			
9	Ghizar E.—	...	114 4		Cross to left bank.	Ghizar bridge.	10000	S. F. G. W. and T. moderate.	Ditto and fort.
		13 ...	118 ...	......	......	Tera ford.			
			121 ...	......	......	Chokhabut bridge.			
			123 4	......	......				

No.	Station	Dist.	Total	Road	Descent	River	Elev.	Supplies	Remarks
10	**Langar**	...	127	.....	.....	Chamarkand bridge.	.....	.....	Alternative route over high pass to Mastuj.
		15	133	Easy ascent to pass	.....	.....	11000	S. and T. nil, F. G. W. procurable.	Jungle.
			138	Pass, long maidan of 3 miles and sharp descent.	Shandur pass down Woghtur ravine.	Shandur Lake	12,000.	.....	.....
11	**Laspur**	10	143	.....	Down Lashpur valley.	.....	9800	Ditto	Hamlet.
			144	.....	.....	Laspur bridge.	.....		
			147	.....	.....	Harchin bed.	.....		
	Rahman	...	150	.....	.....	.....	.....	...	**Path across hills and down Golaud Gol to Chitral.**
12	**Gasht**	9	152	Road over large fan scored by several nalas with steep and narrow ramps.	.....	.....	9000	Ditto	Ditto.
	Chokalrut	...	155	.....	.....	.....	.....	...	First battle fought by Colonel Kelley with Pioneer Regiment and Kashmir Service troops against Chitrali force.
			159	.....	.....	Laspur bridge.	.....		
13	**Mastuj** P. O., E.—	11	163	Road fair	Down Yarkhun valley right bank.	Yarkhun „	7760	S. F. G. W. and T. procurable.	Fort and capital of Kushwakt.
	Nisa Gol	...	169	.....	.....	.....	.....	...	
14	**Sanoghar**	9	172	Road good	Cross to left bank.	Yarkhun „	7000	S. and T. nil, F. G. W. procurable.	**Second battle** fought and defeat of Chitralis. Village.

17

Number of Marches.	Names of Stages.	Distance in miles and furlongs.		Nature of Route.	Main Valleys and Mountain Passes.	River Crossings and Lakes.	Altitude above Sea level is Feet.	Supplies and Transport and Stages.	Remarks.
		Intermediate. m. f.	Total. m. f.						
LXIII	*ROUTE—contd.*								
15	Buni	... ...	17. ...	Road good excepting short part opposite junction of Mulkho river and some bad places in Koragh defile. Road bad and narrow over stone sheets and *debris.*	Called Chitral river.	......	6900	S. and T. nil, F. G. W. procurable.	Village. Junction of Turikho and Yarkhun rivers.
	Koragh defile	11 ...	1·3 ... 190			......	......		
16	Reshun	12 ...	195 ...		......	Reshun nala	6500	Ditto	Small village.
					Cross spur		7200		
17	Barmas E.—	8 ...	203 .	Road fair	......	Barmas nala	6100	Ditto	Ditto.
18	Koghazi	13 ...	215 216		......	Guand Gol	5500	Ditto	Ditto.
19	Chitral P.O., T.O., E.—	12 4	227 228 4	Road very bad and narrow especially 224 and 225 miles through narrow gorge with precipitous sides over kutcha galleries.	Cross to right bank Chitral river.	Chitral bridge.	4980	S. F. G. W. and T. procurable.	Fort and capital of Kashkar. Residence of Mehter of Chitral

From Chitralkala opposite 23 miles on left bank of Gilgit or Yasin River, a track goes up this side by Bubur 36 miles, junction of Ishkoman river 47 miles, 6,000 feet, and up the Ishkoman valley by Chatorkand 63 miles, Imit 78 miles 8,200 feet, Gazkul or Karambar Lake and Ishkoman pass either to Lugar or to Sarhad in Wakhan 138 miles. There are formidable glaciers on this route, which commence at 13½ miles from Imit and are passable only in winter when snow fills the crevasses. The Lake is about 2 miles long at the head of 2 valleys, Ishkoman southwards and Yarkhun south westwards. It is about 33 miles from Imit and about 23 miles from Sarhad across undulating ground covered with grass in summer. From Luspur 143 miles, there is a path southwards over the Tal pass and down the Panjkora valley by Tal and Shiringal to Dir.

LXIII. GUPIS to SARHAD in WAKHAN by YASIN and the DARKOT and BAROGHIL PASSES—*Littledale*.

No.	Place			Road		Bridge	Elevation	Supplies	Remarks
5	Gupis, E.—	...	68	Rough road throughout, but passable for laden animals.	Up Wurshigan valley along left bank to 78 miles where cross to left bank.	Yasin bridge. Wurshigam bridge.	7400	S.F.G.W. procurable, T. moderate.	Small village and fort.
	Gendai fort	... 4	69 73 78						
6	Yasin, E.—	15 ...	83	General direction northwards.	......	......	7765	S. F. G. W. and T. available.	Small town.
	Baraos	... ...	85 90			Ditto.			
7	Mir Wali's fort ... E.—	8 ...	91	...	Cross to left bank.	......	... ...	Ditto	Fort.
	Amchat	... ...	95 98	......		Ditto.			
8	Darkot, E.—	15 ...	106	......	......	... ...	9160	S. F. G. W. and T. moderate.	Village.
9	Camp *at southern foot of pass* ...	10 ...	116	Steep ascent and descent across snow field and glacier with many crevasses.	Darkot pass	......	11050	S. and T. nil, F. G. W. procurable.	Halting place.
		...	122				16000	......	Closed until June.
10	Safer Bek, E.—	15 ...	131	Join road from Mastuj in Yarkhun valley.	Across head of Yarkhun valley.	Yarkhun ford	......	Ditto	Ditto.

NUMBER OF MARCHES	NAMES OF STAGES	DISTANCE IN MILES AND FURLONGS		NATURE OF ROUTE	MAIN VALLEYS AND MOUNTAIN PASSES	RIVER CROSSINGS AND LAKES	ALTITUDE ABOVE SEA LEVEL IN FEET.	SUPPLIES AND TRANSPORT AT STAGES.	REMARKS.
		INTERMEDIATE m. f.	TOTAL m. f.						
LXIIIa ROUTE—contd.			131 ... 137 ...	Notable depression in Hindu Kush range 2 miles wide; easy access on both sides.	Baroghil pass	......	12460	......	Hindu Kush range.
11	Zerkhar	15 ...	146 ...		......	... ...	......	S. and T. nil, F. G. W. procurable.	Hamlet.
12	Sarhad E.—	7 ...	153 ...	Deep snow in December, January and February.	......	......	10450	S. F. G. W. and T. available.	Large village.

From Barmas 40 miles, a rough path westwards by Nalti over the Tui or Moshabar pass 14,700 ft. to Kila Darband in Yarkhun valley 3 marches.
From Darkot 10½ miles, a difficult path eastwards over dividing range by Ishkoman to Imit in the Ishkoman valley 3 marches.

LXIIIb MASTUJ to SARHAD in WAKHAN by BAROGHIL PASS.—*(Approximate) R. G. S. Journal, Robertson's Map.*

NUMBER OF MARCHES	NAMES OF STAGES	DISTANCE IN MILES AND FURLONGS		NATURE OF ROUTE	MAIN VALLEYS AND MOUNTAIN PASSES	RIVER CROSSINGS AND LAKES	ALTITUDE ABOVE SEA LEVEL IN FEET.	SUPPLIES AND TRANSPORT AT STAGES.	REMARKS.
		INTERMEDIATE m. f.	TOTAL m. f.						
13	Mastuj P. o., E.— Chopri	... ...	163 ...	Rough track northwards for laden animals, though difficult in places.	Up Yarkhun valley.	......	7760	S. F. G. W. and T. procurable.	Fort and capital of Kushwaklit.
14	Brep	13 ...	170 ...		......	......	......	S. and T. nil, F. G. scanty, W. plentiful	Village.
15	Miragram	10 ...	186 ...		......	......	......	Ditto	Ditto.
17	Kila Darband E.—	14 ...	200 ...	Eastern track from Yasin by Tui pass and Gazan joins here.	......	......	......	S. F. G. W. and T. moderate.	Village and fort.

									S. and T. uil, F. G. W. procurable.	Halting place.
	Topkhana Ziabeg	10	...	210	...	...	...	...	...	Halting place.
19	Safer Bek ... E.— *Chitrol and Badakshan Frontier.*	22	...	232	...	Ascent to summit 3 miles gentle gradient, plateau 5 miles called Dasht-i-Biughil		...	Ditto	Ditto.
		...	...	235	...	rich pasturage, descent 3 miles	Baroghil pass	...	...	
		...	...	240	...	gentle slope and stage 3 miles beyond — Dasht is		12460	...	Hindu Kush range
20	Zerkhar or Pirkhar ...	14	...	247	...		...	...	Ditto	Hamlet.
21	Sarhad in Wakhan ... E.—	7	...	254	...	2 to 4 miles wide covered by deep snow in December, January and February.	...	Panj ford	10450	S. F. G. W. and T. available.	Large village.

At Sarhad the east and west road used in winter from Sarikol through Wakhan to Badakshan is joined. This starting from Tashkurgan, the capital of Sarikol, 10,250 feet, has the choice of two routes to Gombaz-i-Bozai. *Firstly*, southwards by Zerishtut 20 miles, Kurghan-i-Ujadlshai 30 miles, then westwards across the Tagdumbash Pamir by the Karachunkar pass 65 miles and descends to Gombaz-i-Bozai 110 miles. *Secondly*, westwards from Tashkurgan up rocky stream to Kanshubar 12,980 feet 16 miles, up open valley to Nezatash pass, 14,915 feet 26 miles, descent to Kogachak 12,740 feet 36 miles, and Aktash (white stone) on Aksu river, 12,600 feet 41 miles; thence south-westwards up the Aksu valley through the Pamir Kurud (Little) by Onkul 12,960 feet 65 miles, to Oikul or Gazkul Lake 13,100 feet 90 miles, the source of the Aksu river, 3 miles long by 1½ mile broad; thence descending the open Panj valley mostly along right bank to Gombaz-i-Bozai 12,530 feet 97 miles, where large stream joins in from the east Khajrui pass 16,150 feet, Langar 115 miles, over Daraz Dawan 10,780 feet through open gravelly plain to Sarhad 10,450 feet 140 miles, highest village in Wakhan. Travellers must take supplies for the through journey 8 marches either at Tashkurgan or Sarhad. In winter the Panj river is frozen over and can easily be crossed when required, in summer this river is in flood, and a higher route is taken over many spurs, involving much up and down. Grazing is plentiful and wood fuel pro-urable; the northern hill side being covered with juniper and birch trees.

From Sarhad 140 miles, westwards down Panj valley along either bank to Patnch or Patur, 10,350 feet 145 miles, large village and hot spring 160° Nist 150 miles, Dehgolaman 160 miles, Yur 10,010 feet 163 miles, Vost 1·8 miles, Sas 183 miles, Zom 193 miles, at the junction of the river from the Victoria Lake 13,900 feet (which is the road used in summer through the Great Pamir from Kila-i-Panja to Kogachak on the Aksu river and Tashkurzan) Kila-i-Panja 9,050 feet 196 miles, the residence of the Chief of Wakhan.

From Kila-i-Panja down the Panj valley along the left bank south-westwards is Ishkashim fort, 8,560 feet 270 miles, whence the river Oxus or Ab-i-Panja turns northwards to Kila Wamur.

From Ishkashim, the main road continues westwards over a ridge to Zebak 290 miles, and down the Vardoj valley to Faizabal 3,500 feet 372 miles, the capital of Badakshan.

LXIII. CHITRAL to NOWSHERA—(Approximate.) Maps. Younghusband, Hamilton, Newman.

Number of Marches	Names of Stages	Distance in miles and furlongs — Intermediate m. f.	Distance in miles and furlongs — Total m. f.	Nature of Route	Main Valleys and Mountain Passes	River Crossings and Lakes	Altitude above Sea Level in Feet	Supplies and Transport at Stages	Remarks
	Chitral P. O., T. O., E.—	...	0	Rough and stony bridle road, lately improved, from Chitral through to Malakund and passable for all laden animals.	Down Kunar valley left bank.	......	4980	S. F. G. W. and T. procurable.	Fort, bazar and capital of Kashkar.
	Broz	...	10						
	Gairat	25	15			Shisht bridge.			
1	**Kila Drosh** P. O., T. O., E.—		22	......	......	......	4500	Ditto	Village and Military fort.
2	**Ashreth** E.—	13	38	......	......	......	6430	S. and T. nil, F. G. W. procurable.	Village.
	Gujar	...	47		Lowarai pass		10450		
	Mirga	...	50, 51	Steep ascent and descent over the Lowarai pass.			8400		
3	**Dir** P. O., T. O., E.—	22	60	......	Down Panjkora valley left bank.	......	5650	S. F. G. W. and T. moderate.	Small town.
4	**Chutiatun**	7	67	......	......	Panjkora bridge.	......	S. and T. nil, F. G. W. available.	Small village.
5	**Darora or Gundigar.**	13	80	......	......	......	......	Ditto	Ditto.

No.	Place	Miles	Total	Road	Pass / route	Bridge / canal	Elevation	Supplies	Remarks
4	**Robat**	12	92	Easy ascent and descent.	Up Laram ravine. Laram pass	......	......	Ditto	Village.
7	**Uch** *Serai*	10	98 / 102 / 107	......	Across Swat valley.	......	3500	Ditto	Ditto.
8	**Chukdara** *P. O., T. O., E.—* *Khar*	12	114 / 122	......	......	Swat bridge	......	S. F. G. W. and T. moderate.	Military fort.
9	**Malakund** *P. O., T. O., E.—*	14	128	Steep ascent and descent.	Malakund pass.	......	3500	S. and T. nil, F. G. W. procurable.	Ditto.
10	**Durgai** *E.—* *Shahkot*	9	137 / 141	Cart-road bridged and metalled from Malakund to Nowshera.	......	......	......	Ditto	Village.
11	**Jalala** *E.—*	14	151	Tonga service opened.	......	Alongside Swat canal from Jalala to Hoti Mardan. Across Cabul valley.	......	S. F. G. W. and T. moderate.	Large village.
12	**Hoti Mardan** *P. O., T. O., E.—*	13	164	......	......	......	......	S. F. G. W. and T. plentiful.	Military Cantonment and bazar.
13	**Nowshera** *P. O., T. O., E.—*	16	180	......	......	Cabul boat bridge.	......	Ditto	Small Town and Military Cantonment. Station on N.-W. Railway.

From Dir, 60 miles, there is another route westwards up the Baraul valley by Sarbat 73 miles, thence southwards over the Janbatai pass 9,000 feet 83 miles, Baraul Banda, 3,340 feet 83 miles, Janbatai 85 miles, thence southwards over the Janbatai pass 90 miles, to Kamtat 97 miles, Mundia Khan fort 108 miles, Miankalai 3,530 feet 109 miles; thence eastwards down the Ushiri valley and across the bridge over the Panjkora river to Sado 123 miles, Gamtat 131 miles, and over the Katgola pass 134 miles, to Chukdara on the Swat river 145 miles.

From Baraul, there is another path southwards over the Karposar pass 8,340 feet by Gawargat and Shazadgai to Robat on the Panjkora river.

From Robat 92 miles, the road continues down the Panjkora left bank to Sado 104 miles, and joins the above route to Chukdara 126 miles.

LXIIId CHITRAL to FAIZABAD in BADAKSHAN.—(Approximate) R. G. S. Journals, Maps. LXIIIe CHITRAL to KILA-I-PANJA.

By Dora Pass 14,800 ft.

No.	Place		
19	Chitral 4,980 ft. *Shali at junction of Shogoth and Kunar rivers.*	... / ...	228½ / 234
20	Shogoth 7,230 ft. *Up Lutka valley.*	16½	245
21	Darosh	...	259
22	Lutka, *large village*	14	275
22	Lutka, *large village*	16	275
23	Shah-i-Sholim *Hot spring Eastern foot.*	12	287
	Dora Pass 14,800 ft.	...	293
24	Camp, *Western foot, Sulphur Mine.*	12	299
25	Gazikistan	...	309
26	Sanglich 9,300 ft. *Cross range.*	10	319
27	Tirgaran	20	339

By Agram Pass 16,112 ft. or Nuksan Pass 18,560 ft.

No.	Place		
19	Chitral 4,980 ft. *Chiugar*	... / ...	228½ / 234
20	Shogoth 7,230 ft. *Up Arkari valley. Otes*	16½	245 / 252
21	Shali	12	257
22	Arkari *Darband*	6	263 / 268
23	Agram	13	276
	Agram Pass 16,112 ft.	...	277
24	Daigul *Down Vardoj valley.*	24	300
25	Zebak, *small town 8,550 ft.*	10	310
26	Kobak	16	326
27	Tirgaran	9	335

By Rich or Ochil 18,400 ft. Passes.

No.	Place		
19	Chitral 4,980 ft.	...	228½
18	Koghazi *Gu tond Gol Mori*	12¼	216 / 215 / 211
17	Barnas *Perpish Gol.*	13	203
18	Lun *Gurkir Jani*	10	213 / 215 / 221
19	Kila Drasan 8,640 ft. *Up Turikho valley.*	12	225
	Stari	...	233
20	Rain	16	241
21	Ujnu	13	254
22	Ruah *Rich or Janali Pass 16,700 ft.*	16	270 / 285
23	Kala Yust *On Ab-i-Panja left bank.*	30	300

ANOTHER ROUTE FROM Kila-i-Panja 9,050 ft. (24 ... 324)

No.	Stage		Total
23	Ruah, *Ochil Pass 18,400 ft.*	...	270 / 285
24	Khandut, *On Ab-i-Panja left bank.*	30	300
25	Kila-i-Panja 9,050 ft.	20	320

From Kila-i-Panja 9,050 ft. (24 ... 353)

No.	Stage		Total
28	Chakaran, *Cross Vardoj bridge.*	18	353
29	Khairabad	14	367
30	Faizabad 3,500 ft., *Capital of Badakshan.*	20	387

ALTERNATIVE ROUTE FROM.

No.	Stage		Total
23	Darband	...	368
24	Camp, *Eastern foot Nuksan pass 18,500 ft.*	12	280 / 285
25	Camp, *Western foot*	12	292
26	Daigul	12	304

No.	Stage		Total
28	Tibi, *Cross Kokcha river.*	14	353
29	Jirm 4,800 ft., *Cross hill range.*	16	369
30	Deh-i-Nao	14	383
31	Faizabad 3,500 ft., *Capital of Badakshan.*	16	399

ALTERNATIVE ROUTE FROM. *Does Gogardasht valley.*

No.	Stage		Total
26	Sanglich	...	319
27	Iskitul	16	335
28	Zebak, *small town* 8,550 ft.	9	344
29	Zarkhan	8	352
30	Bazgiran, *Sardob pass.*	8	360
31	Ishkashim Fort 8,500 ft., *On left bank Ab-i-Panja.*	8	368

LXIV GILGIT to YARKAND and KASHGAR by HUNZA and SARIKOL.—

(Approximate.) Maps. Kaight, Conway, Trotter, Cumberland, Dunmore.

Between Gilgit and Hunza, there are bridges over the Kanjut or Hunza river at Dainyor, near Nomal, beyond Gwech, 2 miles beyond Chalt below Gulmit, at Pisan, at Tushot, and at Samaya, also over the Nagar river below Nagar. There is a route along either bank of the Kanjut river, that usually taken is as under :—

Number of Marches.	Names of Stages.	Distance in miles and furlongs.		Nature of Route.	Main Valleys and Mountain Passes.	River crossings and Lakes.	Altitude above Sea Level in Feet.	Supplies and Transport at Stages.	Remarks.
		Intermediate. m. f.	Total. m. f.						
	Gilgit P. O., T. O., C., E.	...	0	......	......	Gilgit bridge	4890	S. F. G. and T. moderate, W. plentiful.	Town, fort, and capital of Gilgit province. Residence of Political Agent.
		...	4	Junction of Gilgit and Kanjut rivers.	Up Kanjut valley right bank.				
	Pitche	...	9	Road to Nomal along sandy reaches and through precipitous rock gorges.	...	......			
1	Nomal E.—	18	18		...	Nalta bridge.	5500	S. F. G. and T. scanty, W. plentiful.	Fort and village.
		...	19						
	Gwech on left bank	...	25	Road to Chalt fair with exception of long Chaichar parri.					
	Chaichar parri	...	30						
2	Chalt E.—	16	31	On united fan at mouths of Chaprot and Garasir nalas.	...	Chaprot "	6120	S. F. G. and T. moderate, W. plentiful.	Fort, village and fields.
		...	36		Cross to left bank, cross	Kanjut "			

	Place					Road			Feet	S. F. G. T. W.	Remarks
3	*Nilt*	...	...	37	4	After crossing steep ridge, road traverses a succession of fans, cut by several deep and precipitous nalas; road fair, though stony, passable for laden animals.	spur from Rakipushi mountain.	8 deep nalas crossed hence to Tushot.	7000	......	Strong fort stormed in Hunza campaign.
	Thol	...	...	45	...		...		......		Fort and village.
		...	...	47	...		...				
	Gulmit *E.—*	15	...	49	...		......		6400	S. F. G. and T. scanty. W. plentiful.	
	Pisan	...	...	52	4		Cross to right bank for Hunza.	Kanjut bridge.	6980	Ditto	Ditto.
	Tushot	...	...	57	4	......		......	7480		
4	**Phakar** *E.—*	10	4	50	4			Kanjut bridge.		Ditto	
	Askordas	...	...	64	...						
	Samayes	...	...	66	4	Junction of Nagar and Kanjut rivers.	......				
5	**Nagar** *E.—* *Or crossing Kanjut river either at Tushot or Samayes.*	13	...	72	4		......	......	7790	S. F. G. T. W. plentiful.	Town, fort and capital of Nagar. Residence of Thum of Nagar.
5	**Hunza or Baltit** *E.—*	13	4	73	...	Road rough and stony to Gulmat, passable for laden animals.	Up Kanjut or Gujal valley.	......	8000	Ditto	Town, fort and capital of Kanjut. Residence of Thum of Hunza.

From Nagar there is a cross path to Hunza about 9 miles in length, crossing both Nagar and Kanjut rivers.

From Hunza, the track continues northwards up the Kanjut valley to Pasu, at the junction of the Shimsal and Gujal rivers. One path goes eastwards up the former valley to the Shimshal pass 17,000 feet, and descends into the Oprang valley, another path goes northwards up the Gujal valley and leads to several passes over the Hindu Kush.

N. W. up the Irshad tributary valley by Reship Jerad and Berdu over 2 passes to Langar and Gombaz-i-Bozai in the Pamir Khurd of Wakhan.

N. up the Gujal valley over the Kilik pass to Tashkurgan in Sarikol as under.

N. E. up a side ravine over the Mintaka pass 14,500 feet, and down by Chudartash and Mazar Said Hassan to Tashkurgan.

N. E. up another side ravine over the Kunjerab pass and down by Mazar Said Hassan to Tashkurgan.

There is deep snow on all these passes from November to March, and a glacier 1½ mile long is crossed over the Mintaka pass. They are free of snow in summer and practicable for laden mules and camels.

Number of Marches	Names of Stages	Distance in miles and furlongs		Nature of Route	Main Valleys and Mountain Passes	River Crossings and Lakes	Altitude above Sea Level in Feet	Supplies and Transport at Stages	Remarks
		Intermediate m. f.	Total m. f.						
LXIV	*ROUTE—contd.*								
	Altit	...	77 ...				...		
	Mahomedabad	...	80 ...				...		
6	Atabad	15 ...	88 ...	......	...	...	...	S. F. G. and T. scanty, W. plentiful.	Village and fort.
7	Gulmat	9 ...	97 ...	Road fair from Gulmat to Pasu.	...	...	...	Ditto	Ditto and cultivated fields.
8	Pasu	8 ...	105 ...	Road through country bare of vegetation, crosses a large glacier shortly beyond Pasu.	Up Gujal valley.	Shimshal ford	8000	S. F. G. and T. moderate, W. plentiful.	Village and fort.
9	Khaibar	10 ...	115 ...	At mouth of grand gorge,	......	......	......	S and T. nil, F. G. scanty, W. plentiful.	Hamlet.
10	Gircha	10 ...	125 ...	winter route along bed of river, summer route over parri spurs. Arduous march to Misgar over huge parris, ever up and down.	......	Cross Gujal river, numerous fords, deep and difficult.	8750	S. F. G. & T. scanty, W. plentiful.	Village.
11	Misgar	12 ...	137 ...		......	...	10200	Ditto	Hamlet.
12	Murkush	13 ...	150 ...	Fairly easy ascent and descent over stony downs on both sides of pass.	Kilik pass, down Wakh.	...	15000	S. and T. nil, F. G. scanty, W. plentiful.	Halting place.
		...	159 ...						

No.	Name	Dist.	Total	Route		Elevation	Supplies	Remarks
13	Kulturuk *nala*	18	168	...ir valley.	......	14600	Ditto	Track west up Wakhjir valley over Khajnui pass 16,150ft. and down Ak Bilis valley to Bozai Gombaz about 50 miles. Track north over Paik pass to Ak-tash 50 miles.
14	Mintaka *nala*	20	178	Track south over Mintaka pass into Kanjut.	......	13000	Ditto	Kirghiz encampment.
	Chadirtash	0 0	189 204	......	......	......	......	Ditto.
15	Kurghan-i-Ujad bai	22	210	Stony road down the Taghdumbash Pamir to Tashkurgan.	Down Tagh-dumbash valley.	12000	Ditto	Old fort near junction of Kunjerab river, road south up latter to pass.
16	Camp	16	226	......	......	......	S. F. T. nil, G. scanty; W. plentiful.	Halting place.
17	Tashkurgan	16	242	Road along plain to Chushman.	Down Tashkurgan valley.	10250	S. F. G. and T. moderate, W. plentiful.	Small town and fort and capital of Sarikol.

Hence are 3 routes, first northwards to Kashgar by Clushman and Tagharma to Little Karakul lake west of Tagharma and Mustagh Ata peaks, thence north eastwards down the Uluart valley and through the Gez defiles, by Tashbalik and Burakatai about 208 miles, or 430 miles from Gilgit.

The second route to Yangi Hissar (midway between Kashgar and Yarkand) as described below.

The third route diverges from Chehil Gombaz 312 miles on second route eastwards to Yarkand, down the Charlang valley to Kiaz Aghzai 6,300 feet, at junction of the Kiaz river 350 miles, then up the latter over the Kara Dawan 9,590 feet 360 miles, and the Kizil Dawan 10,180 feet 367 miles, across the Shaitan-i-gum desert to Yakarik 4,630 feet 422 miles, and through cultivated country to Yarkand 3,923 feet 452 miles.

On each of these three routes, there are variations, which are adopted according to the season, condition of snow in the passes, state of river floods, &c.

Number of Marches	Names of Stages	Intermediate m. f.	Total m. f.	Nature of Route	Main Valleys and Mountain Passes	River Crossings and Lakes	Altitude above Sea Level in Feet	Supplies and Transport at Stages	Remarks
LXIV	ROUTE.— contd.	...	...						
	Tiznf ...	...	242						
18	Chushman ...	...	245	Rough and stony road up ravine and over pass.	Up Karalalak glen.	......	10100	S. F. G. and T. scanty, W. plentiful.	Village.
		10	252	......	Kokmainuk pass.	......	15500.		
19	Chichiklik plain	16	264	Road across plain 5 miles, steep ascent and descent over pass of loose and slipping stones.	Yambulak pass.	......	......	S. and T nil, F. G. scanty, W. procurable.	Halting place.
			268			Toiloboiong Lake.	16000.		
			277						
20	Toilobolong	18	296	Rocky road down ravine, steep and narrow in places over boulders.	Down Toiloboiong ravine.	......	......	Ditto	Ditto.
21	Past Robat ...	13	299	Fair road in valley, very steep ascent and descent over pass, through large rocks.	......	Tangitar ford.	9280	S. and T nil, F. G. procurable, W. plentiful.	Hamlet.
			323		Torak pass.		13130.		
			307				10500	Ditto	
22	Chehil Gombaz	13	312	Steep and rocky ascent and descent.	Kaskam pass, down Kizkol valley.	Charlung ford	2930.		Ditto.
			318			......			

No.	Name	Dist.	Total	Road		Elev.	Supplies	Type
23	**Kinkol** *Sashtaka*	23	335 342	Road fair through defile and emerges on to broad plain.	.....	9455.	S. and T. nil, F. G. scanty, W. plentiful.	Hamlet.
24	**Aktala** *Nizkia*	15	350 356	......	......	7345	Ditto	Village.
25	**Karawul**	12	362	Road fair through cultivated country with villages and orchards.	......	....	S. F. G. T. scanty, W. available.	Fort.
26	**Ighiz Yar** *Karawat*	12	374 390	......	......	5600	S. F. G. T. moderate, W. plentiful.	Village.
27	**Yangi Hissar**	30	404	......	Yangi Hissar bridge.	4320	S. F. G. W. and T. plentiful.	Small town.

From Chushman there is a track northwards up the Karasu valley to Tagharma, and another track eastwards down the Tashkurgan valley to Shindi, and thence north eastwards over the range 14,480 ft., to Past Robat.

From Chehil Gumbaz the Tangi road eastwards to Yarkand branches off down the Charlung valley. It is longer and more difficult than the road to Yangi Hissar, and supplies of all kinds are scarce

Rock salt is said to be found in the mountains bordering the Charlung valley and coal in the Kara Dawan and at Kashetab lower down the Charlung valley. Below the Kara Dawan on the west side, there is a waterfall 400 feet and the road alongside is difficult and dangerous.

From Ighiz Yar 374 miles, there is a track eastwards to Kizyl 398 miles 3,910 feet, which is situated on the Yarkand, Yangi Hissar and Kashgar road, 30 miles S. E. of Yangi Hissar, and 55 miles N. W. of Yarkand 2,923 feet.

Yangi Hissar is thus distant 85 miles N. W. of Yarkand, and 50 miles S. of Kashgar, 4,043 feet by a good road over a fertile country, well watered by canals and cultivated.

LXV   GILGIT to SKARDU by NAGAR and HISPAR.—(*Approximate.*)   Map. Conway, Eckenstein, Wachtmeister.

No.	Name		Dist.	Total	Road		Elev.	Supplies	Type
	Gilgit	*P. O., T. O., C., E.—*	0	...	See previous Route LXIV.	......	4580	.....	Town and capital of Gilgit province.
5	**Nagar**	*K.—*	72	4		......	7790	S. G. W. and T. plentiful, F. scarce.	Town and capital of Nagar.

LXV ROUTE.—contd. 72 4

From Nagar to Hunza 9 miles, the direct route crosses the Nagar river by a rope bridge, the Daung pass 9,200 feet at 2½ mile, and the Kanjut river at 7 miles by a rope bridge.

Between Nagar and Hispar there are two more paths, one up the Nagar and Hispar valleys, about 25 miles, the rest by Hopar are longer. The following is chiefly taken from "Climbing in the Himalayas" by Sir W. M. Conway.

Number or Marches.	Names of Stages.	Distance in miles and furlongs. Inter-mediate. m. f.	Total. m. f.	Nature of Route.	Main Valleys and Mountain Passes.	River crossings and Lakes.	Altitude above Sea Level in Feet.	Supplies and Transport at Stages.	Remarks.
6	Hopar (Ratal) ...	6 4	79 ...	Road from Nagar to Hopar good.	......	......	9220	S., F., G., W. and T. moderate.	Group of 5 villages.
	Bolshal ...	...	80 ...						
	Borpa ...	...	85 ...	Hence to Hispar very rough, crosses several side nalas and glaciers and an intervening ridge.					
7	Paipering Maidan	11 ...	90 ...		......	......	10990	S. and T. nil, F. G. scanty, W. plentiful.	Halting place.
			93 ...		Rash ridge up Nagar valley.				
	Arpi Harrar ...	...	96 ...			Nagar bridge	8620.		
	Darapo ...	...	101 ...			Ditto	9390.		
			103 ...		......				
8	Hispar ...	16 ...	106 ...	After crossing the Garumbar nala, the track ascends along left bank	Up Hispar glacier left bank.	Garumbar bridge.	10320	S. F. G. T. scarce, W. plentiful.	Village.
	Chokutens ...	...	112 ...		......	......	11770	......	Stone huts.

No.	Name	March (miles)	Total (miles)	Route	Description	Features	Elevation (feet)	Supplies	Remarks
9	*Gauder*	...	...	...	of Hispar valley crossing grassy declivities, several side nalas and glaciers from the south, gravel slopes and stony moraines to Haigutum, whence it turns due south up this side glacier, crosses the latter zig-zag up snow field and avalanche slopes over steep snow mound 500 feet above and east of col.	...	13070.	S. and T. nil, F. W. G. available.	Halting place.
	Magorum	12	118	...	...	...	......	......	Ditto.
	Chiring	...	...	...	...	...	......	......	Ditto.
10	**Haigutum or Hyou Kuru**	13	131	Up Haigutum side glacier. Nushik La.	...	...	13880	Ditto	Open only in June, July and August. Ditto 4 huts.
11	**Stiathu Brangsa**	12	139	Down Kero Loongma glacier, keeping generally along right bank.	...	...	17300	S. F. G. T. nil, W. from snow.	Ditto.
	Ding Brangsa	...	143	...	...	...	......	......	
12	**Kutche Brangsa**	10	147	...	...	......	......	S. and T. nil, F. G. W. procurable.	Ditto.
			153						
13	**Arundo** E.—	16	169	Junction and mouth of Kero Loongma and Chogo Loongma glaciers. Down Basho valley right bank.	Descend westwards over snow, rocks, neve by col, striking below latter to level snow field and along moraines to level glacier. Road from Arundo to Tisar fair.	Basho rope bridge.	10000	S. F. G. W. and T. moderate.	Village at foot of glaciers. Another road down left bank, crossing Braldo river and by Kashimal to Shigar.
			178				......	......	
14	**Chutrun** B.—	20	189	Down Shigar valley right bank.	...	Hot Springs	......	S. and T. scanty, F. G. W. plentiful.	Ditto.
	Tisar	...	193	...	...	...	......	......	
			197	...	Difficult parri with 3 ladders and logs.	......	8227	......	Junction of Basho and Braldo rivers.

Number of Marches.	Names of Stages.	Distance in Miles and Furlongs. Inter-mediate. m. f.	Distance in Miles and Furlongs. Total. m. f.	Nature of Route.	Main Valleys and Mountain Passes.	River Crossings and Lakes.	Altitude above Sea Level, in Feet.	Supplies and Transport at Stages.	Remarks.
LXV	*ROUTE.—contd.*	... ...	... 197 ...				.....		
15	Youskil ...	15 ...	204 ...	Road from Youskil to Shigar along sandy reaches, passing several villages.	......	......	.....	S. F. G. W. and T. moderate.	Large village.
16	Shigar E.— ...	16 ..	220 ..	......	Cross to left bank.	Skin raft across Shigar river.	7640	S. F. G. W. and T. plentiful.	Small town.
17	Skardu P. O., T. O., C., E.— ...	14 ...	224 ...	......	......	Indus ferry	7400	S. F. G. W. and T. abundant.	Town and capital of Baltistan.

LXVI GILGIT to HANLE by INDUS VALLEY—*Old Route*. Map. *Conway. Wachtmeister*.

Number of Marches.	Names of Stages.	Distance in Miles and Furlongs. Inter-mediate. m. f.	Distance in Miles and Furlongs. Total. m. f.	Nature of Route.	Main Valleys and Mountain Passes.	River Crossings and Lakes.	Altitude above Sea Level, in Feet.	Supplies and Transport at Stages.	Remarks.
	Gilgit P. O., T. O., C., E.— ...	..	0 ..	See Route LVIII.	......	......	4890	S. F. G. W. and T. moderate.	Fort, town and capital of Gilgit province. Residence of Political Agent.
14	Skardu P. O., T. O., C., E.— ...	...	144 ...	Road across alluvial plateau, along edge of cultivated	Up Indus valley left bank.	......	7400	S. F. G. W. and T. abundant.	Fort, town and capital of Baltistan. Head-quarters of

No.	Stage	m.	f.	Total	Road	Cross	River	Elevation	Supplies	Remarks
	Grapi	:	:	148	fans, round rock parri with stairs, through block house and a third fan green.	...		...	......	Wazir.
	Kepchung	:	.	149	......	...	Kepchung cho.	...	......	Custom-house.
15	**Thurgon** E.—	8	:	152	......	...	:	7530	...	Small village.
	Ghoro	:	:	161	Road over stony maidan, and cultivated plateaux, passed stone blocks with ibex engraved.	...	......	:		
16	**Gol** E.—	13	:	165	Road through fields for 3 miles, rounded parri by staircase road through well cultivated fields of Sermi to Parkuta.	...	Gol cho	......	S. F. G. T. moderate, W. plentiful.	Village.
	Sermi	:	:	169		...	:	7673		Junction of Shayok and Indus rivers.
			4	172		......	Murko cho.			
17	**Parkuta** E.—	12	4	177	Road through fields of Parkuta, across desert, through three villages, rounded parri with several staircases.	4	Kati cho	7870	S. F. G. W. plentiful.	Large village and fort.
	Ghakori	:	4	185		:	Dumsum cho.	:	...	Two old mosques.
	Kinachego	:	4	190		:	......	:		
18	**Totti**	14	4	191	Road on both banks between Tolti and Khurmang, that on right bank more level and best.	Cross to right bank.	Indus rope bridge.	8450	S. F. G. W. and T. moderate.	Village and fort on left bank.

Number of Marches	Names of Stages	Distance in Miles and Furlongs — Intermediate. m. f.	Total. m. f.	Nature of Route.	Main Valleys and Mountain Passes.	River Crossings and Lakes.	Altitude above Sea Level in Feet.	Supplies and Transport at Stages.	Remarks.
LXVI	ROUTE—contd.	...	...						
19	Kartaksho or Khurmang	...	300	From Kartaksho to the Hannu cho the road is very rough and difficult, crossing many spurs and parris abutting on the Indus, involving steep ascents and descents.	Cross to right bank	Indus rope bridge. Gavis cho.	8340	S. F. G. W. and T. available.	Large village and fort on right bank.
	Palpaldo	12	203 4	...	...	...	...	...	...
20	Hamzigund	16 4	208	...	...	Goondi cho	...	S. and T. scanty; F. G. W. available.	Village opposite Tarkuta.
	Marol	...	220	...	...	Gannoka cho.	...	...	...
21	Grugurdo	18	223 4	...	...	Garggri cho	...	Ditto	Village.
	Ourdas	...	228	...	...	...	...	...	Between Ourdas and Sanacha on left bank great gorge of Indus.
22	Garkhun	10	238	...	...	Barorow cho	...	Ditto	Ditto.
	Dah	...	243	...	...	Dah cho.	...	...	...
	Phindoor	...	248	...	...	Phindoor cho.	...	...	...
23	Nubbibranskar or Lower Hanu	16	264	From Hannu cho to Leh the road is	...	Hannu cho	...	S. and T. nil, F. G. W. procurable.	Hamlet.

No.	Name of stage	Dist.		Total	Remarks on road	Direction	Camping ground	Height	Supplies	Description
24	Achinathang	...	...	270	fair throughout and passable for laden animals.	...	Broglow cho.	...	...	...
	Skirbichan *E.—*	14	...	278	.....	...	Kirbuchand cho.	...	S. and T. scanty, F. G. W. procurable.	Village.
	Doomkhar	...	...	284	.....	...	Doomkhar cho.	...	.....	Fort and bridge over Indus river.
25	**Khalsi** *B.—*	16	...	292	Join main road from Srinagar to Leh.	...	Skining cho	10000	Ditto	Village.
26	**Nurla** *B., E.—*	6	...	294	Road through barren country, passing long mani mounds.	Up Indus valley right bank.	Phocha Drokpo	...	S. F. G. W. and T. moderate.	Ditto.
27	**Saspul** *B., E.—*	14	6	300	Good road passable for laden animals.	...	Saspul Drokpo	...	S. and T. nil, F. G. W. available.	Small village and gonpa, cultivated basin.
	Bazgo	...	2	314	New wooden bridge built over Indus river. Hence are two roads to Bazgo, take side valley N.E. passing numerous chortens and inscribed rocks over plateau crossed fertile side valley of Bazgo along stony slope to Nimu; thence stony desert to Phayang, where flowing	...	Bazgo "	11050	S. F. G. W. and T. procurable.	Large village.
28	**Nimu** *B., E.—*	11	4	322		...	Sneme "	...	S. F. G. W. and T. moderate.	Small village.
	Phayang B.	...	2	326		...	Lunachmo Foo.	...	S. and T. nil, F. G. W. procurable.	
	Pitak	...	2	337		...	.....	10500	.....	Village and Monastery.
				340		...				

Number of Marches.	Names of Stages.	Distance in miles and furlongs. Inter-mediate m. f.	Distance in miles and furlongs. Total. m. f.	Nature of Route.	Main Valleys and Mountain Passes.	River crossings and Lakes.	Altitude above Sea Level in Feet.	Supplies and Transport at Stages.	Remarks.
LXVI	ROUTE—contd.	...	340 4						
29	Leh P, O., B., C., E.—	18 2	344 4	water among trees. At Pitak short turf, beyond strip of barren country and vast fan, on top of which are green fields of Leh.	...	......	11500	S. F. G. W. and T. abundant.	Large town and fort. Capital of Ladak.

From Leh, there are routes on both sides of the Indus river to Hanle, and there are wooden bridges at Shushot, Marshalang and Yugu, which are passable for laden animals; also at Hemiya and Tirido, at the mouth of the Tiri ravine from the south. Above Mahiye opposite the mouth of the Puga river, the Indus is generally fordable.

Number of Marches.	Names of Stages.	Distance Inter-mediate m. f.	Distance Total m. f.	Nature of Route.	Main Valleys and Mountain Passes.	River crossings and Lakes.	Altitude above Sea Level in Feet.	Supplies and Transport at Stages.	Remarks.
30	Tikzay	13 ...	357 4	Good road from Leh to Yugu. If transport of pack animals, cross Indus by Marsha-lang bridge and proceed by Puga road.	......	Sabu ravine	11000	S. F. G. W. and T. plentiful.	Large village and Monastery, where there is a Skoo-shok or Mahatma.
	Tangtanka	... ...	362		......	Nang "			
	Opposite Marshalang	... ...	370 ...		......	Chimray river.	......		
31	Yugu	1: 4	374	Footmen only can carry loads over	......	Ugu river	......	S. F. G. W. and T. procurable.	Village.
32	Shera	11	385 ...		......	......	......	Ditto	Ditto.

No.	Name		Miles	Dist.	Remarks on road	Bank	Camping ground	Elevation	Supplies	Remarks
	Ikpa	...	...	388	the precipitous parris or cliffs of the Roug defile between Hemiya and Mahiye.	......	Ikpa ravine.	......	......	Ditto.
	Likehe	...	...	392		......	Tugla „	......		
33	Hemiya	...	14	399		Cross to left bank.	Indus bridge	......	S. T. moderate, F. G. W. plentiful.	Mouth of Tiri foo.
	Kyangyum on right bank	...	...	404	Fair road from Yugu to Hemiya with exception of 2 spurs between Ikpa and Likehe, with stone steps.	Cross to right bank.	Ditto	......	...	Small village.
	Tirido on left bank	...	...	406			......	......	Ditto	
34	Gaik	...	14	413		......	Kumdok foo.	......		Ditto.
	Kumdok	...	...	416	Rough road between Hemiya and Mahiye with many ascents and descents over spurs. The worst part is about half way between Gaik and Ni in rounding a projecting spur with awkward precipices.	......		......	Ditto	
	Etekha	...	...	421		......		......		
35	Gni	...	13	426		......	Nia foo	......		Ditto.
				428		......	Kaiser foo			
				430		......	Yeh foo.			
				438		......	Hot Spring.			
36	Chumathang	...	13	439		......	Chumathang foo.	......	Ditto	Tso Yalse Lake 3 miles up this valley.
				451		......	That foo	......	...	
37	Mahiye	...	14	453	From Mahiye where the Indus valley opens out, the road along the plain to Nowi is fair.	......	Mahiye foo.	13800	S. T. F. G. nil, W. available.	Hamlet.
	Ilokura	...	...	461		......	Polalung foo.	......		
				465		......	Nima foo.			
38	Nima Mud	...	16	469	......	......	Gochin foo	14000	S. and T. nil, F. G. W. procurable.	Two small villages.
				470		......	Gochang foo.			

Number of Branches.	Names of Stages.	Distance in miles and furlongs. Intermediate. m. f.	Distance in miles and furlongs. Total. m. f.	Nature of Route.	Main Valleys and Mountain Passes.	River Crossings and Lakes.	Altitude above Sea Level, in feet.	Supplies and Transport at Stages.	Remarks.
LXVI	ROUTE.—contd.	...	470 ...						
39	Nowi	10 ...	479 ...	From Nowi there are 3 routes up the Hanle valley, rough and stony in the defiles and easy over the plains. Care must be taken to select camps, where the water is not brackish.	Cross to left bank up Hanle valley by left bank.	Indus ford	13900	S. and T. nil, F. G. W. procurable.	Halting place.
	Rhongo	...	486 ...				... ...	......	Village.
40	Chumik	14 ...	493 ...			Chumik ravine	......	Ditto	Ditto mouth of ravine.
	Mankhang plain	...	500 ...			......	......	......	Above Chibra village.
41	Sango plain	14 ...	507 ...			Sangoisang	......	Ditto	Halting place.
42	Hanle E.—	14 ...	521 ...	......	......	......	14276	S. F. G. W. and T. moderate.	Village, large monastery and thana.

LXVII LEH to HARDWAR by TSO MORARI LAKE, SPITI and MASURI—

Number of Branches.	Names of Stages.	Distance in miles and furlongs. Intermediate. m. f.	Distance in miles and furlongs. Total. m. f.	Nature of Route.	Main Valleys and Mountain Passes.	River Crossings and Lakes.	Altitude above Sea Level, in feet.	Supplies and Transport at Stages.	Remarks.
	Leh P. O., B., C., E.—	...	0 ...	Fair road from Leh to Puga, passable for pack animals, yaks chiefly employed.	Up Indus valley along right bank.	...	11500	S. F. G. W. and T. abundant.	Large town and fort. Capital of Ladak.
1	Tikze E.—	12 ...	12 ...	...	......	Sabu foo	11000	S. F. G. W. and T. plentiful.	Large village and monastery.

No.	Name of place	Dist.	Total	Description of road	River crossings	Camping ground, &c.	Height	Supplies	Remarks
	Twaflasha ...	..	16 4	Between Hemiya and Kramang are precipitous parts and cliffs, which can be avoided by taking one of the routes up Tiri valley.	......	Nang foo, Chimre foo.	......		Village.
			24 4		......				
2	**Yugu** *E.—* ...	16	28 4	......	......	Yugu foo	......	S. F. G. W. and T. procurable.	Ditto.
3	**Shera** *E.—* / *Likche* ...	11	40 .. / 43 .. / 47 4	......	...... / ...... / Cross to left bank.	Shera foo, Ikpa foo. Tugla foo, Indus bridge. Indus ,,	......	Ditto	Ditto.
4	**Hemiya** *on left bank E.—*	14	51 .. / 54 ..	Road along both banks of Indus river to Tirido.	Cross to right bank.	Indus ford	......	S. T. moderate, F. G. W. plentiful.	Mouth of Tiri foo.
	Tirido ...	..	62 ..	......	Cross to right bank.	......	......	......	Small village.
5	**Gaik** *on right bank E.—*	14	68 ..	......	......	......	...	Ditto	Path over Kiari La to Tsokar Chumo lake.
	Kundok / *Khetpa Thanbo*	.. / ..	71 .. / 73 ..	......	...... /	Kundok foo. Klatpa Thamba foo	......	......	Ditto.
6	**Kiare** *on left bank* ...	7	75 ..	Road along both banks Indus river to Kramang.	Cross to left bank.	Indus ford	......	S. T nil, F. G. W. plentiful.	On right bank opposite.
	Gui on right bank ...	..	81 ..	......	......	Nia foo	......	......	Hamlet.
7	**Kramang** *on left bank.*	14	89 .. / 99 ..	Leave Indus and ascend Kidmang foo ravine over Sildat La into the Puga valley and across two hill ranges to the Tso Kingr	Sildat La.	Indus ford	......	Ditto	Village, hot springs, sulphur mines, borax fields.
8	**Puga** *E.—* ...	16	105 .. / 109 .. / 111 ..		Naktogoding La. /	Puga foo / ... Zobashi she foo.	15200 18000.	S. G. T. scarce. F. W. plentiful.	

Number or Marches	Names of Stages	Distance in miles and furlongs — Intermediate m. f.	Distance in miles and furlongs — Total m. f.	Nature of Route	Main Valleys and Mountain Passes	River crossings and Lakes	Altitude above Sea Level in Feet	Supplies and Transport at Stages	Remarks
LXVII	ROUTE—contd.	...	...						
		...	111	......	Lanak pass.	Tso Kiagr.	......	......	Lake 1 mile east.
		...	115						
		...	116 4						
9	Shak sang	13	118	......	......	Tso Morari	......	S. and T. nil, G. F. W. available.	North end of lake.
	Pedlo	...	124	......	Along western shore of Tso Morari lake.				
10	Karzok E.—	11	129	Along western shore of Tso Morari.		Ditto	14900	S. and T. scanty, G. F. W. available.	Village and monastery.

From Tirido 62 miles, a route branches off south-west up the Tiri valley by Tiri 66 miles, to Stazuema foo 72 miles, where it forks out up two ravines; the more western track ascends over the Shing bul La and descends southwards along the west side of the Tso kar plateau to Pongo Nagu 86 miles, and along western shore of Tso kar chumo lake to Rignl 94 miles on south side of lake. Hence southwards to Naru chan 106 miles, whence south eastwards over the Karum La 108 miles and down the Nugma foo to Nugma Ninda 119 miles, and then over the Karzok La 128 miles to Karzok 136 miles.

The more eastern track from Stazuema foo 72 miles goes up the other ravine over the Thasang La 76 miles and descends to the same plain on the east side to the Thngg Gondpa 86 miles; thence by Knangrir on eastern side of the Tso kar chumo lake up the Pola Komka foo to Zakti 90 miles, and over the Polakomka La 16,300 feet, 102 miles by Nakpo goding 109 miles, over the Nanak La 111 miles, and Lanak La 116 miles, to Shaksang 119 miles, on Tso Kiagr plain, Pedlo 125 miles, and Karzok 130 miles.

Another track from Polakomka La 102 miles goes down the Puga valley to Puga 114 miles, and onwards to Mahiye 127 miles, where cross Indus by ford to right bank 13,800 feet. F. G. nil.

Another track from Puga to Nima Mud on the Indus is 12 miles in length.

No.	Stage	Miles	Total	Road	Route	Ford	Elevation	Water & Supplies	Remarks
11	Kiangdom E.—	14	143	Road fair to Narbu Sumdo.	......	......	14903)	S. F. T. nil, G. W. scanty, lake water brackish.	South end of Tso Morari lake.
12	Narbu Sumdo	11	146	Road fair to Du-tung crossing many spurs and ravines.	Up Parechu or Parang valley, right bank.	Phirse foo. Parechu ford	15300	S. F. T. nil, G. W. procurable.	Halting place.
	Umdeng		154						
13	Thukrote		156	......	......	......	......	S. T. nil, F. G. W. available.	Ditto.
14	Dutung E.—	18	172	Steep ascent and cross glacier, descent rocky and abrupt, impassable for horses.	Parang La down Spiti valley.	......	16000	S. T. nil, F. G. W. procurable.	Ditto.
		12	184				18300.		
15	Jughtha E.—		189	......	......	......	16000.	Ditto	Large Village.
		10	194						Monastery.
16	Kiwar E.— *ki*		205	......	......	Parlung bi ford.	13400	S. F. G. T. moderate, W plentiful.	Small Village.
		12	206						
17	Kaja E.— *Lidang*		211	Road undulating and in part stony to Dankar.	......	Shilla ford.	......	Ditto	Large Village and Monastery. Capital of Spiti.
		12	215						
18	Dankar E.—		218	If travelling the reverse way take supplies here and at Kiwar to last until Puga.	......	......	12774	S. F. G. T. and W. plentiful.	
		16	226						
			234		Up Pin valley left bank.	Spiti bridge.			
			239						

LXVII ROUTE—contd.

Number of Marches	Names of Stages	Distance in Miles and Furlongs — Intermediate m. f.	Total m. f.	Nature of Route	Main Valleys and Mountain Passes	River Crossings and Lakes	Altitude above Sea Level in Feet	Supplies and Transport at Stages	Remarks
19	Sunam *on left bank* E.—	...	239	Fair road through sterile valley.	Cross to right bank.	Pin ford	.....	S. F. G. T. moderate, W. plentiful.	Large Village.
			257	......	...	Kyokti ford.			
20	Muth *on left bank* E.—	18	252				.....	S. and T. scanty, F. G. W. plentiful.	Small Village.
21	Buldur	8	260	......	......	...	.....	S. and T. nil, F. G. W. plentiful.	Hamlet.
22	Lursa	13	273	Ascent to pass very steep and stony near summit, descent easier.	......	...	.....	Ditto	Halting place.
		9	282						
23	Pustirang *Muling*	10	287, 292, 298	Road through fine forest of firs.	Bhabeh pass. Down Bhabeh Wangar valley.	.....	15000.	Ditto, F. nil	Ditto.
24	Yangpa	12	304	Descent from Yangta to Wangtu very steep.	......	.....	.....	S. and T. scarce, F. G. W. plentiful.	Village where scorpions abound.
25	Wangtu E.—	12	316	Cross Hindustan and Thibet road.	Cross Sutlej valley.	Sutlej bridge	5361	Ditto	Supplies from Sarhan.

From Wangtu there are several routes southwards towards Masurí, by the Pabar and Tonse Valleys, by the Rupin, Gopas and Nalgoon passes down the Rupin and Tonse Valleys and up the Baspa Valley, over the Neela pass and down the Ganges Valley. The Burand Pass route is as under :—

No.	Station	Miles	Total	Road	Direction	Intermediate	Elevation	Supplies	Remarks
			316	Road fair and easy.	Up Sutlej valley left bank.				
26	Kilba ... *F. B.—*	12	328	......	Up Baspa valley.			S. and T. scanty, F. G. W. available.	Forest head-quarters.
	Barang		334						
27	Mulpani	10	338	Steep ascent and descent over rugged pass.				S. and T. nil, F. G. W. available.	Halting place.
			343		Burand pass		15180.		
28	Litim	9	347	Fair road down valley.	Down Pabar valley along right bank.			Ditto	Ditto.
29	Jungli	10	357	......	......			Ditto	Hamlet.
30	Peyki	8	365	......	......			Ditto	Ditto.
31	Chergaon	9	374	Road from Shatul pass joins here.	......	Andretibridge		S. F. G. W. and T. moderate.	Village at junction of Andreti river.
			378	......		Matreti "			
32	Roru *E.—*	10	384	Road from Rampur over Soongri pass joins here.	......	Sikni "		S. F. G. W. and T. available.	Large village.
			390	......		Pursrar.			
33	Hant Kothi or Kaiengarh	8	392	Road from Fagu and Simla joins here.	......			Ditto	Ditto.
34	Shalna	11	403	Road fair ...	......			Ditto	Ditto.

LXVII ROUTE—contd.

Number of Marches	Names of Stages	Distance in miles and furlongs — Intermediate m. f.	Distance in miles and furlongs — Total m. f.	Nature of Route	Main Valleys and Mountain Passes	River Crossings and Lakes	Altitude above Sea Level in feet	Supplies and Transport at Stages	Remarks
		.. ...	403 ...				.....		
35	Jitar	8 ...	411 ...	Road from Simla to Masuri joins here.	.....	Tonse bridge at Timli.	.....	S. F. G. W. and T. available.	Below junction of Pabar and Tonse rivers.

From this point there appear to be two roads to Chakrata, one the forest route goes to Maindroth F.B., 416 miles, Katyan F.B., 426 miles on summit of Jakni Lena pass, Lokar F.B., 432 miles, Manali F.B., 436 miles, Deoband F.B., 445, and Chakrata D.B., 452 miles, which is 2½ miles beyond cantonment. The other ordinary route is as under:—

Number of Marches	Names of Stages	Intermediate m. f.	Total m. f.	Nature of Route	Main Valleys and Mountain Passes	River Crossings and Lakes	Altitude above Sea Level in feet	Supplies and Transport at Stages	Remarks
36	Kanda	10 ...	421 ...	Fair road for pack animals.	.....	.....	.....	S. F. G. W. and T. moderate.	Small village.
37	Bandraoli	11 ...	432 ...	.....	.....	.....	.....	Ditto	Ditto.
38	Deoband	10 ...	442 ...	.....	.....	.....	9000	Ditto	Ditto, Forest head quarters.
39	Chukrata P.O., T.O., D.B., C.E.	7 ...	449 ...	.....	.....	.....	7000	S. F. G. W. and T. plentiful.	Military cantonment and bazar.

From Chukrata there is a road southwards to Saharunpore, passable for carts, 81½ miles long : the stages are Karbeah 9 miles, Saiah B., 9 miles, Kalsi B., 12½ miles (where a suspension bridge over river Jumna) cross Asan river, Fathipur B., 10½ miles, over Timli pass of Siwalik range, Badshah Bagh 12 miles, Kalesa B., 14 miles, Saharunpur, N. W. Railway Station, D.B., 14½ miles.

No.	Place		Miles	Total	Road	Route	Bridge/Ford	Elevation	Water	Remarks
40	Shevalia *D. B.—*	*Nogtat B.—*	11	460 / 463	Bridle road passable for laden animals down hill to the Jumna and thence up hill to Masuri.	Along mountain ridge, crossing the Jumna river.	......	......	S. F. G. W. and T. moderate.	Small village. / On summit of ridge.
41	Lakwar *D. B.—*		11	471 / 475	......	......	Jumna bridge iron suspension.	......	Ditto	Ditto.
42	Masuri *P. O., T. O., Hotels, C., E.—*		15	480 / 486	Good bridle road passable for laden animals down hill to Rajpore.	......	......	6590 / 7133	S. F. G. and T. abundant, water supply limited.	Kempti falls. / Military and Civil Sanitarium, convalescent depot.
	Rajpore Hotels—		...	493	Cart-road metalled hence to Dehra and Saharunpore.	......	......	2996	S. F. G. W. and T. moderate.	Large village.
43	Dehra *P. O., T. O., Hotels, C., E.—*		14	500	Earthen cart-road to Hardwar, very rough in places, crossing stony beds of rivers.	Through Eastern Dun.	......	2347	S. F. G. W. and T. abundant.	Military Cantonment, Civil Station, Town, Bazar, head-quarters of district.
44	Lachiwala *B.—*		11 / 4	511	......	......	Suswa bridge.	1680	S. and T. nil, F. G. W. available.	Hamlet.
45	Kunsrao *B., F., B.—*		8 / 4	519 / 520 / 527	......	......	Motichoor ford.	1360	Ditto	Forest head-quarters.

LXVII ROUTE—contd.

Number of Marches	Names of Stages	Distance in Miles and Furlongs — Intermediate m. f.	Distance in Miles and Furlongs — Total m. f.	Nature of Route	Main Valleys and Mountain Passes	River Crossings and Lakes	Altitude above Sea Level in Feet	Supplies and Transport at Stages	Remarks
		...	527			......			
46	Hardwar P. O., T. O., Canal B., C., E.—	11	531	Situated on right bank of Ganges river, where it issues through the Siwalik hills.	......	......	1050	S. F. G. W. and T. abundant.	Town, bazar, bathing ghats, celebrated place of pilgrimage.

LXVIIa SPITI to HARDWAR by GANGES VALLEY and MASURI—

Number of Marches	Names of Stages	Distance in Miles and Furlongs — Intermediate m. f.	Distance in Miles and Furlongs — Total m. f.	Nature of Route	Main Valleys and Mountain Passes	River Crossings and Lakes	Altitude above Sea Level in Feet	Supplies and Transport at Stages	Remarks
18	Dankar E.—	...	234	Road fair down Spiti valley left bank, undulating, crossing many spurs and shaly slopes.	Down Spiti valley left bank.	......	12774	S. F. G. W. and T. procurable.	Village, fort and monastery. Capital of Spiti.
			237		......	......	......	......	Road to Manirang pass.
19	Pokh	9 5	243 5	....	......	......	......	Ditto	Village.
20	Tabo	6 5	250 2	Road stony, crossing high spurs at both ends of stage.	......	......	...	S. and T. very scarce, F. G. W. available.	Hamlet and monastery.
	Luri	...	253						

No.	Place	Stage m.	f.	Total m.	f.	Road	Crossing	Spiti ford	Height (feet)	Supplies	Remarks
21	Somra	8	1	258	3	Road fair, easy ascent and descent over pass.	Cross to right bank.	......	......	Ditto	Village on right bank of Spiti river. Fort.
	Shalkar	...	...	263	4	......	Lepcha ghat cross to left bank.	......	13628,	......	
22	**Chango** *E.—*	13	5	269	272	......	......	Spiti bridge	10272	S. F. G. W. and T. procurable.	Large village on left bank Spiti river.

Another track starts from Peldo at the north end of the Tso Morari Lake 124 miles down the eastern shore to Lunk Serma 136 miles; thence eastwards crossing Chagarchan La 145 miles, to Ooti 149 miles, whence southwards along the Tegasung plain to Chumar 165 miles 14,000 feet, and down the Parachu valley to Chepzi 177 miles, on the border of Chinese Thibet, entering which Kyuntsang 185 miles, Chagza Sumdo 197 miles, Zampa 205 miles, Karak 212 miles, Sumyal 227 miles, are passed and crossing the border again into British territory, Kuri 238 miles, crossing Parachu river at Shugar by natural bridge of rock to Changrezing 249 miles, and over Changrang La to Chango 257 miles. From Somra 258 miles 3 furlongs, another track follows down the Spiti valley to Huling 264 miles, and crossing the Parachu by the rock bridge at Shugar 274 miles, to Changrezing 280 miles, and Chango 288 miles.

No.	Place	Stage m.	f.	Total m.	f.	Road	Crossing	Spiti ford	Height (feet)	Supplies	Remarks
23	**Naku**	10	...	282	...	Road fair along course of Spiti river.	......	Spiti bridge	11975	S. and T. scarce. F. G. W. available.	Small village on left bank Spiti river.
				284	4		Cross to right bank.				
24	**Lio**	4	...	286		Road commences by a steep zigzag and is then fairly level.	......	......	9600	S. F. G. W. and T. procurable.	Village on right bank Spiti river.
25	**Hangu** *E.—*	8	...	294		Easy ascent to and descent from pass, crossing streams several times.	...	...	11500	S. and T. scarce. F. G. W. available.	Small village.
				300	...		Hungerang pass.	......	14530.		
26	**Sungnum**	12	...	306	...	......	......	......	9920	S. F. G. W. and T. procurable.	Large village, monastery.

There is a more direct track from Dankar 234 miles, by crossing the Spiti river to Mani 242 miles, by Soprona Lake 246 miles, the Manirang pass 18,600 feet 253 miles, and down the Thanam valley to Pamachang 260 miles, Rupa 269 miles, and Sungnum 276 miles. This pass is, however, very high and covered by snow; through supplies and coolies necessary.

Number of Marches	Names of Stages	Distance in miles and furlongs		Nature of Route.	Main Valleys and Mountain Passes.	River Crossings and Lakes.	Altitude abo Sea Level in Feet.	Supplies and Transport at Stages.	Remarks.
		Intermediate. m. f.	Total. m. f.						
LXVIIa *ROUTE—contd.*									
	Tabang E., good	...	306	......					
		...	307	......					
		4	313		Runang pass. Down Sutlej valley right bank.				
		...	318	......	...	Thanam bridge.	14354.		
27	**Labrang** ... *E., bad, stony on shant* *Kola*	14	320			......	10000.		
		...	322	Road rough but passable for laden animals.	...	......	9000	S. and T. scarce, G. F. W. available.	Village.
		...	326			Taitu bridge.			
		...	327	Present terminus of Hindustan and Thibet road.					
28	**Jangi** *R.—* *Akpa*	11	331	Road passes through immense blocks of granite, and through deodar forest.	......		9000	Ditto	Ditto, copper prayer wheel.
		...	335		......	......	......	......	Vines grow here.
29	**Rarang** *E.—*	7	338	Road level for 2 miles, then steep ascent followed by steep descent and level for 3 miles to Pangi	Cross to left bank either at Harang by wooden bridge or at Poari by Jhula bridge.	Kozang bridge.	9068	Ditto	Village, bridge over Sutlej connects with road on left bank.
		...	343	...					

No.	Place	Dist.	Total	Route description	Notes	Notes	Elevation	Supplies	Remarks
30	Pangi *B.—*	8	346	Here leave Hindustan and Thibet road, steep descent to the Sutlej river, cross Jhula bridge and ascend by Poari to Barang.	......	......	8950	S. F. G. W. and T. procurable.	Ditto, pilgrim shrine on Piri peak 14,000 feet.
31	Poari	7	353		......	Sutlej Jhula bridge.	......	Ditto	Ditto.
32	Barang	10	363	Steep ascent followed by level to Meikar, ascend to pass, then rough descent into Baspa valley.	......	......	......	S. and T. scanty, ditto.	Ditto.
	Meikar		367				12000.		
33	Sangla	16	372		Baikart spur. Up Baspa valley right bank.	......	......	S. F. G. W. and T. available.	Ditto, take supplies here for onward journey to Derali.
	Rakcham		379		......		10445.		Hamlet highest in valley.
34	Chitkul	16	387	At Sangla road from Kilba joins and goes up the Rupin pass into the Tonse valley.	......	......	11400	S. and T. nil, F. G. W. available.	Halting place.
35	Suancho	10	395	Road from Sangla through Chitkul and Suancho to Nithal very rough, crossing many spurs and ravines.	......	Raspa bed forded several times.	13000	Ditto	Large plain.
			405					......	
	Denti		413				......		Ditto.
36	Nithal	14	419	At Nithal junction of 2 valleys, eastwards over Gugerang pass into Thibet, southwards over Neela pass, ascend glacier and steep	Neela pass	......	......	Ditto	Ditto.
			427				16000.		
37	Karkuti	18	437		......	......	......	Ditto	Hamlet.
			450			Blagirati bridge.			

Number of Marches.	Names of Stages.	Distance of miles and furlongs. Intermediate. m. f.	Total. m. f.	Nature of Route.	Main Valleys and Mountain Passes.	River Crossings and Lakes.	Altitude above Sea Level in Feet.	Supplies and Transport at Stages.	Remarks.
	LXVIII ROUTE—contd.								
38	**Derali** B.—	...	450 ...	snow field to summit, descend 2 miles to stream and along latter to Karkuti, follow same stream to the Bhagirati river.	...	...	...	S. and T. scanty, F. G. W. available.	Village.
		16 ...	453 ...						

At 450 miles join the Forest road in Ganges valley. The route upwards from Derali goes to the Jangla F. B., 457½ miles ; thence crossing the Jad Gunga, or Nilang river from the Nilang pass, above its junction with the Bhagirati, the road ascends the latter valley to Gangotri temple 10,150 feet 472 miles, and to Gau Mukh 16,000 feet 488 miles, at the mouth of the great Gangotri glacier. Take supplies at Derali. The route down the Ganges or Bhagirati valley from the Ganges bridge at 450 miles is as under :—

Number of Marches.	Names of Stages.	Distance of miles and furlongs. Intermediate. m. f.	Total. m. f.	Nature of Route.	Main Valleys and Mountain Passes.	River Crossings and Lakes.	Altitude above Sea Level in Feet.	Supplies and Transport at Stages.	Remarks.
	Hursil	... ...	450 ...	Road good but narrow.	Down Ganges or Bhagirati valley on right bank.	Bhagirati bridge.	...	.....	Mr. Wilson's bungalow.
39	**Jala** B. C., E.—	... 6 ...	452 4	.....	.....	......	8200	.....	Village. From Jala to Batwari, river confined in narrow gorge.
	Suki	... ...	456 ...	Route to Jumnotri viâ Bandarpunch.	Suki bridge	......	8200		
		... ...	465 ...				8600	S. scarce, F. G. T. W. available.	

No.	Name		Miles	Total	Road	Remarks	Elevation	Supplies	Remarks
40	**Dangala**	...	11	467	...	...	Cross Bhagirati 3 times by bridge.	6500	Ditto	Ditto.
	Itari	...	...	473	...	...	Bhagirati bridge. Sulphur springs.			
41	**Batwari** *F. B., E.—*	...	12	476	...	Road to Junnotri	Bhagirati bridge.	5300	Ditto	Ditto.
42	**Moneri** *B.—*	...	11	479	...	...	Ditto.	4600	S. nil, F. G. T. W. procurable.	Ditto.
	Kota Forest bungalow.	...	...	480	...	...	...			
43	**Barahat**	...	11	499	...	...	...	3900	S. F. G. T. W. available.	Ditto, Hindu temples.
				501	...	Road to Kedarnath.				
44	**Dhunda**	...	12	513	...	...	...	3400	S. and T. nil, F. G. W. plentiful.	Small village.
45	**Darasu** *F. B., E.—*	...	9	522	...	...	...	3300	Ditto	Village.
	Thona	...	...	524	...	...	...	3100	S. available	Ditto.
				527	...	Leave forest road and go across hills S. W. to Masuri.				
46	**Laluri** *E.—*	...	9	531	...	...	...	4000	S. F. G. W. and T. available.	Ditto.
	Mauranah E.—	...	...	538	...	Road fair, crossing many spurs and crest of hill.	...	...	Ditto	Fine view of snowy range.

Number of Marches	Names of Stages	Distance in Miles and Furlongs — Intermediate m. f.	Distance in Miles and Furlongs — Total m. f.	Nature of Route.	Main Valleys and Mountain Passes.	River Crossings and Lakes.	Altitude above Sea Level in Feet.	Supplies and Transport at Stages.	Remarks.
	LXVIIa ROUTE—contd.								
47	**Bhala** *E.—*	: :	538 :	......	Cross Aglar valley.	......	5700	S. F. G. W. and T. available.	
48	**Phedi** *E.—*	10 :	541 :	......	......	......	......	Ditto	Village.
	Seakoti	12 :	553 :	Join here Masuri and Tiri road.	......	......	......	......	
	Lowchaar	: :	558 :	......	Along mountain ridge.	......	7000	......	Convalescent depôt.
49	**Masuri** *P. O., T. O., Hotels, C., E.*	: :	564 :	......	......	......	6500	S. F. G. W. and T. abundant.	Hill Sanitarium.
	Rajpore, Hotels	14 :	567 :	......	Down hill to Dun.	......			
50	**Dehra** *P. O., T. O., Hotels, C., E.*	: :	574 :	Join here cart-road through Dehra to Hardwar.	Through Eastern Dun.	......	2150	Ditto	Military Cantonment and Civil Station.
		14 :	581 :						
53	**Hardwar** *P. O., T. O., D. B., C., E.*	31 :	612 :	......	......		965	Ditto	Chief place of pilgrimage in Northern India. Terminus of branch from Oudh and Rohilkhand Railway.

The Forest road continues from 527 miles to Chann 533 miles 2,700 feet, Kaliasera 544 miles 4,200 feet, Baur 552 miles 4,700 feet, Kandia Gali B., 559 miles 6,800 feet, Kana Tal 565 miles 8,000 feet, Dhansulti B., 573 miles 7,600 feet, Jalki 582 miles, Masari 589 miles 6,500 feet. From 542 miles, there is a direct road to Tiri, the capital of Gurhwal, and a path hence down the Bhagirati valley to Deopryag, junction of the Aluknanda river, and hence down the Ganges valley to Hardwar.

LXVIII LEH to SIMLA by SPITI—

Leh P. O., B. C., E.—	...	0	*See* Route LXVII by Tso Morari Lake and Spiti to the Sutlej valley, where the Hindustan and Thibet road is joined. Take supplies from Leh to Dankar, and from Dankar to Sarhan.
1 to 25	Wangtu E.—	... 316 ...	

From Wangtu upwards this road goes along the right bank of the Sutlej by Chagaon 7 miles, Urni B., 9½ miles 7,900 feet, Rogi B., 20 miles, 9,361 feet, Chini 23 miles 9,196 feet, Pangi B. 30 miles 8,950 feet, Rarang 38 miles 9,068 feet, Akpa 41 miles, Jangi B., 45 miles 9,000 feet, end of road 49 miles, whence rough hill track continues by Kola 54 miles, Labrang 56 miles, Tabang 58 miles, Kunang pass 63 miles, 14,354 feet, Thanam bridge 69 miles, Sungnum 70 miles 8,000 feet, Shaso 74 miles, Charling La 80 miles 14,600 feet, Pooi 90 miles 10,000 feet, bridge over Sutlej river 97 miles, Dubling 95 miles, Khalb 100 miles, Namgea 101 miles 10,000 feet, Naugea Dogri 103 miles, cross two ridges of Kung ma La 108 miles 15,500 feet, to Shipki 112 miles 10,000 feet, a large Tartar village on the frontier of Chinese Thibet. From Wangtu, after crossing the wooden bridge over the Sutlej river, this road continues down the left bank of the Sutlej valley as under :—

No.	Stage			Remarks		Elevation		Supplies
25	Wangtu B.—	...	316	Good road 6 feet wide bridged throughout and passable for laden animals.	Down Sutlej valley left bank.	.....	5361	S. and T. scarce, F. G. W. plentiful	Supplies from Sarhan.
26	Nachar B., E.—	3	319	.....	.....	.....	7125	Ditto	Hamlet.
27	Paunda B.—	4	323	.....	.....	Bridge.	6124	Ditto	Ditto.
28	Taranda B.—	4	325 328	Through fine deodar and elm forest	.....	.....	7015	Ditto	Ditto in Kunawar.

Number of Marches	Names of Stages	Distance in miles and furlongs		Nature of Route	Main Valleys and Mountain Passes	River Crossings and Lakes	Altitude above Sea Level in Feet	Supplies and Transport at Stages	Remarks
		Inter-mediate. m. f.	Total. m. f.						
LXVIII	ROUTE—contd.	...	...						
	Mansapur	...	328	...	......	Bridge.			
	Dralli Cliffs	...	329 330 336	...	Mancoti spur.	......			
29	Sarhan B.—	14	342 345 347	Upper forest road through Soongri branches off here.	...	......	6713	S. F. G. W. and T. moderate.	Large village in Bissahir.
30	Gaura B.—	10 4	352 4	Regular road descends through Gaura to Rampur.	...	Manglud bridge.	6512	S. and T. scarce, F. G. W. plentiful.	Village.
31	Rampur P. O., D. B., C.—	6 4	359 4	Good road bridged throughout and passable for laden animals.	Down Sutlej valley left bank.	......	3870	S. F. G. W. and T. plentiful.	Town and capital of Bissahir State. D.B. one mile north of city.
	Rampur City—	...	360	...	...				
32	Nogri	13	372	...	...	Nogri bridge	......	S. and T. scanty, F. G. W. available.	Hamlet.
33	Nirit	7	377 4 379 381	...	......	Muchara ,, Dera ,,	3660	Ditto	Ditto.

No.	Station	m.	f.	Total	f.	Road	Length	Elevation	Supplies & Water	Remarks
34	Kotgarh *P. O., D. B.—*	10	...	389	...	...	...	5600	S. F. G. W. and T. plentiful.	Tehsil, Mission Station and tea gardens.
35	Nagkunda *P. O., D. B.—*	10	6	396	6	High level road from Bagi joins in here, whence excellent road 10 feet wide fully bridged to Simla.	...	8700	S. F. G. and T. moderate, W. scarce.	Small bazar.
36	Mattiana *P. O., D. B.—*	11	...	399	6	...	...	7690	S. scanty, F. G. W. and T. available.	Village.
37	Theog *D. B.—*	11	2	410	...	...	...	7420	S. F. G. T. procurable, W. scanty.	Hamlet.
38	Fagu *P. O., D. B.—*	5	6	422	6	Leave Sutlej valley and follow to mountain range to Simla.	...	8170	S. F. G. W. and T. moderate.	Ditto. Road to Chor Peak and Masuri branches off here.
	Pabri bazar	...	...	427	4	...	...	...	...	...
	Mohosa neck	...	...	431	6	...	...	...	...	...
	Mashobra toll bar	...	...	433	4	...	...	...	...	...
	Tunnel	...	...	436	...	...	500 feet long.	...	...	...
	Sanjoli bazar	...	...	438	6	...	...	...	...	...
	Lakha bazar	...	...	437	2	...	...	...	...	...
39	Simla *P. O., T. O., Hotel, C.*	12	...	430	6	Carriage road metalled and bridged from Simla to Kalka. Tonga Service.	...	7200	S. F. G. and T. abundant, W. scanty in dry season.	Sanitarium and summer capital of India Town, large bazar. Palace of H. E. the Viceroy of India.
	Kiarighat *D. R.—*	...	...	455	6	...	...	...	...	...
	Solon *P. O., T. O., D. R., C., E. small—*	31	...	470	6	...	...	5000	S. F. G. W. and T. available.	Village and bazar, small cantonment and brewery.

Number of Marches.	Names of Stages.	Distance in Miles and Furlongs.		Nature of Route.	Main Valleys and Mountain Passes.	River Crossings and Lakes.	Altitude above Sea Level in Feet.	Supplies and Transport at Stages.	Remarks.
		Intermediate. m. f.	Total. m. f.						
LXVIII	*ROUTE—contd.*								
	Dharampur D. B.—	... ...	470 6						
		... ...	482 6						
	Kalka P. O., T. O., D. B., Hotel, C., E.—	27 ...	497 6	Hence by rail to Umballa.	...	...	2200	S. F. G. W. and T. plentiful.	Large village and terminus of branch railway from Delhi and Umballa.
	Umballa	39 ...	536 6	...	...	...	1040	......	Large Military Cantonment and Civil Station.

At 345 miles another or high level road ascends the Manglad stream which it crosses by a bridge at 348 miles, gradual ascent through forest scenery by Mashun 351 miles, to Darun B., 356 miles; thence by Tola 360 miles and Nogri bridge 363 miles to Tach; leeh F. B., 366 miles, ascends through fine forest to crest of ridge 371 miles, then level to Bhali B., 376 miles, continues through fine forest to Soonghi B., 386 miles, situated on the ridge where the road from Rampur crosses the neck and descends into the Pabar and Tonso valleys; thence along the ridge to Kudreli F. B., 395 miles, Ragi D. B., 404 miles, and through fine forest under Hatu Pir 11,000 feet, to Nagkunda D. B., 416 miles, where rejoin regular Hindustan and Thibet road.

LXIX LEH to SIMLA by RUPSHU and SPITI—

	Names of Stages.	Intermediate. m. f.	Total. m. f.	Nature of Route.	Main Valleys and Mountain Passes.	River Crossings and Lakes.	Altitude above Sea Level in Feet.	Supplies and Transport at Stages.	Remarks.
	Leh P. O., D. B., C., E.—	... ...	... ...	Road heavy, but passable for laden animals, yaks	Up Indus valley, cross to left bank.	...	11500	S. F. G. W. and T. abundant.	Large town, and fort. Capital of Ladak. Take

No.	Stage	Stage dist.	Total dist.	Remarks on road	Passes and ravines	Rivers, bridges, fords	Elevation	Supplies	Remarks
		...	6	mostly used.	......	......		......	supplies hence to Spiti.
1	**Chushot** B., E.—	...	...	......	......	Indus bridge	10560	S. F. G. W. and T. plentiful.	Village, much cultivation.
	Hanis Gonpa	12	12	Road over sandy desert, with a few green patches.	......	......	......	......	Monastery.
2	**Machalong** B., E.—	13	23	.....	...	......	...	Ditto	Village.
		...	25	.....	......	Shang bridge	...	......	......
3	**Upshi** B., E.—	10	35	.....	Up Gya ravine	......	......	S. F. G. W. and T. moderate.	Ditto.
	Mira	...	43						
	Lotho	...	49						
4	**Gya** E.— *Tiorrenk*	18	53	Steep and stony ascent and descent over pass.	......	......	13500	S. and T. nil. F. G. W. available.	Camping ground.
		...	63		Taga Lung La. Down Debring ravine.	......	17500		
		...	67	......	......	......		......	
5	**Debring** E.—	19	72	......	......	Debring ford	......	Ditto	Ditto.
		...	77	......	...	......	......	......	Branch route by Zara to Zanskar.
6	**Rogchin or Rukchen** E.—	16	88	Road sandy over long plateau in Rupshu.	Up Rukchen ravine and over Kharg chu maidan.	......	15000	Ditto	Camping ground.
	Morchu E.—	...	99	...	...	......	......	...	Ditto.

Number of Marches	Names of Stages	Distance in miles and furlongs — Intermediate. m. f.	Distance — Total. m. f.	Nature of Route.	Main Valleys and Mountain Passes.	River crossings and Lakes.	Altitude above Sea Level in vert. feet.	Supplies and Transport and Stages.	Remarks.
LXIX	ROUTE—contd.	...	...						
7	Sumkyil E.—	...	99	Road rough, ascent over two ridges of pass easy, descent stiff.	...	Crossed 3 streams.	...	S. F. T. nil, G. W. available.	Camping ground.
		93	111		Lachalung La. Up Tsarp valley.	......	16600		
8	Sumdu E.—	20	131	......			...	Ditto	Ditto.
	Giau		139	......	......		...	...	Junction of Tsarp river. Bridge 4 miles off.
			148		......	Tsarp ford	...	...	Ditto.
9	Sarchu Lingti E.—	20	151	Road easy and level.	Up Yunan valley.	...	...	Ditto	Ditto.
	Phalwag Danda		155		......				
10	Kilang E.—	11	162	Long and easy ascent to pass.		...	...	Ditto	Ditto.
			165	...	Bara l'acha pass, down Chandra valley left bank.	Yunan Tso	16200	...	lake

11	Topo *E.—*	18	180	Road rough and difficult.	......	Chandra nala	......	S. and T. nil, F. G. W. available.	Ditto.
12	Topo Koma *E.—*	9	189	......	......	......	......	Ditto	Ditto.
13	Chandra Dul	14	203	......	......	Sam Chikma lake.	......	S. and T. nil, F. G. W. available.	Camping ground.
			210	......	Kunzam pass. Down Spiti valley right bank.	......	14930	......	Ibex ground.
14	Lichu	10	213	......	......	......	......	Ditto	Ditto.
15	Lusar *Hansi*	9	222	Road good along high table-land.	Cross to left bank	Spiti ford ...	13395	S. F. G. W. and T. moderate.	Village.
			229	......	......	......	......	......	
16	Kioto	10	232	......	......	Spiti ford	......	S. and T. scanty, F. G. W. procurable.	Small village.
			234	......	Cross to right bank.	Spiti ford	......	......	Junction of Lagu-darsi river.
17	Hal	11	243	Road good along high table-land.	...	Gyundi ford	......	S. F. G. W. and T. procurable.	Village.
18	Rangrik *Kaja*	10	253	......	Cross to left bank.	Spiti bridge	......	Ditto	Ditto.
			257	......	......	......	......	......	Ditto.
19	Lidang	12	265	Road fair	......	Spiti bridge.	......	S. and T. scarce, F. G. W. available.	Ditto.
			271	......	Cross to right bank, up Pin valley on left bank.	......	......	......	
			273	......	......	......	......	......	Junction of Pin and Spiti rivers.

Number of Marches	Names of Stages	Distance in miles and furlongs — Intermediate m. f.	Distance in miles and furlongs — Total m. f.	Nature of Route	Main Valleys and Mountain Passes	River Crossings and Lakes	Altitude above Sea Level in Feet	Supplies and Transport at Stages	Remarks
LXIX	ROUTE—contd.								
20	**Sunam**	...	273	...	...	Parachu bridge.	.....	S. F. G. W. and T. moderate.	Large village.
	Titang	16	280	.....	.....	Pin "	.....		
21	**Muth**	...	281	...	.....	Ditto.	.....	S. and T. scanty, F. G. W. available	Small village.
	Baddar	8	285	Road fair up wide shingly bed of Pin river.	.....	Ditto	.....		
22	**Lyrsa**	22	289	.....	.....	......	......	S. and T. nil, F. G. W. plentiful.	Halting place.
		...	302	...	......				
23	**Ptiasa**	12	311	...	Bhabeh pass. Down Sutlej valley.	......	15000	S. F. T. nil, G. W. plentiful.	Ditto.
	Mulling	...	323	...	......		......	S. and T. nil, F. G. W. plentiful.	Ditto.
			327						Ditto.
24	**Yangpa**	10	333	......	Cross to left bank.	Sutlej bridge	......	S. and T. scarce, F. G. W. procurable.	Village
	Wangtu B.—	...	345	Join Hindustan and Thibet road to Simla.	......		5361.		

No.	Place		Dist.	Total	Remarks on road		Height	Supplies	General remarks
25	Nachar, B., E.—	...	15	348	......	......	7125	S. and T. scarce, F. G. W. plentiful.	Supplies from Sarhan.
29	Rampur, P. O., D. B., E.—	...	40	388	See previous Route LXVIIIa between Stages 25 & 39.	......	8700.		
33	Naghunda, P. O., D. E., E.—	...	41	429		......	7200.		
37	Simla, P. O., T. O., Hotels, C. E.—	...	40	469	Carriage road bridged and metalled from Simla to Kalka. Tonga service.	......	5000.		
	Solon	...	31	500		......	2200.		
	Kalka	...	27	527	By Delhi-Umballa and Kalka Railway.	......	1040.		
	Umballa	...	39	566		......			

LXX   LEH to SIMLA by LAHOUL and KULU.—

No.	Place		Dist.	Total	Remarks on road			Height	Supplies	General remarks
	Leh, P. O., D. B., C., E.—	...	...	6	Road heavy, but passable for laden animals.	Up Indus valley, cross to left bank.	......	11500 10500.	S. F. G. W. and T. abundant.	Large town and fort. Capital of Ladak. Take supplies to Kailling.
1	Chushot, B., E.— Houses	...	12	12	......	......	Indus bridge	......	S. F. G. W. and T. plentiful.	Village, much cultivation. Monastery.
		...		23					Ditto	
2	Machalong, B., E.—	...	13	25	Road sandy with a few green patches.	......	Shang bridge.	......		Village.

Number of Marches	Names of Stages	Distance in miles and furlongs		Nature of Route.	Main Valleys and Mountain Passes.	River crossings and Lakes.	Altitude above Sea Level in Feet.	Supplies and Transport at Stages.	Remarks.
		Inter-mediate. m. f.	Total. m. f.						
LXX	ROUTE—contd.								
3	Upshi *B., E.— Mtra*	13	25	......	Up Gya ravine	......	......	S. F. G. W. and T. moderate.	Village.
4	Gya *E.— Tharsak*	10	35	Steep and stony ascent and descent over pass.	......	......	13500	S. and T. nil, F. G. W. available.	Camping ground.
		......	43						
		18	53						
		..	63	......	Tagalung La. Down Debring ravine.	......	17500.		
		..	67						
5	Debring *E.—*	19	72	......	......	Debring ford	......	Ditto	Ditto.
		..	77						
6	Zara *E.—*	7	79	Road sandy along wide valley.	Down Zara valley.	......	......	S. F. T. nil, G. W. available.	Here leave route to Lachalung La. Tartar camp.
7	Sangtha	14	93	......	......	......	......	Ditto	Ditto.
8	Loon	9	102	Road through river gorge.	Up ravine	......	......	Ditto	Ditto.
		......	114		Marang La.		......		
9	Takh	18	120	......	Up Tsarap valley.	......	......	S. and T. nil, F. G. W. available.	Hamlet.

No.	Place	Dist.	Total	Road	Route notes	Feature	Elevation	Supplies	Remarks
10	Loon toon nu E.— Gian	9	126	......	......	Hot spring.	......	S. F. T. nil, G. W. available.	Camping ground.
		...	129	......	......	......	......	......	Bridge higher up river.
		...	133	Junction of road from Lachalung La	......	......	......	Ditto	Ditto.
		...	143	......	......	......	......		
11	Sarchu Lingti E.— Phalang Danda	16	145	Road easy and level.	Up Yunan valley.	Taarap ford	......	......	Ditto.
		4	148			......	......		
12	Kilang E.—	11	156	Long and easy ascent to pase.	......	Yunan bridge	......	S. F. T. nil, G. W. available.	Ditto.
			159	......	......	Yunan Teo Lake.	......		
			165	......	Bara Lacha pass.	Suraj Dul Lake.	16200.		
			167	Road good down hill.	......	Bhaga bridge.	......		
			171	......	......		......		
13	Zing Zing bar E.— Tapachand	17	173	......	......	......	......	Ditto	Ditto.
		...	175	......	......	......	13060.		
14	Patsio C.—	9	182	Road fair and passable for laden animals.	Down Bhaga valley right bank.	Bhaga bridge	12464	S. F. T. nil, G. W. plentiful.	Fair held here for Kulu, Lahoul and Thibetan traders.
15	Darcha	9	191	Road level and good, but very dusty all the way to Kailing.	......	Kada Tokpo bridge.	10844	S. F. G. W. and T. moderate.	Village.
		...	192		......				
16	Kulang	10	201	Winding road down hill.	......	......	......	Ditto, F. scarce	Ditto.

Number of Marches.	Names of Stages.	Distance in Miles and Furlongs. Intermediate m. f.	Distance in Miles and Furlongs. Total. m. f.	Nature of Route.	Main Valleys and Mountain Passes.	River Crossings and Lakes.	Altitude above Sea Level is Feet.	Supplies and Transport at Stages.	Remarks.
LXX	ROUTE—contd.								
17	Kailing or Kardang. P. O., B.—	...	201	Road good and easy with many ups and downs.	Up Chandra valley right bank.	Bhaga bridge	10100	S. F. G. W. and T. moderate.	Capital of Lahoul, Moravian Mission.
18	Gundla B., E.—	13	214	Shady from willow trees planted for 4 miles from Kailing.	......	2 hill torrents bridged.	10300	S. F. G. W. T. available.	Village.
19	Sisu E.—	12	226	......	......	Sisu bridge, 5 hill torrents crossed by bridges.	9938	S. F. and T. scarce, G. and W. procurable.	Small village.
20	Koksur B., E.—	9	235	Ascent and descent of pass very steep, very cold and high wind after 9 A.M.	Rotang pass. Down Beas valley right bank.	Chandra bridge.	10300	S. F. and T. scanty, G. and W. plentiful.	Village.
		13	248			......	13500	...	This stage 14 miles long by regular mule road.
21	Rahla	10	258	Good road through lovely scenery all the way to Sultanpur, passable for laden animals and studded with tea and fruit gardens.	...	......	9000	S. and T. nil, F. G. W. available.	Hamlet.
	Palcham	...	261		......	Solung bridge.			
	Barua E.	...	263		......	......		S. and T. available	Village on plain.

No.	Place		Stage	Mile	Road remarks	Direction	River / Camp	Elevation	Supplies	Description
22	Manali	B., E.—	10	268 277	......	......	Manali bridge. Kuish "	......	......	Ditto.
23	Katrain	B., E.—	13	281	......	......	Dobi "	4723	S. F. G. W. and T. available.	Village.
24	Sultanpur	P. O., D. B., E.—	12	285 287 293	Bridle road made and bridged throughout all the way to Nagkunda.	......	Raison " Bandrol " Beas "	4092	S. F. G. W. and T. plentiful.	Capital of Kulu. Town, bazar, tehsil and police thana.
				298	......	—	Ditto "			
25	Bajaora	B., E.—	9	302	......	......	Kandi "	3573	S. F. G. W. and T. procurable.	Small bazar and old ruined fort.
	Badool			305	......	......	Beas "			
26	Larji	B., E.—	12	314	A new and more direct bridle road is being made by the Raja of Mandi to connect Mandi with Simla, starting from Manglaor.	Up Chata valley, cross to left bank.	Synj "	......	Ditto after notice	Hamlet at junction of Synj and Chata rivers.
				316			Chata "			
27	Manglaor	B., E.—	8	322 324		Right bank	Ditto "	3710 5718	S. F. G. W. and T. moderate.	Small village.
	Plach P. O.—			325		......	Ditto "	......		Large village and tehsil.
28	Jibi		9	331	Good climb up hill through woods with pheasants.	......	......	5860	Ditto after notice	Small village.
				338		Jalaori pass. Down Arni valley.	......	10600.		
29	Kot	B., E.—	11	342	Road along west side of hill, cool in morning, steep drop down to nala half way and corresponding rise.		......	7750	S. F. G. W. and T. moderate.	Ditto.
30	Chowai	B.—	9	351		......	Arni bridge	6162	S. F. G. W. and T. plentiful.	Cluster of villages.

Number of Marches	Names of Stages	Distance in Miles and Furlongs — Intermediate m. f.	Distance in Miles and Furlongs — Total m. f.	Nature of Route	Main Valleys and Mountain Passes	River Crossings and Lakes	Altitude above Sea Level in Feet	Supplies and Transport at Stages	Remarks
LXX	ROUTE.—contd	...	...						
31	Dularsh *P. O., B.—*	...	351	Road uphill to pass, lovely views.	Cross spur, descent into Satlej valley.	...	...	S. F. G. W. and T. moderate.	Village.
		8	356	Long drop down to the Sutlej bridge 2 hours by raghandi, similar climb up by short cut on south side.	...	Satlej bridge	2650	.....	Called Lori.
32	Komarsen *B.—*	...	359	...	...	...	...	Ditto	Large village.
33	Nagkunda *P. O., D. B.—*	9	364	Long ascent uphill to join Hindustan and Thibet road, in excellent order along the mountain ridge to Simla.	Leave Satlej valley and follow top of mountain range to Simla.	...	8700	S. F. G. W. and T. moderate, W. scarce.	Small bazar.
34	Muttiana *P. O., D. B.—*	7	368	...	...	...	7690	S. scanty, F. G. W. and T. available.	Village.
		11	386	...	...	...	...	...	...
35	Theog *D. B.—*	11	397	...	...	...	7420	S. F. G. T. procurable, W. scanty.	Hamlet.
36	Phagu *P. O., D. B.—*	5 6	403	...	...	...	8170	S. F. G. W. and T. moderate.	Ditto.

37						Elevation	Supplies	Remarks
	Pokri bazar	...	...	406	6			
	Maskobra toll bar	...	...	411	6			
	Saujoli bazar	...	...	413	...			
	Simla P. O., T. O., Hotels, C., E.—	12	...	415	...	7200	S. F. G. and T. abundant, W. scanty in dry season.	Sanitarium and summer capital of India. Town, bazar. Palace of H. E. Viceroy of India.

From Leh take bulk of supplies and transport (Yaks are best) to Kailing in Lahoul, and from Kailing (calling upon the Assistant Commissioner at Kulang) take bulk of supplies to Sultanpur.

This road is open from June to October.

From Debring 72 miles, the road by Rukchen in Rupshu over the Khiang Chu maidan and the Lachalung La to Gian can be taken if preferred. *See* Route LXIX, stages 5 to 9.

LXXa. KILANG to SULTANPUR by BARALACHA and HAMTA PASSES—

No.	Place	Miles	Total		Road		Elevation	Supplies	Remarks
10	Kilang	...	156	...	Long and easy ascent and descent with long stretch upon summit.	Yunan bridge	...	S. F. T. nil, G. scanty, W. available.	Camping ground.
			159	...		Yunan Tso.	...	......	Lake.
11	Topo	18	168	...	Road rough but passable for laden animals with care over bad places.	Baralacha pass Down Chandra valley along left bank.	16200.	S. F. T. nil, G. W. available.	Halting place.
			174	...			...	...	Ditto.
12	Topo Koma	9	183	...	......	...	...	Ditto	Ditto.

Number of Marches.	Names of Stages.	Distance in miles and furlongs.		Nature of Route.	Main Valleys and Mountain Passes.	River Crossings and Lakes.	Altitude above Sea Level in Feet.	Supplies and Transport at Stages.	Remarks.
		Inter-mediate. m. f.	Total. m. f.						
LXXa	ROUTE.—contd.	...	183 ...				......		
13	Chandra Dul	14 ...	197 ...	......	......	Sum Chikma Lake.	......	S. and T. nil, G. W. available.	Halting place.
14	Karcha	13 ...	210 ...	Hard march over rocks and boulders brought down by avalanches to Chaktru.	......	Chota Shigri torrent and moraine. Bara Shigri glacier and moraine.	......	S. and T. nil, F. G. W. available.	Camping ground.
		...	218 ...						
15	Puti Runi	11 ...	221 ...	Shigri glacier site of huge mountain slip which blocked the Chandra river for some months.	......	......	......	Ditto	Ditto.
16	Chahtru	12 ...	233 ...	Steep ascent, to pass, long and stony and easy descent, fair road through beautiful scenery all the way to Sultanpur.	......	......	......	S. and T. nil, F. G. W. procurable.	Opposite Purana Koksur.
		...	238 ...		Hamta pass. Down Raini valley left bank.		14000.		
17	Chika	13 ...	246 ...			......	......	S. and T. nil, F. G. W. available.	Halting place.
	E.— Hamta	...	254½ ...			......	......		
	Prini	...	256 ...	......	Down Beas valley left bank.	...	......	......	Junction of Raini nala with Beas river.

No.	Name	Inter.	Total	Road	Direction	Bridges	Elevation	Supplies	Remarks
18	Jagat suk *E.—* *Gojra*	12	258	......	......	Doangnu bridge. Splendid cascade. Chaki bridge.	5985	S. F. G. W. and T. moderate.	Village.
19	Nagar *E.—* *Kois*	9	267 272 275	......	......	Beas bridge. Raogi ,, Kois ,,	5780	S. F. G. W. and T. ample.	Small civil station on left bank of Beas river.
20	Sultanpur *P. O., D. B., E.—*	13	280	......	......	......	4092	S. F. G. W. and T. plentiful.	Capital of Kulu. Town, bazar and tehsil on right bank of Beas river.

The drawback to this alternative route is the difficulty of supplies and transport, which must be taken through from Leh and Sultanpur either way. Route open from June to October.

LXXI LEH to JALANDHAR by KANGRA—

No.	Name	Inter.	Total	Road	Direction	Bridges	Elevation	Supplies	Remarks
	Leh *P. O., D. B., C., E.—*	......	0	Road rough and stony, but passable for laden yaks.	Cross Indus valley.	......	11500	S. F. G. W. and T. abundant.	Large town and fort. Capital of Ladak. Take supplies to Kailing.
			5		......	Indus bridge	10560.		
1	Khawuch	10	10	There are no supplies or transport available at the stages between Leh and Padam, and hence onwards both are scarce.		......	......	S. F. G. W. and T. moderate.	Village.
	Zinchan	...	21		Up ravine southwards.	......			
2	Urucha	16	26			......	......	S. and T. nil, F. G. W. procurable.	Hamlet.
			29		Kunda La	......	16211.		

Number of Marches.	Names of Stages.	Distance in miles and furlongs. Inter-mediate m. f.	Total. m. f.	Nature of Route.	Main Valleys and Mountain Passes.	River crossings and Lakes.	Altitude above Sea Level in feet.	Supplies and Transport at Stages.	Remarks.
LXXI	ROUTE—contd.	...	...						
3	Skio	... ...	29 ...	Road ascends Markha valley crossing many spurs and ravines to Gonpa.	Up Markha valley.	Cross Markha river several times.	11120	S. and T. nil, F. G. W. procurable.	Hamlet.
4	Chalak	12 ...	38 ...			......		Ditto	Ditto.
	Markha	12 ...	50 ...		......	......	12510.		Ditto.
5	Gonpa	...	56 ...	......	Up Kuberung Chu.	......		Ditto	Ditto.
		9 ...	59 ...						
6	Camp	10 ...	69 ...	Difficult pass both in ascent and descent.	Ruberung La, down Ruberung Chu.	......		S. and T. nil, F. G. scanty, W. available.	Camping ground.
			73 ...	......	......	Cross Khanuk river.			
7	Khurna Sumdo	15 ...	84 ...	......	......			Ditto	Ditto.
8	Tilut Sumdo	9 ...	93 ...	...	Across Khanuk Valley.	......		Ditto	Ditto.
9	Tomtokh	9 ...	102 ...	......	Up Charcha Chu.	......		Ditto	Ditto.

No.	Stage	Intermediate miles	Total miles	Remarks on road	Rivers, passes and bridges	Height in feet	Supplies	Remarks
10	**Zumlung**	...	109	Pass rough and difficult on both sides.	Charcha La.	......	Ditto	Ditto.
11	**Zozar**	13	115	Join here regular road from Leh to Zanskar by Yelchung.	......	11503	T. nil, S. F. G. W. procurable.	Hamlet and bridge over Zanskar river.
12	**Thonde**	15	130	......	......	11460	Ditto	Hamlet.
13	**Padam**	7	137	Road fair and passable for laden animals to Kargyah.	Tsarap Lingti Chu bridge.	11373	S. F. G. W. and T. procurable.	Fort, village and former capital of Zanskar.

From Gonpa 50 miles, a track continues south-eastwards up the Markha valley by Hankar 67 miles, Nimaling maidan 75 miles, over the Chaksang La 83 miles, to Latho 93 miles, in the Gya valley at 45 miles of Route LXIX.

From Hankar 67 miles another track goes south up the Lantung Chu over the Kurpola 17,050 feet 83 miles, down the Khurna Chu, by Khurnakur 74 miles, Kurto huts 77 miles, up the Omata Chu, by Khanuk 85, over the Yar La 16,180 feet, 103 miles down the Langma Chu to Sangtha 115 miles, in the Zara valley at miles 93 of Route LXX.

No.	Stage	Intermediate miles	Total miles	Remarks on road	Rivers, passes and bridges	Height in feet	Supplies	Remarks
	Bardan Gonpa	...	153	Road along both banks of river from Padam to Pipchu.	Up Tsarap Lingti valley, cross to left bank.	Tsarap bridge. Chema Chekore bridge.	......	......	......
	Pipchu	...	154, 157	......	......	Kern Tokpho bridge.	......	......	......
14	**Reru** E.—	15	161	......	......		......	S. and T. precarious, F. G. W. available.	Hamlet.
15	**Sarieh** E.—	13	174	......	......	......	......	Ditto, F. scarce.	Ditto.
	Clear	...	176	......	......	Junction of Nirichu.	12800	......	Village on right bank.

Number of Marches	Names of Stages	Distance in Miles and Furlongs		Nature of Route.	Main Valleys and Mountain Passes.	River Crossings and Lakes.	Altitude above Sea Level in Feet.	Supplies and Transport at Stages.	Remarks.
		Intermediate. m. f.	Total. m. f.						
LXXI	ROUTE—contd.	...							
16	Tetha E.—	9 ...	176 ... 183 ...	......	Up Kurgyahchu valley.	...... Gian bult bridge.	......	S. and T. precarious, F. scarce.	Hamlet.
17	Kargyah E.—	11 ...	192 ... 194 ...	Hence two roads to Kailing, one over Shingo La, and the other over Phirtse La by Sarchu Lingti.	......	......	13670	S. F. G. W. and T. procurable.	Village and extensive grazing ground.
18	Lakong	9 ...	201 ... 203 ...	......	......	Bilet bridge.	......	S. F. T. nil, G. scarce, W. plentiful.	Halting place.
19	Ramjak	14 ...	210 ... 217 ...	Road fairly easy on both sides of pass.	Shingo La down Lángkyung valley.	......	16722	S. and T. nil, F. G. scarce, W. plentiful.	Ditto.
20	Dak bajan	10 ...	227 ... 236 ...	Road bad for ponies passable with care.	......	Bangyo „	......	S. and T. nil, F. G. W. available.	Ditto.

No.	Station	Stage	Total	Road	Route	Bridges	Elevation	Supplies	Remarks
21	**Darcha** *C., E. on right bank.*	10	237	Here join the Lahoul and Rupshu road. Bhaga valley well cultivated, road very dusty to Kailing.	Down Bhaga valley along right bank.	......	10844	S. F. G. W. and T. procurable.	Village on left bank of Bhaga river.
22	**Kulang** *E.—*	10	247	....	....	......	......	Ditto	Village.
23	**Kailing** *P. O., D. B., C., E.—*	12	259	Road shady from planted willow trees for 4 miles.	Cross to left bank.	Bhaga bridge	10100	S. F. G. W. plentiful, T. available.	Capital of Lahoul Moravian Mission.
			264	Road easy with exception of narrow part round rocks, and	Up Chandra valley right bank.				
24	**Gundla** *B., E.—*	12	274	with many ups and downs and crossing many hill torrents to Koksur.	....	2 Hill torrents bridged.	10300	S. F. G. W. and T. available.	Village.
25	**Sissu** *E.—*	9	280	....	....	Sissan bridge 5 hill torrents bridged.	9938	S. F. T. scarce, G. W. procurable.	Small village.
26	**Koksur** *B., E.—*	13	293	....	....	Chandra bridge.	10200	S. F. T. scanty, G. W. plentiful.	Village.
			298	Ascent and descent of pass very steep, very cold and keen high wind after 9 A.M.	Rotang pass	......	13500.		
27	**Rahla** *B., E.—*	10	303	By mule road 14 miles.	Down Beas valley, along right bank.	....	9000	S. and T. nil, F. G. W. available.	Hamlet.
	Pulchan		306	....	....	Solang bridge.			
	Barcea		308	....	....		......	S. and T. available	Village on plain.

No. of Marches	Names of Stages	Distance in miles and furlongs		Nature of Route.	Main Valleys and Mountain Passes.	River Crossings and Lakes.	Altitude above Sea Level in Feet.	Supplies and Transport at Stages.	Remarks.
		Intermediate. m. f.	Total. m. f.						
LXXI	*ROUTE— contd.*								
28	Manali *B., E.—*	......	303	Road very good through woods and lovely scenery.	......	Manali bridge	......	S. F. G. W. and T. procurable.	Village.
	Baran	10	313			Kuish "			
		......	318			Dobi "			
29	Katrain *B., E.—*	13	326	......	......		4723	S. F. G. W. and T. available.	Near Dwara small town.
30	Sultanpur *P. O., D. B., C.—*	12	338	Road very good up hill to Kuraun.	......	Raison " Beas	4092	S. F. G. W. and T. plentiful.	Capital of Kuln. Town, bazar, tehsil.
31	Kuraun *R.—*	8	346	Easy ascent to pass through grand forest of pines, descent steep and bad.	Rabu pass	......	9480	S. F. G. W. and T. moderate.	Village.
32	Badwani in Mandi *R.—*	10	356	First half of this march fairly level, then stiff descent of 4 miles and climb of 3 miles.	Across Oel valley.	......	6700	Ditto	Ditto, lovely view looking south.
33	Jhatingri in Mandi *B.—*	13	369	.....	......	......	660	Ditto	Ditto B, on top of ridge between two ranges.

No.	Place	Dist.	Mile	Stage	Description of road	Across drainage	Bridge	Feet	Supplies	Remarks
	Guma	......	371 372	....	Cross Ool valley and Mandi hill range in which are the Guma salt quarries, road fair through rice fields and tea gardens, crossing several nalas; cart-road under construction from Guma to Palampur.	...... Mandi range across head of Rana valley.	Ool bridge.	7000.	......	Salt mines.
34	**Dhelu in Mandi** B., E.—	11	373	4	......	......	......	5100	S. F. G. W. and T. available.	Village.
		...	380	...						
35	**Baijnath** D. B., C., E.—	12	392	...	......	......	Binnu bridge	3300	S. F. G. W. and T. procurable after notice.	Cluster of villages. Ancient Hindu temples.
36	**Palampur** P. O., D. B., C., E.—	9	401	4	......	......	......	4050	S. F. G. W. and T. plentiful.	Large bazar and centre of tea gardens.

Hence there are two routes to Hoshiarpur and Jalandhar, one direct across country by Barwaneh 3,198 feet, 407 miles; Juala Mukhi 1,883 feet, 427 miles; Naihon 433½ miles, where cross Beas river by bridge of boats, Kulohah 3,068 feet 447 miles, cross range and Jeswunt Doon to Umb 457 miles, cross Sohan river 461 miles, Gugret R., 463½ miles, where join the main road over Nari pass to Hoshiarpur 1,066 feet 479 miles. The other route *via* Kangra follows the main road and is longer as under :—

No.	Place	Dist.	Mile	Stage	Description of road	Across drainage	Bridge	Feet	Supplies	Remarks
	Makan bazar	...	408 412	2 4	Cart-road from Palampur to Kangra bridged throughout first 3 miles steep descent, rest of easy gradient.	Across drainage from Dhaoli Dhar range.	Nugal bridge	3070. 3000	......	Several tea gardens on Patahar range.
37	**Nugroteh**	14	415	4	......	......	......	2850	S. F. G. W. and T. available.	Bazar.
	Gurkhari	...	418 422	... 4	......	......	Banera bridge	....	......	Road branches to Dharmsala 8 miles north.

Number of Marches	Names of Stages	Distance in miles and furlongs Intermediate m. f.	Total m. f.	Nature of Route	Main Valleys and Mountain Passes	River crossings and Lakes	Altitude above Sea Level in Feet	Supplies and Transport at Stages	Remarks
LXXI	ROUTE.—contd.	...	422 4						
38	Kangra P.O., T.O., D.B., C., E.	9 4	425 ...	Bridle road partially bridged from Kangra to Hoshiarpar and passable for laden animals.	Down Bangunga valley.	......	2300	S. F. G. W. and T. plentiful.	Ancient fort, large town and bazar. Devi temple frequented by pilgrims.
	Dandatpur	...	426 4	......	......	Bangunga bridge.	2100	...	Large bazar.
		...	430 4	......	......	......			
		...	434 4	......	......	Ditto.			
39	Ranital B., C., E.—	11 ...	436 ...	......	......	......	2000	S. F. G. W. procurable, T. nil.	Small village.
		...	440 4	......	Bhagrot saddle.	......			
40	Gopipur Dehra P.O., D.B., E.—	13 ...	449 ...	......	Across Beas valley.	Beas bridge of boats. Gopipur rao.	1400	S. F. G. W. and T. available.	Town, bazar, tehsil and schools.
		...	452 ...						
41	Bharwain	11 4	460 4	Road crosses wide raos in the Jeswunt Doon which are very	Summit of Sewalik range.	......	3000	Ditto after notice, W. scanty.	Small village.
	Kinno	...	463 4		......	... ...	2400	......	Ditto.

No.	Place				Road remarks				Water supply	General remarks
42	Gugret, B., C., F.—	13	...	471	4	sandy and heavy.	Sohan ford	......	......	Road 3 miles E. to Umb.
				473	4	......	Cross Jeswunt Dooa. Nain pass.	......	Ditto	Hamlet and shops.
43	Manguwal, B., E.—	7	...	476	4	......	......	......	......	Halting stage.
				480	4	Easy ascent and descent.	Southern base of Sewalik hills.	......	S. and T. nil, F. G. W. procurable.	
44	Hoshiarpur, P.O., D., B., C., E. confined—	8	4	483	...	Hence cart-road bridged and metalled to Hoshiarpur, where dák gharis are procurable.	Maskara rao.	......		
				489	...		Choea rao	1045	S. F. G. W. and T. ample.	Small civil station, town and bazar.
45	Adampur, Nasrala	14	...	501	...	......	......	880	Ditto after notice	Small village.
				508	4	......	Nasrala rao.			
46	Jalandhar, P.O., T.O., D.B., C.,E.	11	...	512	...	......	......	778	S. F. G. W. and T. abundant.	Station on N.-W. Railway. Civil station and military cantonment.

A new line of railway will shortly be commenced to connect Hoshiarpur with Jalandhar.

LXXI*a*. KHURNA SUMDO to CHAR—

No.	Place				Road remarks				Water supply	General remarks
7	Khurna Sumdo...	...	84	.	Very rough and difficult path.	......	......	S. T. nil, F. G. scarce, W. plentiful.	Halting place.
8	Lapurba	8	...	92	...	......	......	......	Ditto	Ditto.

No. of Marches	Names of Stages	Distance in miles and furlongs — Intermediate m. f.	Distance in miles and furlongs — Total m. f.	Nature of Route.	Main Valleys and Mountain Passes.	River Crossings and Lakes.	Altitude above Sea Level, in feet.	Supplies and Transport and Stages.	Remarks.
LXXI	ROUTE—contd.	...	...						
9	Niri Sumdo	...	92	Steep and difficult ascent and descent over snow fields.	Shapo dak La, down Niri Chu valley.	......	18530.	S. T. nil, F. G. scarce, W. plentiful.	Halting place.
10	Niri	16	100	......	......	......	......	Ditto	Ditto.
		12	108	Road crosses on high spur.	......	......	......	......	
			120	......	Shingri La. Down Niri Chu valley left bank.	......	......	......	
11	Shadi	10	126	Road fair and passable for laden yaks.	......	Niri Chu bridge.	......	S. and T. nil, F. G. W. procurable.	Village.
	Tantak Gonpa		130	......	......	......	......	......	Monastery.
			134	......	Cross to right bank.	Botkung bridge.	......	......	
12	Yaytah	11	139	......	......	......	......	Ditto	Hamlet.
			141	......	......	......	......	......	
13	Phooktal Gonpa	8	149	......	......	Niri Chu bridge.	......	S. F. G. W. and T. moderate.	Monastery.

| 14 | Char | ... | 6 ... | 155 ... | ... | Tsarap Lingti 12800 Chu bridge. | Ditto | Village at junction of Niri Chu and Tsarap Lingti Chu. |

From Botkang bridge 139 miles, there are paths either up the Shoon river or over the Nialo kontse La and Gotconta la 16,500 feet, to Kormooch 153 miles, Mane Leh 159 miles, Satak 166 miles, Takh 173 miles at mile 120 of Route LXX leading to Lalhoul.

LXXII. LEH to AMRITSAR by KISHTWAR and CHAMBA—

No.	Place	Dist.	Total	Route	Notes	Notes	Elev.	Supplies	Remarks
	Leh P. O., D.B., C., E.—	...	...	On main road towards Dras and Srinagar as far as Nimu.			11500	S. F. G. W. and T. abundant.	Town, fort and Capital of Ladak.
	Pitok	...	4 7						
1	Nimu	18 2	18 19	Cross Indus river and ascend Zanskar valley, road fair passable for yaks.	Up Zanskar valley.	Phayang Dokpo. Indus bridge.		S. F. G. W. T. moderate.	Village. Below junction of Zanskar and Indus rivers.
2	Ezas E.—	15 6	34	......	Up Sumdak foo.			S. and T. nil F. G. W. available.	Small village.
3	Drogulika E.—	9	43	Long easy ascent and descent from pass.				Ditto	Ditto.
4	Hinjoo E.—	10	53	......	Choke la		13513.	Ditto	Ditto.
5	Phanjila E.—	9	62	Here joins road from Lama Yuru to Zanskar.				S. and T. nil, F. G. W. procurable.	Village.
	Soondoo	...	65						

Number of Marches	Names of Stages	Distance in Miles and Furlongs		Nature of Route	Main Valleys and Mountain Passes	River Crossings and Lakes	Altitude above Sea Level in Feet	Supplies and Transport at Stages	Remarks
		Inter- mediate. m. f.	Total. m. f.						
	LXXII ROUTE—contd.								
6	Honupatta E.—	...	65 .	Road good and passable for laden animals.	......	......	12400	S. F. G. scarce, W. plentiful, T. nil.	Village.
7		7	69		Sir Sir La.	......	10372.		
	Photaksur E.—	13	78	Road through the hills, crossing numerous spurs and ravines and with easy ascents and descents over passes.	......	......	13900	S. F. G. W. procurable, few coolies.	Ditto.
	Maling	...	82		......	......	......	......	
		...	90		Singi La.	......	16600.		Cultivated valley 6 miles.
		...	94		......	......	......		
8	Yelchung E.—	16	98	......	Chochu Bori La.	......	12730.	S. precarious, T. nil, F. G. W. scanty.	Small village.
			100 4	......		Zanskar bridge.	10819.		
			103	......					
9	Naerung	6	104	Road fair through low hills inland	Nera La.	......	16000	S. and T. nil, F. G. W. procurable.	Ditto.
			110	......			......		
10	Pangot	10	114	across a bend of the Zanskar river.	......	......	......	Ditto	Halting place.
11	Khurmafoo	10	124	......	Chelong Labho.	......	13050	Ditto	Ditto.
			129			......	14530.		

No.	Stage		Dist.	Total	Route		Bridge	Elevation	Supplies	Remarks
12	Zang la	...	13	13?	......	......	......	......	S. F. T. scarce, G. W. plentiful	Village on right bank Zanskar river.
13	Zozar	...	6	143	Leave main Zanskar road and continue up left bank of Doda river.	Up Doda valley on left bank.	Zanskar bridge.	11583	T. nil, S. F. G. W. procurable.	Village and bridge over Luna Sampu or Zanskar river.
14	Kursha	...	12	155	......	......	......	......	S. F. G. W. and T. moderate.	Village and monastery opposite junction of Doda and Luna Sampu rivers.
	Tungriug	:		165	Here join road from Zanskar to Suru.	Cross to right bank.	Doda bridge.			
15	Ating	...	16	171	......	Up Kardur valley	......	12020	S. F. G. W. procurable, few coolies.	Village.
	Senekun Gonpa			177						
16	Gowra *E.—*	...	10	181	Continuous glacier and snow fields from Huttra to Bujwas.	......	......	13542	S. F. T. nil, G. W. procurable.	Halting place.
	Huttra	:		187				16109.		
				191	Steep ascent to pass, over glacier and snow fields, level plateau and steep descent.	Umasi La. Down Bhetna valley.	......	17370	......	Open 3 months June to August inclusive.
17	Bugjan Hiwan *E.—*	...	13	194	......	......	......	15500	Ditto.	Ditto.
18	Bujwas *E.—*	...	7	201	......	......	......	11570	S. T. nil, F. G. W. procurable.	Ditto.
	Sumjam	:		205	Easy path from Sumjam through cultivated valley to Atholi, passable for laden animals.	......	......	11000	.....	Sapphire mine in vicinity.
19	Machail *E.—*	4	8	209				9700	S. F. G. W. and T. moderate.	Village.
20	Kundhel Umshil	:	11	220	......	......	Bhetna bridge	7660	Ditto.	Ditto.

Number of Marches.	Names of Stages.	Distance in Miles and Furlongs. Intermediate m. f.	Distance in Miles and Furlongs. Total m. f.	Nature of Route.	Main Valleys and Mountain Passes.	River Crossings and Lakes.	Altitude above Sea Level in Feet.	Supplies and Transport at Stages.	Remarks.
LXXII	*ROUTE—contd.*								
21	Atholi or Gulabgurh. E.—	...	220 4	From Atholi difficult path, high above river, crossing numerous side gorges with considerable ascents and descents, practicable for unladen ponies to Bagni, whence easy road to Kishtwar.	Down Chandra Bhaga valley left bank.	Bhetna bridge and Chandra Bhaga rope bridge.	6360	S. F. G. W. and T. moderate.	Village and fort, chief place of Padar.
22	Siri	11	231 4	...	...	......	8700	S. and T. nil, F. G. W. available.	Hamlet.
23	Piyas	14	245 4	...	...	......	6320	Ditto.	Ditto.
24	Bagni	9 4	255 ..	...	...	......	......	S. scanty, F. G. W. plentiful, T. available.	Small village.
25	Kishtwar P. O., E.—	11	266 ..	From Kishtwar road fair and narrow in places, following the windings of the Chenab river and passable for laden animals.	...	......	} 5400 5000	S. F. G. W. and T. ample.	Town, fort, bazar on elevated plateau head quarters of district.
26	Joshni E.—	13	279 ..	...	...	......	......	S. T. nil, F. G. W. procurable.	Village.
27	Janglwar E.—	15	294 ..	......	Ascend hill range. Chira gully.	Karney Gad bridge.	3670	S. F. G. W. and T. available.	Ditto.

No.	Stage	Miles	Total	Remarks on road	Route / pass	River crossing	Elevation	Supplies	Remarks
28	Jaorá E.—	8	308	Summer road rises to ridge of hill, along which it keeps to Chinta, then descends to Budhawar, winter or lower road by Jagrul.	......	......	......	S. F. G. W. plentiful, T. procurable.	Ditto.
	Chinta	...	322						
29	**Budrawar** P. O., E.—	17	325	Road good and passable for laden animals, crossing several small streams up cultivated valley.	......	Neru bridge	5427	S. F. G. W. and T. ample.	Capital of Budrawar, Jagir of Raja Sir Amar Singh, K. C. S. I. Town, fort and bazar.
30	**Thenala**	8	333	......	Padri pass. Down Kandi Mari valley.	......	3000.	S. and T. nil, F. G. W. plentiful.	Iron mines.
31	**Langera** *E. on roof of huts,*	14	347	Long ascent to pass and steep descent down stony bed of stream.	Down Shoon valley.	......	5082	Ditto	Hamlet.
32	**Bhandal**	12	359	Road rough, hilly and stony to Chamba.	......	Shoon ferry.	5679	S. F. G. W. and T. available.	Large village.
	Digi	...	364						Ditto.
33	**Manjeri** B. E.—	14	373	......	Across Sachi valley.	Sachi bridge	......	Ditto	Ditto.
	Rajanger	...	380		Cross Rajnager spur.				
34	**Chamba** P. O., D. B., B., C., E.—	16	389	......	......	Ravi bridge	3000	S. F. G. W. and T. abundant.	Capital of Chamba, residence of Raja. Large town and bazar.

Number of Marches.	Names of Stages.	Distance in miles and furlongs. Inter-mediate. m. f.	Total. m. f.	Nature of Route.	Main Valleys and Mountain Passes.	River Crossings and Lakes.	Altitude above Sea Level, in feet.	Supplies and Transport at Stages.	Remarks.
LXXII	ROUTE—*contd.*								
35	Rareri	... ...	389 6	Road difficult but improved, with steep descent from pass for 5 miles.	......	......	......	S. F. G. W. and T. procurable.	Village.
	Mankot	6 ...	395 6		Mankot gully				
36	Chuari *B. C., E.—*	... ...	400 ...	......	......	......	......	Ditto	Customs post.
	Joji	12 ...	407 6			Chuki ford.			
37	Nurpur *P. O., D. B., B., C., E.*	... ...	414 ...	......	......	......	......	S. F. G. W. and T. ample.	Ancient fort and town. Large bazar and tehsil.
		16 ...	423 6	Join cart-road from Kangra to Pathankot.		Jubber Khud	2050		
38	Puthankot *P. O., T. O., hotel, C., E.*	... ...	432 6	......	......	Lyall viaduct	1300		
		16 ...	439 6				250		
	Gurdaspur	23 2	463 ...	By Amritsar branch of North Western Railway.					
	Batala	20 ...	483 ...						
	Amritsar *P. O., T. O., hotel, C.*	24 ...	507 ...					S. F. G. W. and T. plentiful.	Town and large bazar, terminus of branch railway.

XXIIa ZOZAR to CHAMBA by POAT LA and SACHI PASSES—*Map, Rose.—Distances approximate.*

No.		Stage	Dist.	Total	Route remarks	Direction	Bridge / Ford	Elevation	Supplies	Remarks
13	...	Zzar	...	143	This route though shorter is much more difficult and crosses much higher mountain passes.	Up Doda valley right bank.		11583	S. F. G. W. procurable, T. nil.	Hamlet and bridge over Zanskar. or Luni Sampu river.
14	...	Thonde *E.—*	7	150				11460	Ditto	Small village.
15	...	Padam *E.—*	9	159		Up Tsarap Lingti valley.	Usarap Lingti bridge.	11373	S. F. G. W. and T. procurable.	Village and Fort, former Capital of Zanskar.
		Barden Gonpa		165				.....	.....	Monastery.
16	...	Chemo Chekore...	10	169		Up Tema Tokpho valley.		.....	S. and T. nil. F. G. W. available.	Hamlet.
		Chimi Chenmo	...	174						
17	...	Kanjoo	11	180	The glaciers and snow fields extend from Kanjoo to the Camp at head of the Kilar nala about 43 miles. The ascent and descent of Poat La are not difficult, but the ascent and descent of Shinkil pass are extremely rough, steep and difficult.			.....	Ditto	Halting place.
				187		Poat La	18752			
18	...	Danga	19	199		Across head of Danlong valley. Shinkil pass. Down Kilar valley.	Danlong ford.	.....	Ditto	Ditto.
				211						
19	...	Camp	24	223				.....	Ditto	Ditto.
20	...	Kilar *E.—*	9	232		Cross Chandra Bhaga valley.	Chandra Bhaga bridge.	8411	S. F. G. W. and T. procurable.	Village in Pangi.

Number of Marches	Names of Stages	Intermediate m. f.	Total m. f.	Nature of Route	Main Valleys and Mountain Passes	River crossings and Lakes	Altitude above Sea Level in Feet	Supplies and Transport at Stages	Remarks
	LXXIIa ROUTE—contd.	...	232 ...		...	...	...		
21	Halias	9 ...	241 ...	Steep ascent from Chandra Bhaga river and easy descent. Long and narrow glacier on summit.	Sachi pass	...	14328.	S. and T. nil. F. G. W. available.	Halting place in Chamba.
		...	247 ...	......	Down Sachi valley.	...			
22	Alwas *E.—Baira*	15 ...	256 ...	Road fair and stony to Chamba down Sachi valley to Tikri, thence branching up Chanju valley to near Chanju,	......	Debri nala.	6997	Ditto	Hamlet.
		...	262 ...						
23	Tisa *E.—Tikri*	12 ...	268 ...		Up Chanju valley.	Makna „	...	S. F. G. W. and T. moderate.	Large village.
		...	275 ...						
24	Kalel	12 ...	280 ...	crossing a low range of hills and down the Hul valley to the Ravi.	......	Chanju bridge	5060	Ditto	Village.
		...	286 ...		Panjah pass, Down Hul valley right bank.				
25	Masrund	9 ...	289 ...			......	6376	Ditto	Ditto.
26	Chamba	12 ...	301 ...	......	Ravi valley	Ravi bridge	3033	S. F. G. W. and T. abundant.	Large town and bazar. Capital of Chamba State. Residence of Raja.

P. O., D. B., C., E.—

LXXIII LEH to JAMMU   by ZANSKAR and BUDRAWAR—*See ROUTE XVII.*

LXXIV LEH to SRINAGAR by DRAS and SINDH VALLEY—*See ROUTE LI.*

       Ditto   by SURU—   *See ROUTE LII.*

LXXV LEH to GILGIT   by INDUS VALLEY—   *See ROUTE LXVI.*

LXXVI LEH to SKARDU   by SHAYOK VALLEY. *Drew, New, Knight, Wachtmeister.—Distance approximate.*

Stage			Total	Road	Route	Name	Elevation	Supplies	Description
Leh P. O., D., B., C., E.—	...	...	0	Follow ordinary road towards Srinagar as far as Khalsi, then instead of crossing bridge keep down Indus valley to the junction of the Hanu valley.	Down Indus valley right bank.	......	11500	S. F. G. W. and T. abundant.	Large town and fort. Capital of Ladak. Palace of Gialpoor Raja.
Pitak	...	...	4			......	10500	......	Village and Monastery.
1 **Phayang Dokpo** B.—	7	2	7	......		Lamachmofoo	......	S. and T. nil, F. G. W. procurable.	Ditto.
Nimu B., E.	...	2	18			Nimu Drokpo.	......		
2 **Bazgo** B., E.—	15		22			Bazgo ,,	11658	Ditto	Large village.
Taratse	...		29 / 32			Likir ,,	......	......	Likir Monastery, 2 miles up valley.
3 **Hemis Shukpa**	15	6	38	Road rough and in bad order to Nurla, crossing low hills and through a gorge to the Indus.		......	......	S. and T. scanty, F. G. W. available.	Village and Monastery on high plateau, grove of pencil cedars.
Timisgam	...		45			......	......		

Number of Marches	Names of Stages	Distance in miles and furlongs — Intermediate m. f.	Distance in miles and furlongs — Total m. f.	Nature of Route	Main Valleys and Mountain Passes	River crossings and Lakes	Altitude above Sea Level, in feet	Supplies and Transport at Stages	Remarks
	LXXVI ROUTE—contd.	...	...						
4	Nurla *B., E.—*	11	45	...	...	Phocha Drokpo.	......	S. F. G. W. and T. moderate.	Village.
5	Khalsi *B.—*	6	49	Road fair along the Indus crosses many spurs and ravines.	Keep to right bank.	Skinning Cho.	......	S. and T. scanty, F. G. W. procurable.	Ditto.
	Doomkhar	...	55			Indus bridge Doom Khar Cho.	10000	......	Fort and bridge over Indus river.
			57						
			65						
6	Skirbichan	16	71	...	...	Kirboo Chand bridge. Brogiow.	......	S. nil, T. scanty, G. F. W. available.	Village, cultivation.
	Achi natung	..	79	...	...				
	Nubbi bramkar	...	84	...	Up Hanu valley.				
7	Goma Hanu *E.—*	18	89	Long and easy ascent to and descent from pass.	... Chorbat pass. Down Chorbat Loongma.	......	16696.	S. F. G. W. and T. moderate.	Village.
8	Cam'	21	102	...	...	...	...	S and T. nil, F. scarce, G. W. plentiful.	Halting place in Baltistan.
			110						

	Name		Miles	Road	River	Encamping ground	Elevation	Supplies	Remarks
9	Piun or Paxfain E.—	9	119	Road fair and stony, crossing many spurs and ravines.	Down Shayok valley left bank.	......	......	S. F. G. W. and T. procurable.	Picturesque village.
	Kustang	..	123	.....	.....	Kustang Brok.	......		
	Kubar	..	126	.....	.....	KubarLongma	......	Ditto	Village on hill.
10	Dau	10	129	.....	.....	.....	......		
	Lunkha	..	133	.....	.....	Lunkha Brok.	......		
11	Sirmu	11	140	.....	.....	Sirmu Brok.	......	S. and T. nil, F. G. W. moderate.	Small village.
12	Khapalu E.—	7	147 / 149	Road good and sandy.	Cross to right bank.	Shayok ferry or skin raft.	8400	S. F. G. W. and T. moderate.	Large village and Raja's palace.
13	Kerka E.—	10	157	Road fair along irrigated terraces.	.....	Narul Loomba	8356	S. and T. nil, F. G. W. moderate.	Large village.
	Possawu	..	161	.....	.....	Thulle „	......	......	Road branches by Tusserpo La to Shigar. Village.
14	Kuru	16	173	Path over sand along the Shayok river.	.....	Kuru „	7992	Ditto	Large village.
15	Kiris E.—	9	182	Path over sandy hills high above the Indus, views very striking.	Down Indus valley right bank.	Kiris „	......	S. W. and T. moderate, F. G. scarce.	Large village.
	Ghoro	..	185 / 193	.....	.....	Ghoro „	7673	......	Junction of Shayok and Indus rivers.
16	Narh E.—	14	196	.....	.....	Narh „	......	S. and T. scarce, F. G. W. moderate.	Village.

Number of Marches.	Names of Stages.	Distances in Miles and Furlongs.		Nature of Route.	Main Valleys and Mountain Passes.	River Crossings and Lakes.	Altitude above Sea Level in Feet.	Supplies and Transport at Stages.	Remarks.
		Intermediate. m. f.	Total. m. f.						
LXXVI *ROUTE—contd.*									
	...	...	196	...					
		...	206	Join Shigar and Skardu road over sand, gravel and dust.	Cross to left bank.				
		...	209 4						
17	**Skardu** *P. O., T O., C., E.—*	17	213	...	...	Indus ferry.	7400	S. F. G. W. and T. abundant.	Town and fort, capital of Baltistan.

Take supplies from Leh to Goma Hanu, hence to Pinu, hence to Khapalu, and the same on the reverse way. Summer route open from June to October.

Winter route by Indus valley, crossing at Khurmang to the Dras and Skardu road.

Marches 11 and 12 of 18 miles can be shortened to 14 miles by avoiding Sirmu, though the short cut is rough and stony over an hill spur.

LXXVIa LEH to KHAPALU by SHAYOK VALLEY—*Map, Thomson.—Distances approximate.*

Number of Marches.	Names of Stages.	Distances in Miles and Furlongs.		Nature of Route.	Main Valleys and Mountain Passes.	River Crossings and Lakes.	Altitude above Sea Level in Feet.	Supplies and Transport at Stages.	Remarks.
		Intermediate. m. f.	Total. m. f.						
	Leh *P. O., D. B., C., E.—* [*Patak*]	...	0	Ordinary road from Leh to Phayang Dokpo whence turn up a side valley to its source under the Lasirmou Peak over the Thanglasgo	...	...	11500	S. F. G. W. and T. abundant.	Capital of Ladak. Town and fort. Palace of Gialpoor Raja.
1	**Phayang Dokpo** *E.—*	7 2	7 2		Up Lanachmo foo.	Lanachmo foo.	......	S. F. G. W. and T. procurable.	Monastery.

No.	Halting place	March	Total	Road	Direction of march	Camping ground	Height in feet	Supplies	Remarks
	Chena	12	14	La and down this and the Palzampin ravines to the Shayok valley.	......	......	......	S. and T. nil, G. F. W. scanty.	Halting place.
2	**Lunachmo**	6	20	......	Thanghago La. Down Thanghago ravine.	......	16960.	Ditto	Ditto
3	**Brok Guma**	......	25	......	......	......	......	......	......
	Wachan	23	43	......	......	......	......		
4	**Hungar** *left bank* E.—	13	46 / 56	Road fair to Umuaru, and rough to Koro, where it branches up aside valley crossing many spurs to Waris.	Down Shayok valley left bank.	Palzam piu Loongma.	10300.	S. F. G. W. and T. moderate.	Large village and orchards.
5	**Thaise** *left bank*	11	67	......	Cross to right bank.	Shayok ford	......	S. and T. nil, F. G. W. available.	Village.
6	**Umuaru** *right bank* E.—	8	75	......	......	Unmari Loongma.	......	S. F. G. W. and T. moderate.	Ditto.
7	**Koro** *right bank*	10	85	......	Up Waris Loongma.	......	10300.	S. and T. nil, F. G. scanty, W. plentiful.	Halting place.
8	**Waris**	10	95	Hence it rises sharply over 2 main spurs and descends again to the Shayok river.	......	Waris Loongma.	12494.	Ditto	Hamlet.
	Zhong potas	......	98	......	......	......	......		
	Skepa	......	100 / 102	Ascent and descent of passes very steep and abrupt.	Lagopo La Down Biagdang Loongma.	......	13143.		
9	**Biagdang** *right bank*	10	105	Road fair and easy with many ups and downs.	Down Shayok valley.	Biagdang Loongma.	11700.	S and T precarious, F. G. W. plentiful.	Village.

LXXVI a ROUTE—contd.

Number of Marches	Names of Stages	Distance in Miles and Furlongs — Intermediate m. f.	Distance in Miles and Furlongs — Total m. f.	Nature of Route	Main Valleys and Mountain Passes	River Crossings and Lakes	Altitude above Sea Level in Feet	Supplies and Transport at Stages	Remarks
10	Chalunka right bank ...	...	105	...	......	Chalunka. Loongma.	....	S. and T. precarious, F. G. W. plentiful.	Village.
11	Turtuk left bank ...	10	115	...		Shayok bridge, Turtuk "	......	Ditto	Ditto.
12	Prahnu right bank E.—	9	124	......		Shayok "	8740	S. F. G. W. and T. moderate.	Large village, well cultivated.
13	Piun left bank E.—	14	138	Join summer route from Leh by Chorbat pass.		...	.....	S. F. G. W. and T. procurable.	Village.
		12	150						
16	Khapalu left bank	28	178	See Route LXXVI, marches 9 to 12.			8400.		

LXXVII KHAPALU to SHIGAR by THULLE LA or TUSSERPO LA.—Distances approximate.

Number of Marches	Names of Stages	Distance in Miles and Furlongs — Intermediate m. f.	Distance in Miles and Furlongs — Total m. f.	Nature of Route	Main Valleys and Mountain Passes	River Crossings and Lakes	Altitude above Sea Level in Feet	Supplies and Transport at Stages	Remarks
12	Khapalu ...	...	147	Road good and sandy.	Cross Shayok river from left to right bank.	Shayok ferry or skin rafts.	......	S. F. G. W. and T. plentiful.	Large village and Raja's palace.
13	Kerko ...	8	155	......	Up Thulle valley.	....	8356	S. F. G. W. and T. moderate.	Large village.

	Dowani	...	159	...			
14	**Harangur**	11	160	......	......	Road rough and stony, crossing many spurs and ravines.	S. F. G. W. and T. procurable.	Village.
15	**Bukma**	12	178	11323	......	......	Ditto	Ditto.
16	**Dubla Khan**	7	185 / 193	16679.	......	Tisserpo La down Tiath lung.	Very steep ascent and descent over pass, cross small glacier.	S. and T. nil. G. F. W. available.	Halting place.
17	**Tapsa**	18	203	......	......			Ditto	Ditto.
	Basmakarel	..	205				
18	**Shigar**	12	215	7640	......	......	On left bank Shigar river.	S. F. G. W. and T. plentiful.	Fort and large village, garden cultivation.

From Bukma 178 miles is a cross track up the Tunthul nala over the Laggo La 16,785 feet down the Kiris Loomba to Kiris about 24 miles in length.

From Dubla Khan 185 miles there is a shorter but steeper track over the Thulle La 192 miles, down the Yaltsa Loomba to Bauma Karel 202 miles in the Tiath lung valley.

From Khapalu there is another track northwards up the Husabe valley along right bank to the glaciers at foot of the Masher Brun Peak in 3 short marches to Muden (opposite to Huldi 8,867 feet on left bank) 12 miles, Kande 13 miles, and Husae 10 miles.

From Huldi at junction of Husabe and Saltoro rivers, another path goes eastwards up the Saltoro valley by Chino 9 miles Dumsun at junction of Kandus and Saltoro rivers 8 miles, Goomba Khan 11 miles, Ghyari up the Ghyari Loomba 13 miles, Ali Brusa 9 miles at foot of the Bilafun glacier and pass, an old route, now unused, over the Mustagh Karakoram range towards Yarkand.

From Khapalu eastwards there is another track by Sirmu, which crosses the Shayok river by skin raft at 8 miles to Goortse 13 miles; thence up left bank of the Saltoro river, past Dumsun 12 miles, Pilid 9 miles, where it crosses a bridge over the Saltoro river to right bank and joins the previous route at Goomba Khan for the Bilafun pass.

LXXVII LEH to YARKAND and KASHGAR by NUBRA VALLEY, KARA KORAM PASS and KILIAN PASS.

Tabistani or Summer route. Drew, Trotter, Bellew, Biddulph, Lansdell.—Distances approximate.

Number of Marches.	Names of Stages.	Distance in miles and furlongs. Inter-mediate. m. f.	Distance in miles and furlongs. Total. m. f.	Nature of Route.	Main Valleys and Mountain Passes.	River crossings and Lakes.	Altitude above Sea Level, in feet.	Supplies and Transport at Stages.	Remarks.
	Leh P. O., D. B., C., E.—	...	0	Road tough and stony.	Up ravine north of Leh.		11500	S. F. G. W and T. abundant Take through supplies and transport to Yarkand.	Large town and fort. Capital of Ladakh. Palace of Gialpoor Raja. Residence of Wazir and British Joint Commissioner.
	Ganles	...	5						Halting place.
1	**Camp**	12	12	Ascent to pass by a very steep and stony zigzag, descent down a steep snow field over moraine banks and down a mountain torrent to the Shayok valley.	Khardong or Laochi La, down ravine, cross Shayok valley and up Nubra valley along left bank.	......	15000	S. and T. nil, F. G. W. scarce.	
							17800	......	Yaks necessary over this pass.
2	**Khardong** E.—	15	27			......	13500	S. and T. nil, F. G. W. available.	Village on plateau.
	Khartsar	...	38						
3	**Satti** E.—	12	39	Road fair down Shayok valley and then up Nubra	......	Shayok ferry	10430	Ditto.	Village in fertile and cultivated valley.

Stage	Place	Miles	Total	Description	Intermediate	Pass	Elevation	Supplies	Remarks
	Tirit	...	46	valley, passing several populous villages, well cultivated.	...	...			
4	**Tagar**	15	54		Sumur Loongma Chamsing „	...	10030	S. and T. scarce, F. G. W. procurable.	Ditto, orchards and much cultivation.
	Chamsing	...	59			..			
	Popchick	...	61	.....					
5	**Panamik** *E.—*	13	67		Hot Springs	.....	10840	S. F. G. W. and T. moderate.	Ditto, complete supplies here for onward journey.
	Pokozhu	...	69 75		Poka chu Tutyalak „				
6	**hunglung** *E.—*	11	78	Here leave Nubra valley. Steep zigzag ascent and descent over pass.	Hot Springs	Up Tutyalak ravine over Karawal Dawan	10760 17000	Ditto	Village last to be met in Ladakh.
		...	81		.....				
7	**Tutyalak or Pangdongsta.**	11	89	Road most difficult and dangerous from snow avalanches, moraine slips and sudden floods.		.....	13000 15500	S and T. nil, F. scarce, G. W. plentiful.	Halting place under glacier.
	Sartang	...	97	Cross 2 glaciers 10 miles long on watershed between Nubra and Shayok valleys. After crossing Shayok ford, turn eastwards up deep gully to Chungtash and down		Saser pass Cross Shayok valley	17500	......	Yaks essential.
8	**Brangsa Saser** *E.—*	15	100 104 105		Shayok fort.		15204	S. F. G. T. nil, W. plentiful.	Huts on right bank Shayok river. Winter route up and down latter. Lake.
	Chongtash	...	112			Up Ront side valley.	.....	......	

22

Number of Marches.	Names of Stages.	Distance in miles and furlongs.		Nature of Route.	Main Valleys and Mountain Passes.	River crossings and Lakes.	Altitude above Sea Level, in feet.	Supplies and Transport at Stages.	Remarks.
		Intermediate. m. f.	Total. m. f.						
LXXVII ROUTE—contd.									
9	Bulak-i-Murghai ... *Barte* ...	... 10 ...	112 114 127	stony gully to Murgai. Hence road narrow, difficult and risky from stone avalanches.	....	....	15100 16000.	S. F. G. T. nil, W. plentiful, springs.	Halting place.
10	Kizil Langar ... *E.—*	16	130 136 144	Ascend by steep and stony gorge to high plain, cross this barren plateau over	Dipsang plateau, cross Chipchak valley.	......	16700 17800.	Ditto	Camping ground.
11	Daulat Beg Uldi ... *Chajesh jilga*	20	150 158	spongy soil and descend by wide and deep gully.	......	Chipchak ford.	16880	Ditto	Ditto. Winter route from Leh joins here.
		...	163	Gradual rise to pass over gravel and clay soil, then ascent sudden and steep, similar descent, then gradual down shingly gully.	Karakoram pass	......	18300		Practicable for laden horses.
12	Balti Brangsa ... *E., Rock Shelter—*	22	172		Down Yarkand valley.		17180	Ditto	Halting place.
	Wakab Jilga ...	...	186	Road good	......	......	16000.		

No.	Stage	Dist.		Total		Road	Direction	Fords	Elevation	Supplies	Remarks
13	Aktagh or Malik Shah *k.:—*	28	...	200	...	Road gradually rises over arid stony plateau to foot of pass.	Leave Yarkand valley.	......	15,590	Ditto, a little grass in summer.	Winter route diverges by Kugiar.
14	Chibra	10	...	210	...	Road ascends gradually to the	......	......	16480	S. F. G. T. nil, W. scarce.	Halting place.
				216	...	Suget pass, flat on top for 3 miles and descends steeply down ravine, over moraine banks and granite boulders.	Suget Dawan. Down Suget and Karakash valleys.	......	17618	......	Yaks necessary, air rarefied.
15	Suget	21	...	231	...	Road follows course of Suget stream, then crosses Karakash river and along right bank of latter.	......	Cross Suget stream several times. Karakash ford.	12970	S. and T. nil, F. G. W. plentiful.	Junction of Suget and Karakash rivers.
				235	...	......	......	......	......	......	Old fort erected by Maharaja of Kashmir. Kirghiz Camps around.
16	Shahidula	8	...	239	...	......	......	......	11500	Ditto	
	Aidak	...	...	244	...						
	Toghra Su	...	...	247	...			Toghra Su ford.			
17	Ali Nazar Kurgan	11	...	250	...	......	Up Kilian or Dair man-luk valley.	......	......	Ditto	Kirghiz Camps and Fort.

Hence are 3 routes over the Kuenlun range to Kargalik and Yarkand.

1. By Toghra Su valley, Kilik pass and Tupa Diwan, path little known and closed by the Chinese authorities, grass and wood procurable at every stage, said to be the best for foot passengers.

II. By Kilian valley, Kilian pass and Kilian city, summer route as under.

III. By Karakash valley, Sanju or Grim pass and Sanju city, also summer route as in **LXXIX.**

The Chinese authorities sometimes block II, and at other times block III.

Number of Marches.	Names of Stages.	Distance in miles and furlongs. Inter- mediate. m. f.	Total. m. f.	Nature of Route.	Main Valleys and Mountain Passes.	River Crossings and Lakes.	Altitude above Sea Level in Feet.	Supplies and Transport at Stages.	Remarks.
	LXXVII ROUTE—contd.								
18	Bostan	...	250	......			......	S. T. nil, F. G. scanty, W. available.	Halting place.
19	Kara Chaglan Aiaghe.	10	260	Ascent and descent of pass steep, but not difficult, men and horses suffer	......	......	......	S. T. G. T. nil, W. available.	South foot of pass.
		18	278						Yaks necessary.
20	Tsch Kun Kilian.	16	294	from dam or mountain sickness through the rarefied air.	Kilian Pawan. Down Tazgun valley.		17000	S. F. T. nil, G. scanty, W. available.	North foot of pass.
21	Basilik Aghse	12	306	...	...	Crossed Tazgun torrent several times.	...	Ditto	Camping ground.
22	Chiguluk Aghse	15	321	...	...	...	...	Ditto	Ditto.
23	Akshor	15	336	Road fair	...	...	...	Ditto	Hamlet.
	Sargh Aryk	...	346						
	Yat Kuduk	...	350			Tazgun ford.			
24	Kilian	20	356	Road through r'ch ly cultivated valley, then over sandy soil and mu-	......	Tazgun ford.	7000	S. F. G. W. and T. moderate.	Large village of 150 houses, where re- new supplies.

No.	Name of place	Miles	Total	Remarks (road)		River or ford	Elevation	Supplies	Description
25	Bash Langar	14	370	dulating ground.	......	......	......	S. F. T. nil, G. W. available.	Village, buy fruit.
	Doghri Kuprik	...	377						
26	**Bora**, *Oasis*	14	384	Road gradually rises over undulating ground for 8 miles and then along a chul flat to Kargalik.	......	......	......	S. and T precarious, F. G. W. available.	Village in oasis, well cultivated, where join route from Sanju.
27	**Besh Aryk**	25	409		......	......	......	S. and T. nil, F. G. W. moderate.	Village.
28	**Kargalik**	6	415		Across drainage of Tarim valley	......	4500	S. F. G. W. and T. plentiful.	Large town and bazar, 1000 houses.
	Kulchi	...	422	Road from Kargalik to Yarkand through cultivated and watered country.		Tezab ford.			
29	**Yak Shambeh**	11	426		......	......	......	S. F. G. W. and T. moderate.	Village, 300 houses.
30	**Posgam** *C., E.—*	13	431 / 439		......	Tiznaf ford.	4200	Ditto	Large village, 600 houses.
31	**Seh Shambeh**	9	448		......	Yarkand or Zarafshan ferry, Zulchak river	......	S. T. nil, F. G. W. plentiful.	Hamlet.
	Longar Alim Akhoon	...	454						
32	**Yarkand** *P. O., E., C., E.—*	8	456 / 460	Good road through gardens and cultivation well shaded by trees for 9 miles from Yarkand, traversed by arbas.	......	Opah bridge.	3950	S. F. G. W. and T. abundant.	Large and ancient city, Fortress, bazars. Residence of Governor, centre of trade.
33	**Kok, Robat,** *oasis*	25	481		......	......	3830	S. and T. nil, F. G. W. plentiful.	Village, 400 houses.
34	**Ak Robat** *B.—*	15	496	Road through chul or stony desert.	......	......	......	Ditto, W. brackish.	

Number of Marches.	Names of Stages.	Distance in Miles and Furlongs. Intermediate. m. f.	Distance in Miles and Furlongs. Total. m. f.	Nature of Route.	Main Valleys and Mountain Passes.	River Crossings and Lakes.	Altitude above Sea Level in Feet.	Supplies and Transport at Stages.	Remarks.
	LXXVII ROUTE—contd.								
35	Kizil, oasis C., E.—	... ... / 15	496 / 511	Good road through oasis, then over a chul or stony desert.	...	Kizil ford	3910	S. and T. nil, F. scanty, G. W. available.	Large village, 300 houses, iron works.
36	Topaluk	14	525, 526	...	.....	Shahnaz Bridge	.....	S. F. T. nil, G. W. available.	Small village, iron works.
37	Yangi Hissar B., C., E.—	16	541	Good carriage road 25 feet wide traversed by arbas. The road is lined by trees and runs through a well watered and cultivated country, 6 miles from Yangi Hissar, 10 miles round Yapchan, and 9 miles from Kashgar.	...	Shahnaz Bridge	4320	S. F. G. W. and T. plentiful.	Large town and fort, 600 houses.
	Seghelac		556						
38	Yapchan	25	566		...	Crossed several branches of the Gez river.	4210	S. F. G. W. and T. plentiful.	Large village, 250 houses.
	Tazgun		571		...	Tazgun bridge.			
	Karasu		575		.....	Karasu „			
39	Yangi Shahr	15	581		.....	Kizil Su or Kashgar river.	4060	S. F. C. W. and T. abundant.	New city and fortress.
40	Kashgar P. O., B., C., E.—	5	586	...	...	...	4043	Ditto	Capital of Chinese Turkistan. Large and ancient city, bazars, centre of trade.

There are 3 improvements being made on the Kashmir side in this road from Leh.

A new road over the Khardong pass with an easier gradient to summit, avoids the glacier on further side and descends to Shayok valley with a fairly easy gradient.

Blasting of a road (¾ mile through solid rock) up the mouth of the Tutyalak ravine to circumvent the Karawal Dawan, to avoid this high spur and shorten the distance.

New approaches on both sides to the great glaciers on the Saser pass.

From Yarkand, a road branches westwards to Tashkurgan in Sarikol by Yakarik 20 miles, over Shaitan kum desert to Kiziltagh 23½ miles, Arpalik 15½ miles, crossing two low passes, Kizil Diwan and Kara Diwan to Khaizak 21 miles, on the Charling river and up this valley by Tashkerim 14½ miles, to Chehil Gombaz 19 miles, over Torat pass 13,400 feet, to Past Rohat 9,370 feet 9 miles, Tarbashi 11,515 feet 8 miles, Shindi 17 miles, Tashkurgan 10,270 feet 19 miles.—Total Yarkand to Tashkurgan 188 miles.

From Yangi Hissar another road branches south-westwards and joins the foregoing at Chehil Gombaz 10,310 feet, by Ighizyar 19 miles, Aktala 17 miles, Sasak Taka 13 miles, Kaskasu 14 miles over Kaskasu pass 13,000 feet to Chehil Gombaz 8½ miles.—Total Yangi Hissar to Chehil Gombaz 71½ miles and to Tashkurgan 124½ miles.

From Tashkurgan 10,270 feet these roads continue in the same direction S. W. by Khanshabur 12,980 feet 17 miles, over Nesa Tash pass 15,000 feet, to Aktash 12,000 feet 18 miles, Ghazkul lake on Little Pamir 13,200 feet 46 miles, Langar 12,530 feet 25 miles, Sarhad 11,150 feet 24 miles, Kila Panja 55 miles.—Total Tashkurgan to Kila Panja 185 miles.

LXXVIII LEH to YARKAND or KASHGAR by SHAYOK VALLEY, KARA KORAM and YANGI DAWAN PASSES.

Zamistani or winter route when Shayok river is frozen over with thick ice. Dren, Trotter, Beller—Distances approximate.

Leh *P. O., D. B., C., E.—*	...	...	...	Up ravine north-east of Leh.	11500	S. F. G. W. and T. abundant. Take through supplies and transport to Yarkand	Large town, fort-capital of Ladak. Palace of Gialpoor of Raja. Residence of Wazir and British Joint Commissioner. Huts.
Solu ...	5 ...	10 ...	Ascent to pass steep and rough, descend a long stony slope covered with snow, then over bogs and moorland. Road fair.	...	...	...	...
1 **Polu** "	10 ...	10 ...		...	17900	S. F. T. nil. G. W. scanty.	Yaks necessary.
2 **Digar** ... *E.—*	14 ...	14 ...	24 ...	Digar or Laswan La, down Lang thung Loong-ma.	13080	S. F. T. scanty, G. W. plentiful.	Village on plateau.

Number of Marches.	Names of Stages	Distance in Miles and Furlongs. Intermediate. m. f.	Total. m. f.	Nature of Route.	Main Valleys and Mountain Passes.	River Crossings and Lakes.	Altitude above Sea Level in Feet.	Supplies and Transport at Stages.	Remarks.
	LXXVIII ROUTE—contd.								
3	Agham, *left bank* E.—	8 ...	24 ...	Road fair eastwards to Chang jungle, whence it turns northwards and becomes rough, in places rugged.	Up Shayok valley	Cross Shayok river 24 times between this and Murghai.	10500	S. and T. nil, F. G. W. plentiful, spring.	Village on left bank of Shayok river. Complete supplies here.
4	Pakra, *right bank* ...	12 ...	44	...	......	......	11000	Ditto	Camping ground.
5	Chimchak, *right bank,*	10 ...	54	...	...	......	11600	Ditto	Ditto.
6	Lamakyont, *right* or Shayok, *left bank.*	8 ...	62	The river bed where crossed is sandy or gravelly.	......	Shayok river frozen over 4 months in winter above this, when people travel over the ice.	12200	S. and T. nil, F. G. scanty, W. plentiful.	Village on both banks.
7	Chang Jungle, *right bank.*	18 ...	80	Between Agham and Manifarlik little snow falls, but above Mandarlik to Brangsa continual snow in winter though the road is never closed.			12800	N. and T. nil. F. G. W. plentiful.	Pasture ground.
	Changthang Jilga ...		83				......		Junction of Chang Chenmo and Shayok road eastwards by Chumurti to Rudok.
	Kabstar Khotea		89 ...						
8	Dong Aylak, *left bank.*	19 ...	98			...	13000	Ditto	Halting place.
	Yarghuluk Fort		108 ...						

No.	Name	Miles	Total	Remarks	Direction of road	Game	Height	Supplies	Camping ground.
9	**Mundarlik,** *right bank.*	20	118	......	...	......	13300	Ditto	Camping ground.
	Yartni ...	...	121	......	...	Kura Jilga.	......	Ditto	Ditto.
10	**Kutaklik,** *left bank.* E.—	12	130	From Kutaklik up Rout valley to Bulak-i-Murgai about 14 miles, where join summer route over Dipsang plain, or continue up Shayok river on the ice through a narrow and winding strait, between the glaciers on right bank and the cliff opposite on left bank to Gapshan.	...	Rout nala.	13500	Ditto, spring	Ditto.
11	**Sultan Chuskum,** *left bank.*	15	145			...	14000	S. and T. nil, F. G. scanty, W. plentiful.	Ditto.
	Branqsa Suser on right bank opposite.		155			...	15000.		Ditto.
12	**Dani-Murghai or Kamdan,** *left bank.*	18	163			......	......	Ditto	Ditto.
13	**Gapshan**	9	172	Road rough, crossing many spurs and ravines.		......	......	S. and T. nil, F. G. scanty, W. plentiful.	Ditto.
14	**Daulat Beg Uldi** E.—	15	187	Lower approaches gradual and upper approaches sudden and steep on both sides.	Up ravine northwards. Karakoram pass.	Chipchak fowl.	16880	S. F. G. T. nil, W. available.	Join summer route.
	Chepoch Jilga ...		195			......	18300	......	Marble slab in memory of A. Dagleish.
			200						
15	**Balti Brangsa** E., *Rock shelter*	22	209		Down Zaraf-shan or Yarkand valley to Kulan Uldi.	......	17180	Ditto	Camping ground.
	Wulsab Jilga ...		223			......	16000.		

LXXVII ROUTE—contd.

Number of Marches.	Names of Stages.	Distance of Miles and Furlongs. Inter-mediate m. f.	Total. m. f.	Nature of Route.	Main Valleys and Mountain Passes.	River Crossings and Lakes.	Altitude above Sea Level in Feet.	Supplies and Transport at Stages.	Remarks.
16	Aktagh or Malik shah. E.—	28	223 ... 237	Road rough down Yarkand valley to Kulan Uldi, thence northwards across Kuenlun range, head of Tiznaf	......	......	15590	S. F. G. T. nil, W. available, a little grass in summer.	Leave summer route here.
17	Khufe lung	20	257		......	......	......	S. and T. nil, F. G. W. available.	Camping ground.
18	Kashmir Jilga	12	269	valley and intermediate range and down Kugiar valley to Kargalik, passable throughout for laden animals.	......	......	......	Ditto	Ditto.
	Khirghiz Jangal								
19	Kukat Aghzi	26	295		......	Cross Yarkand river several times.	12870	Ditto	Ditto.
20	Kulan Uldi	15	310	Up narrow, torrtuous and deep gorge with easy ascent and descent to pass. Along course of Tiznaf river.	Up ravine northwards. Yangi Dawan. Down Tiznaf valley.	Yarkand ford	12650	Ditto	Ditto.
21	Chiragh Saldi	12	319 ... 322			......	15800. 14200.	S. and T. nil, F. G. W. procurable.	Ditto.
	Kirghiz Tam		325				......	S. and T. nil, F. G. scarce, W. procurable.	Kirghiz Camps.
22	Gurunj Caldi	14	336	......	......	Cross Tiznaf numerous times, in winter frozen over, in summer	11900	S. F. G. T. nil, W. available.	Ditto.

No.	Name	Dist.	Total	Nature of road	Direction	River	Elevation	Supplies	Remarks
23	Duba	9	345	......	......	floods are dangerous.	10000	S. T. nil, F. G. W. plentiful.	Pasture ground.
24	Khoja Mazar	6	351	......	...	...	9250	......	Pakhpa camps.
25	Chighlic	18	369	3 miles up river at Kughda-su are copper mines and works.	Tura Dawan	Tiznaf ford	8250 / 10200	S. F. T. nil, G. W. available.	Grassy flat with willows and poplars.
26	Ak Musjid *Postar*	12	375 / 381	Very steep rise between hills of loose dust and similar descent very dusty.	Down Kugiar valley.	Kugiar ford	8500	S. F. G. T. nil, W. procurable.	Camping ground. / Huts.
27	Kugiar, *oasis C., E.—*	24	399 / 405	Road fair over gravelly waste and sandy desert, traversed by sandy ridges to about 3 miles of Kargalik, where cultivation begins.	...	...	6460	S. and T. nil, F. G. W. available.	Village of 100 houses.
28	Yolaric, *oasis*	12	417	...	...	River bed	...	Ditto	Hamlet.
29	Besht Aryk, *oasis*	12	429	...	......	Ditto	...	Ditto	Ditto.
30	Kargalik *B., C., E.—* *Kuteki*	20	449 / 461	Road good, 20 feet wide through well watered and cultivated country.	Across drainage of Tarim valley.	Tiznaf river.	4370	S. F. G. W. and T. plentiful.	Town, 1,000 houses.
31	Yakshamba *bazar B.—* *Posgam C, E*	16	465 / 470	Over cultivated plain with farms, meadows and marshes.	......	......	... / 4200	S. F. G. W. and T. moderate. / S. F. G. W. and T. plentiful.	Village, 300 houses, bazar. / Large village, 600 houses, and bazar.
32	Yangichak *B—*	18	483 / 484	Over cultivated plain, well stocked with trees.	......	Yarkand or Zarafshau river.	...	......	Settlement.

NUMBER OF MARCHES	NAMES OF STAGES	DISTANCE IN MILES AND FURLONGS		NATURE OF ROUTE	MAIN VALLEYS AND MOUNTAIN PASSES	RIVER CROSSINGS AND LAKES	ALTITUDE ABOVE SEA LEVEL IN FEET	SUPPLIES AND TRANSPORT AT STAGES	REMARKS
		INTERMEDIATE. m. f.	TOTAL. m. f.						
	LXXVIII ROUTE—contd.								
	Langar Ali Akhoon ...	......	484	......	......				
33	Yarkand P. O., B., C., E.—	12	490	Road good, 20 to 25 feet wide, lined with trees near the towns passing through a well watered and cultivated country. Road traversed by arks.	......	Zilchak bridge.	3923	S. F. G. W. and T. abundant.	Large town and fortress. Centre of trade, numerous bazars. Residence of Amban.
			495						
			499		......	Opah bridge.			
34	Kok Robat, oasis C., E.—	25	520	Road traversed by arias.	......	......	3530	S. and T. nil, F. G. W. plentiful.	Village, 400 houses.
35	Ak Robat	15	535	Crossed stony desert.		......	......	S. F. T. nil, G. W. procurable.	Halting post.
36	Kizil, oasis	15	550	Alternate cultivation and sandy plains.		Kizil ford	3910	S. G. W. T. moderate, F. scanty.	Village, 300 houses and a few shops. Iron mines and works.
37	Topaluk	14	564 / 575	......		Shahnaz bridge.	......	S. F. T. nil, G. W. scanty.	Iron works
38	Yangi Hissar	16	580	Road good through cultivation with 10 miles of pasture ground in middle of stage.		......	4320	S. F. G. W. and T. plentiful.	Fort and bazar. Town of 600 houses.
	Sitta	...	590			Crossed several branches of the Giez river on both			
	Khanka	...	594						

No.	Name			Remarks (road)			Elevation	Supplies	Description
39	**Yapchan** *Tuzgun*	25 ...	605 ... 610 ... 614 ...	Road good through irrigated country watered by canals. Garden cultivation commences 3 miles from Yangi Shahr.	... ...	sides of Yap-chan. Tazgun ford. Karasu bridge.	4210	S. and T. nil, F. G. W. plentiful.	Village, 250 houses.
	Yangi Shahr	:	620 ...		...	Kizil su or Kashgar river.	4063		New fortress and city.
40	**Kashgar** *P. O., B., C., E.—*	20 ...	625 ...	......	...	......	......	S. F. G. W. and T. abundant.	Capital of Turkistan. Large town and bazars, Residence of Taotai. Centre of trade.

LXXIX LEH to YARKAND and KASHGAR by CHANG CHENMO, AKTAGH and SANJU PASS.

Uvee, Biddulph, Trotter, Bellew, Henderson.—Distances approximate.

No.	Name			Remarks (road)			Elevation	Supplies	Description
	Leh *P. O., D., B., C., E.—*	... ...	0	Road good ...	Up Indus valley on right bank.		11500	S. F. G. W. and T. abundant. Take through supplies and transport to Yarkand.	Large town and fort. Capital of Ladak. Palace of Gialpoor Raja. Residence of Wazir and British Joint Commissioner.
1	**Tikze** *Tangtanda*	12 ... :	12 ... 18 ... 4	Road fair, for 12 miles, leave Indus and path turns up Sakti valley well cultivated.	......	Salm foo. Nang „	......	S. F. G. W. and T. plentiful.	Large village and Monastery, much cultivation.
2	**Chimre** *E. bod*	17 ... :	24 ... ; 20 :	......	Up Sakti valley.	Sakti „	11800	S. F. G. W. and T. moderate.	Ditto.

Number of Marches.	Names of Stages.	Distance in Miles and Furlongs.		Nature of Route.	Main Valleys and Mountain Passes.	River Crossings and Lakes.	Altitude above Sea Level in Feet.	Supplies and Transport at Stages.	Remarks.
		Inter-mediate. m. f.	Total. m. f.						
	LXXIX *ROUTE—contd.*								
	Sakti	... ...	29 ... 4						
3	**Zingral** *E.—*	8 ...	33 ...						
		... ...	37 ...	Gradual ascent and descent over pass, winding through rocks and boulders.	......	......	15780	S. and T. nil, F. G. W. available.	Halting place.
		... ...	41 ...	......	Chang La Down Changl ravine.	......	17690	......	Kailas range.
4	**Tsultak**	8 ...	45 ...	......	Up Sushal valley.	Sushal bridge	15950	Ditto	Lake, ditto.
	Durgo	... ...	53 ...	Road along both banks of river to Tankse.	......	......			
5	**Tankse**	14 ...	57 ... 4	......	......	Sushal ford.	12900	S. F. G. W. and T. plentiful.	Large village and store house.
			50 ...	......		......			

From Chimré 29 miles, there is a route northwards up the Muegri branch of the Sakti nala, to Tagnuk 10 miles, cross Waris La 17,300 feet, an easy pass of the Kailas range dividing the Indus and Shayok valleys, to Tayar 20 miles, where a cross road is joined starting from Satti on the Shayok river opposite Khar char eastwards and up valley to Agham 20 miles, Tayar 13 miles, cross Noblok La to Durgo 24 miles, and Tankse 6 miles.

From Durgo there is also a branch road northwards 10 miles long to Shayok on the left bank of the Shayok river.

From Zingral 37 miles, there is another shorter route to Tankse 57 miles by the Kay La, 17,900 feet and Kay Tso down the Kay Loomba, but the pass is more difficult for laden animals.

From Tankse are paths southwards over high passes leading to Ugu and Shera on the Indus.

No.	Name			Road	River	Elevation	Water & Supplies	Hamlet
	Moglib	...	...	Road from Tankse through gorge for 6 miles, then in open valley.	......	......	......	......
6	Chakar Talao	14	67	Road fair	......	......	S. and T. nil, F. G. W. procurable.	Tank dry in summer.
7	Lukong	7 ¼	73	Road over pasture ground.	......	14130	Ditto	Two miles distant from N. W. end of Pangong Lake. W. salt.
8	Chagra	8	80	Road over undulating ground.	......	15090	S. F. T. nil, G. W. plentiful.	Stone huts.
			88	Gradual ascent and descent over pass.	......	18400.		
9	Rimdi	13	99	Lunkar La or Marsimik pass. Down Rimdi valley. Across Chang chenmo valley and up Ku-graug branch valley		17500	Ditto, F. scarce.	Camping ground.
			101		Chang Chenmo river.			
10	Pamzal	13	111	Road becomes very stony.	......	14790	S. and T. nil, F. G. W. plentiful	Ditto, road westwards down Chang chenmo valley, left bank to Sha-yok river about 40 miles.
			114	Road good	......			Ditto.
11	Gogra	12	127	Road good, with several steep ascents and descents over tributary streams.	......	15570	S. G. T. nil, F. W. plentiful.	
			133		......	......		Road branches northwards over Chang lung Barma La.

LXXIX ROUTE—contd.

Number of Marches	Names of Stages	Intermediate m. f.	Total m. f.	Nature of Route	Main Valleys and Mountain Passes	River Crossings and Lakes	Altitude above Sea Level in Feet	Supplies and Transport at Stages	Remarks
	LXXIX ROUTE—contd.	...	133 ...						
12	Kota Jilga	8 ...	135 ...	Road gentle ascent through a broad stony ravine for 4 miles and then steeper			16730	S. and T. nil, F. G. W. procurable.	Camping ground.
13	Pangtong	7 4	142 4	Gentle ascent to pass, high table land one mile, and bad road along ravine.	Chang lung pass.	...	17250 / 18910	Ditto	Ditto.
			147 ...						
14	Sumzungling	15 ...	157 4	Gentle ascent to high table land, road fair	...		17310	S. F. T. nil, G. scanty, W. available.	Ditto
			162 4						
15	Dehra Compass	19 ...	176 4	...	Cross west end of Lingzi thang plain. Dehra pass	Branch Kara-kash ford Kaaakash ford.	17890 / 18160	S. F. G. T. nil, W. scanty by digging.	Ditto.
			178 ...	Road good but stony.					
			182 ...						
16	Shinung or Dang lung	18 ...	185 ...	...	Down Kara-kash valley.	...	17030	S. G. T. nil, F. W. plentiful.	Ditto.
			194 4	Road bad and stony across ice beds, slippery and difficult for laden animals.					

No.	Name of stage	m.	f.	Total distance	Nature of road	Direction of route	Rivers	Height in feet	Supplies	Remarks
17	Kizil Jilga	14	4	239	......	......	Karakash river.	16360	S. and T. nil, F. G. W. procurable down valley. F. G. W. available.	Ditto.
	Khushk Maidan			257	Road stony and bad.	......	......	.....		
18	Chung Tash *E.—*	23	4	262	......	......	......	15740	S. F. G. T. nil, W. available.	Ditto.
	Rock shelter			264	Road leaves Karakash river, and ascends tributary, bad for 3 miles, and then across plain.	Up ravine	Cross stream several times.			
19	Shor Jilga	14	4	276	......	......	......	17710	Ditto.	Ditto.
				281	Road up ravine rough to pass with short sharp descent into open plain.	Karatagh pass.	......			
20	Karatagh	9	·	285	......	......	......	16590	S. G. T. nil, F. W. procurable.	Lake.
	Tamba			296	Road good over level plain.	......	......			
21	Aktagh or Malik-shah *E.—*	22	4	308	On right bank Yarkand river. Road over arid stony plateau.	Yarkand valley. Up ravine.	......	15590	S. F. G. T. nil, W. available.	Junction of Karakoram route.
22	Chibra	10	6	318	......	Suget Dawan. Down Suget valley.	......	16480	S. F. G. T. nil, W. scanty.	Few stone enclosures.
	Kutas Jilga			324	......	......	......	17600		
				330	Gradual ascent to pass, steep descent into ravine, crossing high moraines of granite boulders on right bank Suget stream.	......	......			
23	Suget *E.—*	21	4	339	......	......	Cross Suget stream several times.	12970	S. T. nil, F. G. W. plentiful.	Camping ground.
				343	......	Down Karakash valley.	Cross Karakash river	.....	......	Junction of Suget and Karakash rivers.

Number of Marches.	Names of Stages.	Distance in miles and furlongs.		Nature of Route.	Main Valleys and Mountain Passes.	River Crossings and Lakes.	Altitude above Sea Level in Feet.	Supplies and Transport at Stages.	Remarks.
		Intermediate. m. f.	Total. m. f.						
	LXXIX ROUTE—contd.								
24	Shahidula Khoja	...	343 ...	On left bank Karakash river, continues down this winding valley by a rough road.	......	twice. Ditto, three times. Toghra ford.	11780	S. T. nil, F. G. W. available.	Old fort erected by Maharaja of Kashmir. Kirghiz Camps around.
	Toghra su	8 ...	347 ...		......				
	Ali Nazar Kurgan	...	352 ...				......	......	
		...	356 ...	......					Junction of valley, up which road diverges to Kilian pass.
	Kilian su	...	357 ...		......	Kilian ford	......		Pasture flat.
25	Pillata gach	14	361 ...	......	Up ravine.	Forded Karakash river twice.	......	Ditto	
	Mazar Mirza Abubakar	...	367 ...	Left Karakash valley turning up narrow glen to left, ascending a tortuous gully by a steep, narrow and rough path.					
26	Kichik Kara Koram.	10	371 ...	Falling stones, dangerous ascent up a narrow, wind-	......	Crossed torrent several times.	12050	S. F. G. T. nil, W. melted ice.	Halting place in gorge.
	Zakongra	...	374 ·		Sanju Dawan or Grim pass.	......	16300	......	Yaks necessary.
	Koramlik jilga	...	378 ...						
		...	382 ...						

No.	Place		Miles	Total	Route	Valley	River crossing	Elevation	Supplies	Remarks
27	Gachaka	...	18	389	ing, rocky gully over landslips and great rocks. Ice field on top, then sudden drop down steep slope liable to avalanches of snow and along rapidly falling defile.	Down Sarighyar valley.	Crossed Sarighyar river by numerous fords.	10100	S. F. T. nil, G. W. available.	On Sarighyar river, Kirghiz camps in vicinity.
28	Tam C., E.—	...	10	399		.....	.....	8750	S. T. nil, F. G. W. available.	Hamlet, cultivation on Sarighyar river.
	Chichi glen	...	...	404	Road down narrow and winding defile.	.....	.....	.....	.....	Road to Chuchu pass 11,850 ft. on right and down Arpalik valley to Sanju.
29	Kiwaz	...	16	415	Road down an expanding valley for 4 miles and through fields and gardens to Sanju.	.....	Sarighyar ford.	.....	Ditto	Detached huts in flat sandy basin.
30	Sanju C., E.—	...	12	427	Cultivation extends for 12 miles up and down river. Road chiefly through desert over sand and gravel to Besh Aryk.	.....	Sarighyar ford.	6070	S. F. G. W. and T. ample.	Town of 1,200 houses on Sarighyar river. Country well cultivated, orchards and gardens.
	Langar	...	...	443						
31	Kush tak	...	25	452		.....	Kilian ford	.....	S. T. nil F. G. W. moderate.	Village on Kilian river.
32	Oi Tograk, oasis	...	20	472		.....	.....	5760	S. and T. nil, F. G. scanty, W. plentiful.	Settlement.
33	Bora, oasis	...	12	484	Road good through irrigated fields.	Across Tiznaf valley.	.....	5340	Ditto	Centre of farms along course of stream.
	Beshi arghi, oasis	...	...	489						

Number of Marches	Names of Stages	Distance in miles and furlongs		Nature of Route.	Main Valleys and Mountain Passes.	River Crossings and Lakes.	Altitude above Sea Level in Feet.	Supplies and Transport at Stages.	Remarks.
		Inter-mediate. m. f.	Total. m. f.						
LXXIX	**ROUTE—contd.**								
34	Kargalik B., C., E.—	...	499 ...	Road through populous and highly cultivated tract with occasional strips of marsh, tamarisk jungle and waste.	......	......	4370	S. F. G. W. and T. plentiful.	Market town of 1,000 houses.
	Yak chaonba bazar C.—	22 ...	506 ...		......	......	......	......	300 houses.
		...	518 ...		......	......	......		
		...	523 ...		......	Tiznaf ford.	......		
35	Posgam E.—	25 ...	531 ...	Road good fit for arbas.	Across Yarkand valley.	Yarkand or Zarafshan river.	4200	S. F. G. W. and T. moderate.	Large village and bazar of 600 houses.
		...	534 ...		......	......	......		
	Iawgar Zilchak	...	543 ...		......	......	......	......	Aygachi boat ferry few miles below ford.
36	Yarkand P. O., B., C., E.—	17 ...	548 ...	Extensive garden cultivation.	......	......	3958	S. F. G. W. and T. abundant.	Large city and fortress, centre of trade, residence of Amban.
	Sughu chak	...	552 ...	......	......	Opah bridge.	......	......	Post stage.
	Rabat chi	...	558 ...	......	......	......	......		
		...	563 ...	Road over sandy waste interspersed with green patches or oases of cultivation.	...	......		...	Village of 200 houses.
	Kok Robat, oasis... B., C., E.—	25 ...	573 ...				3830		

No.	Stage / Place	Total miles	March	Road	Crossing	Bridge / Ford	Height	Water & Supplies	Remarks
	Ak Robat	589	……	Road over gravelly desert.	……	……	……	2 Wells, W. brackish	Post stage.
38	**Kizil** B., C., E.—	603	30	Road over 10 miles of thin pasture, and then over waste and desert to Shahnaz.	……	Kizil ford	3910	S. and T. nil, F. G. W. available.	Large village of 500 houses, iron works, brought from hills, 2 marches west.
	Topaluk	617	……	……	……	……	……	……	Village.
	Sogat Bulak	623	……	……	……	……	……	……	Post stage.
	Shahnaz	628	……	……	Kayragh ridge.	Shahnaz bridge.	……	……	
39	**Yangi Hissar** B., C., E.—	633	30	Road over thinly cultivated country and saline plain or sandy wastes, with isolated scattered homesteads.	……	Crossed two canal bridges.	4320	S. F. G. W. and T. moderate.	Small town of 4,000 houses and fort.
	Soghoilue	648	……	……	……	Khan Aryk bridge.	……	……	Garden.
		652	……	……	……	Kusan ″	……	……	
		655	……	……	……		……	……	
40	**Yap chan** B., C., E.—	658	25	Road over plain of sandy waste, and marsh to the Karasn river, and then through high cultivated tract with orchards and gardens.	Across Tazgun valley.	Three canal bridges.	4210	Ditto	Large village.
	Tazgun	663	……	……	……	Tazgun ″	……	……	
	Karasu	667	……	……	……	Karasu ″	……	……	Large village.
	Yangi Shahr	673	……	……	……	……	4043	……	New fortress and city.
41	**Kashgar**	678	20	……	……	……	……	S. F. G. W. and T. abundant.	Large city, capital of Turkistan; residence of Taotai or Governor

LXXIX₄ GOGRA to SHAHIDULA by LINGZITHANG PLAINS, CENTRAL CHANG CHENMO ROUTE—*Hayward, Drew.*—

Distances approximate.

Number of Marches	Names of Stages	Distance in miles and furlongs Inter-mediate m. f.	Distance in miles and furlongs Total m. f.	Nature of Route.	Main Valleys and Mountain Passes.	River crossings and Lakes.	Altitude above Sea Level in Feet.	Supplies and Transport at Stages.	Remarks.
	Gogra	...	127	Road good and passable through-out for laden animals from Chang Chenmo valley up the Kugrang valley, then branching up the Chang lung valley to the north-east, steep ascent and gradual descent, winding hill side, crossing many spurs and ravines.	Up Kugrang and Chang lung valleys.	......	15570	S. T. nil, G. scarce, F. W. plentiful.	Camping ground.
		...	133		......	Hot springs.	......	...	Path up eastern ravine to Chann lung Yokina La.
		...	136		......		......		Ditto.
12	Shamal Lungpa	12	139		Chang lung Burma or Cayley's pass.	......	17020	Ditto	Ditto.
		...	146			......	19300.		
13	Nischu	13	153			......	18030	S. F. G. T. nil, W. available.	Ditto.
	Kala Pahar	4	159		......	......	19300	...	Sumahal plain.
14	Lingzi thang	16 4	169 4	Road good	Across the Lingzi thang plain.	......	17680	S. G. T. nil, F. scarce, W. by digging.	Halting place.
15	Jangal	17 4	186 4	Ditto	......	......	......	S. F. G. T. nil, W. precarious.	Small ford.

No.	Stage	Stage miles	Total miles	Road and remarks on route	Down valley	River crossing	Height	Water and Supplies	Remarks
16	Sumna	21	202 4	Gentle ascent and descent.	Kizil Diwan. Down Kizil Jilga ravine.	......	17290	S. T. nil, F. G. W. procurable three miles down.	Camping ground.
17	Kizil Jilga	9	208	Road good	......	......	17150	S. T. nil, F. G. W. plentiful.	Two huge red rocks on Karakash river.
			217	Road excellent ...	Down Karakash valley.	......	16360		
18	Khushk Maidan	17	222	Water disappears from ground for 1½ miles. Road good	......	......	......	S. T. nil, G. scarce, F. W. plentiful.	Numerous springs.
19	Chungtash	7	231	Road through narrow gorge in parts stony and bad.	......	......	15740	S. F. G. T. nil, W. plentiful.	Camping ground.
			241						
20	Sumnal	13	247	Valley opens out for 3 miles, then narrows and road is obstructed by huge boulders and masses of débris.	......	Hot springs	15500	S. T. nil, F. G. W. plentiful.	On right bank of Karakash river. Junction of Nala.
	E. good—		254			Cross Karakash river often.	15540		
	Zurfin		257						
21	Tak Marpo	11	265	Valley opens out and road good.	......	......	15000	S. T. nil, F. scarce, G. W. plentiful.	Yellow rock on left bank.
	E. good—								
22	Pulong Karpo	21	286	Road branches up broad valley over the Kuenlun range by Ilchi or Yangi Diwan pass to Khotan (80 miles distant).	......	......	14600	S. T. nil, F. G. W. abundant.	Huge rock on left of valley.
	E. good—		294						
23	Sora	15	301		......	......	14000	Ditto	Natural salt pans.
	E. good—								

Number of Marches	Names of Stages	Distance in miles and furlongs		Nature of Route.	Main Valleys and Mountain Passes.	River crossings and Lakes.	Altitude above Sea Level in feet.	Supplies and Transport and Stages.	Remarks.
		Inter-mediate. m. f.	Total. m. f.						
	LXXIXa ROUTE—contd.								
24	Kara Jilga	... ...	301 ...	Road bad	.....	Kara Jilga	.....	S. T. nil, F. G. W. abundant.	Mouth of small ravine.
25	Sumgal E.—	17 ...	318 4	Road hence N. E. to Khotan 10 days' march, crossing Kuenlun range by Hindu tagh pass over glacier, 17,379 ft.	.....	.....	.....	Ditto	Camping ground on right bank Shayok
		25 4	343 4						
			348 4		.....	Numerous springs.			
	Fotash F. left bank		350 4	Path up Fotash ravine over difficult pass to Tumba thus avoiding Suget pass.	.....	.....			
26	Gul bashem	17 ...	369 4		.....	.....	12390	Ditto	Kirghiz ditto on right bank of Karakash river.
27	Bulakchi	10 ...	370 4	Pass jade quarries at foot of Kuenlun range, join road from Suget pass, road good.	.....	.....	.....	Ditto	Ditto.
			376 4	......					
28	Shahidula E.—	13 ...	383 4		.....	......	11780	Ditto	Old fort on left bank of Karakash river.

LXXX   LEH to KHOTAN by ILCHI or YANGI DEWAN PASS—*Johnson.—Distances approximate.*

No.	Place	Dist.	Total	Road	Route	Notes	Elev.	Supplies	Remarks
1	Leh	...	...	Road good and passable for laden animals.	Up Indus valley.	......	11350	S. F. G. W. abundant.	Capital of Ladak, large town and fort. Palace of Gialpoor Raja.
	Tikze	13	13	......	......	...	......	S. F. G. W. plentiful.	Village and Monastery.
2	Chimre	16	24	......	Up Sakti valley.	...	......	S. F. G. W. and T. moderate.	Ditto.
	Sakti	...	29	......	......	......	......	......	Large village, well cultivated.
3	Zingral	...	35	Very steep ascent from Sakti to Zingral.	......	......	......	S. T. nil, F. G. W. available.	Halting place.
		11	40	Ascent to, and descent from, pass easy.	Chang La. Down Chang ravine, up Durgul valley.	......	......	......	
4	Durgu	...	44	Road on both banks of Durgul river.	......	......	*	S. T. nil, F. G. W. procurable.	Small village, well cultivated.
		15	55	......	......	......	......	......	
5	Tankse	7	62	......	......	Cross Durgul river several times.	......	S. F. G. W. and T. plentiful.	Small village, central store depôt.
	Muglib	...	60	......	......	......	......	......	Hamlet.
6	Sowar or Chiri	13	75	......	......	......	......	S. T. nil, F. G. W. available.	Small lake, no houses. Pangong Lake western end.
	Lrokara	...	85	......	Up Loonkur valley.	......	......	......	

Number of Marches.	Names of Stages.	Distance in miles and furlongs. Intermediate. m. f.	Total. m. f.	Nature of Route.	Main Valleys and Mountain Passes.	River Crossings and Lakes.	Altitude above Sea Level, in Feet.	Supplies and Transport at Stages.	Remarks.
LXXX	ROUTE—contd.								
7	Chagra	...	85	Road good	......	......	14917	S. T. nil, F. G. W. available.	Shepherds' Camp.
		15	90	Descent boggy from snow.	Marsimik La	......	18860	......	Pang lung range.
8	Rimdi	11	97		Across Chang Chenmo valley	.	......	Ditto, F. scarce.	(Grazing ground.
9	Pamchalam	14	101	......	......	...	......	S. T. nil,	Ditto.
10	Kiam	12	115	On left bank of Chang Chenmo river. Road level	......	Hot spring 179°, Sulphur and Soda. Cross Chang Chenmo river several times. Chang Chenmo ford.	17045	F. G. W. plentiful. Ditto	Ditto.
11	Lumkang	18	145	On right bank of Chang Chenmo river.	Up ravine	......	17501.	S. T. nil, F. G. scarce, W. plentiful.	Halting place.
			153	Road good and ascent gradual.	Lum kang La	......	19501.		
12	Nischu	20	165	Road good	......	......	17680	Ditto, G. nil.	Ditto
13	Burcha thang	18	183	Ditto	Lingzi thang plains.	......	17425	S. F. G. T. nil, W. available.	Ditto

No.	Name		Miles	Total	Road	Route	Ford	Elevation	Supplies	Remarks
14	Tso thang	...	20	203	Soil covered with 6 inches saltpetre.	......	......	17024	Ditto	Small lake, salt.
15	Huzak har	...	15	218	Road fair	......	......	16684	Ditto	Small lake, fresh spring.
16	Mapothang	...	16	234	......	......	......	15959	S. F. G. T. nil, W. brackish.	Small lake, water brackish.
17	Yangpa	...	25	259	Ditto soil covered with 9 inches saltpetre.	Up ravine ...	......	15279	Ditto, W. brackish.	......
				267		Khatai Diwan.	......	17500		
18	Kara Kash *river*	...	18	277	Road hence along left bank of Karakash river to Shahidula.	Across Karakash valley.	Karakash ford	15491	S. T. nil, F. W. plentiful, G. scarce.	Stone huts.
				286				19092	......	Kuenlum range.
19	Tash	...	19	296	Ascent to pass steep and difficult, much ice, descent rugged, road steep and bad, passable in June, July and August.	Yangi Diwan. Across Yanga valley.	......	15583	Ditto	Stone huts.
20	Kush lash Inngar	...	13	309	......	Yangpa ford.	......	15048	S. F. G. T. nil, W. available.	Ditto.
								18080		
21	Brinjga	...	22	331	Road bad, ascent to pass steep over large glacier, descent abrupt over glacier through granite rocks; road rocky and dangerous.	Nain Khan pass.	......	11755	S. T. nil, F. scarce, G. W. plentiful.	Grazing ground. Wild senna plant.
22	Kapas	...	10	341	......	Down Yurung Kash or Khotan valley.	......	10650	S. T. nil, worse grass and reeds, W. plentiful.	Stone hut.
23	Karangotak	...	16	357	......	Cross spur	......	8735	S. T. nil, F. G. W. moderate.	Village of 500 houses, trees and cultivation.
				364	......	......	Khotan ford.			

Number of Marches	Names of Stages	Distance in Miles and Furlongs. Intermediate m. f.	Total m. f.	Nature of Route.	Main Valleys and Mountain Passes.	River Crossings and Lakes.	Altitude above Sea Level in Feet.	Supplies and Transport at Stages.	Remarks.
LXXX	ROUTE—contd.	...	...						
24	Pisha	...	364	......	......	......	8643	S. T. nil, F. G. scarce, W. available.	Village, 20 houses.
25	Buia	8	372	Ascent and descent of spur very steep, road bad, down rocky bed. Road good	Up ravine Bisha Diwan. Down Siri-su ravine.	......	7692	S. T. nil, F. scarce, G. W. plentiful.	Village, 100 houses.
		10	382				10000		
26	Yangi langar	29	411	On right bank Sirian.	......	......	5930	Ditto	Village, 30 houses.
27	Kumat langar	5	416	Road sandy through well cultivated plain.	......	......	5790	Ditto	Village, 150 houses.
28	Bozilia	10	426		......	......	4678	S. F. G. W. and T. plentiful.	Village and bazar. 1,000 houses.
29	Ilchi B., C., E.—	11	437	Town on left bank of Khotan river.	......	Khotan ford difficult.	4320	S. F. G. W. and T. abundant.	Capital of Khotan, population 40,000. Town, fort, large bazar, country well cultivated.

Mr. Drew gives from Tso thang 17,100 feet, to Lokzhung 17,200 feet 16 miles, Thaldat 16,300 feet 15 miles, Yangpa 16,200 feet 30 miles, E. Karakash valley 15,000 feet 24 miles, Shahidula 11,500 feet 81 miles, as taken by Adolphe Schlagintweit. Also a diversion as taken by Dr. Cayley from Thaldat 16,300 feet, to Patsalung 16,400 feet 20 miles, Camp 15,900 feet 21 miles, E. Karakash valley 15,000 feet 12 miles.

LXXXa KARGALIK to KIRIA in KHOTAN by ILCHI—*Johnson, Lansdell.—Distances approximate.*

No.	Place	Int. dist.	Cumul. dist.	Remarks	Ford	Elevation	Supplies	Description
	Kargalik	...	0	Carriage road over cultivated ground to Khush Langar, and thence over alternate chul and sandy desert, stony and arid to near Guma.	......	4370	S. F. G. W. and T. plentiful.	Large town of 1,000 houses.
	Lob	...	8		......	......		
	Yakin Langar	...	13		...	......		
1	**Khush Langar** *B.—*	17	17		...	......	S. F. G. T. nil, W. scanty.	Picket station.
2	**Chulak Langar** *B.—*	16	33	......	......	......	Ditto	Walled garden.
	Silak Langar	...	42		......	......		
3	**Hajif Langar** *B., E.—*	14	47	......	......	......	Ditto	Garden.
4	**Guma** *B., C., E.—*	9	56	Traversed about three miles cultivation and plunged into sandy desert and chul to Janghnia.	Kilian ford	4340	S. F. G. W. and T. moderate.	Large town and bazar.
	Cholo	...	59		Branch of Kilian ford.	......		Village of 60 houses.
	Makhi La Langar	...	66		......	......		
	Cheda, oasis	...	68	......	......	......		Large village.
			76					
5	**Moji,** *oasis*	25	81	Hence road fifteen miles to Sanju.	......	4290	S. T. nil, F. G. W. available.	Ditto and bazar.
	Koska Langar	4	85		......	......		
	Kosulla Langar	4	91		......	......		

Number of Marches.	Names of Stages.	Distance in miles and furlongs. Intermediate m. f.	Distance in miles and furlongs. Total m. f.	Nature of Route.	Main Valleys and Mountain Passes.	River Crossings and Lakes.	Altitude above Sea Level in Feet.	Supplies and Transport at Stages.	Remarks.
	LXXX. ROUTE—contd.								
6	**Janghnia**	......	91 4	Hence road to Sanju, traversed some cultivation and then all sandy desert.	......	......	......	S. F. G. W and T. moderate.	Village, fort and bazar.
7	Pialma C., E.—	14	95	Cultivation for two miles then region of sand hills for three miles.	......	......	4342	S. T. nil. F. G. W. available.	Small village and bazar.
8	Ak Robat	22	117		......	......	......	Ditto, deep well.	Mazar or tomb of Imam Mohamud Shah.
	Tobackas Langar B.—	15	132						
		......	142						
9	**Zawa Kurghan** C., E., oasis.	13	145	Road fair through cultivated country.	......	Bridge	4430	S. F. G. W. and T. moderate.	Small town walled, customs post.
	Ak Serai B.	......	159	......	......	Karakash ford.	......	......	
	Do Shambeh	......	174	Road through irrigated fields, orchards and gardens.	......	......	......	......	Bazar.
10	Ilchi B., C., L.—	20	165	Road good through cultivation to Dol Langar, then	......	......	4390	S. F. G. W. abundant.	Capital of Khotan, large town and fort. 40,000 population.

No.	Stage	Stage miles	Total miles	Road	Ford / River	Elevation	Supplies	Remarks
	Yurung Kash	...	168 4	sandy plain covered with jungle.	Yurung Kash ford.	4121	......	Bazar of 500 shops.
	Lob	...	179		......			
11	**Dol Langar**	17	182	......	......	4420	S. T. nil, F. G. W. available. Ditto	Village, 150 houses.
12	**Beshtoghrak Langar.**	15	197	......	......	......		Halting place.
13	**Chira** B., C., E.—	20	217	Takla Maklan desert three miles north.	......	4220	S. F. G. W. T. plentiful.	Town of 600 houses.
14	**Karakia**	25	237 242	......	Chira ford.	...	S. T. nil,	Village, 10 houses.
15	**Kiria** B., C., E.—	28	270	Road sandy until Kiria river, then through cultivations and gardens.	Kiria bridge.	4580	F. G. W. available. S. F. G. W. and T. ample.	Large town of 7,000 houses on right bank of Kiria river.

The Sorghak goldfields 7,060 feet, are distant 64 miles from Kiria eastwards in 3 marches.

From Kiria there is a frequented track southwards by Polu, 8,430 feet 55 miles, over the Kuenlun range by the Diwan pass to Ghubolik 16,960 feet, Lake with sulphur mines 43 miles, and across the Chantang and Chang Chenmo plains by the Yeshil kul 16,160 feet, the Tashhak kul 16,620 feet, and the Mangtza lakes to Noh 245 miles, and Rudok 20 miles—Total distance from Kiria by Noh and Tankse to Leh 550 miles.

LXXXI   LEH to RUDOK by PANGONG LAKE—*Map, Johnson.—Distances approximate.*

No.	Stage				
	Leh	...	...	...	See Route LXXX towards Chang Chenmo valley and Khotan.
5	Tankse	...	...	62	

Hence there are two routes to Rudok, one north and one south of the Pangong Lake.

Number of Marches.	Names of Stages.	Distance in miles and furlongs. Intermediate. m. f.	Distance in miles and furlongs. Total. m. f.	Nature of Route	Main Valleys and Mountain Passes.	River Crossings and Lakes.	Altitude above Sea Level in Feet.	Supplies and Transport at Stages.	Remarks.
	LXXXI ROUTE—contd. *Muglib*	... ...	62 70			......	......		
6	Chakar Talao ...	14	76	From Tankse, road up valley, which narrows to a gorge and then opens out by Muglib, crosses grassy swamp and ascends two miles among rocky boulders.	Up Pazar valley.	......	......	S. T. nil, F. G. W. scanty.	Shallow pond, dry in summer.
7	Lukong	7 2	83 2	From Chakar Talao road continues up valley to the plain at end of Pangong Lake.	Up Loonkur valley.	......	14130	Ditto	Two miles, N. W. end of Pangong Lake. W. salt.
8	Chagra	8	91 2	Road good all the way to foot of pass.	...	......	15090	S. T. nil, F. scanty, G. W. plentiful.	Pasture ground.
9	Charkang	8	99 2	Gradual ascent to summit, whence road turns eastwards over elevated ground called the Kieu La into the head	Marsimik La	......	......	S. T. nil, F. G. W. procurable.	Southern foot of pass.
		...	100		Kieu La.	......	18420.		
		...	104	La into the head Kieu valley.	Down Kieu valley.				

No.	Name				Road	Pass / Valley	Water	Elevation	Supplies	Remarks
10	Pangur Gongma	10	6	110	of the Kieu valley which drains down into the Pangong Lake.	......	Kim Stream is difficult to cross in summer.	17670	S. T. nil, F. G. W. scanty.	Eastern foot of pass.
	Ningri	...	:	:		......				
11	Niagzu	13	:	123	Good road up this branch valley to the head, where it crosses two passes and descends into the Tal valley.	Up Tso Kiok valley.	......	16250	S. T. nil, F. G. W. available.	Junction of three valleys.
12	Kaisarpo	12	:	135		......	......	15390	Ditto	Halting place.
		:	:	143		Tso Kiok La	......	17300		
13	Gonu	:	:	144	Road along river bed and then crosses Salam spur.	Demjor La Down Tal valley.	......	17700	S. T. nil, F. G. W. scanty.	Frontier post.
		12	:	147		......	......	......		
14	Chuzan	13	:	160	Road fair over the pass and down the ravine.	Up ravine Dingo La. Down Toba Ruberg ravine.	Springs	15840	S. T. nil, F. G. available, W. springs.	Grassy plain.
		:	:	166						
15	Pal	20	:	180	Stony road along northern shore of two fresh water lakes, Tso Rum and Tso Nyak.	......	"	......	Ditto	On northern shore of Pangong Lake.
16	Dobo Nakpo	8	:	188	......	......	......	14020	S. T. nil, F. G. W. scanty.	On northern bank of Tso Rom.

No. of Marches	Names of Stages	Intermediate m. f.	Total m. f.	Nature of Route	Main Valleys and Mountain Passes	River crossings and Lakes	Altitude above Sea Level in Feet	Supplies and Transport at Stages	Remarks
	LXXXI ROUTE—contd.	......	188 ...				......		
17	Noh	9 ...	207 ...	......	......	Naichu Loomba.	......	S. T. nil, F. G. W. scanty.	On northern bank of Tso Nyak, small village of 25 houses.
18	Rudok	20 ...	227 ...	......	......	......	......	Ditto	Village and chief place in Rudok.

Or along southern shore of Pangong Lake, 40 miles long by 2 to 4 miles broad 13,336 feet. W. salt.

No. of Marches	Names of Stages	Intermediate m. f.	Total m. f.	Nature of Route	Main Valleys and Mountain Passes	River crossings and Lakes	Altitude above Sea Level in Feet	Supplies and Transport at Stages	Remarks
7	Lukong	...	83 2	Fair road, but stony along the southern margin of the Pangong Lake, which is here quite open to Thakung.	......	......	14130	S. T. nil, F. G. scanty	Two miles from N. W. end Pangong Lake. W. salt.
	Spang mik.—	...	90 ...						
8	Mang south bank	13 6	97 ...	......	......	......	13940	S. T. nil, F. G. W. available.	Hamlet.
	Mirak.—	...	104 ...				......	......	Small village.
9	Kark pet south bank	10 ...	107 ...	......	......	......	14000	S. T. nil, F. G. W. scanty.	Hamlet.
10	Thakung south bank	7 ...	114 ...	Hence the mountain spurs come	......	Saka Loongma.	......	S. T. nil, F. G. plentiful.	Halting place.

								W. scanty.	
11	**Yula** *south bank*	15	129	down close to the Lake and the road along the shore is winding and rough.	......	Yula ravine	......	S. T. nil, F. G. W. precarious.	Ditto.
12	**Aot** *south bank*	15	144	At east end of Pangong Lake, which is connected with the Nyak Tso by a long narrow channel fordable at Aot. Hence good but	......	Pangong ford	......	S. T. nil, F. G. W. plentiful.	Pasture ground. About 3 miles, N. W., is the ruined fort of Kharnak. Camping ground.
13	**Dal** *north bank*	12	156	stony road continues along northern shore of Nyak Tso to Pal,	......	Dal Loomba	......	Ditto	Ditto.
14	**Pal** *north bank*	21	177	and thence along northern shore of 2 small lakes,	......	Pal „	......	Ditto	Ditto.
15	**Noh**	20	197	Ram Tso and Nyak Tso, to Noh.	......	Naichu „	......	S. T. nil, F. G. W. scanty.	Small village of 25 houses.
16	**Rudok**	20	217	Rudok is on the southern side of the latter lake.	......	......	......	Dito	Village, chief place of Rudok.

From Noh, there is route northwards up the Naichu valley over the Kiang la, by the Maug Tza lake, 16,600 feet, over an extensive elevated plateau 16,880 feet, and the Diwan pass by the Chubolik lake and sulphur mine 16,960 feet to Polu 8,430 feet and Kiria in Khotan 4,580 feet in length.

Colonel Trotter, R. E., writes that, according to Mr. Moorcroft, this was part of an ancient highway from Kohistan northwards to Turkistan starting from Nujinabad (whence a branch railway has just been made 15 miles to Kotdwara at foot of the hills), 210 miles long to the Niti pass 16,676 feet, thence crossing the Sutlej river at Toding 12,200 feet, where there is an ancient iron suspension bridge, and crossing the Bagro la 19,210 feet into the Indus valley at Gartok 14,240 feet, it follows this river to Demchok and crosses the Jara pass northwards to Rudok and Noh about 275 miles.

From Noh to Kiria in Khotan is 343 miles, from Kiria to Kargalik 270 miles and from Kargalik to Yarkand 42 miles—Total 1,140 miles.

LXXXII.—LEH to GAR.—*Map, Montgomerie, Drew.—Distances approximate.*

Number of Marches	Names of Stages	Distance in Miles and Furlongs.		Nature of Route.	Main Valleys and Mountain Passes.	River Crossings and Lakes.	Altitude above Sea Level in Feet.	Supplies and Transport and Stages.	Remarks.
		Inter-mediate. m. f.	Total. m. f.						
	Leh *P. O., D. B., C., E.—*	... ...	... ...	See Route LXXX towards Chang Chenmo valley and Khotan.					
5	Tankse	... ...	62 ...	Ascent S. E. valley, road rough and stony; passable for laden animals.	Up Harong valley.	......	13900	S. F. G. W. and T. plentiful.	Junction of 5 valleys.
6	Erad	9 ...	65 ...	......	......	Chumik Loongma.	...	S. T. nil, F. G. scanty, W. plentiful.	Huts. Neck over spur projecting into valley.
7	Bulchen	10 ...	71 76 ...	Road easy along wide plain extending to the head at Kangta La, the approaches of	Harong La. Up Harong or Kailung valley.	Bulchen Loongma. Kailung do.	...	Ditto	Tartar camp.
8	Loi yugma	12 ...	81 ...	which are easy on both sides. The road thence descends down the	......	......	...	S. T. nil, F. G. W. available.	Pasture ground.
9	Burma	9 ...	87 ... 93 ... 102 ... 106 ...	Yara ravine to the Shushal plateau.	Kangta La. Down Yara	......	...	Ditto	Ditto.

No.	Name		Road description	Route	Water	Elevation	Supplies	Remarks
10	Shushal *Thinn—*	16 — 118 126 ·· 4	......	ravine, up Shushal valley.	Spring and Bobsang nala.	14200	S. F. G. W. and T. moderate.	Village and store house. Road branches W. to Mirpa Tso 13 m. Halting place.
11	Dachung	16 — 134 140	Ascent and descent over pass easy.	Tsaka La. Down Tsaka valley.	......	15200.	S. T. nil, F. G. W. available.	Halting place.
12	Ralmang	11 — 145	......	......	......	......	Ditto	Hamlet, Gonpa Lama, Serai 1 m. distant.
13	Dungti	12 — 157	Road on both sides of the Indus river.	Up Indus valley.	Indus ford	......	S. T. nil, F. G. scanty, W. plentiful.	Bend of Indus river where it turns from S. W. to W. course.
14	hang	12 — 169	Hence road ascends left bank of the Indus in a broad valley and through low hills between Tashigong and Demchok.	Ditto left bank.	Indus „	......	Ditto	Halting place.
15	Khangra	12 — 181	......	......	......	......	Ditto	Ditto.
16	Tashigong	10 — 191	......	......	Koyul Lungpo	......	Ditto	Kashmir territory.
17	Demchok	26 — 217	Hence upper valley narrows with a lofty range of mountains on the western side.	......	......	......	......	Chinese, Thibet whence road northwards over Jara La to Rudok.
18	Tashingong	20 — 227	......	......	......	13020	......	Chinese Thibet.
19	Junction of Singh-Gi-Chu.	8 — 235	Road up the left bank of the more western branch,	......	......	......	...	Eastern branch of Upper Indus.

Number of Marches.	Names of Stages.	Distance in miles and furlongs.		Nature of Route.	Main Valleys and Mountain Passes.	River crossings and Lakes.	Altitude above Sea Level, in Feet.	Supplies and Transport at Stages.	Remarks.
		Inter-mediate. m. f.	Total. m. f.						
	LXXXII ROUTE—contd.	... ...	235 ...						
20	Gar Gunsa	26 ...	261 ...	general course downwards from south to north.	......	......	14140	......	Chinese Thibet, centre of trade in winter.
21	Longong	20 ...	281 ...	......	......	......	......	......	Chinese Thibet.
22	Gartok	30 ...	311 ...	......	......	......	14240	......	Chinese Thibet, centre of trade in summer.

From Gartok there is a road south-westwards over the Bogo La 19,920 feet 25 miles, to Totling 12,190 feet 22 miles, in the Sutlej river, across which there is an ancient iron suspension bridge, thence southwards by Daba 25 miles, to the Niti pass 16,570 feet 23 miles, on the British Frontier—Total distance from Gartok 95 miles.

Firstly.—LXXXIII **LEH to HANLE**.—*Maps, Montgomerie, Drew.—Distances approximate.*

There are 3 routes from Leh to Hanle :—
    I by Tankse and Shushal.
    II by Indus valley.
    III by Rupshu and Puga.

	Leh									
5	Tankse	...	...	62	See Routes LXXX and LXXXII.					
10	Shushal	...	...	118	Hence there are two routes to the Indus at Mahiye and Nowi.					
12	Ralmang	...	...	145	Hence there are two routes to the Indus at Nowi and Nima Mud.					
13	Nowi right bank	16	...	161	Road fair and passable for laden animals.	Up Hanle valley left bank.	Indus ford waist deep.	13000	S. T. nil, F. G. scanty, W. plentiful.	Huts.
	Rhongo		...	167						
14	Shol fo	8	...	169	......	......	...:	......	Ditto	Halting place.
15	Chibra or Mankhang.	12	...	181	......	......	......	......	Ditto	Ditto.
	Sangoisang plain	...	...	187	......	......	Sangoisang nala.	......	Ditto	Ditto.
16	Hanle	19	...	200	......	......	......	14276	Ditto	Village and Monastery.

From Shushal there is a road northwards down the Shushal valley to Thakung on the Pangong Lake about 10 miles long.

From Shushal there is a track direct eastwards along the Pangoor Tso by Laungmar and Zhungja to Rudok about 70 miles in length.

From Shushal another track goes southwards over the Thato La to Mahiye on the Indus, the stages are Mirpa Tso, fresh water lake, 13 miles, cross Thato La 16,950 feet 3 miles ; by a very stony road to Ghale 8 miles, and passing two small lakes, Khan Tso and Yahe Tso, to Mahiye 13,800 feet 12 miles—Total 36 miles.

From Ralmang there is a path southwards over the Belung La and down the Gachang ravine to Nima Mud on the Indus about 18 miles in length.

Secondly.—**LEH to HANLE by INDUS VALLEY.**—*This is the shortest route of the three—*

Number of Marches.	Names of Stages.	Distance in miles and furlongs. Intermediate. m. f.	Distance in miles and furlongs. Total. m. f.	Nature of Route.	Main Valleys and Mountain Passes.	River Crossings and Lakes.	Altitude above Sea Level in Feet.	Supplies and Transport at Stages.	Remarks.
	Leh	... ...	... ...						
8	**Mahiye** *on right bank*	... ...	108 4	See Route LXVI, Road fair along right bank of Indus valley to Nima Mud, where it crosses the Indus by the most convenient ford, thence up a defile joins the road up the Hanle valley to Hanle.	stages 29 to 37. Up Indus valley.	37. Mahiye foo Polalung ,, Nima ,,	13500	S. F. T. nil, G. W. available.	Pasture on left bank.
			116 4						
			121 4						
9	**Nima Mud** *ditto*	... ...	124 4		......	Ciachang ,, Indus ford.	14000	S. T. nil, F. G. W. plentiful.	Two small villages.
			132 ..		......				
			137 ..		Sangthung La.				
10	**Shol foo**	13 4	138 ..	......	Up Hanle valley left bank.	......		S. T. nil, F. G. W. procurable.	Halting place.
11	**Mankhang** ...	12 ..	150 ..	......	......	......		Ditto.	Ditto.
12	**Hanle**	19 ..	169 ..	......	......	...	14276	S. F. G. T. W. moderate.	Village, large Monastery and Thana.

Thirdly.—**LEH to HANLE by RUPSHU and PUGA.—**

No.	Place	Dist.	Total	Road remarks	Intermediate	Elevation	Supplies	Camping ground
5	Leh	...	...					
	Debring *in Rupshu*	...	72	*See* Route LXIX, stages 1 to 5. Down Debring valley. Road good and sandy down an opening valley to an extensive plain, where it passes round north and east of the Lake and ascends a ravine to the pass.	Debring ford.	...		
6	**Pongo Nagu**	13	85	......	......	14900	S. T. nil, F. G. W. plentiful.	Camping ground north of Tso Kar Chumo, Tartar Camp.
	Thugji	...	89	Up Pola Konka ravine.	Tso Kar Chumo.			
7	**Zukti**	16	101	Ascent and descent over pass very gradual for three miles down a narrow rugged valley with masses of boulders to an undulating plain, encrusted with salts, thence through a narrow winding gorge with rocky cliffs on both sides to the Indus.	......	......	Ditto	Halting place.
		4	103	Pola Konka La, down Rulang Chu valley.				
8	**Puga**	13	114	......	Hot springs	15200	S. T. nil, F. plentiful, G. W. scanty.	Sulphur and borax fields.
	Kaldang	...	119					
9	**Mahiye** *on right bank.*	13	127	Road along left bank of Indus very rough and stony, crossing many spurs which project down to river.	......	13800	S. F. T. nil. G. W. available.	Pasture on left bank.
	E. on left bank.							

LXXXIII ROUTE—contd.

Number of Marches.	Names of Stages.	Distance in miles and furlongs. Inter-mediate m. f.	Total m. f.	Nature of Route	Main Valleys and Mountain Passes.	River Crossings and Lakes.	Altitude above Sea Level in Feet.	Supplies and Transport at Stages.	Remarks.
10	Nidar on left bank...	.. ..	127 ..	Crosses road which leads southwards to Ooti and Chumar.	...	Nidar foo	.....	S. F. T. nil, G. W. available.	Opposite Nimu.
11	Takalung on left bank.	12 ..	139 ..	Road fair, leaves Indus river and goes southwards through a rocky gorge and up a stony valley over a low ridge and down a ravine to the Hanle valley, then ascending latter over long gravelly plain and turfy saline meadows.	Up ravine	Takalung "	.....	S. T. nil, F. G. W. available.	Halting place.
12	Chumik	10 ..	149 ..		Sangpoche La. Down ravine up Hanle valley left bank.	Chumik "	.....	S. T. nil, F. G. W. scanty.	Spring 4 miles up ravine.
		12 ..	156						
			161						
13	Sangoisang	13 ..	174		......	Sangoisang "	.....	Ditto	Halting place.
14	Hanle E.—	13 ..	187		...	......	14276	S. F. G. and T. moderate.	Village, large Monastery and Thana.

APPENDIX A.

The tables of routes leading to Turkistan in Central Asia may be of interest in considering the question of the best route for trade.
Taking Delhi and Amritsar in India and Yarkand in Turkistan as the termini, the length of the chief route, so far as known at present, may be thus shown approximately.

Route.		By Rail.	By Road.
Foot Notes of LXXXI / Ditto and LXXXa	**Delhi to Kotduara**		
	Kotduara by Gartok to Keria in Khotan ...	187	811
	Keria by Kargalik to Yarkand ...	......	322
	Total ...	187	1133
	This route is at present barred by the Chinese, though according to W. Moorcroft it was formerly the highway for trade.		
LXX / **LXXVII**	**Delhi to Kalka**		
	Kalka by Simla, Kulu and Lahoul to Leh ...	162	473
	Leh to Yarkand ...	......	456
	Total ...	162	929
	If a railway be made from Kalka to Simla, 60 miles, the rail distance will be increased and the road distance decreased by this length.		
LXXXI / **LXXVII**	**Amritsar to Jalandhar**		
	Jalandhar by Palampur, Kulu and Lahoul to Leh ...	52	512
	Leh to Yarkand, summer route ...	......	456
	Total ...	52	968
	If a railway be made from Jalandhar to Hoshiarpur, 25 miles, the rail and roads distance will be lengthened and shortened accordingly.		

ROUTE.		BY RAIL.	BY ROAD.
LXXII **LXXVII**	**Amritsar to Pathankot** ... Pathankot by Chamba and Kishetwar to Leh Leh to Yarkand, summer route ...	67	440 456
	Total	67	896

If a railway be made from Pathankot by Kangra to Palampur, 90 miles, the rail distance will become 175 miles and the road distance from 558 miles.

		BY RAIL.	BY ROAD.
LXXI and **LXXVII**	Palampur by Kulu, Lahoul, Zanskar and Leh to Yarkand.		
XLII and **LI** **LXXVII**	**Amritsar to Rawul Pindi** ... Rawul Pindi by Srinagar to Leh ... Leh to Yarkand, summer route ...	211	441 456
	Total	211	897

		BY RAIL.	BY ROAD.
LXI **LXIV** and Foot Note to **LXXVII**	**Amritsar to Kala Serai** ... Kala Serai by Abbottabad and Chilas to Gilgit ... Gilgit by Hunza and Sarikol to Yarkand ...	231	203 426
	Total	231	719

If a railway be made from Kala Serai by Abbottabad to Balakot in the Khagan Valley, 90 miles, the rail and road distances will be increased and decreased accordingly.

To every route there are variations, which are adopted according to season, the state of the passes, the river floods and ice, and the condition of the water, fuel and grazing at the stages.

The routes by Srinagar and Leh are at present resorted to, as Srinagar and Leh are entrepots of the trade, where the goods can, if required, change hands, and both supplies and transport are abundant.

The Abbottabad, Gilgit and Sarikol route is now being opened out and the road distance being the shortest, is likely to be favoured, especially if Gilgit were to become an entrepot of trade.

It is probable that all the routes, except the first, by Simla, Kangra, Chamba, Srinagar and Gilgit will continue to be used, as wool, fuel and grass for pack animals on each is limited and would be exhausted in time, if one route only were adopted.

In time a railway from Kala Serai, Haripur, for Kela Derband and Gilgit would form the best approach to command the trade of Central Asia. The distance by railway would then be roughly, Amritsar to Kala Serai 231 miles, Kala Serai to Derband in Indus valley 50 miles, Derband up the Indus valley to Bunji 4,631 feet 250 miles, Bunji up the Gilgit valley to Gilgit 4,890 feet 40 miles—Total by rail 511 miles, and by road 426 miles.

396 INDEX.